The Artist Wears Rough Clothing

The Artist Wears
Rough Clothing

Robert Wexelblatt

LAMAR UNIVERSITY press

ISBN: 978-0-9911074-7-6
Library of Congress Control Number: 2014942295
Manufactured in the United States of America
Cover Art: "Landscape in the Style of Li T'ang" by Qiu Ying (16th Century)
Book and Cover Design: Heather Odom

Lamar University Press
Beaumont, Texas

Acknowledgments

I am grateful to the editors of the following publications for publishing some of the stories in this book.

Amarillo Bay
Dislocate
Kansas Quarterly
Michigan Quarterly Review
RE: AL
Sou'wester
South Dakota Review
Talking River
The Massachusetts Review
Waccamaw
Western Humanities Review
Witness

Fiction from Lamar University Press

Gerald Duff, *Memphis Mojo*
Mimi Ferebee, *Wildfires and Atmospheric Memories*
Gretchen Johnson, *The Joy of Deception and Other Stories*
Christopher Linforth, *When You Find Us We Will Be Gone*
Tom Mack and Andrew Geyer, eds, *A Shared Voice*
Harold Raley, *Louisiana Rogue*
Jim Sanderson, *Trashy Behavior*
Jan Seale, *Appearances*
Melvin Sterne, *The Number You Have Reached*

www.LamarUniversityPress.Org

Books by Robert Wexelblatt

The Derangement of Jules Torquemal
Losses
Zublinka Among Women
The Decline of Our Neighborhood
Professors at Play: Essays
Life in the Temperate Zone

CONTENTS

1   Hsi-Wei's Skull

7   Double Concerto

29   Tinderbox

51   The Avramarash Negotiations

73   Citizenship

89   Delusion

121   Blessant and the Dutchman

137   Arno Meer

159   Z

175   Steppe Story

183   On The Boughs Our Bodies Shall Be Strung

189   Elected Silence

207   Leuterre

225   Salisbury

247   The Artist Wears Rough Clothing And Carries Jade Inside

Hsi-Wei's Skull

Chen Hsi-Wei was born in the latter half of the sixth century, at the close of the troubled period of the Six Dynasties and at the beginning of Sui rule. His verses, though original, are characteristic of the times, except for his frequent use of vulgar idioms and southern dialects. Recently a curious manuscript of Chen Hsi-Wei's has come to light.

According to a brief preface added by an unknown hand, it was at the request of a certain lady-in-waiting that Chen wrote this account of a well-known but perplexing poem of his. The lyric is popularly called "My Skull" after its last words. Evidently composing this explanation especially inspired Chen Hsi-Wei because he supplied something more than was requested, virtually an account of his becoming a poet.

Freely translated, the poem reads as follows.

> In Pingyao, as they began to lash my back and chest,
> I could just hear little girls chanting "Rice-Bowl-Rice":
> Through green doors, across red pavement, that jolly song.
>
> When they dragged me off to be questioned in Nanyang
> Melancholy music wafted from Three River Tavern,
> Just the sort to make barge men soften like medlars.
>
> I curled up contentedly by a great sow near Chuchow,
> No less warmed than she by our soiled straw,
> Our cradle rocked by Feng's fierce horsemen tramping by.
>
> Wuchow's streets ran with festive dragons, crackers burst,
> Women warbled, children cheered and babies bawled as
> General Fu ran his so-eager finger over my skull.

Honored Lady, deeply touched by your request, I rush to fulfill it. Please overlook my awkwardness; put it down to my haste to gratify your curiosity.

You must first know that I was born a peasant. My people lived in a village not far from the capital. In fact, you may have at some time enjoyed a banquet supplied from our farm which used to be famous for its ducks.

There was nothing unusual about my rearing or indeed about me, save for one peculiar capacity which I will mention presently.

In those first days of the new dynasty the Empire was still riven by strife. Warlords threatened the peace on every hand. Ruthless bandits terrorized the countryside. One of the greatest problems with which the new government had to cope was the getting and sending of letters and dispatches. Under the conditions of the period, no postal system could be counted on.

It happened that the Emperor's ministers needed to get a message through to our southern army. Apparently, nothing less than the survival of the Empire itself depended on the safe delivery of this message; moreover, disaster could be counted on should the information fall into the wrong hands. But to get to the southern army, a messenger must pass through vast lawless lands and many regions under the thumb of one or another warlord.

The Emperor's ministers knew that an armed force sent south with the message would only call attention to itself and, whatever its strength, was bound to fall prey either to warlords or bandits. Nor could couriers be trusted, for they were only too likely to be captured along with the message. I am told that the stratagem adopted was suggested to the First Minister by an old scholar who had come across it in an obscure history of the Chou dynasty.

A decree was put about the vicinity of the capital that the Emperor required a healthy young man with three qualities: bravery, illiteracy, and fast-growing hair. Rewards were promised to any family that should supply such a man.

You will recall my mentioning that in my youth I possessed only one noteworthy peculiarity. This was that my hair grew so quickly it needed cutting every week. While I cannot claim to have been especially brave, I certainly could neither read nor write.

Peasants are not only illiterate but also poor, My Lady. My parents were poor indeed, and when they heard the decree of the Emperor read out in the marketplace they did not hesitate to bundle me off to the capital. They even gave me a duck for the Emperor's minister. I carried it on my back.

Of course I was not the only peasant lad to show up in the palace's outermost courtyard on the appointed morning. There were scores of us. The guards, who instantly relieved me of my duck, made us wash our faces in great vats of water then lined us up in ranks. "Stand straight!" they roared at us and we did so for half an hour until a group of distinguished personages issued from a doorway. I wonder if you, My Lady, can imagine our awe when I tell you that the First Minister personally walked among us and, as we had been forbidden to kowtow, looked directly into our faces. I had never seen anyone like him, so grand and wise, so haughty and disdainful, draped in silks and taking little steps on shoes that elevated him well above even the tallest of us. We trembled before him—beneath him I should say, for the tiled roofs of the palace, the height of its walls, the scornful regard of the First Minister, everything looked down on us and made us feel stuck to the earth like beetles.

Many were dismissed at once. Some looked weak, had coughs or boils. Some were too fat, had bowed legs or thin hair. A few city boys, dressed up by their parents to look like peasants, in terror of the First Minister confessed that they could read. They too were sent packing. About forty of us remained. We were conducted into one of the palace's stables. The place looked to me vast enough to hold my whole village. Here we knelt six at a time. A small patch on the back of our heads was shaved. Then we were each issued a tiny bowl of rice with a few vegetables and locked into the stable for the night with our guards. Anyone heard groaning with discomfort or complaining about the food was immediately seized and sent away.

Those of us who remained were fetched out at dawn and told to race to some privies several hundred yards away. Note was taken of our speed. Nature's call being particularly insistent that morning, I ran faster than most. Once we had accomplished what was necessary at the privies, the guards again commanded us to wash in the vats of water, except for our heads that were to be kept dry. Once again we were arranged in ranks. "On your knees! Bow your heads!" yelled the guards. This time the First Minister did not participate. Instead, we were examined by clerks who held rods to the shorn spots on our heads. Each clerk had a scribe behind him to record our names and the results of the night's growth.

An hour later, two guards escorted me trembling with fright into the palace itself. I walked through magnificent galleries, down burnished and lacquered corridors into a magnificent room with a high teak desk and many opulently cushioned couches. On one of these couches, raised upon a low dais, reclined the First Minister.

I kowtowed.

"Explain matters to him in plain language," said the Minister gravely to one of his attendants.

This the attendant did and plainly enough. The crucial message to the army in the south, the communication on which the whole of the Empire depended, was to be entrusted only to me. There would be no scroll to deliver, no words for me to memorize. Scrolls can be taken away, memorized words divulged either in one's sleep or under torture. No, the message was to be inscribed in indelible ink on my shorn skull. The moment my hair had grown back sufficiently to hide it, I should depart for the south. I would travel on foot but as rapidly as possible and as inconspicuously too. I was to be given barely enough money for the journey and should take on the role of a peasant lad forced on the roads after being thrown out by his family. I must expect to be threatened, captured, even tortured along the way. At all costs, though, I must get through and never tell anyone except General Fu himself about the secret message on my head. The general would himself write a message for me to take back.

This, they told me, was the command of the Emperor himself and therefore my mission was divine.

Perhaps you can imagine how dumbfounded I was yet also how proud. It was as if I had been suddenly shown some special merit in myself. Looking back now, I wonder how many of us boys might have listened to that speech, felt the same shocked pride, how many were sent into the cauldron of the warring states and whether I was just the only one to make it all the way to Wuchow and back. I wonder also about that message I could not read but which I, in a sense, was. I wonder how essential it actually was, and whether it arrived in time. In Wuchow General Fu said nothing to me. I might have been a scroll. He simply directed a scribe to paint a few characters on my freshly shaved skull and kept me under close guard for the few days it took for my hair to grow back.

And so, My Lady, the poem about which you were so gracious as to be curious merely records a few images from my journey. However, the first of my travels introduced me not only to the vastness of the Middle Kingdom and the variety of its peoples, but also to the grandeur of civilization and the cruelty of barbarism. I learned something else as well. I learned the diversity of tongues and what I might call the weight of words.

I returned to the capital as illiterate as when I had departed so many months before but with an inextinguishable burning to become educated. I who had borne language on my empty head yearned to master its secrets. That is why when the Emperor's clerks offered me gold and land and concubines I begged instead to be taught. This made them howl with laughter. They must have informed the First Minister because he sent for me.

"I am told that all peasants dream of is land and money and women. Why do you, a peasant, wish to be educated?"

Though I lay prostrate before him, I replied with an audacity I must have somehow picked up on my journey. "Your Excellency, would you consent to surrender your education, to forget not only all you have read but even how to read, for land you could not describe, wealth you could not count, or a woman with whom you could not intelligently converse?"

The room grew hushed at this unheard-of temerity, but lucky for me the First Minister, notwithstanding his contempt for peasants and despite his haughty smile, replied seriously. "I see your education has already begun, boy. Very well. We shall see that it continues, but there shall be no land or gold or women."

There was never, My Lady, a truer prophecy.

I was assigned a stern tutor, the Master Xu Shuang, with whom I spent the next eight years at hard intellectual labor. I seldom saw my parents, though they did me honor for the gifts they received from the Emperor. My first nephew is named Hsi-Wei.

In the end I became a poor poet, which is just what I wanted to be. I believe the happiest moment of my life was the first time I overheard "The Yellow Moon at Lake Weishan" sung in a tavern by some students far gone in their cups.

Yet I confess to you here, My Lady, how little has altered since my fate was first decided. A poet too is a sort of messenger from the Emperor; he too must remain faithful to his mission, inured against the hardships of his travels. To this day I still make my way through the wide world in search of General Fu with mysterious characters I myself cannot always understand inscribed upon my skull.

Double Concerto

By the time he sat in Bert Forster's downtown office and signed the contract Katim had been to bed with Amalia Amati twice and felt he had come back to life. Out of sheer exhilaration and the wish to brag he put it to his skeptical friend Schulman: "Could anyone resist a woman with the name of Amalia Amati, even if she was half as gorgeous, talented, and willing?" Schulman had known the Amatis for years, Katim too. He mused ruefully to himself that, so far, hardly anybody had managed to resist Amalia. It had become a commonplace at several points of the compass that Amalia Amati might have served as the model for Botticelli's Aphrodite, lacking only the balance to stand naked on a half-shell in a marine gale. Even though the fair Amalia touched her knees and breasts inopportunely and went through men the way a six-year-old with a cold does a box of tissues, to call such a charming young woman either neurotic or promiscuous would be brutal. Her sister Annabelle was not so charitable. She had disapproved of Amalia ever since their parents brought her home from the hospital; and, when exasperated with her sister, Annabelle did not hesitate to use strong, unclinical words. Queenly Annabelle was brunette, censorious, a clenched fist wedded to an architect. Easy-going Amalia was blond, generous, light-hearted, an open palm and single. Humanly speaking the sisters' characters were incompatible, but when they played, their antitheses synthesized into high art. From their debut recital in their teens no audience had for a moment even considered resisting them.

One of Katim's quirks was the assigning of nick-names. Some of these were quite wicked. A former nun who directed a well-regarded chorus by hollering at it he dubbed "Twisted Sister"; a famous female cellist he christened "Legs Akimbo." So, when Katim was telling his friend about his transaction with the famous Amati sisters, Schulman was not surprised that he had nicknames for both. Amalia was "Dite" because, Katim explained, he could hardly call a woman with hair like that "Aphro." In Katim's opinion, Annabelle had the air of an earnest Soviet schoolgirl and, what with the rimless spectacles, he called her "Mrs. Strelnikov". Schulman laughed. Katim was unaware that he, Schulman, was responsible for arranging the commission Katim had received from the Amatis.

Schulman was Katim's closest friend, likewise the only one who also composed music. Because Schulman wrote for the movies and did not take what he did seriously, Katim was at ease with him and talked eagerly of his own work, dreams, miseries, needs, and sorrows. Though he was both, Katim considered himself anything but professionally petty or competitive. On the contrary, he professed to be disgusted by the "it's not enough that I succeed, everyone else must fail" attitude so common among musicians. Schulman observed with amusement that his friend's magnanimity took the form of simply ignoring the existence of his contemporaries; the only composers of whom Katim ever spoke were defunct. Schulman was the ideal companion for Katim. He indulged the worst of his faults, was amused by his less venal ones, and appreciated his talent in the sort of detail demanded by Katim's vanity and insecurity. Schulman was, in a sense, Katim's good angel, though Katim was blithely unaware of it. It was Schulman who held Katim's hand when his wife Julia left him, Schulman who helped him plan out the weekly visits with his daughter Felice that so terrified him, and it was Schulman who, alarmed by his friend's descent into dejection and lethargy, had the notion of convincing the Amati sisters to commission the concerto from him. Moreover, he had some ideas of his own for such a piece.

Still in their twenties, the Amati sisters were well established, had already recorded a good chunk of the two-piano repertoire, were much in demand for concerts and recitals. Their parents' and teachers' confidence had always been such that the sisters never doubted themselves. They took their success as a matter of course, a sort of historical inevitability. Five years earlier, after one look and one listen, the A-list manager Bert Forster knew it too; but Forster also understood that the girls would have to stick together. The world is willing to support only a limited number of piano-duos and, much as he loved them, he knew that neither Amati was up to the standards of a De Larrocha or Argerich. Forster was a prudent, hard-headed man who had a horror of over-promising. He was fond of using the word *niche* with his clients. "It's all about finding your niche," he would say. Curiously, Forster didn't know that this word was a metaphor until, over dinner one evening, when he was laying out his plans for the next stage of their career, Annabelle's architect husband looked up from the tortellini to explain. *"Niche* literally means *nest,"* the architect had said with the air of delivering a very short lecture then went back to the pasta. "No kidding," said Forster, not in the least embarrassed. With the cultured, he found it wise to appear crude but shrewd. "My two little chicks in their little nest– how cozy," he added, beaming at the sisters.

"Chicks?" warned Annabelle with a raised eyebrow while Amalia giggled demurely and touched her left breast. Amalia was fond of Bert; after all, he was a man.

Schulman was anxious about Katim's affair with Amalia. He should have foreseen such a development. It couldn't end well. Katim had been in a bad way ever since Julia split; he had avoided women and produced no work for months except for three piano preludes, all in minor keys. These whining pieces weren't to Schulman's taste ; however, they did show his friend could write for the keyboard in a neo-Romantic mode. And so, when he found himself chatting with the Amati sisters at a downtown reception, he had brought up his concerto idea. Now Katim was all wrapped up in Amalia and appeared almost manic.

It was with some vague notion of cutting catastrophe off at the pass that Schulman invited Katim to take a break from his Muse and eat a seafood lunch with him. Donnelly's Nantucket Tavern, which Schulman affectionately called "Donnelly's Soi-Disant," was about five blocks from his condominium and looked more Westwood than Nantucket, though not for lack of effort. It was festooned with phony New England décor, but the food was fairly authentic. Since his wife's death Schulman had become a luncheon regular and was treated as such, which was the chief reason he went there so often; that is, he went because he went. Then too there was his regular waitress, Cassie. He had been a widower for less than two years but already thought of himself as an old bachelor. That old bachelors should relish being restaurant regulars served by comely young women is hardly surprising. He was warmed by Donnelly's familiar greeting, the pint of his favorite microbrew that he didn't even have to ask for, still more by Cassie's banter and ministrations. Cassie was from Indiana, like him, and impressed that he wrote soundtracks, even if he had never actually won an Oscar.

"Hey there, Karl," Donnelly called from behind the bar. "Same for your friend?"

"Sure."

9

Robert Wexelblatt

They took a booth and Cassie brought the menus. "Chowder first?" she suggested.

"This is Cassie," said Schulman to Katim. "She ought to be a star."

Cassie made a face. "Just as soon as he gets me a screen test."

Schulman blushed. "You know I can't do that, Cassie."

"Sure, sure."

"Karl always does what he says he will, Cassie," Katim assured her.

"That's just the problem. He never says he will."

Schulman shrugged. "Why would they listen to me? I'm just the tune-plumber."

Cassie smirked at this but patted his hand before going to fetch the chowder.

"Cute girl," said Katim.

"Don't say it."

"What?"

"Never mind."

"Okay, then. I only wanted to tease you. So, what's up?"

Schulman cleared his throat. "I want you to know Amalia Amati is a very special young woman. I mean to *me*. Don't you dare hurt her."

"*Hurt* her? Why would I? I'm too grateful."

"Look, it's fine your period of celibacy's over and all that but I worry. No offense, but you can be rather—" Schulman paused, as he'd been on the point of saying jealous but this was too exact—"possessive."

"Who, me?"

Not for the first time Schulman thought that if his friend should ever experience a moment of genuine self-knowledge his head would probably explode.

"She's very, well, generous," Schulman said. "She makes a lot of men grateful."

"You're telling me she's a slut?"

Schulman frowned. He didn't like what he was doing. "Look, I've known her since she was nine. Her parents are friends of mine."

"Then, what?"

"Well, how can I put it? Amalia's like one of those resealable plastic bags. There are women like that—innocent whatever they do, as if their virginity grew back overnight."

"Like Prometheus' liver?" Katim laughed. "Well, I guess I know what you mean."

10

"You do?"

"Certainly. You're saying Amalia's not so much fickle as good-hearted."

The distinction was so much like insight that Schulman was surprised. "That's it."

"*La donna non e mobile, ma* . . . what's the Italian for generous?"

"*Generoso?*"

"*Ma generoso.* Sounds like an Italian gun-moll from the thirties."

Katim laughed but Schulman didn't.

Why should it matter to Schulman that Katim went to bed with Amalia Amati? And why should he worry about Katim hurting her when it was so much more likely to be the other way around? It was late in the day to protest the virginity of Nick and Francesca Amatis' darling younger daughter, though he believed her honor was intact and that was more important than a hymen. Was it that he didn't approve of Katim mixing business with pleasure or was it the decade of difference in their ages? Only the hard-boiled are immune to vulnerability. Maybe the problem was that he couldn't think of two more childish people than Katim and Amalia.

Mama and Papa Amati were retired to Arizona now. They were the first friends Schulman made after his emigration. Nick was a studio musician and Francesca a successful painter of flowers and landscapes, Eastern Italo-Americans who ran down New York to New Yorkers and California to Californians. They adored their daughters and drove them to perfection, Nick especially, albeit in the fondest way. Perhaps Schulman had made too many friends. Why was that? He wasn't particularly gregarious, didn't care for the social ladder or being seen at the right events. He'd always assumed his hectic social life must be Claire's doing, that crowded address book, all those receptions and dinner parties. The shock of her death was followed by perplexity that his social calendar didn't go blank, not even after a decent interval. Could it have been that all along it had been Schulman people sought and not Claire? If she had suspected this his wife had concealed her resentment. When Claire died, Schulman supposed he would become a recluse. It was a surprise that people went on phoning him, wanting him as their friend, confiding in him even more than before. Perhaps widowers are deemed particularly trustworthy. It might have been because people sensed Schulman meant them well, a rarity in the capital of Schadenfreude, or maybe it was because people saw Schulman as both dependable and non-threatening, as Katim did. In any case, he soon found himself transformed into Schulman the sympathetic amigo, the benevolent, quasi-involved narrator, the asexual repository of gossip, just as, professionally, he went on being the serviceable Schulman who could be relied on to make chase scenes chasier and love scenes lovier.

He was worried because he didn't know exactly what was worrying him. Was it Julia and Felice who worried him, that Katim was somehow betraying them with Amalia? That was preposterous. Julia had already married Jack Hunt, a perfect gentleman and long-time divorcé who loved her and had proved himself an impeccable stepfather. Katim, having more or less driven Julia away, nevertheless held a grudge, believed she had let him down; for a while he even claimed, in the melodramatic manner he affected, that Julia had "wrecked his life." But this was self-indulgence. For years Katim had lived off Julia's money and Julia's energy, took her for granted, put her and Felice deep in second-place behind his beloved Muse. Perhaps what troubled Schulman was that his friend thought that, having been abandoned by Julia, he had earned a free pass with Amalia and so might revenge himself by treating her badly. But Amalia was the butterfly, not Katim.

Schulman was feeling anticipatory guilt about what might happen. Claire used to make fun of him on this point. "You feel responsible when the sun doesn't come out, for the Santa Anna winds, the fires and the mudslides," she had said after one self-lacerating soliloquy. What Claire didn't understand was that guilt is independent of responsibility. It's entirely possible to feel the former while being innocent of the latter. Maybe that's what irritated her, what that dear, unbigoted woman called half-mockingly his *being such a Jew*.

"Does Annabelle know?" he asked Katim over the baked scallops.

"About me and Amalia? I don't suppose so. Why?"

"Because she might object."

"Why should she? What business is it of hers? Anyway, according to Amalia, Annabelle doesn't approve of anything she does, saving her legato. Look, I'm happy, at least for now. And I'm writing, writing damned well. I'll show you. I think you should be happy for me—and for Amalia too."

"And what about the future? You thinking of having one?"

Katim frowned then laughed. "Are you asking whether my intentions are honorable? Jesus, Karl, why do you always have to be the ant?"

12

"Because you're such a grasshopper."

"Look, you know how I tried with Julia. I cared too much. It was too one-sided."

"That so?"

"Isn't it obvious I loved her more than she loved me? And even Felice. I mean, couldn't she at least *pretend* to hate Jack a *little*?"

So that was the solace he'd settled on, thought Schulman, a grievance narrative.

Annabelle's husband had built a dream house up near Santa Monica, not ostentatiously large and certainly not on the beach but back in the arid hills where pet owners worry about coyotes and gardeners get discouraged. The clapboards were stained to look like cherry wood, as if the place were a breakfront; the red-tiled roof was cantilevered. A floor-to-ceiling window faced west; the furniture looked like a set of Platonic ideas. Most of the rooms were small, except for the living room with its great window and baby grand. There were three walls of bookshelves, the tomes punctuated by pre-Columbian faces and vases with dried flowers and small cacti. The bookless wall was covered by a huge abstract painting in deep reds— "Hell on a Good Day," Katim decided to call it. Two thick white rugs completed the *Architectural Digest* mis-en-scène.

It was late afternoon. Amalia had suggested they all go down to the beach to eat at one of the clam shacks after Katim made his presentation. Annabelle had called Katim to set up the meeting. She told him it was time for a progress report.

Amalia phoned Katim right after Annabelle. "Not too soon, is it, Sweetcakes?"

"Not at all," Katim had boasted. He had superstitiously resolved not to tell Amalia about the piece and she hadn't pressed, which disappointed him. On the other hand, he talked it over with Schulman nearly every day. Schulman had been encouraging and even made some practical suggestions. The fact was he had been working better than he had in two years, was fulminating with ideas, and the concerto was taking shape quickly, which he told Schulman is always the best way, or, as he said, "the only way I really can trust." Katim had often spoken to Schulman of Handel with his cataracts cobbling *Messiah* together in twenty-four days, and in Dublin weather. He envied Handel those twenty-four days.

Amalia had been arch. "Think we should show up together?"

Katim recalled Schulman's long face. "Probably not."

So the sisters were waiting for him when he pulled up the gravel driveway. Amalia met him at the door with a big wink. Katim was wearing old jeans and a black turtleneck and she whispered he looked like a young Paul McCartney.

Once inside, Katim got straight to the point.

"The concerto's going to have four movements."

"Like Brahms' *Second*," said Amalia.

"But not, I hope, quite such a bear to play?" added Annabelle nervously.

"Nothing beyond the two of you," Katim flattered.

"So, four movements," said Annabelle.

"The third's going to be the most extraordinary. No orchestral accompaniment." This was one of Schulman's notions.

"No orchestra? What will all those people do?" teased Amalia.

"They'll be listening to you, of course, rapt and ravished."

Annabelle was curious. "What is it, an interlude?"

"Think of it as an extended cadenza."

"Does it soar? Is it very romantic?" asked Amalia expectantly.

"Oh, romantic to the max. Bitter, sweet, lyrical, tragic, *molto cantabile* and with a roller coaster of a fugue at the end. Ten, maybe a dozen minutes." The roller coaster metaphor was Schulman's, too.

"And this, I take it, will be the *heart* of the piece?" asked Annabelle, beginning to appreciate the focus such a movement would put on them.

"You understand perfectly. Heart, kidney, lungs and all."

"And then?"

"And then the orchestra will have to come back to life—like the frozen people in Sleeping Beauty's castle—and play the finale. That's going to be *prestissimo*—like a bullet train. Oil up them magic knuckles."

Annabelle wanted to know how the concerto was to begin.

Katim leapt to his feet. "May I?" He crossed to the piano. "I can give you the first two themes. The movement's going to be neo-classical, a sonata-allegro. The dominant will turn into a minor and the tonic to a major by the end."

Later, Annabelle would tell herself that it was while Katim played the concerto's opening theme that she first thought of leaving her husband.

"*Katim Olympics —Les Olympiques Katim—Die Olympiade Katims*" read the home-made sign that hung across the entrance of her father's apartment, complete with the five interlocking rings. Felice considered it dubiously. "Olympics?" she said. "You mean games?"

"Several," Katim assured her.

"Like what?"

"Well, let's see. There's hide-and-seek of course, the indoor-outdoor hard-candy hunt, the fudge-making contest, the hopping race, then my old favorite, Is It Beethoven, Bach, or Brahms, and finally *your* favorite, role-reversal. What'd ya think?"

The way to overcome his panic over Felice's visits lay in improvisation. This is what Schulman had advised. Put yourself out for her, make things fun. Katim taught Felice to sing mock-fugues with him; they recorded them in the bathroom for the sake of the acoustics. He made up a series of adventure stories about a little girl named Elisa May. Elisa May's father was an explorer named Rolf Tarzansky, fearless and partial to balloons and iced coffee. Elisa May's mother was always reluctant to let Tarzansky take Elisa off on a dangerous journey, but then gave in and waited anxiously for her safe return. Katim composed all sorts of riddles, songs, and epigrams for Felice.

> There was a young lady named Katim.
> If her daddy weren't, she might date him.
> Well, at least she doesn't hate him!

He made up doggerel aimed at mutual reassurance.

> Felice's daddy writes silly tunes
> And he blows up enormous balloons.
> C'est vrai! Daddy adores his Felice
> Lots more than if she were, say, his niece,
> Likes her more than the Cat in the Hat,
> And will even when he's old and fat.

Best of all he wrote musical parodies for her such as "Für Felice" and "The Half-Minute Waltz."

Though Katim worried about his daughter's mental state, in fact Felice handled the separation and divorce better than he did. For a few weeks she suffered from stomach aches and threw the occasional tantrum, but this was perfectly normal, according to the pediatrician. Then one

Saturday it all just stopped. Felice thought of it as waking up when she woke up. Not without some guilt over abandoning her post, she gave up spiting her mother, blaming her father, and pretending to resent Jack Hunt. From that day, her stomach behaved itself and she became as philosophically detached as a seven-year-old can. It was, Julia explained joyfully to her new sister-in-law Susan, as if all on her own Felice had resolved to accept the New Order and make the best of it.

"Kids are resilient," mumbled Susan blandly, phone in the crook of her neck, as she stirred the red sauce and watched her own baby toss Cheerios from the high chair.

"I'm so relieved. I read that a divorce at this age can cause *permanent* damage," said Julia. From the moment she became a mother, she had begun to worry about her daughter. This was the reason for the girl's name. Though Katim objected that any literate people she met would always think of the woman Kafka jilted, Julia insisted on the name Felice so that her child would always be happy. "Names are stories," she said as if she really believed in magic.

"Maybe," Katim had said, "but the story always comes second."

Julia's labor had lasted fourteen hours. "Look at me," she commanded from her hospital bed. "Give in."

"Okay. You win," Katim said, then spoiled it with a joke. "Why is it that mothers always have moral superiority when Strindberg said that fathers can never be sure?" He giggled. "You do realize her initials are going to be F. K."

"You're a monster," sighed Julia.

Then they both stared with terror and wonder at the seven-pound being who was going to be Felice ever after.

After a lunch of grilled cheese and tomato soup, Felice had quickly found all five items in the treasure hunt, the last being a balled-up pair of socks Katim had stuffed in the oven.

"Two minutes, five seconds," he announced, looking at his watch. "You're getting too good at this, kid. What next? The park? A movie? Or, how about we zip over to Paris and pick up a decent baguette? We could maybe get a little onion soup too, and four or five bottles of perfume."

Felice wasn't buying it. "I haven't got any friends around here," she complained, hitting the socks against her palm like a blackjack.

Katim's heart fell.

"Mommy and Jack have a real house. How come you live in this poky little apartment?"

This was bad but he let her go on. Silence isn't a bad tactic while you're waiting for a strategy.

"I mean there's your piano and *it's* nice but it takes up practically the *whole* room. And everything's so old and not very . . . very *clean*. All the toys here are worn out, and how come you never make your bed properly?"

Katim sat down on the piano stool. This way they could look each other in the eye.

Felice was trembling. Her speech had gotten away from her and swollen to an enormity. It was nearly too much for her.

Katim felt unmoored but he had an idea that it would be smart to de-personalize the issue, whatever it really was.

"Tell me, sweetie, would you rather not come here to see me?"

"I didn't say *that*," she said in a small, lawyerly voice.

Katim raised an eyebrow. "Are you missing a big soccer game today? Is that it?"

"Daddy, you know I hate soccer."

"Oh yes. All that running and you can't use your hands."

"It's not *fair*, that's all."

"What's not fair, honey?"

She made a face. Honesty took a lot of concentration, a lot of nerve. Why did loving her father make her say bad things to him?

"What?" he insisted.

"Mommy and Jack are happy and rich and *you're* not either. It's not fair."

"Oh?"

"Yes, and you always try so *hard*, Daddy. I mean you try so hard it makes me sad."

"You think I'm unhappy?"

"Aren't you?"

Katim made a show of examining his two hands, lifted his left foot and scrutinized it, then the right. "Well, nope. I'm not all that unhappy, actually. I agree that this little nest may not be very splendid but it suits me fine. Remember what I told you about overhead?"

"Always keep it low," she repeated, the dutiful second-grader.

"Right! Of course, I miss *you* when you're not here—you know that—

and naturally there are times when I'm less than bursting with joy, when I fill up with a sort of yearning—"

Felice kept her distance. "What's *yearning*?"

"Yearning, young lady," said Katim, knitting his hands over one knee, "yearning is a romantic form of longing."

"What?"

"Okay. Listen to this."

Katim turned on the stool and played his daughter the opening theme of the concerto. "*That's* yearning."

Felice threw herself down on the sofa. "Oh, Daddy. I'm only seven, you know."

Katim joined her, pulled her to him, stroked her hair.

"Once upon a time a daddy took his little girl out for a walk. It was a lovely spring day. After they'd walked a while the little girl asked her daddy why the grass is green and her daddy said, 'I don't know, honey.' Then he took her hand and they walked a little further. 'Daddy?' said the little girl. 'Why's the sky blue?' 'I haven't a clue, sweetheart,' answered her daddy. When they got to the beach the girl asked, 'Daddy, why are there waves?' and her daddy answered, 'Really couldn't say, darling.' They walked along the sand. 'Daddy?' said the little girl. 'What is it, sweetie?' 'I hope you don't mind my asking all these questions.' 'Not at all,' said her daddy. 'How are you going to learn if you don't ask questions?'"

Katim had been working like a fiend, perhaps as hard as Handel. He scrawled, played, crossed out, wrote more. Over a two-day period he didn't answer his phone or even visit Schulman, slept about five hours, and ate whatever was left in the fridge, including an overripe cantaloupe. After drinking up all his coffee, he switched to tea. It was all prestissimo now. Never before had it gone like this for him, a prolonged, agonizing, joyful opening out, childbirth without labor. It would be stupid and ungrateful to stop. Schulman, he thought, was going to be blown away. The last call he had taken was from Amalia. She insisted on coming over on the grounds that, technically, she was his boss. "Stay away," he warned, but she came anyhow and they made love as if the Big One were going to hit any moment. Then he shooed her away. "Go, go," he implored. "Work, I've got to work. Nothing personal. You'll see." He had once shown her his parodies for Felice. "Well, thanks for the Half-Minute Waltz," she joked as he shoved her out the door.

Sunday afternoon. Felice had gotten back from her overnight with Katim at eleven and asked her mother if she could invite her best friend, Nancy Grillo, over for the afternoon. She craved her dyad; she was at that stage. The girls were on Felice's bed going through their respective doll wardrobes, negotiating trades. Felice let Nancy see that she was glum and waited impatiently for Nancy to ask why. Something was up with her father, she said; she didn't know exactly what. He was distracted, not himself, or rather he was more like his old self, the one that didn't care so much about her. Anyway, it was weird.

Nancy gave the matter her consideration. Back in kindergarten, she pointed out, there had been hardly any kids with divorced parents but by now it was the other way around. Lots of sour mommies in big cars dropping off sad kids. "At least you've got two parents," Nancy said on the compare-down-not-up principle, though her own parents had never had so much as a trial separation, a fact which she occasionally regretted.

"I have three, actually," corrected Felice and examined a minuscule sequined skirt.

Nancy fell quiet for a while, picking through the tiny clothes. "We'll do it better, you know. We'll do it right," she said with determination and an anger that surprised Felice.

The concerto was as good as finished and Katim felt used up. It was a masterpiece. It was going to make him famous. He wanted to call Julia and boast and then talk to Felice, sounding weary and triumphant and tender, and ring Schulman and just crow. Instead, though it was only noon, he collapsed on his bed, wondering for an instant why it hadn't occurred to him to telephone Amalia, the obvious choice. Then he lost consciousness.

Amalia had her own key. Though the apartment was full of California light and Katim was a light sleeper, he didn't move when she burst in with two bags of groceries or when she dumped the groceries, doffed her clothes, slid into his bed and climbed half on top of him. In a few moments she had him aroused yet not quite awake. Poor dear, she thought with amusement, he'll imagine he was dreaming; well, that's nice too. Amalia moved her mouth from his chest to his stomach and played arpeggios with her right hand.

Katim's apartment was in a squat thirties-style building, the Egmont Arms. Katim claimed to have chosen it not merely because it was cheap, but because the name reminded him of Beethoven's incidental music. For a time he called it the Armless Egmont and later the Nathanael West Memorial Flophouse. The place had no security arrangements, no buzzers from below and certainly no doorman. So Annabelle was able to walk right up the stairs and knock on Katim's door, which her ardent sister had neglected to close tight behind her.

I hardly recognize myself, Annabelle thought with excitement and disgust as she knocked three times, each time harder. With the last, the door swung open.

On the drive over in her Saab, the street map laid out beside her on the passenger seat, she decided that all she needed was just one afternoon in bed with Katim and she'd be cured of the obsession that had seized her. One afternoon—just one hour—then everything could go back to normal and she and Amalia could resume their sexual division of labor. Mrs. Strelnikov was beyond thinking of Mr. Strelnikov, beyond thinking of calling ahead.

Schulman seldom had to show up at a studio more than a couple times a week. It was generally accepted that his work was only delayed by time spent with producers or, worse, with directors. All the equipment he needed was crammed into the big sound-proofed studio of his condominium. He and Claire had bought the place around the time condos were invented. They had, so to speak, gotten in on the ground floor by buying the top floor of the five-story building. Schulman had no idea how much the place would be worth on the market now but, from what his friends said, he gathered that it could be traded in for a small nation in the southern hemisphere. He was house rich. Claire had remodeled the place a few times over the years and Schulman had assented to all her requests, on the sole condition that his studio remain off-limits to the decorators. The joint had always been capacious but now, with Claire gone, it felt cavernous, far too large for a widower edging toward retirement or a coronary. But he owned it outright, the location couldn't be beat, and it was home. Anyway, he couldn't imagine working anywhere but his studio. He badly needed to work, too, though no longer for the money. From the time he had read them as an undergraduate he had never forgotten Freud's words, that nothing else "attaches the individual so firmly to reality as laying emphasis on work." He also remembered that Freud had to admit most people will do almost anything to avoid labor. That's just how it was with him. He used to joke—he yearned for nothing more than to work yet there wasn't anything he wouldn't do to escape it.

Schulman's attitude toward his vocation resembled that of a good plasterer. He did it to please others, professionally and without pomposity. He respected what he did though not himself for doing it. Artists he revered and forgave anything, as he forgave Katim. He had the odd custom of putting on a coat and tie before going into his studio each morning. When Katim discovered this he told Schulman that he reminded him of the Englishman in a Maugham story who lived alone in the middle of the Malayan jungle but dressed for dinner every night.

Once, at a dinner party, Schulman had been badgered by a reviewer about his low opinion of movie music. Schulman had quoted Norman Rockwell, who insisted he was nothing but an illustrator and rejected the label of artist. The critic, who thought movies the non plus ultra of Western civilization, objected. "Either you overestimate art or undervalue yourself, Schulman," he said, smiling at his own turn of phrase. The remark wasn't intended as a compliment and Schulman shrugged. But Claire, who agreed with this disagreeable fellow, leaned across the dinner table and made it worse. "The two aren't mutually exclusive," she said.

Katim agreed with Schulman about what he did. In fact, he listened to Schulman's opinion of his work precisely because he had so little regard for Schulman's. As the *Double Concerto* took shape Katim had come over more and more, ostensibly to seek Schulman's praise, but he ended up with a lot of advice. The rigmarole was rather childish. Katim would announce how he planned to manage some passage then raise his voice at the end. Bright, curious children operate the same way. They propose a hypothesis and wait to be corrected. "Cows give milk through their big noses?" "Lightning is God taking pictures?"

When the bell rang at eight-thirty in the morning Schulman was still in his pajamas. He assumed it must be Katim, who had been showing up at all hours, but the voice that came through the security box was female.

"It's Cassie," it said, breathy and anxious. "From Donnelly's."

"Cassie? Come on up."

What could he do? There wasn't time to get dressed. Schulman ran to the bedroom, grabbed his robe, thought of opening the door for her then yelling in from the bedroom, begging her to wait until he had made himself decent.

Schulman had never seen Cassie except in the ridiculous outfit

Donnelly insisted his waitresses wear, demure skirt, white apron, tiny mobcap. Now here she was at his door in a short black skirt, tights, and a purple blouse under the kind of wool coat you don't see in California. Though she was pulling a suitcase behind her, what drew Schulman's eye was her hair and legs, both longer than he expected. Cassie looked very pretty, but distressed and embarrassed. She parked the suitcase by the door and stepped into the apartment in a sort of submissive crouch with her little fists held in front of her.

Schulman wanted to dress, to offer her a cup of coffee, ask how she found him and why she'd bothered, to tell him what her problem was and about the suitcase. This was too much all at once and, anyway, before he could say anything, Cassie was apologizing and bursting into tears, the little fists coming up to her eyes.

For a moment Schulman rocked back and forth on his L. L. Bean slippers then he stepped forward and took her in his arms. It was a conditioned reflex.

He led Cassie into the living room, sat her down on the couch, left to fetch a box of tissues, came back, sat down beside her, got up again, then sat down again. He didn't say a word, not even "there, there."

Cassie's age was a subject to which Schulman had devoted little thought. To him she was simply one of the young and that was enough. She claimed to be an aspiring actress from Indiana and if she wanted to be a cliché that was okay by him. At the restaurant they could play displaced Hoosiers together; it made a pleasant bond and justified his huge tips. He was a widower, a Hoosier Jew, and she was nice to him. If Cassie went to the trouble to track him down she would certainly tell him why. Even in his pajamas he could be patient, but he was bound to speculate. There was that suitcase by the door. Obviously the girl was in some sort of trouble. Pregnant? Raped? Abusive boyfriend? But why did it have to be sex trouble? Maybe she just needed money. Of course he would give it to her and then she would go away.

Cassie pulled herself together. She rubbed her fists into her eyes, those little fists. "You haven't asked me anything." That was the first thing she said.

Schulman replied with a tenderness that surprised him. "Why should I?" Tenderly is how one talks to a good-looking young woman who barges into your living room and weeps.

Cassie looked at him and managed a half-laugh. He remembered

Claire doing the same thing—the stifled little chuckle that marks Niagara's end. "*Look* at you," she said. "You're not even dressed." It was a way of apologizing. Schulman blushed and stood up yet again.

Cassie patted the sofa and he dutifully sat down next to her. The patting, he noticed, had somehow shifted things and put her in her control. "Look," she said, "my parents were in a car accident last night. My father was killed and my mother's still in intensive care. I got the call an hour ago. I'm on my way to the airport. I don't know when I'm coming back or even if."

"That's terrible, Cassie. You need a ride, anything?"

"You think I came to ask for a ride?"

"Do you need any money?"

Cassie slipped out of her Indiana coat, then out of her purple blouse.

"I'm thirty-two. I'm unhappy and I just realized I'm crazy about you. Because I was about to leave."

"What? Cassie, this—"

"Shut up. Look, I'll be gone before you know it."

This proved untrue.

Ten minutes after she left in a cab, Bert Forster telephoned.

At the last minute the Amati sisters had cancelled a recital in San Francisco. The sponsoring agency called him, angry; that's the way he found out. Forster was alarmed, embarrassed, and he wanted an explanation. Was somebody sick, or worse? He phoned Annabelle but got her answering machine. Then he called Amalia who said, "Sorry, Bert. Ask my bitch of a sister," then hung up.

He tried the architect at work. He was about to go into a meeting and could only spare a minute. Yes, there had been quite a spat. Annabelle had said some harsh things about Amalia. No, he hadn't a clue what was behind it, unless it was the last three decades. So that's why San Francisco was out. You know how sisters can be. No, nothing like this before but no doubt they'd make it up in a day or two. Sorry but he had to get to his meeting.

Annabelle had retreated to her bedroom, feeling like a sore that needed lancing, all suppuration and pus. She kept seeing Amalia with Katim's robe half covering her, more shameless than if she'd been stark naked. That robe was a catalyst; years of floating rancor and resentment crystallized in a moment. She had slapped Amalia then fled to her car and cried like an idiot all the way up the Pacific Coast Highway. She hadn't wanted so much, had she? Hell, this was California. One man for one afternoon. Amalia always got everything that mattered: the blond hair, Daddy's partiality, bigger breasts, first to get rid of her virginity. The irrationality of her jealousy, the shock of her hatred, divided about evenly between her sister and herself, overcame Annabelle the way mudslides did the mansions, sweeping everything down in a tide of foulness.

That night she had denounced her sister in a great screed. Annabelle had always wanted to throw Amalia out of the nest; now she would demolish their niche.

Forster sounded apologetic and fretful, rather as Cassie did when she'd come through his door. Still in his pajamas, still dumbfounded, Schulman could think of little else than Cassie sweeping into his sanctum like a wet dream. But when she left what he felt wasn't guilt or shame but perplexity and joy. For a few minutes he'd bounced off the walls, then went into the bedroom to see if he could still smell her on the sheets. That's what he was doing when Forster called. He'd run to the phone; it might be Cassie on her cell from the taxi. She would tell him that he hadn't been dreaming and she'd be back, wait and see. Or that he should drop everything and come with her to Indiana.

As Forster began to explain who he was Schulman collected himself. "I know who you are, Mr. Forster. You represent half the people I know—the better half, incidentally. What can I do for you?"

"Well, I'm not exactly sure what and it isn't exactly for me either. I asked around and everybody says you're Katim's best friend."

"Katim?"

"I suppose you know about the commission for the concerto? For the Amatis?"

"Yes?"

"I always thought you had something to do with that. Well, there's this problem."

"Deadline for the premiere? I think the piece is about done, if that's it."

"No, not that. The problem's that there may not be any premiere."

"Why not?"

"Look, I'm telling you this because I'd rather tell you than Katim. Frankly, I think he's the problem."

"How's Katim a problem?"

"I don't even know that. All I know is that the Annabelle and Amalia aren't speaking to each other and they just canceled a recital up in San Francisco and if they break up, which is what they're telling me they're doing, then I won't be making any money off them and they won't be making any money at all. The other thing is that Katim might want to read his contract."

"What about the contract?"

"It says that the Amati sisters own the sole and exclusive right to the concerto for three years after the first performance which, of course, they also have the exclusive right to give."

"So?"

"So the way the thing's written, if they don't premiere it your friend's magnum opus is going to wind up on the shelf. I mean, indefinitely, as far as the eye can see."

Schulman was horrified. "But that's completely ridiculous."

"That's never a problem for the lawyers, I've found."

"You think Katim's responsible for whatever's happened between the sisters, that he can patch things up?"

"Call it a hunch. Anyway, I was really looking forward to hearing that concerto. I imagine you were too."

"What do you want from me?"

"I really don't know."

Schulman paused. "Why do you think I'm so eager to hear it?"

"Just another hunch," said Forster. "Bye-bye, Mr. Schulman."

By now it has probably occurred to you that this has been a first-person narrative masquerading as the other kind. What's true of me is true of many so-called omniscient narrators. The difference is that usually the teller preserves the illusion by never disclosing himself and so his unreliability, his human finitude.

I set out to tell the story of a piece of unheard music. I'm not sure why I did it in quite this way, whether out of idleness or compulsion, or why I didn't do a better job of keeping myself out of it. It was always Marlow I identified with, never Lord Jim, always Nick, never Gatsby. Now I'm not even sure whose story I've been telling—the concerto's, Katim's, the Amatis', Felice's, or my own. Maybe this just means that I've told the story ineptly, as a circle without a center. Anyway, I'm not honest enough to write an autobiography. Have I made Katim up, then? Has Katim served me as a sort of living pseudonym, an alter-ego devised to preserve the separation of art from illustration? No, it's not so bad as that. I assure you Katim really does exist. In fact, I'm still in touch with him. And he's still a composer too, and not such a bad one, within his limits.

Katim never acknowledged how much of his work I proposed, shaped, directed, and outright did for him. Like all deeply vain people, he reasoned deductively. Even when I first met him Katim had already forged a religion of his talent. This amused me but I was also drawn to his self-assurance. Like Keats, Katim wanted nothing but immortality, that his name should not be writ on water, and he was sure he deserved it. Katim's axioms ruled out the idea of his having an equal, let alone a collaborator, and so I found I could contribute as much as I liked to his work because, by definition, I had nothing to contribute. It was easy to let him think I was only humbly putting forward the most minor suggestions—a diminished chord here, a modulation there, perhaps this little tune could go in just here. Soon I was writing whole passages which, because of his logic, he regarded as negligible. This suited me perfectly. I'm not saying I composed Katim's stuff. It would be more accurate to say we composed together. After all, collaboration's a complicated business; the frontiers of identity can be as shifty as the ones drawn across the Sahara.

Not everything I've said about Katim and the others is verifiable; nevertheless, I believe it's true. When Julia, at the time executive secretary to a big-shot producer pal of mine, asked me to help her husband she probably meant help him to do what I did, make money by writing for the movies. This I admit I never did. I acquiesced in Katim's ambition; I entered into it. I can't say when my little nudges blossomed into something more. Perhaps it was just my wish to see how far I could go. What Katim wrote was good; it inspired me. Working with him satisfied an ambition whose tousled little head I thought I had long before held under the waves.

Out here people only take seriously the culture that was fabricated yesterday. It's part of California's charm; the state motto, rendered into Latin, could be from Henry Ford, "History is bunk." But this puts demands on people; the lotus-eating is overemphasized. It's much harder to make a good movie than a bad concerto. We have first-class museums, theatrical revivals for the nostalgic and intellectual, but that kind of stuff isn't serious because it doesn't pay and whatever doesn't pay is self-indulgence. Either art dolls itself up, gets itself liposucked, democratized, and industrialized or it's a hobby—or, worse, a monument. All Henry James' stories about artists are cautionary tales. There's the one about the author who can't succeed because every potboiler he tries to write turns into a masterpiece; there's the one about the young writer conned out of the girl by the master he reveres, and the one who's advised to be as dead as he can be. I was careful; I never even told Claire how far things had gone with Katim.

Julia and Katim had what I call a San Andreas marriage, one with lots of little fissures running through it and one big fault. Katim, paralyzed by faith in his talent, was a feckless provider, an indifferent father, and, worst of all, self-righteous about his shortcomings. Didn't Nietzsche say a married philosopher is a bad joke? Julia stuck it out longer than anyone could have expected. The divorce might have gone smoothly, Julia finding happiness with the stalwart Jack, Katim with his solitary art. The fly in the ointment was Felice who went on loving her father long after her mother had given up doing so. It's a peculiarity of such situations that men like Katim sometimes do better at being fathers when better is likely to do the most harm. They rouse themselves to perform. "Für Felice," and "The Half-Minute Waltz" are just such performances.

I attended the Amati sisters' first recital; their parents had invited me. The girls opened their program with Milhaud's delectable *Scaramouche*, followed it with Brahms' four-handed *Waltzes* then three *Hungarian Dances*. Huge applause. After the break, the girls pulled off the difficult Rachmaninoff Suite. Wonderful to hear and watch, the two glossy pianos, the two sleek girls: Annabelle staring so intently at the keyboard she might have been searching it for lice, Amalia, head on the move, flirting with the house as if we were all her father.

The *Double Concerto* is the best thing either Katim or I have ever done. It's a passionate piece and I suppose this quality must have derived from what was deepest in us at the time, our respective losses and dispossessions. Yearning is a romantic form of longing. Forster's prediction came true; the piece never has been performed in public and to this day languishes in legal limbo, like a soul awaiting redemption. This is the kind of irony at which I could afford to shrug, but not Katim. He craved the fame of having written while I wanted only the pleasure of writing. Once I thought Katim a holy fool but maybe he's simply a talented fool. In any case, what we made belonged to the sisters Amati and now belongs, in effect, to nobody.

Here's how things turned out.

Annabelle suffered a sort of nervous collapse, was briefly hospitalized, recovered, gave birth to twin boys sired by the architect, the designer of her new niche. She no longer plays the piano in public.

Amalia, ever the virginal femme fatale, dropped Katim, moved on to other men and a third-rate career as a second-tier soloist, no longer represented by the perceptive and redoubtable Bert Forster.

I helped Katim get a job teaching music at Indiana University. You could say I sent him back where I came from. The University has given him an email account, so I hear from him from time to time. He still composes a little and gets his stuff performed at student concerts. For the last year he's been seeing the secretary of the philosophy department. Felice has visited him twice. Unfortunately, I gather neither occasion went well.

I'm tempted to leave Cassie out of this final roundup but if I did you'd conclude she's just an aging man's Hollywood fantasy, and a derivative one at that. Perhaps so. As I say, I'm not honest enough to write autobiography. However, the fact is that right now Cassie is lying on my living room couch watching an old movie. I wrote the score. The film was a hit when it came out, a love story with a happy ending. The novel on which it's based ended in murder and insanity but the focus group demanded a better outcome for the heroine, or the charming actress who played her, so the last reel was rewritten and I got to compose something sweet. Who's to say humdrum happy endings are less worthy of belief than melodramatic catastrophes?

TinderBox

Most people believe the entire city was consumed, nothing left but cinders, blistered ruins, cremated citizens. But if you hold a match to, say, an oak leaf, even one that's brown and withered, something will be left, black veins that once carried life-giving water and nutrients, the leaf's armature. Even the hottest fires don't wipe out a forest. Things survive in secret places, by cunning or by luck. I was lucky.

I had wanted to be a composer, not an inspector of houses, enumerator of debris, uncoverer of cadavers, avoider of dogs. That was my case, more or less, but I couldn't complain. In those days the moment you even thought of grumbling about your own renunciations the complaint turned as weightless as the breath enveloping it. Now that everyone had grasped the fragility of cities lamentations too crumbled, blew away like burnt leaves. It's possible we had no Jeremiah because we were all Jeremiahs.

Nights made you think of the Dark Ages. Moonlight glinted off metal that twisted out of heaps of bricks. It had been a city of bricks. Countless bricks.

People used to say of something reliable that it was solid as a brick wall. Now it was painful and funny to think of the making, firing, transporting, and laying of bricks in thousands of courses, the spreading of mortar between them, the strings painstakingly stretched to keep each course straight, walls plumb, the fastidious work around windows, the aching backs of hod-carriers. Bricks. All that work and in the end they might just as well have been playing cards.

I had my room and my life. I was young and resilient so I expected something to turn up. One morning I went out into the streets, into the rubble and stench. Something did turn up and right away, a piece of paper affixed to a scorched pole. A piece of paper that had not burned. I tore it off and headed south.

There was no one else around. The distribution of people was completely changed. Many remained in hiding but if you looked around you'd assume most were dead. Near the corner of what had been Ockham and Broad Streets I encountered a big policeman who glared as if he held me personally responsible for all his unpaid overtime. He ought to have been glad to see me, I thought, glad for me and for him. But he was not. For him depopulation had not raised the value of remaining lives, rather the contrary. With no partner, backup, no jails, courts or paddy wagons, he was law and order. Or perhaps he felt ridiculous in his uniform, patrolling a beat that no longer existed.

His hostility made me polite. "Excuse me, officer, can you tell me where to find the Office of Emergency Housing?" I quickly held up the flyer so he wouldn't suppose I was selfishly looking to the government to put me up. No, I was here to serve, just like him; I wanted to do my bit, whatever I could. No need to mention the promised two meals a day. Hadn't we all suffered? Hadn't we all felt the same things at the same time, like an audience in the hands of a master playwright whose tragedy had gotten out of hand and overflowed the stage?

His thumb was huge, good for squashing roaches and ex-would-be composers. He jerked it contemptuously over his burly shoulder. "How is it you're alive when X and Y and Z aren't?" There was no need to say it aloud.

The Office of Emergency Housing was established, fittingly, in a firehouse. The ground floor of the solid old building was still standing, no doubt rescued by its inhabitants. Several offices occupied the first floor, empty now of fire trucks but with the old brass pole still extending upward into thin air. These were not proper offices, no more than a few metal desks and some filing cabinets. I looked the place over. Below a window covered with cardboard a pale, corpulent man sat despondently. His desk had a sign reading Registry of Deeds taped to it. Across the cracked gray floor representatives of the Sanitation and Water departments argued desultorily with one another while, nearby, a representative of the Electric Company—for all I knew it could have been the Director himself—sat staring into space. These men were dressed haphazardly, in the vestments of indifference and defeat. By contrast, in the middle of what had been the garage, batting away at old manual typewriters, sat three vibrantly dressed young women, complete with make-up. They alone had eyes wide open and held themselves erect, moved with purpose, typing what could only be pointless dispatches, reports, letters, forms, appeals, minutes, communiqués, press releases. In the corner, on a low table that must have been salvaged from somebody's living room, a coffee pot simmered away over a heating element. These people have a generator, I thought. They had coffee. I did not begrudge the government a bit of electricity or even real coffee. On the contrary, I was impressed; electricity itself was a kind of hope. I would have been grateful to be offered a cup of coffee, but no one took any notice of me.

I went up to the Registrar of Deeds and stood at attention before him, in my head a phrase remembered from old movies, "Reporting for duty, sir."

"Well?" he said morosely. "What do you want?" His words suggested impatience but his soft body was in the grip of inertia, of gravity. Balding, pale, overweight, he sat sunk in his gray rolling chair as if paralyzed by the question of what to register.

"I'm here about this, sir," I said, trying to hand him the flyer.

He gave it the merest glance. "Downstairs." His voice sounded like pebbles in a narrow lead pipe, high but rough and muffled.

How does one become a Registrar of Deeds? A snug berth for politicians' brothers-in-law, I thought resentfully, spoil of a stupid loyalty. Was he in mourning for his family or his records, all burnt up? The poor guy looked to me like a man with no mettle left to test. I turned away with relief, the way you do after coming out of the funeral of somebody at least a generation older than yourself.

The cement stairs were in good shape. The basement was cooler and everything smelled of smoke, of course, but there was also a reek of damp. Still, it was lively. Beneath the pipes, now useless, the walls were covered by big street maps and no less than three desks were piled high with papers. People sat at these but not like the invertebrate Registrar upstairs. Here they perched like birds on a branch, eyes bright as sparrows' because they had work to do. These people had resilient spines and spring in their legs. I felt a wave of optimism. I was so young I'd have seized on anything and, really, just to look at these people was refreshing. They even had a functioning telephone; I heard it ring. What had wrecked the departments upstairs had invigorated theirs. It's better to count what's left standing than to wail over the ruins.

Except for one dignified, rather gaunt man in a gray suit coat, everybody in the Office of Emergency Housing was young, more or less my own age. My youth resonated sympathetically with theirs. We would remember the same music, the same movies. They chattered as they bustled back and forth among the three desks and the wall maps on which little areas were shaded in various colors.

I approached the thin man whom, because of his age and dignity, I took to be the chief.

He looked up from his desk and watched me approach. He was evidently not one to miss anything. I prepared to be challenged, disparaged, dismissed.

"I hope you aren't looking for a place to live," he began apologetically. I was surprised and touched. It was nearly a greeting.

"No, sir." I held up the flyer.

"Ah, an applicant. Splendid luck! Fifteen minutes ago and I'd have sent you packing but I've just been told we need somebody to replace—who is it, Babette?"

"Smithson," Babette barked over her shoulder and went on coloring in a corner of one of the maps. "Falling I-beam," she added.

"Smithson," sighed the chief in a tone of mild regret. "All right. You're here so you're hired. You get a clipboard, an identification badge, three pens, and two meals a day at the government canteen. For now, just soup and bread. When we can, if your work's good and when cash is worth something again, we may pay you some money. See that good-looking young fellow over there?"

The good-looking young fellow occupied the third and smallest desk. He was not all that good looking or even all that young but you could see he had plenty of energy and the purposive look of the practical idealist; he could have been an officer in the Salvation Army. Amazingly, he was wearing a white shirt and a striped tie. Wasting no time mustering me in, it took him only seconds to extract a new clipboard from a drawer and a sheaf of forms from a stack on his desk. These he crisply inserted under the clip; then he poured three plastic ball-points from an open box, laid them neatly on the clipboard, and passed everything to me.

"My last name's unpronounceable," he said with precise enunciation, standing up and holding out his hand. "Call me Vikram. Yours?"

I told him my name and he wrote it down on yet another clipboard. Then he printed it on a blank identification badge. I liked the way he wrote my name; it was painstaking rather than petty, as if my name mattered.

Vikram had punctilio.

"Good. Smithson's section—yours now—that's roughly the area from Rheinach Park to the docks. Know it? No? Here, I'll show you. Follow me."

He leapt from his desk, brushed neatly by Babette, and took me over to one of the maps of the city-that-was, of what had been built up over centuries with only sporadic attempts at planning, streets divided on either side into tiny plots with tinier numbers in them, unnamed alleys snaking like little wayward brooks through the orderly grid. Vikram drew an imaginary square with his finger. "Your area," he declared with a smile. "Your responsibility." Then he explained my duties.

Once I had dreamed of writing symphonies.

I was young. I set out into the silent, smoldering city with my clipboard, badge, and pens like the youngest son.

Stillness did not settle over the city at once. All through those days sparks spun in the foul winds and there was the noise of walls crashing down, undermined by unextinguished fires, unnecessary sirens. The little help that arrived in the first days didn't help. During the first night and day hundreds of survivors had camped out in Rheinach Park. That was where I decided to begin my work.

No one occupied the park any longer, only heaps of abandoned trash, rags, and plastic bottles. The campers had made it easy for the evacuation trucks and I don't doubt most were happy to go. It's an old ritual, a Biblical cliché, people streaming out of destroyed, judged cities. Women with hands over their eyes, men with mouths set, stunned children. Can the god of deserts hate cities so much?

The trees closest to the streets were like burnt hands reaching desperately skyward but those further in looked normal, except that they were covered with ash. I stared for a full minute at an ancient oak, reassured by its indifference. It's still growing, I remember thinking; sap hasn't boiled, cells still dividing, going right on turning sunlight into oak.

We learned later how the people in the suburbs, maybe with shame, had quietly prevailed on the authorities to end the evacuations. As a result the larger urban shelters that were still intact—some school gymnasia, theaters, museums, train stations—were full to bursting. I suppose the plan was to disperse the overflow throughout the city, even though this would create difficulties for the distribution of food and water. But I only thought this out later. At the time I focused on the task before me. I had my badge and clipboard and pens. I had my responsibility and was glad of its limits.

Despite the fate of Smithson, whom I anyway imagined as much older than myself, I didn't consider my job dangerous. I had merely to work my way through the desolation looking for any places that might serve to house people. These I would record on the forms using my clipboard and one of my pens. There really were places here and there in the ruins that had been preserved. No one really understands how this happens, how what is all-consuming doesn't consume all. Vikram had instructed me to keep my eyes peeled for these pockets of potential utility, no matter how small. He called them "the whims of Mr. Nobel," a little joke I didn't get at the time. The very first tenement into which I ventured had a wholly intact bathroom, not a tile disturbed. I picked my way to it over charred timbers and rippling linoleum, bed springs, a blackened refrigerator, tried the taps and the toilet but of course there was no water. In the medicine cabinet I found reminders of the weakness and vanities of the flesh they had outlasted. There was a bottle of astringent, a jar of cold cream, patent medicines for hemorrhoids and backache, children's aspirin, three lipsticks, a tin of bandages, hair cream, and a rusted razor. I thought of taking the children's aspirin.

It was as though people had decided to collect in one place as much combustible material as possible and then blithely forgot about it, never asking which generation would see the inevitable conflagration. Naturally, no one thought of it as inevitable; no one thought of it, period. Even a small city breeds the illusion of control, confidence in human mastery over not just the environment but events too. We had grown up to think of nature, which can be insidious and vengeful, as so powerless that we had to build little parks to preserve it. And was it so different with our own natures, our own urges? No one looks over his city and thinks of it as a target, at least not for long. It's not normal to reckon with squares and apartment blocks in terms of sudden oxidation, except perhaps for fire inspectors. But even those experts' worries are on a small scale; they'd be anxious about wires with stripped insulation, or newspapers piled near boilers, old paint cans. To urbanites, city life is normal and what's normal must be stable. City life is interesting because it's complicated, characterized by all sorts of reticulated connections, like all those pipes that now lay punctured and cracked. People run into one another, eat together, get married and divorced, go to galas, movies, balls, discos. They have cousins, high school pals, lovers, business associates, mortal enemies. Even if you live alone, you're still stuck on a tremendous web made out of countless tiny ones. No one can disentangle a city, no more than people could untie Gordius' knot, which likewise proved suddenly vulnerable in the end.

I wasted the whole morning rooting through two blocks of tenements. I came on three corpses, all partially buried, all unrecognizable. The first made me jump and I vomited right there in the open, but I was prepared for the second and third. On my own authority, I made a note of each body's location; Vikram had neglected to tell me what to do in such eventualities or what Smithson had done. Perhaps I was being officious but it was an aspect of my youth to have a sense of duty that exceeded my instructions. As for the addresses, these I could only approximate. From the point of view of physics, burning may be an orderly process, but from any human angle it messes everything up; stuff flies around, half of one building tumbles on top of another. Street numbers, names on mailboxes, any little signs of human identity are blotted out.

The work was hard. My clothing was smudged and my hands black. My back and legs ached from awkward climbing and I was thirsty. There were ravenous dogs to avoid, though they had not yet gathered into packs. It was just dawning on them that they were no longer pets. I soldiered on. People were counting on me; I had a responsibility.

The south end of the city appeared to be deserted and for good reason. I had been working all morning and had yet to come on any building that might, even under the most generous interpretation, be deemed habitable. I seldom ran across anyone and when I did encounter some straggler or displaced person, they glanced at me anxiously and shuffled quickly away. In the middle of one block, however, an old man with wild eyes jumped up from a naked stoop and challenged me. He gripped a length of pipe. "Hold it right there, sonny. Neighbors are away, see, so I'm taking care of the neighborhood. Watching over things. I don't know you. What're you doing around here?"

I hastened to show him my badge and told him what a fine job he was doing. He turned my badge over suspiciously but eventually gave it back without my having to ask.

"All right," he said with an air of authority. "Okay, sonny. Get on with you now."

I turned a corner and came on a large property surrounded by a wrought iron fence, the old-fashioned kind whose palings are spears. The lot seemed too large for the city, at least half an acre. Skeletons of hemlocks and maples stood forlornly in the colorless yard. The grass was a horrid blackish gray.

The house would have been grand, though probably not recently. It was one of those piles conjured up over a century ago by tycoons with large guts, fierce appetites, and vast families, the sort of pompous edifice that epitomized its proprietor's convoluted life and commercial dealings—thousands of square feet of space, probably topped by crenellations and turrets, all burned away now. I pictured a generous porch extending on three sides, mature rhododendrons and yews pressing up against the railings, children playing croquet as women in long white dresses watched from the shade, gossiping.

The front door, massive and often painted, still stood but was about as useful as the Maginot Line, as the walls around it had collapsed. I just walked in. Bare traces of three stairways remained, the nearest of them immense. Once upon a time there would have been a library, a conservatory, servants' quarters, larders, back and front parlors, dressing rooms, nurseries, broom closets, sewing and lumber rooms, an attic crammed with bandboxes, steamer trunks, desiccated toys, musty finery, forgotten sheet music. Fuel galore. It had been a mammoth among houses. Single families had not lived in such places for a long time, at least not in the city. What with income taxes and depression the house would have been divided into apartments generations ago.

Everything I saw suggested crude metaphors. The three stairways rose part way into nothingness. Segments of the interior walls stood like one-legged bathers resisting an undertow. Shards of glass and slate shingles lay all over like scattered tablets in a pyramid. Looking at the scorched, flowery wallpaper was like viewing a corpse's underwear; seeing the dangling wires and pipes like peering into a mortal wound.

The kitchen was several times the size of my own room. I found a door in one still-standing wall. I opened it, took one step into the semi-darkness and fell, "ass over teakettle" as my grandfather the master sergeant would have said. I misjudged the distance between the risers, which were uncommonly narrow, as if made for children's feet, and pitched forward. Fortunately, my shoulder took the brunt of the fall on the stone steps or I could easily have snapped my neck, another Smithson. I saw my clipboard fly above me, the top form whipping up like a broken wing.

"Shit."

"Watch your language."

"What?" A little dazed, I had an impression of someone seated at a card table. The voice was female—no, feminine.

"Can you get up?" She sounded less concerned than impatient. I supposed she was frightened.

"I think so," I said unthreateningly.

"Okay. Do it. Then go away."

I got to my knees.

"Don't be afraid," I said as one might to a trembling puppy and reached for my badge.

"Afraid of you?" She laughed—no, cackled. "Fire, rats, dogs, gangs maybe." At least she didn't add "but not you."

I didn't want to frighten her and yet felt humiliated that I hadn't. The male ego is perverse, though easily understood if considered as a wine glass.

"It was the steps. I'm sorry."

"You sure are."

She hadn't moved. The light was peculiar, soft, liquid. She had an oil lamp on the table. Her face was just behind it and so in shadow. Then she leaned a little forward, maybe to check if my leg was broken. I estimated that she was a bit older than myself, maybe thirty. She had on a pair of blue jeans and a loose pullover that was either tan or gray. Her long hair was uncombed. It looked sort of red but that was owing to the lamplight. She stood up and put her hands on her hips. She looked pretty cocky with that snub nose of hers.

Though I would have liked to have scared her at least a little, I was relieved to see she wasn't holding a lead pipe or a wrought-iron spear.

She bent down and picked up my clipboard which had wound up nearer her than me. "What's this about? You taking a census or something?"

Facetiousness, I thought, suggested sanity. I didn't think mad people could be ironic.

"Not exactly a census," I said, getting gingerly to my feet and vigorously rubbing my shoulder. "A census of houses, of rooms, not of people."

"It isn't obvious enough that there aren't many left of either? Oh, I see. We need to count to know exactly how bad it was. Or to say it wasn't all that bad, after all. Could have been worse."

I fumbled with my badge and held it out to her. She ignored it so I looked on the floor for my pen.

In the shadows I could see a mattress, a Styrofoam cooler, four large jugs of spring water, an open cardboard box with cans in it and a lot of closed cartons. There were paper towels, two bags of briquettes, blankets, books piled in the corner. In some ways it resembled my own room, cramped but cozy, though I was not prepared for a siege. Also, my own room was above ground, an open boat on the ocean of ash, while she had a den, a burrow.

"You're staying here, alone?"

She sighed. "You going to leave now?"

I considered the question seriously as I rubbed my shoulder. I admit I could have used a little sympathy. "Not quite yet, if you don't mind."

She sighed again, sat down at the table, then bounced right up.

"I only have the one chair. You'd better use it."

"I'm all right. Really."

"You don't look it. Your cheek got a cut. The way you fell, it wasn't very funny."

"Funny? Not very funny? Just a wee bit funny?"

She moved away from the chair, back to her cartons. I sat down and turned toward her.

"Then you're all alone here?"

She still wasn't frightened. "To be alone in a city is really to be alone," she said softly.

"That's true," I admitted. It was a serious remark and I paused to let it settle. "Yes, alone, but, well, I'm here. The government—"

"Which you represent?"

"Well, I suppose. In a way. Actually, I got hired this morning. Just went into the office. Anyway, the government's trying—"

"To take this away from me. Right?"

"No, of course not. I'm just responsible for making a list—"

"Of places to commandeer. It's martial law now, isn't it?"

"Why won't you let me finish a sentence?"

"You finished that one." There was no getting the better of her.

"Anyway, what do you suppose the list is for? Do you even know?"

Did I? "No, I don't. I think they want to find places for people who—"

"Exactly. For other people."

I tried to reassure her with logic. "Why other people when you're already here?"

"Other people may be better connected. Are you going to write down that I'm here?"

I made an executive decision. "No. I'm not going to write down anything at all."

At this she smiled. It made her look more sane. "Really? You promise?"

The morning was hardly gone and already I was taking liberties with my duty. I nodded.

"Want some water? You better have some water."

I looked at the jugs. I had forgotten how thirsty I was.

She took a glass from a shelf and, expertly tipping one of the demijohns, filled it for me. I would have offered to help but it seemed pointless. Her self-sufficiency was perfect and yet, somehow, it wasn't, like a masterpiece that close up turns out to be full of cracks.

"Did you live here before?"

"Not in the basement."

"I meant—"

"You meant to be inquisitive."

"I suppose so. At least it's unofficial."

She leaned back against her tower of supplies and crossed her legs at the ankle. It was then I noticed that her hair wasn't really red but a sort of honey brown, a bit like maple syrup, only lighter.

"Did you lose anyone?" she asked suddenly. The question took me by surprise. It didn't match with her truculence, but I also felt grateful. No one else had asked me; people don't when everyone has lost so much. It made a connection, gave permission. Still, I didn't want to specify.

"Yes," I said. "And you?"

"Me? I misplaced everybody. It's beyond careless." She shrugged, actually shrugged, as if to say she might have had a family, a lover, a husband, a child, but all that had now become a matter of indifference.

I had already learned that excessive grief is mute. In those days people behaved like refugees, scraped little hollows and buried their

39

feelings along with other inedible valuables —photos, jewelry—in the vague hope of retrieving them later.

"Family?" I ventured, knowing that I was going too far but doing it anyway because I wanted to push, to probe, to get underneath that shrug.

She looked at me and crossed her arms as well as her legs, the better to defend herself. Then she shrugged yet again but differently this time; it was more like a shiver. To have a family, said this movement, is a requirement of nature, but to ask about one is not in good taste.

What else could I do? I punished myself by saying, "My parents, my little sister, most of my friends. So far as I know."

I was glad she didn't say she was sorry. Instead she said something unexpected.

"Will you visit me again?"

Hard to say if it was a challenge or a plea.

That afternoon I covered four more blocks and found three buildings with a total of fifteen rooms worth reporting. I filled in my forms. I was as diligent as a lunatic clearing an avalanche with a spoon. I came across a dozen people on the march with their suitcases and parcels, bicycles and little red wagons, all heading north. A simple technology, the wheel. The city had returned to the Middle Ages, back to basics. Nobody spoke to me.

I got back to the firehouse at sunset. Only the Office of Emergency Housing was still open. Vikram was there, spirited as ever. He examined my forms and declared himself delighted with my work. "Really," he said beaming, "you've done splendidly. I think you're our best!" He handed me two tickets and told me the canteen for city workers was at the courthouse two blocks away. "The second ticket is for breakfast tomorrow. Get here bright and early."

As I left he patted my aching shoulder. "Good work," he said.

Dinner was soup and bread and weak tea. "We're expecting a truck in tomorrow morning," said the weary woman in a kerchief who filled my bowl.

"Thank you," I said, and meant it.

People sat in couples or all alone. There was little conversation, just the dull andante of matter-of-fact exhaustion.

Back in my room I lay on my bed and stared at the ceiling. It was lit by two candles I had found the day before. Somehow they had not melted. I tried to think up themes, tonic and dominant. I tried to read but my eyes were strained from the smoke they had been looking through for so long. I ended by thinking about the woman in the basement. She puzzled me. Why was I sure she wouldn't tell me her name if I asked? Why had she stayed in the ruined house and where did she get all those supplies? Above all I considered why she had asked if I would visit her again.

I recalled those forlorn words that already seemed to me a private proverb: To be alone in a city is really to be alone. The thought of this woman whose grief I assumed was beyond telling, whose loneliness was disconsolate, a sphere without a fissure, filled the vacuum of my suddenly emptied world.

At breakfast—soup and bread again—everyone was handed a bag of cookies, the kind with vanilla cream between chocolate wafers.

"Cookies?"

The flat-headed man with rolled flannel sleeves who was distributing the bags snapped at me. "You want 'em or not?" No doubt he too had hoped for bacon and eggs and steak and potatoes and leeks and lettuce. But there was strong coffee and I had two cups. My body rewarded me with a resilience that felt like just like optimism. Even the stiffness from my fall nearly went away in deference to the great god caffeine.

Before heading off to the firehouse to check my orders with Vikram, I sneaked a second bag of cookies.

It was simple. I would give her a treat and, in return, she would tell me her name.

Upstairs at the firehouse the mood was still gloomier than the day before. Even the brisk secretaries were drooping. No one greeted me. I went straight downstairs.

Vikram was not there. Babette was and the chief and a couple other people.

"Where's Vikram?" I asked.

The chief looked embarrassed, Babette furious.

My heart had misgivings. "What happened?"

The chief rose. "I'm afraid Vikram's gone."

"Gone?" Vikram a deserter? Impossible.

"He hanged himself last night," said Babette mercilessly and pointed

41

Robert Wexelblatt

to one of the overhead pipes. "Right here. Pinned a note to his chest and hung himself right here."

"I can't believe it," I said, as if I had the right to doubt anything at all.

The chief, a compassionate man, came closer to me. "If you strike a light bulb just right," he observed in a thin voice, "it burns brighter for a short while. That's how it was with Vikram. Last night he stayed on, insisted he wanted to work late . . . . His family. You understand? Wife, two little girls."

Why, in the midst of all these deaths, of the city's destruction, the deaths of people I knew and loved, why should it have been Vikram's that I felt most deeply? A last straw? An emblem of despair? Was it that he alone chose to die? He was a stranger, after all. I had spent hardly a quarter of an hour in his company and yet I had liked him a great deal, had reposed my confidence in him, been warmed by his praise, relied in some way on his energy and efficiency. Vikram had buttressed my youth; that is, he had made me believe we'd pull through and that, even after such a trial as this, there was still a prospect of living happily ever after.

"May I see the note?"

The chief's eyebrows rose. Behind me Babette made an unpleasant noise.

The chief went to his desk and took Vikram's note out of a drawer.

The handwriting was appallingly neat. He had used one of the emergency housing forms, keeping carefully to the lines for addresses. It was short.

"My dear colleagues, I deeply regret causing you further difficulties. Please try to forgive me. I thought I could go on."

The chief sent me out into the city. "Your duty," he said solemnly, echoing Vikram, shaking my hand.

But I no longer cared. What sense did canvassing make? The city was like a defunct god; the feral dogs and cats, once pampered and cleaned up after, so many maggots on the colossal corpse, baffled and angry. Emergency housing? The very phrase rang false. The emergency is that there isn't any housing. Anyway, a house is the opposite of an emergency; it's permanence, dependability, roofs, walls, warmth, dryness. What did it matter if here and there a few cells had neglected to die? Who could nestle into such necrotic cavities of plaster and lath? There would be a

42

future. I couldn't deny it. Eventually help would come; help that really helped would stream in with powerful machines and new wires, plenty of determination and government contracts. Still, no vision of resurrection attracted me. I could already foresee that for us survivors the reconstruction would feel like an offense, like building an amusement park over a cemetery. It would be like saying "There, there" to Vikram. And, when the moment came that we forgot ourselves, happiness would leave a bad taste in our mouths.

Nevertheless, elation was what I felt as I made my way to her basement hideout under the mansion. I tried to shake the joy off me but it stuck.

She was wearing an oversized sweatshirt over a denim skirt. She sat at her table, a book open in front of her.

"I didn't expect you," she said guardedly. "At least not yet."

"You're all right?"

She made a motion with her arm. The sleeve of the sweatshirt covered up her hands and made her look like a child. I wondered whose it had been.

"I sleep and eat. I'm breathing. I can stand. See?" And she stood up. "By the way, congratulations."

"What for?"

"Not falling down the steps."

"Have you been out?"

"Outside? No reason to. I got all this the first day." She pointed to her hoard.

"How'd you move it?"

She grimaced at me. "Magic."

I remembered the cookies, dropped my knapsack and pulled out the two bags. "Here, a present."

She took the packages and looked at them hard, as if I had given her a photograph and she was trying to identify the people in it.

"Ada adored these. We called them Ada sandwiches."

"Who's Ada? Where is she?"

She ignored the foolish, improper question.

"Ada would eat a whole bag if we didn't take it away from her. And then she'd cry. Ada had a condition."

"A condition?"

"Ada couldn't do things. She couldn't walk or talk. She was my sister."

"What was her condition?"

"A punishment? I don't know. An accident? Who does know? You think the world makes sense? Not to me. Ada wasn't sweet tempered. She was greedy for everything, not just cookies. Once, when we were putting her to bed she threw a fit. It happened from time to time. She'd hit anybody who got near her but the screaming was worse. You know why? Because it was silent."

I fumbled for something to say. I wanted her to go on talking. "Was Ada older or younger than you?"

"Older. No, younger."

"You aren't sure?"

"I said younger. My poor, grasping little sister Ada . . . . Tell me, which do you think is worse, not being able to talk or not being able to walk?"

"But," I said, "you said Ada couldn't do either."

"True. Ada didn't have a choice. But what if you did?"

"Not being able to talk would be worse for me."

"How about being blind?"

"Blindness terrifies me."

"Me too. I'm even afraid of blind people. You always think for a moment it might be catching." She returned to her game. "Which is worse, having a family or not having one."

She was a text I couldn't make out. Was she verging on hysteria or infinitely beyond it? Or was she simply teasing me? Yesterday her reticence had made me jumpy, now her speaking did.

I suggested we open up one of the bags of cookies and eat some Ada sandwiches.

All the rules were gone along with the cars and the street signs. The city was lawless but in those first days too bewildered to fall into murderous anarchy. It hovered between the state of nature conceived as war and that other nature, the benign one which is universal sympathy. More exactly, there was neither peace nor war, neither courtesy nor rudeness, only desolation which a Roman called peace when he meant war.

What I mean is that I had no idea of the right way to behave with her.

Because there was only the one chair we seated ourselves side by side on the steps. I was careful to leave a distance between our hips. She didn't seem to care.

She bit into the cookie and nodded. "Good."

"What were your reading?" I hazarded.

"Reading?"

"When I came in. That book on the table."

"A fairy tale."

"Fairy tale?"

"Somebody's favorite."

"Ada's?"

"No, of course not. Ada couldn't understand stories."

"I thought it was just walking and talking."

"And stories."

"Whose favorite then? Yours?"

"You're pretty pushy, you know."

"Yes. Pushy. I know."

Long pause then she said, "I'm a witch. I do magic. I'll bet you want to know my name."

"Yes."

"Strega." She cackled as she had the day before. "Hexe. Sorcière. Venefica. You can take your pick. Witches can walk and talk and they can follow stories so what is it they don't do drown—or burn?"

"I don't know. Maybe they didn't eat cookies."

"Had to be burn."

"Couldn't be. Witches were burnt at the stake."

"Never drowned, or beheaded?"

"Beheaded?"

"In the story the soldier cuts off the witch's head with his sword."

"Whose favorite?"

She didn't answer. We sat quietly for a while, eating the cookies. I was thinking of going. I could head toward the docks, review some more ruins, see how the dogs were getting on.

"You like fairy tales?" she asked.

"I liked them when I was a kid, I guess. Don't think about them much. Actually, I did yesterday. The world out there reminds me of the time those stories came from."

"Dark woods? Princesses in towers? What I think is we're all

45

children of those horrid stories. They're like shadowy parents, I mean shadows speaking from behind our parents. But then the parents too were poisoned by the tales, weren't they? I mean when they were kids. Then they forget and turn nostalgic and that's how the stories get to go on and on. The parents forget the prejudices and fears and the sheer insidious nastiness of them. All they remember is snuggling up under the covers and Mommy's voice, so sweet . . ."

"So you think fairy tales are dangerous?"

"Anything powerful is dangerous. Hatred, love, gunpowder, a match. Powerful like a tinder-box."

"A tinder-box? I remember a story by that name. Is that the one you were reading?"

"We never really get over the stories. I used to know people, grown-up people of forty and fifty, who saw themselves as Cinderella or Jack going up his beanstalk. The stories are like molds. People pour themselves into them. We shouldn't read them to children."

I felt a sudden desire to take her hand but it was hidden up her sleeve.

"Why'd you call yourself a witch?"

"Because I didn't burn up. Because I live underground and do magical things. Everything burnt up but not me. And then I'm terribly wise, of course. I know things."

Was she teasing? "I think the fairy tales were meant to teach."

"Do you? Teach what?"

"I don't know. Virtues, I guess. Loyalty. Perseverance. Honesty and bravery."

"In Copenhagen there's a monument to Andersen. He's surrounded by all these kids. I saw a picture of it once. He's smiling even more innocently than the children, simpering like a dope pusher."

"He was poor. Children love his stories, and not only children."

"The innocence is phony. Sure, he was poor. He had the resentment of the deprived, always pushing his face up against the shop windows of Copenhagen. 'The Little Match Girl.' You think that's innocent? A little primer in virtue? Revolution maybe. Andersen knew the worst of people and all his stories are protests, even against his heroes . . . . Only what's dangerous endures."

I was feeling lost but determined to hold up my end. "Or what's dull. Like the pyramids. Pyramids last. You can't knock them over."

She became agitated. I was contradicting her. "No, no! The pyramids are—extremely dangerous, full of dog-gods and curses and rotting spirits."

"Who loved 'The Tinder-Box'?"

She slumped and lowered her voice. "How well can you remember the story?"

"Let's see. A poor soldier gets hold of a magic tinder-box that lets him call up big dogs. They bring him money and food and in the end he marries a princess."

"Just what a boy would remember."

The way she said "boy," while hardly a compliment, was not without pity.

"Did I leave much out?"

"Only the murderous cynicism." Close as we were, hip to hip, almost the last woman and the last man in the world, she wouldn't look at me. "Don't you remember how he gets the tinder-box, where it comes from? How the people treat him well when he's rich and badly when he's poor? Don't you remember what he does to get the princess or how shallow she turns out? Hell without flames. Nope. Witches don't burn; you have to cut off their heads because that's where all the wisdom is."

My heart began to ache more than my shoulder but I was as merciless as Babette. "Who is it that loved the story?"

She sighed. Sighing, shrugging, cackling—these were the modes she used not to communicate what was beyond language.

I couldn't resist putting my hand on her shoulder and she let it stay there a moment before shrugging that off too. She got up and took two steps to the card table where the lamp stood by the book.

She read in a voice that was sweet and furious:

> What are you going to do with the tinder-box? asked the soldier.
> That is nothing to you, replied the witch; you have the money,
> now give me the tinder-box.
> I tell you what, said the soldier, if you don't tell me what you
> are going to do with it, I will draw my sword and cut off your
> head.
> No, said the witch.
> The soldier immediately cut off her head, and there she lay on
> the ground.

"That enough for you?"

"What do you think she was going to do with it?"

"When he meets her he calls her 'old witch.' I mean she's just an old woman and right off the bat he calls her a witch."

"But a witch is what she is."

"How would the soldier know that?"

"It's just a story."

"Oh sure. And this is how it ends. Happily most people would say. They're about to hang the soldier for stealing the princess in the night. He abducts her with the dogs and, for all we know, rapes her. Why not? You have to read between the lines. I certainly wouldn't put it past Andersen. Anyway, the soldier's about to be hanged but he tricks the king into letting him light his pipe. The last smoke. The foolish king forgets that fire's always dangerous, even tiny fires." She turned the page, her voice oozing sugary disgust.

> The soldier took his tinder-box, and struck fire, once, twice, thrice, and there in a moment stood all the dogs; the one with eyes as big as teacups, the one with eyes as large as mill-wheels, and the third, whose eyes were like towers. Help me now, that I may not be hanged, cried the soldier.

> And the dogs fell upon the judges and all the councilors; seized one by the legs, and another by the nose, and tossed them many feet high in the air, so that they fell down and were dashed to pieces.

> I will not be touched, said the king. But the largest dog seized him, as well as the queen, and threw them after the others.

> Then the soldiers and all the people were afraid, and cried, Good soldier, you shall be our king, and you shall marry the beautiful princess.

> So they placed the soldier in the king's carriage, and the three dogs ran on in front and cried, Hurrah! and the little boys whistled through their fingers, and the soldiers presented arms.

The princess came out of the copper castle, and became queen, which was very pleasing to her.

"Who's the worst?" she shouted at me. "The greedy, homicidal soldier, the disloyal, craven subjects, the possessive, arrogant king, or the vain and fatuous princess? Not the witch, that's for sure. Not her."

We had a difference of opinion. She thought she was a witch but I thought she was a princess, and, of course, both of us were wrong.

"Whose favorite story was this?" I asked almost for the last time.

To this day she's never told me.

The Avramarash Negotiations

The northern city went briskly about its business under a faint December sun. Already ice was hardening at the edges of its bottomless lake and the surrounding mountains sparkled hygienically with snow. I found the place cold. It was an indoor life, not at all like that of the crowded alleys, boisterous markets, and swarming nomadic clans of our homeland. There was nothing to smell. Toward us, the well dressed local population was neither over-friendly nor indifferent, merely polite. In fact, we attracted little attention except from members of the press, and even the reporters thinned out after a few days. The local bankers and shop-keepers, the foreign salesmen and tourists, all seemed sophisticated to me. The tall, blue-eyed women walked about confidently sheathed in fashions that seemed to me impregnable. But we had nothing to complain of. The formal welcoming ceremony was presided over by the mayor, who made a resoundingly hopeful speech; the city council, magistrates, and vener-able syndics sat behind him on a platform. We were made welcome, to be sure, but decidedly taken in stride. I sensed that the ceremony was a ritual the city had often laid on before. Perhaps it was a point of pride for the populace to show how used they were to hosting conferences like ours. In a practical sense, this indifference was ideal, for it decreased the pressure on everyone and minimized distractions. On the other hand, the city's attitude was a little disappointing too, especially for the youngest among us who had never worked abroad and so had romantic notions. Without any precise ideas we had privately anticipated adventure, romance; perhaps we wished to be fussed over, wanted it acknowledged that ours was a life-and-death task.

As experts on hydrological and border issues respectively, Pethos and I were not required for the day's session. Nevertheless, we had been instructed to remain on hand. We were lounging in the corridor at eleven o'clock when the high doors of the main conference room swung open and everyone streamed out. The undersecretaries looked solemn and the ambassadors were red in the face. Everyone else acted like kids suddenly let out of school.

Pethos grabbed Marjusa by the arm.

"Hey, what's up?"

Marjusa, who was not yet twenty-four, made a perfunctory attempt to appear put out in case her boss should be watching. "Temporary impasse," she declared, shrugging off Pethos's hand. Hired fresh out of an American university as a public relations officer, Marjusa had already picked up the habit of speaking in headlines. "Three-day suspension of all talks."

Pethos cast his eyes up toward the ceiling and whistled like a falling bomb.

Marjusa turned to me. In her blue business suit, her rosy cheeks and stylish hair, she looked like a precocious barrister. "Practically a paid vacation. What'll you do?"

Three days off? I imagined myself spending them at the Excelsior where our delegation was handsomely housed. The hotel was luxurious. Though I had been too busy to find them, Pethos told me there was a pool and a gym, even a spa that offered massages. I imagined three sybaritic days.

Before I could reply to Marjusa, Pethos interrupted. "I know. What do you say we all go for a hike this afternoon?" He elbowed my ribs. This was to let me know I was to agree and then beg off so that he could be alone with Marjusa on whom he had designs.

"Hike?" Marjusa was dismissive. She tossed her head, throttled up her outboard engine and left us in her sparkling wake. "Shopping for me. Bye-bye." She waved over her shoulder.

"Playing hard to get," said Pethos with determination.

It was true that the official talks had been put on hold, but the three days were hardly empty for me. I was either in meetings or preparing for them from eight in the morning straight through to sunset. No treadmills or chlorinated laps, no hikes in the mountains or decadent rubdowns. I was the delegation's technical specialist on the frontier question. I had walked the Avramarash Valley from end to end, knew both sides of the disputed border, had stayed in its villages, forded its streams, surveyed its hills; I had entered into the lives and huts of its people, heard its tall tales, studied its dialects, puzzled out its oral histories, kicked balls with its toddlers, admired its women, hunted with its men. I had eaten the local millet cakes, drunk fermented honey, chewed the inimitable meat dish called lammenflek; I had inquired of the weavers about their designs, trekked into the mountains with shepherds. Not unlike the population I had studied—some of whom identified with my nation, others with its rival, while most did not dare to utter an opinion about politics—I felt pulled this way and that. Border skirmishes, artillery duels, night raids, sniping, and one all-out war had made them cautious and resentful of both sides. One old almond farmer told me of a dream his dead wife had. In this dream the whole Avramarash Valley rises up into the air and floats away to a far-off sea. As the farmer put it, "There we are an island with no neighbors to love us to death." I had grown fond of these people and wanted what was best for them, which was surely a peace settlement; nevertheless, I was worried about what the two neighbors who loved them might arrange. For whatever happened I would now bear some measure of responsibility, however small. Who else knew the place as well as I? Who else's love was so disinterested, so free of covetousness? The people of the Avramarash breathed and worked and laughed in my memory. I could easily summon up the picture of an onion field with tough, bearded Baghrat hailing me, the adolescent Dunyasa who shyly showed me her collection of local love poetry; there was the endearingly crafty merchant Soroky who bragged of getting the better of my countrymen, and above all the saintly Karlus Chawnic at whose clinic I lived for a week. I had flirted with Avramarash girls and had been giggled at by its children. For me the maps spread across the conference table were a thickly peopled landscape and the names of villages, hills, and rivers were stories.

I was overjoyed at my appointment to the delegation, certain that my superiors would aim at a fair and beneficial settlement. I soon realized that both parties were looking for something they could call a compromise but that would be nothing of the kind. Greed and national pride were to blame. Negotiations, I reminded myself, are the continuation of war by other, better means. I needed to recollect that I too had a side; that rival countries were playing a game and one of these countries happened to be my own. I reminded myself that there could be no third side. Nevertheless, when I leaned over the maps I found myself patiently explaining details that were more ethnographic than topographic. I did my utmost to convey the complication of the human situation on the ground, the networks of trade, the reticulations of intermarriage and criss-crossed customs, clan loyalties and deadly vendettas. I demonstrated the lines of force that radiated from every village to every other, even though these were visible only to me, and only counted for me. My boss took me aside and impatiently dressed me down for wasting people's time with trivial local considerations. I came to grasp that the negotiations were less about peace and still less about the people than about mineral and petroleum deposits. At one meeting I fought down my bitterness and spoke from the heart. "Please listen," I begged. "The Avramarash is a solar system, a precarious balance of gravitational forces. It is like a great raw diamond and if it is clumsily cut it will crumble to dust." This speech only exasperated my boss while some of the others laughed at me. I could really have done with a massage.

The first time I saw Andrew Broadbent was at a meeting of our delegation. This was on the second day of the suspension. My boss had admonished me an hour earlier, reminding me of "the limitations of my function." The tycoon must have hopped on his private jet the instant word of the hiatus in negotiations reached him.

It is no secret that the Avramarash Negotiations were Broadbent's doing. He pressured his own government to call for them, urged ours and our rivals' to attend; Broadbent selected the venue, saw to the accommodations; his staff even drew up the preliminary proposals. Broadbent picked up the tab for everything from mineral water and telephone calls to limousine rentals and room service. Though he made no effort to keep his involvement from the press, he did try to minimize his contribution so as not to offend too crudely the dignity of sovereign states. Broadbent understood when not to put himself forward, but about his motives he was remarkably candid. "Of course," he told one interviewer, "I want to do whatever I can to bring peace to this long-troubled region, this international running sore. It's my duty. But I'm no saint, not if sainthood demands entirely disinterested motives. The Avramarash Valley is potentially rich; my people tell me it's got chromium deposits, petroleum, and lots of natural gas. I admit I want to make a development deal, a fair one, but it's obvious nothing's going to happen until the borders are fixed and the troops are out. Once that's done it's a quadruple win. The local population will benefit, so will the two countries and, yes, if I can make a deal, my stockholders will profit too, as will the world economy. Let's face it, the time's past when economics had to take a back seat to politics. In my opinion that's a good thing. Look at the twentieth century and ask yourself which is more likely to bring about human happiness: free economic development or traditional hatreds and misplaced national pride?"

In person Andrew Broadbent is not quite as large as he appears on a television screen, which he dominates with his enormous forehead and fierce eyes; yet in person he is even more vital, more charismatic. Dressed with elegant informality in slacks, a turtleneck sweater, and leather jacket, he commanded the room as soon as he entered it. He has a Caesarian aura, a kind of electrical glossiness, the refulgence of his dollars, I suppose. He seemed to own everything. Energy spirals from Broadbent, as though he were the center of swirling currents, a dynamo, the eye of one of those huge storms that dominate whole quadrants of the planet. He swept into the conference room like a gust of wind—a bracing northern one—and filled it up with his words and will. He didn't bother with introductions, I noticed, and I saw how this disregard of formalities intimidated my superiors, for whom protocol is almost the paramount concern of life. Whatever they babbled in response to his rapid and angry questions sounded dispirited and apologetic.

"Look," he said brusquely, "I'm going to meet with the other sons-of-bitches in fifteen minutes. I can't lay down the law, though I'd like to, so just tell me what you think is wrong with their position and then I'll find out from them how they think you're screwing things up. We'll move on from there and see whose face needs saving." The ambassador, with help from my boss, gave him a point-by-point answer after which Broadbent nodded once, turned his leather-jacketed back on us, and began to walk out. He stopped by the door. "Oh, by the way, I've arranged a little treat for tonight, a special recital. You're all invited. Tickets for everybody are waiting at the hotel desk. Eight o'clock." He mumbled a question to one of his minions, a young man in a blue suit, then nodded at his reply. "At the Opernhaus. Should be quite an event. Rudolf Wehenbrock's going to play. Out of retirement just for you, for us, for the cause of peace." I was surprised that Broadbent should be excited about a recital or think that piano music could advance the negotiations. Was this captain of industry also an aficionado, the admirer of a legendary name, or was he merely showing off?

In our best clothes we marched up the floodlit stairs to the baroque Opernhaus like a victorious brigade going to occupy the enemy's citadel.

Our morale was high. Well-fed and excused from work, people laughed, sporting new ties, dresses, and shoes.

Pethos had contrived to maneuver Marjusa over to one end of our phalanx while I was caught in the center overhearing two conversations. On one side Ostermann, the chief flack and Marjusa's boss, was eagerly telling fabulous tales of Broadbent in a tone of admiring envy to the geologist Gromelius.

"They say he's got a whole fleet of Mercedes and Porsches and mistresses on every continent, all beauty contest winners, movie actresses, or ballerinas."

"Except for Antarctica, presumably," said Gromelius dryly.

Ostermann's credulity knew no bounds. "Who knows? He may have an underground castle at the South Pole, you know, just in case."

To my other side an undersecretary was quietly bawling out his assistant.

"And another thing, since I'm being frank with you for a change. I really don't care for those little jokes about my wife. It's one thing for me to talk about her that way, quite another for *you*."

"But sir—"

The two ambassadors were, of course, not to sit with us underlings. Broadbent had arranged for them to be picked up by limousines and escorted by ushers to a box presided over by himself. I saw them as soon as I entered the theater, up there under the ceiling with its fresco of Apollo and the Muses on twin-peaked Parnassus. Broadbent was without even a single mistress. In well-pressed evening dress he turned this way and that, at his ease. He was saying something and the ambassadors were laughing deferentially, as if his jokes had been spoken directly by two or three billion dollars.

The delegations were seated down in the first three rows of the orchestra. My ticket placed me several seats from Pethos and one seat over from Marjusa. Broadbent had arranged alternate seating for the two delegations the better to encourage fraternization. Pethos had stolen a look at his prey's ticket and, ascertaining that I was closer to her, asked me to exchange seats. I was one seat from the aisle. To my left was a man of about forty with a black mustache that dominated his face like a successful parasite. I had seen him several times across the negotiating table. I suspected he was a military officer in mufti. He never spoke above a whisper and then only into the ear of his ambassador, who paid close attention. "Good evening," I said. "Evening," muttered the mustache. He sat stiffly, palms on thighs, back straight, clearly prepared to give only name, rank, and serial number. The seat to my right, the one on the aisle, was empty.

Though I am not much of a music lover even I had heard of Rudolf Wehenbrock. Pethos, who had studied piano in his youth, filled me in before we left. Wehenbrock's had been one of the grand careers of the century, triumphs all over the globe, brilliant recordings, uninterrupted adulation. According to Pethos, Wehenbrock had been a bon vivant but also a great signer of humanitarian petitions, a citizen of the world who, after a series of mysterious illnesses, had purchased a villa overlooking the lake and retired to this city. It was rumored that he practiced for two hours every day; nevertheless, he had not performed in public for years. Pethos put him in his early seventies. This recital really was a major musical event, just as Broadbent said. Critics had flown in from New York and Tokyo.

"That Broadbent was able to get him to perform is astonishing. God, he must have offered the old man a pile."

"Perhaps he appealed to his humanitarian sentiments. Maybe Broadbent convinced him that if he played for us, and played well enough, there would also be peace and harmony in the Avramarash."

"Don't be cynical. It doesn't become you."

"I'm serious."

"Performing for peace? Well, perhaps you're right. Joshua and Jericho. The universal language and all that. Maybe musicians under-estimate what music can accomplish."

"Maybe billionaires don't."

I looked up at the men in the imperial box. It was all conviviality up there. Broadbent lacked the cautious attentiveness of a mediator. As usual, he looked like a proprietor. The ambassadors, distinguished senior officials, were doubtless patriots, but they were likewise men-of-the-world. I was beginning to understand the contradictory condition of diplomats who must appreciate more than their compatriots the humanity of foreigners, who must therefore be able to grasp their wishes and needs, doing them a kind of justice. Diplomats, I had begun to think, constitute a class apart, a subculture of cosmopolites, even if they are occasionally called upon to perform like meat-eating jingoists for the domestic press. Their language is all coded, subtle, cryptic, at once esoteric and public.

They carefully balance a sense of subordination with independence of mind; they slip their private judgments under official lines; for they are never without ideas of their own, pragmatists by experience if not inclination. Perhaps the best that can be said of them is that they cannot afford the luxury of demonizing their adversaries.

As I observed that trio up under the classical cerulean sky, a disgraceful question suddenly bubbled up in my mind: might Broadbent try to bribe them? Had Pethos been seated beside me I would impulsively have asked his opinion and he would have laughed. As it was, I felt no compunction about entertaining such suspicions. What was worse, though—worse, that is, for my conception of myself—was that I should wonder whether bribery in such a case might not be such a bad thing. I felt a little nauseated, adrift on deep and heaving seas. Was corruption, then, or the tolerance of it, a coming to terms with the world; was this that passage into realism my father loved to predict for me? As I pondered this there came that magical transition, the moments when an audience forgets its existence as the lights begin to dim. In this theatrical dusk a tall young woman wearing a striking purple dress exited a door at floor level just to the right of the stage. In a nearly stately fashion, she hastened up the aisle and took the seat next to me. Before I could get a good look at her, darkness fell over the hall and the old man, the great Wehenbrock, walked stiffly on to the stage to an eruption of applause and polyglot cheers.

Wehenbrock's frame was long and angular, his hair wispy and white. He was dressed in tie and tails, and looked like a virtuoso from the time of Liszt. He held himself erect with a difficulty he only partially succeeded in concealing. The applause did not abate. The young lady at my side did not clap; she leaned forward tensely on her seat, as though ready to make a dash for the stage.

Above the din I asked her boldly, "Are you his nurse?"

She turned, surprised and, I thought, regarded me with some interest. Perhaps she was less startled by my question than that I had dared to ask it. She nodded. "Yes. His nurse." I liked her low, oddly accented voice.

Wehenbrock bowed his head to the audience, then, with a rigid turn, to the lords up in their box. They were on their feet applauding and all three nodded back. Hear no evil, speak no evil, see no evil.

I leaned to my right. "Why's there no program?" The nurse's hair did not smell in the least medicinal.

"Shh. He only decided this afternoon."

Wehenbrock strode to the piano on which he leaned with one hand while holding up the other and waited for silence. "Busoni's arrangement of Bach's *Praeludium and Fugue in D-major*," he said in a firm voice. Then he sat down and built a roller coaster for us; he summoned thunder. His playing was more passionate than precise, but then, as I later discovered, Busoni's Bach is a gutsy, spiritualized Romantic, a Bach who sat at the feet of Beethoven, and no Lutheran rationalist. With the final cadence the audience jumped to its feet and so did I. Wehenbrock could have been a rock star.

I stole a glance at the nurse. She was about Marjusa's age but more attractive. The astonishing purple dress perfectly suited her dark hair and ruddy cheeks. I took note of a resolute chin and somewhat flat nose. It was too dark for me to make out the color of her eyes.

Behind us somebody shouted, "He's lost nothing." And another retorted, "Why did he retire?"

Gradually, we settled down. Wehenbrock stayed seated at the piano. He turned to us and again held up his hand. "Beethoven's Opus 109."

"He's already so tired," sighed the anxious nurse, not exactly to me.

The first movement of the sonata made me think of riding in a coach through a novel by Jane Austen early on an April morning, while the second movement summoned up an appreciation of Napoleonic fury. But it was the long meditative lines of the third movement's variations that almost brought me to tears. Wehenbrock convinced me Beethoven had recorded a supreme act of resignation.

Tiring as all this must have been, Wehenbrock allowed no intermission, as if he didn't dare to catch his breath. He concluded his comeback by playing two pairs of Scarlatti sonatas with exactitude and wit, but not without feeling for the emotional range of these sturdy miniatures. Such playing made you think about music almost as if you were a musician. The applause went on and on and, only after a refusal by the audience to cease, something the anxious nurse seemed barely able to endure, Wehenbrock gave us two encores, a delightful piece by Ravel I actually recognized and a Rachmaninoff prelude which made me wonder if he had sprouted ten more fingers.

The crowd was practically giddy with delight and went on applauding and yelling bravo for fully ten minutes, all of which the old man bore like a not unhappy Stoic.

Even the nurse clapped with the rest of us. So, he was not going to collapse after all. In her relief she turned to me and smiled. There was no one else to whom she could express the joy people feel in the face of demonstrated mastery.

"I've never heard anything like that before," I said in the direction of her ear.

She said something inaudible.

I leaned still nearer. "Pardon me?"

"I said I hear it every day."

"Really?"

"When he practices."

The noise of the crowd began to moderate.

"Oh, of course. I'm an idiot."

"Are you an idiot?"

"It's beyond question. From time to time, at least."

"That's a coincidence."

"Yes?"

"I'm a nurse . . . from time to time."

"Is he very ill?"

"He was. Now just—from time to time."

"Look. Can I see you again?"

She was amused. "You have romantic designs on me?"

I held up my palms and shrugged. "You've seen right through me."

"It isn't difficult. Men don't like it though, in my experience. Men want to be opaque. They enjoy games with rules and usually prefer the rules to the games. I have to go now."

It is an interesting nurse who philosophizes in this way, I thought. I touched her bare arm and was surprised to feel a small electrical thrill. I continued leaning toward her, magnetized.

"Tell me your name."

"Rachel."

"Rachel what?"

"Rachel Wehenbrock."

"Wehenbrock? Then—?"

"His granddaughter every day—his nurse only. . ."

We concluded the sentence together, soprano and baritone, "From time to time."

"I really have to," she said, pulling away like Cinderella.

"Wait! Here!" I handed her my pen and held out my hand. She paused. I put my hands together and begged.

She took my hand and, with some care, inscribed a phone number on my palm. Rachel Wehenbrock was left handed.

As if spurred on by the excellence and wisdom of Wehenbrock's playing, the negotiations resumed the following morning in a spirit of concord and proceeded with breathtaking velocity. The new proposals laid on the table by each side were similar and, on their face, reasonable. However, I thought them disastrous from the standpoint of the inhabitants of the Avramarash. During a break in the corridor I went so far as to ask for a moment with my chief to lodge a protest. He pushed me into the men's room.

"Before you say anything about boundaries, let me remind you again of your own. You don't approve or disapprove our proposals. You only support them in the highly improbable event that somebody asks for your view. You're an advisor and your advice is to be offered only when required. Today, nobody's asking. Now, get back to work."

I could see how things stood. The valley would be partitioned in such a way that roughly half the chromium deposits and half the petroleum would go to each country. This would result in a frontier that separated clans, split up traditional commons, ruined pastoral customs, and made a hash of the valley's complex water allocations. Even the fairness to each state was, in my opinion, only apparent; the real beneficiary would be Broadbent who would be able to play each nation off against the other in working out the price of his concessions. The sudden amity, I concluded rashly, was inspired not by Wehenbrock's sublime music but Broadbent's bribes, which, if I were right, must have extended to the highest reaches of both governments.

I opened up to Pethos over dinner. He did not share my concerns, to put it mildly. His opinion was that matters were finally moving and that was splendid; the direction was of little concern to him. As for my bribery theory, he warned against such loose talk, especially since I had no evidence—"though," he added shrewdly, "if you actually *did* have any evidence it would be much worse for you."

Pethos' belief in the felicity of momentum might have had something to do with the progress of his siege of Fortress Marjusa. "She's agreed to go to a disco with me tonight," he crowed. "You wouldn't care to join us, would you?"

It was a double negative invitation. I teased him. "What if I said yes?"

"Then I'd have to lower my estimation of your intelligence and that would pain me."

"Don't worry. I'll stick around the hotel. They may want me."

Pethos smirked. "Perhaps someone'll offer you a bribe!"

Before leaving the opera house I had transferred Rachel's phone number from my palm to my ticket, worried that sweat might blur the figures. Once back in my hotel room I had copied the number from my ticket on to the pad with the Excelsior's crest that lay ready by the telephone. There it stayed, as if radioactive, while I worked up my nerve and tried to calculate the best time to call and what to say. I could hardly ask Wehenbrock's granddaughter to a disco.

The call worried me all the following day. I was like a schoolboy. Freed early, at only five o'clock, I returned to the hotel, showered, changed clothes, sat on the bed and stared at the phone.

The call could not be called easy, but neither was it interrupted by any awkward silences.

Rachel herself answered, which was an immense relief.

"This is the man with your number on his palm," I said as lightly as I could.

"My grandfather's number, actually. Unlisted, of course. Well, I've found out about you," Rachel said in a manner both teasing and torrential. "For example, your name, which you neglected to mention last night. I also know you're an expert on the Avramarash Valley, quite respectably educated, from a solid bourgeois family. Your father is a physician and your mother teaches French at a private school. You have an older sister who, unlike me, is married. Safely and happily, I hope?"

"How—?"

"Your photograph's linked to your country's website. You didn't know? The whole delegation's there, from old and reliable to young and eager, complete with résumés and head shots. Yours isn't so bad."

This, I realized, must be the work of Marjusa and company.

"Our families too?"

"No. For that I made my own inquiries. Sorry, my sources are strictly confidential."

"You had me vetted?"

"A girl can't be too careful. You're a foreigner and a man who freely confesses to having romantic designs on me."

"And all I know about you is that you occasionally nurse your grandfather who is a great artist."

"Not true. You also know I look good in purple."

"And that you're left-handed."

She laughed. "Bravo."

She suggested a bar where we could meet.

"Do you drink a lot?"

"From time to time," she said coquettishly.

It is stretching things only a little to compare my infatuation with Rachel Wehenbrock to one of Bach's preludes and fugues since it began with a sort of playful cantabile, this giving way to a divagation of voices in lines at once harmonious and contentious, impossible to disentangle, and it wound up in a finale of exact confusion. These days I often listen to Bach, the true Bach, without Busoni's inveigling, ardent, lily-gilding passions.

The bar Rachel chose for our rendezvous was called Torheit. Eager to see her and afraid of missing the address, I was early. But, like the cuckoo in the clock on the wall, Rachel showed up right on time. She wore a violet blouse, blue jeans, a leather jacket, all three rather tight-fitting.

The Torheit crowd was young and professional so the noise level was comparatively low. We found a booth; I went to the bar for beers. As on the phone, the conversation was fluent, challenging, swift, yet unsatisfying. Rachel made a joke of disclosing only as much about herself as would not spoil what she called "my very own feminine mystique." She insisted that, for me, she appeared exotic, though she did not grant the same allure to me. I learned that she was visiting with her grandfather only for a month after which she was to be relieved from her post, so to speak, by an aunt. So she would be leaving before Christmas. When I asked where she would be going then, she said simply, "Home, of course."

"Are you a musician too?"

"No. I only play the flute—"

"From time to time?"

"Precisely. From time to time."

"What *do* you do, then?"

She was evasive. "I've only been out of university for two years. Give me a chance. And you? You're an anthropologist?"

"I'm whatever the website and your sources say."

She laughed. Every trace of her gravity of the night before had vanished. "You know, linguistically, anthropology is the opposite of gynecology."

"But it isn't, is it?"

She asked a few pointed questions about the negotiations but I answered only vaguely.

We drank two beers each and halfway through the second I suggested some food.

There was a little place down the street, quiet and rather dark, and over the local sausages I told her about the Avramarash Valley. I wished I had photographs of the landscapes I clumsily described, but she was more interested in the people, particularly in the friendship I had struck up with the saintly Karlus Chawnic, a doctor and a Baptist.

"He sounds interesting. Are you religious yourself?"

"No."

"Then you aren't a believer?"

"Not since I was twelve."

She nodded. "And, assuming he asked you about it, what did your Dr. Karlus have to say to that?"

"He did ask, as a matter of fact, and I confessed."

"What did he say?"

"He said he knew two things about atheists."

"Really? Do you remember what they were?"

"I remember almost everything Karlus said to me. First, he said you always have to ask atheists which God it is they don't believe in."

"That's good! He's a wise man, your Saint Karlus. And what was the second thing?"

"He said that atheists often do the good even if they can't bring themselves to speak it."

She put down her fork. "Even better! You know, there was an old rabbi who said something quite like that. You've just reminded me. I wish I could quote the whole thing correctly. It was beautiful."

"Try, then."

"Let's see. He said that all our capacities are created by God for some purpose and so the same must be true of disbelief."

I smirked. "All our capacities? Even the worst, the basest ones?"

"Yes, even those, because he was a saint too, you know. For example, he said that when greed is uplifted it becomes a hunger for salvation, hatred becomes zeal for virtue, and lust the love of the divine."

"And what exactly is 'uplifted'?"

She laughed, brushed fetchingly at her hair, and shrugged. "I don't know. Ask a saint."

"All right. So what did this rabbi say about God's purpose in making me an atheist?"

She turned serious. "You have to be careful about such things. The rabbi never said God made anybody not believe in Him, only that because some people are atheists He must have created the capacity for disbelief. Including yours, of course."

"Yes," I said impatiently, "but to what purpose?"

"That was the most beautiful part. I remember the phrase 'deeds of charity.'"

"Ethics without God? Some rabbi!"

"Yes, some rabbi. An observant one. He said that, faced with people in distress, believers all too readily hand them empty pieties. You know. They say things like 'Have faith. It's God's will. Put your troubles into God's hands.' That sort of thing. Well, atheists never do that. They can't. And this rabbi, who was a really pious man, this rabbi who ran his life by hundreds of laws, concluded that we should act as if there were no God. He said to act as though you were the only one who could help—only yourself."

I was impressed but also perplexed and a little annoyed. Religious talk always irritated me. How had our light, flirtatious teasing turned so solemn? In my state, I couldn't help feeling that she meant to tell me something, something about my duty. If there were no God, if on top of that there were no negotiators, no governments, no multinational corporations, if the fate of the Avramarash and its people were up only to me, what would I do then? The good believer acts as if there is no God yet believes in his heart that there is; the bad atheist—and perhaps I was one—believes in his heart that there is no God yet acts as irresponsibly as if He not only existed but were answerable for everything in the world. Rachel's story felt to me like a reproach. It smarted.

"Are you a Jew?" I asked her bluntly.

She smiled.

I tried teasing her. "What? Only from time to time?"

She looked at me pensively. "Well, only around Gentiles."

Seeing that I was beginning to brood over her story, Rachel herself made light of it. "Perhaps I find it easier to believe in God than in saints. Do you enjoy hiking?"

So two days later we bundled up and climbed to the top of one of the shorter alpine foothills and there we kissed and I felt lost and found.

I was summoned at six o'clock. "Get over here," said my chief. I phoned Rachel at once to say I wouldn't be able to meet her after all. There was a film she wanted to see, and she had hinted that she would be coming back to the hotel with me afterwards.

All our delegation's big shots were there. The ambassador was eating a beef steak at one end of the long table and there were trolleys with the ruins of other meals. Empty beer and wine bottles stood on the low window sill as if waiting for someone to shoot at them. Most of the conference table was covered by a map of the Avramarash. When I came in my boss gave me a stern look conveying both a prayer and a commandment: "Thou shalt not object."

A red line twisted crazily through the valley from northeast to southwest, zigzagging, curling, meandering, as if a child had drawn it while watching television.

What do they want from me? I wondered.

Looking alternately sheepish and peremptory, the ambassador, in his shirtsleeves, wiped his mouth with a napkin. He said he would like my answer to one small question. He glanced toward my boss who must have tried his best to keep me out of the room.

The ambassador got up, joined me over the map and pointed to the highlands, to two villages; he wanted to know how things stood between them. "Do they, you know, get along? I'm thinking of those famous Avramarash vendettas."

Perhaps he was thinking of foreign contract workers caught in a crossfire. I didn't care. I repressed my indignation, seasoned no doubt by missing my date with Rachel, and told him the truth, that the two villages had been feuding for three or four generations.

He seemed more curious than alarmed. "I see. Over what?"

"Water. Women. Land. A drunken brawl. Whose baker makes better bread. Something that happened at a wedding, or didn't. Nobody remembers."

He nodded as if to say, "Typical. Ignorant peasants, what can one expect?"

I yearned to be asked for my opinion of the crazy red line. I wanted to denounce it in a splendid geyser of vituperation, to mock the very idea of considering such a ridiculous outcome to the negotiations; but my boss rushed me out as quickly as he could and shut the door behind me.

I hurried back to the Excelsior in a cold drizzle. In the lobby I spotted Pethos lounging in a club chair, paging through a magazine.

"No Marjusa tonight?"

"I'm tired of her," he said defensively. "Anyway, the word is we'll be leaving in a couple of days."

"Back to your wife, then?"

"So, what about you?" he growled.

He meant what about me and Rachel Wehenbrock.

I excused myself without answering. It was still early, almost early enough for the film, and there was plenty of time for the promised aftermath, for intimacy, discovery, relief. And yet I would have to go home soon and Rachel herself was to leave in days and so what were we really about? I told myself to be light-hearted, that what is without consequence is trivial, comical. But my feeling for Rachel was no more comical than what I felt for the valley of Avramarash. Could I do anything about either? Just me with no help from even an untrustworthy God? Because there is love must there be a consequence? Were Rachel and I just like Pethos and Marjusa? Why should I care? I had not shown myself so scrupulous in the past, when I found leaving women every bit as gratifying as starting up with them. But Rachel was unprecedented and non-negotiable. It was as though some fate were making fun of me, giving and taking away with the same hand, spouting contradictions: you can have her, you can never have her, yes, no.

My conception of Rachel was bound up with her grandfather's recital. I believed she was deep and serious, like the purple of that becoming dress, like Beethoven's resignation. Just because she was not forthcoming, wouldn't declare herself in headlines like Marjusa, I thought what she kept back had to be significant, her own feminine mystique. Love begins as curiosity not ownership; that is, it seeks to penetrate and so there is always a drop of cruelty in it. It was as Rachel had said; for me she was exotic, and I wanted to pierce that strangeness, to get inside. And what was I to her? Impossible to see oneself as exotic; in fact, I felt merely displaced, like those pitiable refugees who had fled the Avramarash during the war.

I took the elevator up to my room and seized the telephone. A woman answered. I didn't recognize her voice and was shocked to realize this must be the aunt. Time was that short. I asked for Rachel and was told that she and her grandfather were dining out. I gave my name and number and, to show I was someone of substance, not one to be ignored, added that I was at the Hotel Excelsior. The woman replied irritably that she would leave the message somewhere but that she herself would be going to bed soon. She sounded peevish, dyspeptic or jet-lagged.

I stayed in my room, faithfully at my post, but there was no call from Rachel.

The light precipitation of the night had become steadier by morning. Only a couple of degrees colder and it would have been the first snow of winter, something less dismal than the last downpour of autumn. I lay in bed, half awake, listening to the rain against the window. The phone rang and I grabbed at the receiver with both hands, as at a promise of bliss.

It was my boss. "Listen. Deal's done. Understand? We're all to meet in the Conference Hall for the reporters and cameras at nine o'clock. Wear your best suit. Try to look exhausted and delighted." He himself sounded neither delighted nor exhausted; he sounded hostile. It amused me that he thought I had more than one suit.

I was shaving when Pethos knocked at my door fifteen minutes later.

"What did I tell you? Party's over."

"It's ridiculous," I said, "a scandal."

"The agreement?" He shrugged. "Well, not if it really means peace."

He had a point, one I had perhaps not adequately considered. Could such a settlement actually produce the greatest happiness for the greatest number rather than just the cheapest stainless steel and air-conditioning for Broadbent? Even fugues in minor keys eventually resolve themselves.

"Hurry up," said Pethos, looking at his watch. "If we're late Marjusa will have a fit." His irony was one tick shy of bitter.

We arrived at five of nine. The hall was already crammed with television crews and their enormous lights; the place was loud with reporters. Could they all have flown in that morning?

At one end of the hall a dais with a long table had been set up with plenty of room for the two delegations to stand—picturesquely weary, smiling, and well dressed—behind the ambassadors with their genial pens. But only our own delegation was there. I spotted Broadbent's man off to one side. He watched everything like a security guard making sure nothing would go wrong. To him we were all suspect. The great man himself was tastefully not on hand. Perhaps, I mused, he's at the bank with the ambassadors filling up unnumbered accounts.

Suddenly there was a hubbub at the door. It was the rival ambassador plenipotentiary, ashen-faced, stiff, wet from the rain. He was alone and looked it. Entourageless. A handful of reporters rushed him, thrusting out microphones, yelling questions. He ran this gauntlet looking stricken, holding up his hands as if in surrender.

He made his way to the dais and began to speak, but no one could hear him. The reporters shouted for a microphone. I was standing behind him and to his left. I noticed his socks didn't match.

A microphone was brought forward. The old man, his damp grey hair slicked back vampire-style, spoke briefly and to the point.

"Ladies and gentlemen. I have to apologize. Four hours ago there was a coup in my country. Our prime minister has resigned and fled the country. The generals now in power have renounced the treaty negotiated here. Obviously, I do not speak for the military government; in fact," he added pathetically, "I no longer occupy any official position at all."

The roar of questions arose even before he stepped back from the microphone looking unhinged, unofficial, even unbribed.

Marjusa stood between me and Ostermann. Over the tumult I heard her excitedly formulate a headline for her chief, "Renewed War in Avramarash Valley."

My flight departed the following morning. The big shots had already gone. At the Excelsior everyone rushed about doing things with that air of significance one gets from a crisis. Marjusa was positively flying. In general, people were exhilarated; our delegation enjoyed the vain felicity of believing we had succeeded. Hadn't we made a generous agreement? Hadn't we behaved like statesmen? The military coup just proved the intransigence and bloody-mindedness of our adversaries. What more could we be expected to do? The whole world could see the difference between us and them. Nothing could be clearer. Now the Avramarash would be patriotically defended, all of it reclaimed as our own; its people were now our brothers and sisters threatened by oppressive generals. The valley would be torn apart; people would murder each other; children would flee in terror to frantic mothers. The girls I had flirted with would be raped. I could see it already.

Pethos stopped by my room to say he was going to the spa.

"Join me? Last chance."

"No," I said glumly. He nodded sadly, as if he understood.

I called for a taxi to drive me up to Wehenbrock's villa.

The rain had slackened and the air turned warmer. Humidity fogged the cab's windows. I felt enervated, as if I were breathing the humid exhalations of Mediterranean stevedores. Unable to see the mountains, always an invigorating and humbling sight, my thoughts were shut in by the taxi. Rachel and I had avoided the most serious topics. No, that wasn't quite right. We had skirted them. I thought of us as two people walking side by side through a famous museum. We both recognized the great works, the ones that counted most; we even nodded to one another to acknowledge their greatness and our recognition of it, but we moved on silently, wary of committing ourselves to any serious judgment that might be disputed. One evening, we disagreed about a certain novel, though calmly and with detachment, as if it hardly mattered that we thought differently, as if we were not talking about anything like the possibility of a possible future in which we might possibly, somehow, be together. Possibly.

As the cab rose above the city I thought of the people of the Avramarash, my hospitable friends, the foxy Soroky, the saintly Karlus, and what might already be happening to them. The pride of nations and the control of resources were grindstones, heavy and inexorable. What could I do to stop their momentum? Of what use was I with my half-hearted sense of responsibility, my petty emotions?

So a prime minister had fled, displaced, bribed or not. I too felt I was fleeing, running to Rachel like a hurt child rather than as a disgraced leader. I was all feeling now. I longed for her.

Rachel was gone. She had left that morning, had flown off to a city bristling with glassy office towers, full of green trams and networks of clacking computers. It was the old man who told me. He was practicing when I arrived, softly playing chorale preludes like an abstracted theologian mumbling into his beard. The aunt, an overweight woman in a floral housedress, would have turned me away at the door but Wehenbrock stopped playing and called to her, asking who was there.

He gave me ten minutes of his time.

I wanted to ask him straight off about Rachel but instead I told him how much I had enjoyed his playing. He began to talk of himself. I suppose it was what he was used to.

"I gave it up at first because I fell ill but then, when I was better, I thought I had had enough and ought to make way for the young. I didn't want to be kept alive by adulation or to have the applause survive my talent. It was also to please my dear wife. She disliked my traveling so much and was terrified of a relapse. Then she died. Four years ago." He nodded toward the next room, where the fat aunt was fussing with some knick-knacks, and lowered his voice. "Now they take turns visiting me, as you see. I allow it because it seems to make them feel better."

"Why did you give that recital?"

"Because Rachel asked me to. Could I refuse her anything? Could you?"

"Rachel asked?"

He nodded his big head with its long wisps of hair. "A favor." He looked at me with restrained pity and I saw that he intended to be more Bach than Busoni.

"Rachel's a businesswoman, one of these child-entrepreneurs one hears so much about. Do you know she started her own firm even before she was out of school?"

I was amazed.

"She didn't tell you, then? I suspected as much. She researches under-exploited natural resources. Her clients are chiefly big companies. Quite a success."

"She works for Broadbent?"

"It was he who invited us to dinner last night. It was to be a celebratory banquet. Wonderful food most of which I didn't dare touch. He was very nice to me, by the way, not a bit stiff or deferential—knows a good deal about music too. I honestly believe the man means well. Rachel wouldn't have anything to do with him otherwise. She's a very ethical girl, Rachel, surprisingly religious too. Lit the Chanukah candles every night." He gave a rattling laugh. "'And why shouldn't God concern Himself with economic development?' she said to me."

Robert Wexelblatt

"Then she was here because of the negotiations?"

Wehenbrock shrugged his bony shoulders. "I suppose it was conven-
ient. Very nice for me to have her around, of course. Nice for you too, I
imagine. My impression is that she liked you very much. She certainly
spoke highly of you. I do hope you didn't fall in love with her." He paused.
"Very sorry about the negotiations, by the way. I heard the news this
morning. It's a great disappointment."

I looked at the old artist, at the humane eyes that were somehow
cold, at the mottling on his powerful hands. I do hope you didn't fall in
love with her. It was something a corpse might say. He stood up and
extended his hand to bid me goodbye, to wish me well, to send me home
to the foolish war.

I didn't know what to reply. A sentence came into my mind and for
some reason I said it. "Without music life would be a mistake."

"Ah," he answered, recognizing the quotation with pleasure. "Yes,
yes, and even then . . ."

Citizenship

She was posed sideways on some sort of cushionless banquette, perhaps even a slab of marble. The background was likewise cold and blank, a clinically lit wall or scrim. No texture or curves but those of young female flesh. Her dark hair appeared freshly washed and blown dry. It had apparently been disposed with some care to fall both over her inclined back and beside her face. The latter had been carefully made up, especially the eyes which were turned full on the camera. Her expression at first struck him as sheer pretense, a facsimile of the fashion model's bored and supercilious pout. Later he imposed other interpretations, some sillier, others more sinister. Her legs were drawn up beneath her; her left arm extended so as to conceal her breasts. Technically, the picture was of high quality, glossy and professional, the regulation eight-by ten. In his childhood such pictures were found in forbidden books of "art photography," but probably few people under seventy would still call this black-and-white picture erotic. Was it sexy? The sinuous expanse of bare thorax, hip, thigh, calf, and ankle has been unerogenized by ads for depilatories and skin lotions. Nevertheless, the young woman was naked, brazenly examining the viewer, and the photo shocked him more than a page of Danish pornography would have. True, some might even call the picture tasteful, nothing sexy about it. And yet. And yet it was one of his students. It was Marcia Rodriguez.

At thirty-three Gregory Vollbart thought of his adulthood as a locomotive. A dozen years back, he had jolted into motion pulling nothing but a light caboose. He shot down a level track for four years, stopping only briefly to couple on a shiny Pullman named Sheila. But then quite unexpectedly he derailed. A year later he was up and running, Pullman-less, puffing, chugging more doggedly, and on a different track. Such things happen often in a world become professionally fluid; careers are fungible and stockbrokers turn into potters, drill sergeants teach elementary school, high school whizzes are captains of industry, actors morph into presidents. There are switches everywhere. Re-invention is not such an odd buzzword when you come to think about it. Something that exists because it was invented goes on existing by being re-invented, remains itself only by transforming itself. Steel companies go into financial services; military contractors manufacture child seats; telephone companies produce movies. America is the home of reinvention. Here people have always loved to sport a badge proclaiming themselves self-made. Alexander Hamilton, Abe Lincoln, Ulysses Grant, Sam Goldwyn, Harpo Marx, Bob Dylan. Change your name, your spouse, your religion, your wardrobe, your address, your metaphysics, your portfolio, your ethnicity. To remain true to yourself remain true to nothing else; constancy of change demands changing constancies.

Vollbart's second-generation, vestigially Jewish father, a thoracic surgeon, liked to tell old jokes about fouled-up assimilation, immigrant jokes from the Lower East Side he had heard as a boy. Lipschitz, heavy accent and all, goes to City Hall, legally changes his name to Kelly, then goes back a week later and changes it to Smith. The week after, he introduces himself to a WASP businessman as Smith. The Establishment laughs. "Smith? Come now. What was it before it was Smith?" And ex-Lipschitz says brightly, "Kelly."

Vollbart had gone to Georgetown, delighted the priests and professors, aced all his courses, then the foreign service exam too, married the pretty young upstate New York woman he met when he was a senior, was posted to Ankara, to Manila, to Geneva. He was brilliant yet reliable. Everybody said so. On the fast track. Then, in Switzerland, Sheila began drinking and acting out at parties. She had three affairs that he knew of. He had an affair too. She suffered. He suffered. His work suffered. Then came the divorce and almost simultaneously his resignation. Everything happened so quickly it really did feel like a train wreck.

He spent a year living off his savings in a studio apartment back in the District, depressed, muddled, fending off his panicky parents. He read a lot at random, history, novels, even poetry. "Such an end from such a beginning," wrote Whitman glumly. "There's a certain slant of light," Dickinson chimed in. He finally pulled himself together, talked his way into a Ph.D. program at his alma mater and worked demonically, harder and faster than anybody else. In four years flat he landed a good job with prospects in Ohio, three courses in the Fall, only two in the Spring. Professor Gregory Vollbart, historian, philosopher, political scientist, scholar and essayist, measured optimist in public, hesitant pessimist in private, divorced bachelor. "He can teach anything," beamed his chairman when he took Vollbart by the arm and introduced him around. His first year had gone well.

Vollbart had had enough of thinking about himself during his year in Washington and so he thought about big things, geopolitics, philosophy, ancient history. On his return to Georgetown he had improved his Latin to the level of his excellent French and German, above his passable Russian. He was only in his early thirties, not too old to be an assistant professor and his chances of tenure looked excellent given his mounting reputation and list of publications. The four years in the diplomatic corps lent him a certain prestige among his colleagues, as if he had been a prizefighter or a first-baseman. He was a popular teacher too, judging from the encomia his students wrote about him that first year. He knew he deserved their praise. He cared about his students properly, one at a time. He was a good adviser. The ignorance of the young stimulated him; as for their innocence, he took it for granted that his job was to disturb it. He invented new courses and pedagogical strategies to lay before them like an inspired chef, just as he had dreamed up Professor Gregory Vollbart, the fellow in the black turtleneck and sprucely clipped beard.

Vollbart laughed at himself. Hercule Poirot minus mustache wax and Belgian conceit, but it was so; he had deduced. The plain manila envelope containing the photograph of Marcia Rodriguez had been slipped under his office door between approximately five-thirty Tuesday afternoon and eight-fifteen Wednesday morning. He had left his office at four-thirty. Had the article in question been deposited during the next hour Alfonso Pentilento would have found it when he came to empty the waste basket. He would have placed it on Vollbart's desk as he often did term papers and memos. Vollbart and Pentilento were on familiar terms. The janitor was a Filipino and back in September they had sat around gossiping for nearly an hour about the Marcoses, Aquinos, and Jeeps. Pentilento wound up complaining about why he had to get away from the islands. "No chances," he said, shaking his head. "Here they offer my daughter free tuition someday. But there?" He shook his head again. Then he started on the overseas Chinese. "They own everything. They try to act like us but also, you know, they keep to themselves. They change their names but nobody's fooled." Another double-play: Lipschitz to Kelly to Smith. The Jews of Asia.

Knowing approximately, or even precisely, when the envelope had been placed under his door was of no use. The real questions were who put it there, why, and what to do about it. Should he run to the Dean, even file a charge of sexual harassment, and so cover his untenured ass? Or ought he to invite Ms. Rodriguez to his office and—keeping the door wide open and arranging for a female colleague to sit in—confront her with the picture? This was too much, he felt; it seemed embarrassing and brutal. Wouldn't it be better to do nothing at all, ignore the provocation or invitation or whatever it was, pretend never to have seen it? Might that be dangerous? He thought of the young women in his undergraduate classes at Georgetown. Sheila had been one of them, blonde, inexperienced, with those ravishingly open Rochester vowels. Vollbart had been naïve about Sheila, or at least about her capacity for discontent with life on the move, with his careerism, with him. Was it possible Marcia had a crush on him and would choose this way of announcing it, advertising her availability? Maybe he was still naïve about females. He shook his head like the exiled janitor.

Vollbart decided against going to the Dean. He could see the prudence of doing so but it bothered him to throw the responsibility, and probably Marcia Rodriguez as well, into the bureaucratic machinery, even the soft, student-centered, therapy-pushing motor that ran the University. Once, in London, he had been taken to see a cricket match. The bowler bowled, the batter stood still, the ball missed the wicket. The man beside him rose and applauded. "Oh, well not hit," he said. He was the professor. He would decide. It was his responsibility and the responsible thing was to do nothing. Well not hit.

Still, he had to interrogate himself on a crucial point. Was he the least bit tempted? A smidgen turned on? There had been a couple of women in his life in D.C. but he had been celibate for nearly eleven months now. This condition was not a matter of principle but owing to a fervent dedication to work and the accident of not meeting anybody he cared to pursue since pulling into Ohio. Might his condition undermine his judgment in some way? Even if the picture did not affect him in any inappropriate fashion what was the appropriate one? Inappropriate was the nation's current euphemism for sexual. Inappropriate touching, language, relationships. Clinton had chosen the word for the same reason Nixon preferred incursion to invasion back in 1970, because it made hard things soft. The private was now famously the political. Everybody knew the code and the consequences of being inappropriate were severe. Third-graders who kissed classmates got suspended. Stolen smooches are inappropriate, like ethnic jokes and offhand threats to blow up buildings. Anyway, his feelings towards his students were paternal not amorous. No, the photograph stirred him not a bit. Professor Vollbart knew the limits of the appropriate and approved of them. He embraced the mores and restrictions of his profession and was disgusted by professors who contracted affairs with students, even the former graduate students they left their spouses for and had grandchildren with. That the erotic leached into teaching, that the emotional bled into the professional, these things he was conscious of only the better to ignore them.

He put the photograph back into its envelope, threw it in the bottom of a desk drawer, and covered it with some folders. He had other things to think about.

Listening to Helen Chou's complaints about her parents reminded Vollbart of stories he had heard as a child, tales of the second generation tearing itself free from the first.

"I mean I love them, of course, but they just don't get it. They say I have to marry a Chinese. I started hearing that when I was about five. I have to speak Chinese at home or they won't answer me, even though their English is fine. I have to be in by eleven. I have to get straight A's. Like if I get a B my father just about goes into cardiac arrest and my mother starts this silent crying and shaking her head and talking about all their hopes and the bad example I set for my little sister. They're just so rigid, you know? I can't even use make-up. Naturally they hate all my friends. I have to show respect, that's really huge. Respect means bowing my head and doing whatever they want. Respect means ancestor worship only the ancestors are still alive."

College boy. That's what Vollbart's grandfather had called his son whenever he was disgusted with him. College boy. He remembered his father doing an imitation of the way his father said it, addressing himself to the sympathetic minyan perched on his left shoulder. College boy. It summed up all his immigrant's fear, inadequacy, frustration, resentment, but also his pride. All bricks for the monument of mutual ambivalence Vollbart's forefathers had built together. Was Napoleon Bonaparte a hero for making Jews citizens or a villain for setting in motion the process that led to Vollbart's father marrying a shiksa? College boy, or girl. Think they

Robert Wexelblatt

know it all. Can't wait to be like the Goyim, the round eyes, the blond and blue-eyed set, the slackers, the country clubbers. Vollbart père had married an Irish girl and wouldn't go near a synagogue. He even let his red-haired wife take his boy to church. He didn't keep the Sabbath, not even the high holy days; all he kept were the jokes. Jokes were the essence of Vollbart's ethnic patrimony. A Jew newly arrived in New York tries to put on airs. He affects what he thinks is an English accent, stops a native on the street to ask how to get to the subway. "I say, old chappie, how might one get underground?" And the New Yorker snaps back, "Drop dead."

Helen Chou could have been his aunt. It was the same generational battle, the same want/don't want, the same tug of war between identity by inclusion and exclusion, the hope of acceptance, the terror of being told to drop dead.

"They hate me going to the mall. They can't stand my music. I can't even tell them who I go out with here. And there's like all this pressure, Professor Vollbart. Grades, grades. It's all they care about. I'm going to crack up."

He hardly knew what to say, having already granted her an extension on her paper.

"Think about this, young man. If you marry a Gentile you're the same as Hitler. You're carrying on his work." This from the local rabbi in 1964, his father told him. "He thought assimilation's as big a threat as genocide. Hell, he believed it is genocide. So, what do you think, half-breed? You know what they say, don't you? The son wants to remember what the father wants to forget. That true for you?"

"What do I do, Professor? How do I make them see I love them but I'm just not them?"

"Your parents love you, Helen. They'll forgive you, even for things you don't believe you need to be forgiven for. They're confused too. Parents see their children's worries; kids seldom see their parents'. They're just afraid of losing you, or of your losing yourself. So keep reassuring them. Remember, they're in America too. As for your grades, why not just get all A's and make them happy?"

Pathetic and pallid advice. Hardly edification. Such pabulum should have disgusted her, though she smiled and said he'd made her feel better. And yet Vollbart was deeply interested in what was happening to students like Helen. How did they manage the schisms, he wondered.

78

Vollbart devoted the night before the second photograph appeared on the floor of his office to working on a paper that was giving him stomach cramps. He was to deliver it at a conference between Christmas and New Year's. This was no ordinary conference but an interdisciplinary extravaganza sponsored by three of the snootiest of scholarly journals. Speaking there ought to have been a coup, grease for the tenure case to come. But the letter accepting his proposal sounded to Vollbart like a threat. "Your idea has provoked considerable interest on the organizing committee," wrote the chairman, "so much that we plan to give your paper pride of place. We would like you to deliver it in the hotel's banquet hall on the first day at one p.m. It is our intention that no other papers be scheduled at that hour so you can expect an audience of two or three hundred. The panel of respondents is not yet settled, but I can promise you they will all be distinguished scholars. We are thinking of a group of three: a historian, a classicist, and a philosopher. You will no doubt be pleased to learn that Professor Geoffrey Pryme, a member of our committee who reviewed your proposal, has requested to serve as the historian." No doubt pleased? Geoffrey Pryme crushed specialists with his erudition and was notorious for his slice-and-dice reviews. Vollbart was scared. Of his thesis he was now uncertain and it seemed to him that the "considerable interest" it had provoked on the committee was the kind foxes took in chickens.

What he had proposed he could not prove. He could find no smoking gun, only smoke which he imagined Pryme blowing away with gales of sarcasm, gusts of derision. He had a nightmare in which the three Fates swooped from their perches on the dais behind him, talons and beaks flashing, and bit off his head and hands. It was scholarly castration.

Vollbart had proposed a paper on the stability of the Roman Empire, the durable status-quo and Pax Romana that Europeans had never gotten out of their systems and were still trying to reproduce. Vollbart's thesis was that the chief reason for the persistence of the Roman system was the decision to extend citizenship to non-Romans. His point was going to be that this inspired policy required an intellectual shift achieved by no other ancient society and, indeed, by hardly any subsequent ones until the founding of the United States of America.

The customary historians' accounts described how during the late Republic Romans first offered citizenship selectively throughout Latium; that is, to people much like themselves in appearance, mores, religion, and language. To Vollbart's thinking the historians made too little of the Social War of 90-88 B.C. when the more distant Italian allies rebelled because Rome had refused to grant them citizenship. After all, Drusus had promised it to them before his assassination and there were substantial benefits attached to the franchise. The war ended with a victory for Roman arms but also with all the Italians south of the Po getting their citizenship. According to Vollbart a new, enlightened, progressive idea had entered the world at the moment citizenship became a matter of adopting certain institutions rather than of race, ethnicity, or residence.

As usual, the economic reductionists had solid and dispiriting arguments. To them, the extension of citizenship was initiated by self-interested agribusiness in Rome while the Italians desired citizenship only so as to claim a bigger share of the spoils they had helped to generate. The granting of citizenship was merely one of several tactics the Romans deployed for colonial domination. In the end the Empire became a sort of multinational corporation with stockholders spread across the map, all eager to defend the Establishment and keep the profits rolling in. Various emperors advanced the process by fits and starts until in 212 Caracalla made all freeborn inhabitants of the Empire full citizens. According to one mordant, undemocratic historian, what Caracalla did "devalued the privilege of citizenship so much as to make it worthless." These scholars loved to season their accounts with all kinds of arcane distinctions: *civitates liberae* vs. *stipendiariae*, *colonia* vs. *municipia*, *peregrine* vs. *municeps*. They relished showing how the process accelerated during the civil war between Caesar and Pompey when, as they cynically reckoned, both generals dispensed citizenship to potential allies as bribes. It astonished Vollbart that none remarked on the cosmopolitanism, the anti-parochialism, the universalist vision, the decency, tolerance and rationality that, in his opinion, must be behind this unprecedented policy. What fascinated him was the good idea that kept the system running for so long, an idea that Serbs, Croatians, Germans, Indonesians, Japanese, and Rwandans had yet to grasp.

Like all ideas this one had a history of its own, a history more philosophical than political. And it was this history Vollbart proposed to trace in his paper. "Socrates said he was not an Athenian or a Greek, but a citizen of the world," wrote Plutarch. So he would begin with Father Socrates, even though he preferred death to exile from the city he tormented and loved and could lose his way even in the suburbs.

Cosmopolitanism had nothing to do with travel. From Socrates he would go to the Cynics, begotten by Socrates through his pupil Antisthenes. "Asked what country he came from Diogenes replied, 'I am a citizen of the world,'" quoth Diogenes Laertius. Cosmopolites. Socrates begat the Cynics and the Cynics begat the Stoics and Stoicism was more or less transferred to Rome in the first century B.C. which was when citizenship really began to spread. Stoic virtue was Roman virtue, civic-minded, indifferent to wealth, dignified, tough. The head of the Stoic school in Rhodes was Posidonius who served as ambassador to Rome from 87 to 86 B.C. He got to know the tribune Gaius Marius and befriended Pompey who later visited him in Rhodes. Above all, Posidonius spent time with his old student Cicero and it was Cicero, contemporary of the citizenship-strewing Caesar and Pompey, who universalized the concept of Roman Law, explicitly distinguishing between a transcendent idea of justice and mere local ordinances and customs. To become a citizen of Rome was to live under the most advanced legal system the world had yet devised or would for the better part of two millennia. The climax of Vollbart's paper, philosophically, would come with Epictetus, the ex-Greek slave who wound up as a Roman professor. At the end of the first century Epictetus asked: "What is a man?" He gave this extraordinary answer: "A part of a commonwealth; first and chiefly of that which includes both gods and men; and next, of that to which you immediately belong which is a miniature of the universal city . . . . You are a citizen of the universe, and a part of it." The universal city, the cosmos, was Rome.

What made the extension of Roman citizenship possible? Vollbart could not believe it was merely necessity, policy, or greed. His idea was that it was Stoicism, the sole Greek philosophy dreamed up by a non-Greek, that it was Stoicism with its strain of oriental monism and pantheism. "You are a distinct portion of the essence of God," Epictetus lectured his students. "Why do not you remember, when you are eating, who eats and whom you feed? . . . You carry a God about with you . . . and know nothing of it." Stoicism was Roman virtue plus theory. Stoicism gave Rome centurions indifferent to the heat of Africa, the snows of the Alps, the damp of Britain, incorruptible administrators who cared only for their duties. Seneca said "we are born for others," that all relationships determine responsibilities and it is for these we should live. Stoicism reinforced the networks of patronage on which Rome ran. It founded marriage on duty rather than infatuation. In short, Stoicism offered the noblest solution to the problem of how to live a happy, meaningful life in a vast, corrupt empire. But above all Stoicism said all men are created equal, since all are portions of God.

Vollbart meant to enforce his point by contrasting the Roman idea of citizenship with that of Athens. For the Athenians the polis was exclusive. At the height of the Golden Age they adopted a law restricting citizenship to the legitimate offspring of parents who both came from citizen families. Compared to the Romans, the Athenians were tribal. True, their city welcomed immigrants from all over the Greek world, offered them economic opportunity and social acceptance, but citizenship could be granted only by vote of the Assembly and this was both grudging and rare. There was no procedure for naturalization. Even Aristotle never became a citizen.

Vollbart might add that Aristotle's most distinguished pupil, Alexander the Great, may have had a vision of supra-tribal equality, of an inclusive rather than exclusive state, when he conceived of a nation made of Greeks and Persians. But this notion was unpopular with his Macedonians, with the Greeks, perhaps with the Persians as well. It was an idea whose time had yet to come. It died with Alexander, as did his empire. What could you expect from a people whose word for anybody unlike themselves was barbarian?

Vollbart intended to conclude his paper with an explanation of why human equality, an idea that ignited revolution in the eighteenth century, buttressed the status-quo in the first. He would explain how Stoic fatalism did not make Epictetus think of breaking his bonds but only of being the best slave he could be, and made Marcus Aurelius, Rome's paragon of good government, indifferent to his position, but faithful to his duty. Epictetus himself provided the perfect metaphor: God who is Nature hands out the parts at the stage door. You have no choice whether you play Hamlet or Polonius, only whether you perform well or badly. The Stoics were masters of emotional toilet training; it is the source of their stolid dignity. Care only about what you can control, your attitudes, your will. Rebellion pits you against the universe, against God. Epictetus says that one should "accede to whatever happens; it is for the good of the universe or of the state." Only a Roman would equate the two. And he mocks the whining of Greek tragedy. God is not outside nature and history; there is no evil, there are no miracles, or rather the miracle is the status-quo. But the main point Vollbart would make is that since God is in all human beings Romans are not better than Spaniards, Britons, or Gauls. Thus all can be citizens together. Excellence alone is a genuine distinction and maestria is where you find it. Long ago Nietzsche pointed out that, notwithstanding their ruthlessness and the lions in the Coliseum, the Romans had it all over the Christians when it came to tolerance and magnanimity. Their persecutions were like the rub-outs in *The Godfather*: "Nothing personal, just business."

Vollbart imagined his paper taking the structure of a triumphal arch. But he knew the reason Roman arches stood up so well was that the builders were obliged to stand beneath them when the scaffolding was removed. His arch, it now seemed to him, was built of vaporous speculation, a light enough material until it fell on your head.

Like the first, the second photograph arrived in an unmarked manila envelope, was eight-by-ten, black and white, technically proficient. Against the white background Helen Chou lay on her back, naked, one knee bent, smiling at the camera. Vollbart was stunned. This was the Helen who had been asking for advice and an extension in his office only the day before, who got in trouble for hanging out at the mall, whose curfew was eleven o'clock.

The fact of a second picture changed things. If he were to go to the Dean now there might be an awkward question about the delay. Also, a second picture of a different student meant that the first had not been put under his door by a smitten Marcia Rodriguez, not unless there were some bizarre conspiracy between her and Helen. No, it was more likely the photos had been left by the photographer. Vollbart quickly conjured up a male student, wealthy, handsome, and twisted, with straight blond hair and connections who had seduced these girls into posing for him, then made prints to slip under his door. But why? Maybe it was an initiation prank or some perverted proof of power; perhaps he did it out of disgruntlement over a grade or personal malice toward Vollbart, toward women, particularly Chinese and Hispanic ones, or maybe it was to show the teacher, the intellectual, the superiority of gonads to neocortex. "They listen to you because they have to, but look what they will do for me." It had to be a male, didn't it? Anyway, it was unfathomable. But why assume it was only under his door that these photographs were slipped? It was almost a kind of vanity to think so. How many of his colleagues might also be receiving these pictures, or pictures like them, and keeping mum about it? He could hardly ask around.

Before concealing it in his desk drawer Vollbart contemplated the picture of Helen Chou. It pained him to see her unclothed. She was so young and slim and vulnerable. Why would she consent to such a thing? He imagined her taking off her clothes for some spoiled red-faced frat boy. He could just see this monster arranging her, telling her to bend her left knee like that, directing the lights on her. She would have been nervous. With alarm Vollbart realized the devil must have given her alcohol or drugs, just as he had Marcia Rodriguez.

Three more pictures showed up in November, a dreary month hardly redeemed by Thanksgiving. Vollbart spent the break making a hash of his own paper and grading his students' instead of going home as his parents begged him to do. All three pictures were of female students in his introductory ethics class. He could no longer doubt they were aimed at him alone. Worse still, the photographs had become more provocative. There was prim Luciana Agrigenti touching herself, shy Tiffany Kim peeling a banana, the earnest Suzanne Schulman and bookish Brina Grossman on the point of kissing. Was it possible they were all so corrupted, that they knew these pictures were being delivered to their professor? Did the whole class know? Were they all waiting for him to respond, to explode, to melt down at the lectern?

He no longer left the pictures in his desk. It was too dangerous. He took them home, put them under his sweaters, and tried not to look at them. He had to concentrate on his paper, which was disintegrating under his hand like wet toilet paper. Stoicism, he had told his students back in October, is everything you're not. But that's it's appeal, the lure of the anti-self. He tried to be Stoical himself. In the will alone is virtue, in the will alone is vice. We eat God, we feed God. Pleasure and pain are matters of indifference. God takes the pictures, God poses for them, and God looks at them. What the hell were they trying to do to him?

Blocked, he went back to the historians who always made things worse. "Even by the close of the first century Roman citizenship had lost most of its advantages," one Oxford mandarin wrote. "As soon as the lower classes attained citizenship the law began to distinguish less between citizens and non-citizens and more between wealthy and poor, regardless of citizenship." Reading this depressed Vollbart. It was all too plausible, too drearily familiar. Of course the Romans never gave up their sense of hierarchy, of insiders and outsiders. Nobody does. Even here, in Jefferson's experiment, in the middle of Whitman's democratic vistas, wasn't it much the same? Hadn't he foolishly overestimated the Romans' achievement? Maybe pantheism had nothing to do with it. Couldn't greed, ambition, lust of power, lust itself account adequately for Rome's mafiaesque ripping off of the world?

He wrote a note: "Humility befits the millennium. No good society can be perfect and no society that aims at perfection can be good. Freedom without security breeds license; security without freedom spells totalitarianism. Merit without equality turns into oppression; equality without merit dulls motivation. Even the best societies, particularly the best, are fields of tension." He threw the scrap of paper on the floor and went to bed, defeated, desolate and flat as Carthage.

The following night Vollbart turned to his notes on Posidonius, who is supposed to have written nearly eight hundred books, all lost. None of his views could be cited with certainty. Yet one scholar wrote confidently that "... contrary to the general Stoic dogma he taught that passions are not simply false judgments but an irreducible force in human nature." A Stoic who respects emotion? Again the arch wobbled.

The week following Thanksgiving the weather turned cold. One morning there were a few inches of snow on the ground. Vollbart welcomed the chilly weather; he was glad football season was over, that the semester would soon come to a close and he would never have to look at the duplicitously fresh-faced undergraduates in his ethics class again. They would disperse without anything being said, probably go home and have sex in their parents' rumpus rooms. He had not taken the bait. He had acceded to all that happened.

Still, each morning Vollbart approached his office door as if it might blow up. In your face, Professor. Did he want an envelope to be there or not? Was he relieved or disappointed when they finally ceased showing up? He felt himself in the absurd position of a man who collected pornography yet was disgusted by it. This was not exactly hypocrisy but something very like it. Perhaps, he thought, a good citizen requires a little hypocrisy, needs to be able to despise in public what he practices in private and to approve in public values he privately violates. He was both shocked and perversely pleased by this idea.

By the final week of the semester he loathed going to class, all his classes, and his dread undermined his teaching which became less

Robert Wexelblatt

imaginative, supple, responsive. He no longer bothered inviting discussions or walked about the room patiently drawing out his students, forcing them to answer in paragraphs; he barely made eye-contact. In the semester's last faculty meeting he flinched when the Dean referred to the student body. Around his colleagues he felt himself becoming furtive. For over a month he had eaten his lunches alone unless forced to join some jolly clutch of his young colleagues, all private idealists who in public competed at cynicism. Vollbart felt singled out, baffled, marked, as if he no longer belonged.

Come now, what was it before it was Smith? Was it perhaps Agrigenti, Schulman, Grossman, could it have been Rodriguez, Kim, or Chou?

The phone rang the night before the final examination in Vollbart's ethics course. He expected it would be his mother, checking up yet again on his flight at the end of the month, after the conference, which he was thinking of getting out of by claiming to have come down with something along the lines of cholera or pellagra. The voice at the other end was not his mother's. It identified itself as Helen Chou's. He stiffened.

"I'm so sorry to bother you at home, Professor. Are you very busy?"

"Go ahead, Helen."

"Well, a bunch of us are here studying together." A bunch of them? The whole harem? "And we had a question. I know we should have brought it up at the review session but—"

"It's okay, Helen. What is it?" He trembled. Was it possible she would mention the pictures?

"It's about the Tarasoff case."

Vollbart had used this landmark lawsuit earlier in the semester, back when he was still trying to provoke discussions. Tarasoff was a young woman murdered by her boyfriend who had previously confided to his therapist his intention to kill her as soon as she returned home from a vacation in Brazil. Owing to what they considered the obligations of professional confidentiality, the therapist and a consulting psychiatrist did not report the threat to the woman, her family, or the police. The family sued.

"We all checked our notes but none of us wrote down what the court actually decided."

"That's because I didn't tell you."

86

There was a pause. Helen the grade-grubber. Helen under her mother's deceived gaze, her father's misplaced thumb. Helen of the bent knee.

"Then we don't have to know it for the exam?"

"No. But I could ask you to write what you would decide and why, using one or more of the philosophers we studied to support your answer."

"Oh." There was some fumbling with the receiver; he heard muffled words.

"Professor? It's Luciana. How are you?"

"I'm fine, Luciana."

"Look, about this Tarasoff case. You said there was a conflict between values. Right?"

"Yes?"

"Well, we're not exactly sure what they are."

Vollbart was silent for a few seconds. To his own surprise he asked, "Who else is there?"

"What? Who else?"

"Yes."

"Tiffany and Suzanne and Brina. We all live in the same dorm. We're a study group."

Vollbart could see them in the dorm room, the white wall, a banquette pulled in from the lounge, the tripod and lights.

"You never study with any of the men?"

"Well, sometimes. Why?"

"Just wondering."

"Oh, Brina wanted me to be sure and tell you how much we all loved your course. We think you're amazing."

"Awesome," somebody said in the background. Sincerely? Facetiously?

Vollbart pushed this tainted praise aside. "Let's get back to Tarasoff, okay? On the one side you have the rules of professional confidentiality and the risk that if they aren't upheld by the court mentally disturbed people would be discouraged from seeking help."

"Wait a minute. I'm trying to get this down."

"All right. What do you think would go on the other side of the ledger, Luciana?"

"I don't know. The Tarasoff girl's life?"

"Yes. Our duty to respect the lives, persons, and rights of all our fellow citizens even if it means violating the ethics of our professions or our private promises and wishes."

"Oh, I see."

"Do you? Do you, Luciana?"

Vollbart spent the night after he turned in his grades reconstructing his paper, trying to pull together a conclusion that might anchor the rebuilt arch firmly enough for him to risk standing under it. There was nothing he desired more than to finish his paper, but there was nothing he wouldn't do to avoid working on it. He paced around his apartment, paged desultorily through his books, scrubbed the kitchen counter, lay down on his bed, took a walk in the cold air.

After midnight he pushed his notes off the desk and scrawled the following.

"Citizenship guarantees protection but also entails the obligation to protect. Citizenship includes and excludes, but the principles by which it does one or the other matter enormously. It is foolish to expect even the noblest human conceptions to be immaculate, detached from the base impulses of human nature, appetite, cupidity, rapaciousness. The great thing is that self-interest should sometimes coincide with a noble idea, that passion should not always drag reason into the mud but elevate itself by correcting calculation with compassion for those superficially unlike ourselves, even for the venal, the licentious, the barbarous. The universal city is not limited to seven hills and the Romans proved we can all be citizens of it. What will make us citizens of the world in the end is not the law or imperial policy or even reason. It is passion, the worst in us but also the best, the lightest and the heaviest. The Stoic Posidonius respected this feeling. He gave it a sublime name. He called it cosmic sympathy."

Delusion

1.

In June 1932 the psychiatrist Arno Balassa moved into a small but decent apartment not far from the bookstalls that lined the left bank of the Seine. Three and a half years earlier he had taken similar lodgings in Vienna, having left his native Budapest with a new medical degree and a tidy legacy. He had gone to Austria in order to learn psychoanalysis. Young Balassa revered the personal example of Sigmund Freud and could imagine nothing more splendid than to become his disciple.

Upon completing his studies in Vienna he did not think of returning to his homeland whose mixture of energetic parochialism and lazy cosmopolitanism did not appeal to him. His parents were dead and there was nothing to draw him back to Hungary. Even his former sweetheart had married; indeed, according to a post card he received from a mutual friend, she was already a mother. He was free to go where he wished. Psychoanalysis was an international movement. Fluent in French and provided with letters of introduction to the leading analysts there, he chose Paris to be his future home, the city of light, Western antipode of the East's religious obscurantism, antidote to its imbecile chauvinism.

Balassa had many books, but the greatest treasure in his luggage was a personal note from Freud himself commending *The Case of Herr B.*, a case study he had written in emulation of the Master.

This patient had been referred to him by a Dr. Rath who claimed to be too busy to deal with him, but Balassa saw it as a test. If so, he had passed *cum laude*. Herr B. was a respectable shopkeeper who had dismembered his wife's cat and left it in the oven for her to find. He had consented to see Balassa only so that his wife would not leave him. It had taken many months to overcome his resistance but in the end Balassa skillfully discovered the cause of his patient's behavior. One day the man confessed—in a voice both fearful and ashamed—that he had to kill the cat because it was a malign spirit preventing his wife from becoming pregnant. Such a delusion was a plausible way of coping with Frau B.'s unwillingness to conceive an heir, but Balassa had not been convinced. After a few more sessions, he discarded the idea that the fellow was desperate to become a father or even that his wife lay at the bottom of the matter. From the Master he had learned that delusion is, so to speak, an editorial function, a way of correcting the text of reality by deleting whatever cannot be borne and replacing it with ideas that suit one's wishes or allay one's fears. Balassa's hypothesis was that Herr B. feared he was incapable of engendering a child. Putting the blame on the cat would ease that anxiety. However, this theory was dashed when Herr B., now eager to treat Balassa as his confessor, disclosed that, a few years prior to his marriage, he had been responsible for the pregnancy of a young woman, a servant in his parents' home. His training had taught Balassa to look far into his patients' past for the source of derangement. Not for nothing, he understood, was Freud a collector of antiquities, an amateur of archaeology. The analyst, too, must delve into the layers buried beneath the veneer of civilized adult reasoning; for psychically nothing ever dies. The breakthrough came when Herr B. recalled how one day when he was about ten he had gone through his father's desk and came across a bundle of love letters from a woman, a dancer. These letters had shocked the boy and marked him for life; he had grasped that in them lay the source of the unhappiness that made his home tense and prevented his mother from loving him as he wished. Balassa even worked out how the subsequent affair with the housemaid was an effort to identify with the father while at the same time seeking revenge upon him, since Herr B. suspected his father of also lusting after the young woman. It is always the telling detail for which one must search, the detail that is the magic key. Those love letters the dancer had sent to his father were signed *Kätzschen*—that is, Kitty. Balassa had burst through appearances; he had passed his final *viva voce*. The root of the man's problem was not marital, the young doctor had triumphantly concluded his case study, but Oedipal. He knew the Master would be pleased.

Balassa was proud of the way he had dealt with this case; it had given him confidence. In the letter he wrote thanking his young colleague for the case study Freud had suggested that Balassa make a special study of delusion. There was a great deal of work to be done in this field, he observed. And so, in Paris, Balassa let it be known among his new confrères that, while fully qualified to cope with all kinds of cases, it was with delusions that he intended to make his name. He would, of course, be most obliged for any referrals in that line.

2.

The weather was sultry and overcast on the first Monday of August. Balassa, weary of reading and feeling bored, decided on a walk by the Seine. The leaves of the trees hung motionlessly. Notre Dame appeared to him more forlorn than majestic on its little island; the Eiffel Tower so much geometrical space limned by rusting iron. Along with the humidity, loneliness had settled over Paris.

Balassa sighed. He had put nothing into his stomach all day except a cup of coffee, not so much as half a brioche. The night before he had tried a new restaurant whose *boeuf en gelé* had proved greasy and persisent. In fact, he felt completely out of sorts. The city was deserted. The only patient he had so far secured, Mme. Desmoulins, had gone off to Cannes with her spectacularly unfaithful husband and their two daughters. Though desolated to have to discontinue her sessions for three whole weeks—an eternity, she said!—Mme. Desmoulins could not conceal her pleasure at getting away and having her husband all to herself. "Even that goat understands the rules," she explained, referring to her due as his wife and the mother of his daughters. This disruption was almost more than she could bear, and just when they were making such progress, but there was no help for it. Her unresolved conflicts would have to be packed away with the lotions and bathing suits, but he was not to worry about her. She would be sure to write down all of her dreams for him. See? She had purchased a special leather-bound notebook expressly for the purpose. Her dream-diary. Indeed, there was no telling what buried traumas from her Norman childhood might be stirred up by the proximity of the sea. Could she write to him if necessary? He would promise to answer by return post?

Balassa yawned; his arms hung at his sides. He had hoped the walk would refresh him but he felt drained of energy. Climbing steps almost like an old man, he went up to a kiosk, bought three cigars—the Master's own specific stimulus—and a newspaper. Trouble in Germany, as usual. The French journals reveled in any bad news from that quarter and doubtless made things out to be worse than they were. He ought to make a note on the commonplaces of journalistic delusion and their implications for

91

international diplomacy.

Did he need a woman? Since arriving in Paris he had sought out a prostitute only once, just to clear his head for work. He got little pleasure on that occasion. Cheap hotel rooms in Vienna were cleaner and the women less hard. Here the putains referred to their private parts as purses.

As he walked Balassa began to go over a conversation he had had a couple weeks earlier at a dinner party. It was with André Florel, a psychiatrist with a considerable reputation and his own clinic at Rambouillet. Though Balassa knew better than to be excessively earnest at a soirée, he was eager to make an impression on the man. No doubt he had talked more shop than he ought to have but Florel had provoked him.

As usual, Balassa mentioned his interest in cases of delusion, speaking with enthusiasm about Freud's theories and his ambition to make a substantial contribution to the profession's understanding of the disorder.

Though Florel did not exactly patronize him, Balassa felt his reply to be disagreeable. Florel remarked that, though he had personally treated a mere dozen such cases (Balassa had seen only Herr B.), he had found the prevailing theory of delusion not altogether useful or, to be frank, interesting. "Freud's general account of delusions—that is, why people might be motivated to embrace them—doesn't interest me as much as the particular form of a patient's delusion, which does not always conform to the theory. Please correct me if I'm mistaken, but in his most recent work Freud appears convinced that delusion is a form of escapism, another blind tactic in a doomed quest to evade unhappiness. To be candid, Dr. Balassa, I don't see why a delusion cannot itself be illuminating. I grant that my experience is limited but, as I see it, delusion is itself a sort of theorizing, an attempt to interpret reality—an unsuccessful one, to be sure, at least from the viewpoint of social norms. But I am not making myself clear. I accept that the ego may be defending itself by delusion, of course, but this defense may also be based on interesting insights and speculations. You know as well as I that, in the course of time, many views thought to be delusory have been confirmed. The history of human thought is littered with delusions, including the history of science which prides itself on being immune to them. For how many generations before Lavoisier did scientists believe in phlogiston? And didn't Aristotle remark that the chief function of the brain is to cool the blood? Who can say how much of what we believe now is also a delusion?"

Balassa had smiled and shaken his head at this, as if the elder man had made this long speech especially to tease him. Though Florel's experience greatly exceeded his own, here it was the seasoned clinician who was pleased to be fanciful, while the young theorist stuck by hard distinctions and remained faithful to orthodoxy.

"But Doctor," he said, "you fail to differentiate between scientific error and mental derangement. Aristotle's theories of the brain, of reproduction, or of astronomy are not delusions but simple mistakes and the proof is that, were he to be confronted with better evidence, he would surely alter his opinions. The deluded, on the other hand, always ignore the evidence. Delusion is static and self-defeating while science is dynamic and self-correcting. People suffering from delusions wish to rearrange reality. Our job is to bring them back from their fantasies, back into the real world. Naturally, I agree that to understand the particular form of a delusion is essential, but only because each delusion reveals its motive and only through discovering their concealed motives can we help our patients to get well. Without a general theory of delusion how could we proceed?"

Florel had remained quiet through this rather fervent speech, as though respectfully allowing the younger man every opportunity to lay out his case. Balassa hoped the smile frozen on Florel's face was good-humored rather than condescending.

"So, you would say the trick is to stay free of delusions, then?"

"Pardon me?"

"Well, if I follow you, we analysts are men of science and it is forbidden for scientists to have delusions."

"In so far as we are scientists, certainly."

"I see. But didn't Freud himself say that all of us mortals correct some aspect of reality which we cannot bear or do not like, that we all cobble together some wish or other and, like a virus, inject it into reality?"

Balassa was aware of the passage, of course, and had not been untroubled by it. In theory, he was willing to grant that abnormality lies on a continuum with normality. Indeed, he judged this principle to be one of Freud's greatest contributions to the scientific study of madness. However, Balassa drew a bold line between a man of science doing science and a man of science behaving irrationally; that is, like any ordinary mortal. To him, delusion was delusion, error error, sanity sanity. Florel's view appeared to him corrosive of these indispensable distinctions.

He had wanted to reply sharply but, remembering his position, overcame his instinct for polemics and responded humorously instead. "Well, we do have to be on our guard, Dr. Florel. It wouldn't do to be won over by our patients."

Gratifyingly, Florel had taken his hand, laughed, welcomed him to Paris, and wished him every success in his new practice.

Sweating and thirsty, Balassa began to look for an open café, some dark interior space with a marble table on which to cool his hands, something cold to drink. The first place he came across was closed but the second was just what he had in mind. He went inside and asked for a beer. As his eyes accustomed themselves to the dark he saw that there was one other customer, a woman approximately his own age. She was eating an omelet by herself in a corner.

He found the woman attractive. Straight dark hair worn longer than was fashionable in Paris with bangs nearly down to her eyebrows, a blue summer dress, breasts more ample than was chic at the moment. It is to the secondary sexual characteristics that humans attach the idea of beauty, Freud had written. But what arrested Balassa's gaze was the woman's face. It was remarkably still and, as she was looking down at her food, he was able to study it. Strong chin, rounded cheeks—no, not, he thought, a French face. He had found that French women, even elderly ones, made it a point to appear vivacious even in repose. They aspired to a sort of permanent levity, called *esprit*. He guessed that this woman's height would be almost equal to his own. She was not heavy but large, a substantial presence; he thought the word queenly suited her.

He was sufficiently attracted to turn shy but, resisting the impulse to turn away, he took a seat at the table nearest hers. She glanced over at him without altering her expression. Again he felt that this was a serious person, like the female students he had met in Vienna; but for them he had never felt more than comradeship. One would have to be careful approaching such a woman, cautious yet at the same time direct. To become involved with her might even be dangerous.

He waited until he had finished half his glass of beer before speaking. "Excuse me, mademoiselle. You aren't French, are you?"

She did not look over but she did reply. "Is that of any importance?" Her speech was slightly accented, her tone nearly resentful.

"No, not especially. You see, I'm not French myself and—" He was intending to make some clever remark about all the Parisians having abandoned Paris when she got to her feet.

"Excuse me," she said briskly. "I have an appointment."

For a moment Balassa actually considered following her.

3.

Julie Kregel and her family had moved to Paris from Frankfurt in 1925. When her father died five years later her mother, unable to cope with his loss, became a semi-invalid. Julie lived with her mother and younger brother in the Faubourg St.-Germaine. Monsieur Kregel had left his family well off.

Balassa was told all this two days after the encounter in the café, though he was not yet aware that the woman who had so impressed him was Julie Kregel. Over those couple days he had often found himself thinking of her, even to the point of regretting that he had not followed her out to the street, had been unable to say anything that would interest her in him. It was not like him to be distracted by women and he put the preoccupation down to frustration. The article he had intended to complete by September was stalled. The opening paragraphs had come so easily that he had been filled with confidence, certain that he could complete the work in a single uninterrupted burst of insight. He had imagined a glorious month of productivity and a paper that would make his reputation.

While he was able to work solitude had been welcome; the moment he stopped loneliness oppressed him. "That's why I keep thinking of her," he told himself, "because I can't work. I'm looking for distraction, that's all." And he reflected on the curious fact that one may want more than anything to write and yet seize on anything to keep from doing so.

The phone call was from Emile Janvier. Balassa had paid him a courtesy call soon after arriving in Paris, and they had talked congenially for a half an hour about Vienna, where Janvier had also studied. Though they had hit it off Balassa had not spoken with Janvier since. He was surprised to hear from him.

"Glad to find you in, Dr. Balassa. I wonder if you could perhaps take on a case for me. You see, I'm leaving the city tomorrow. We're to join my sister-in-law's family for the rest of the month. The sea, you know, near Toulon."

Balassa tried not to sound too eager. "I would be more than happy,

Dr. Janvier."

"Then you're not going away yourself?"

"No, I'm staying in Paris."

"Excellent. Well, here's as much as I know . . ."

The appointment Julie Kregel was rushing off to that day in the café had been genuine; it was with Janvier. She had gone to consult him about her brother Max who had begun to behave strangely, showed signs of an unhealthy withdrawal and, when he did talk, said the most peculiar things. Madame Kregel was distressed and she herself was deeply concerned for her brother's stability. Julie had confided in an old friend of her father's and he had referred her to Janvier.

"If I remember correctly," said Janvier, "you have a special interest in delusions."

"Yes, that's correct."

"Then, from what Mademoiselle Kregel told me, this might be just the thing for you. I'll have her telephone, if that's all right."

"I'm most grateful, Dr. Janvier."

"Not at all. You'll be doing me a favor. What do you say we get together next month?"

Balassa began to feel better at once; even his digestion improved.

4.

"Dr. Balassa? My name is Julie Kregel."

"Yes, Mademoiselle Kregel. Dr. Janvier told me you might call."

"And he's told you why?"

"As much as he was able, I think."

"You can see me?"

"I will be happy to see you, as soon as you like. I presume you would like to discuss your brother with me rather than bring him along?"

"Oh, he wouldn't see you."

There was something familiar about the contralto, a timbre, an accent.

"I see. Would I be wrong to assume your brother is unaware of your concern about him?"

"No. Max knows perfectly well I'm worried and Mother too. He just doesn't believe anything's the matter with him, and he refuses to talk about it. In fact, he is talking less and less."

Balassa nodded to himself. The authentically deluded are never aware of their condition; they are more apt to think that normal folk are deluded and, in extreme cases, will even avoid intercourse with them. Their false ideas dominate their lives, yet the instant they are made to recognize that they are deluded, they are free. This is the moment toward which the analyst must struggle, uplifting his patient, so to speak, like a sober man with his arm around a drunkard.

"When would you like to see me, Mademoiselle Kregel?"

"Is tomorrow morning too soon?"

"Ten o'clock then?"

"Where is your office?"

Balassa was embarrassed. He could not yet afford a proper office but had fixed up his sitting room with a desk, wing chair, and long leather couch; all the furniture was used but presentable. He had hung his diplomas and certificates on the wall, also the letter from Dr. Freud which he had had framed in black wood. On the long wall opposite the couch he had placed a painting that caught his eye in a gallery during the spending spree of his first week in Paris. Though it was an extravagance, he thought the price too reasonable to pass up; it was such an attractive work. The gallery owner explained that he was charging so little for such an appealing picture because he had picked the canvas up in a lot from a dealer who could not fix its provenance. The artist was obviously talented but had, alas, neglected to sign the work.

It was a large modern piece, four-by-six feet, an imaginary landscape, the sort of picture in which the artist's liberated fancy flirts with allegory and fools with tradition. Balassa liked its surreal precision and the wit of its images. The foreground was an impasto of green and orange, a fence or border of high grass setting off a swirling dream park. At the center two blue spruces leaned in, as if to catch what a statue (Apollo? Dionysius?) was whispering to an elongated cat. Balassa had been reminded of Herr B.'s kitty. Rushing through the middle ground of flowers, tree trunks, and gamboling animals, a high wind whipped whorls in hare's-tail grass. Up top a preternaturally blue sky was punctuated by three suns—dawn, afternoon, sunset—suggesting to Balassa the riddle solved by Oedipus. To the left four larks wheeled in a perfect arc, as if being juggled by the extended branches of a big copper beech. In the background lay a long purple pond dappled with pink and yellow waterfowl. Amusing details were scattered through the picture. An old sycamore at the left sported a bandage on one branch; nearby a toddler was dumping his diaper behind a privet. Over on the right two rabbits copulated gleefully beside a white herm of the nature god Pan. The initial effect was of complexity and joy, as if the exuberant painter wished to suggest not nostalgia for a lost Eden, but an almost manic hopefulness that the whole of foul Creation might be transfigured by some unexpected stroke of luck into surging, ebullient innocence. Looked at more closely, the picture actually invited all sorts of interpretations. At times Balassa could see in it visualized hysteria. At others it appeared to him a wry commentary on the pointless vitality of nature, or a concretization of the pantheism that was paganism's last gasp, or an inchoate, not-quite-intelligible allegory of sexuality.

He was very pleased with this picture, had it well framed, and, as he was hanging it up, thought of it as his personal homage to Freud, a modernist counterpart to the Master's antiquities, his little Cupids and Aphrodites.

The following morning Balassa was seated at his desk, despondently turning the pages of his abandoned manuscript, when the buzzer went off. It startled him, even though he had been anticipating the sound for ten minutes. He leapt for the door.

Everything crucial, all that would be most consequential for what followed, happened within two minutes.

He recognized her at once, and just as quickly, before he could utter some crass word he would have wished to recall, saw that she recognized him too. Both were astonished. In her surprise, Julie let her purse fall to the floor. The doctor bent to retrieve it, but she did the same and their heads collided. Julie fell to the side with a little cry and Balassa, instinctively reaching out for her arm, lost his balance as well. The upshot was that his hand brushed her chest and they both tumbled in a heap on his threshold. Neither had said a word as yet and for a few moments they remained dumbfounded, stunned like fallen toddlers. Balassa was chagrined by the physicality of the episode and embarrassed by his clumsiness. Then, quite unexpectedly, Julie began to laugh. His professional dignity in tatters, he jumped to his feet. As he helped her up he began to apologize while rubbing his forehead.

She took his chin between her fingers and scrutinized his face. "You're going to have quite a bump there," she declared. "I believe you got the worst of it, Doctor."

"I'm sorry. Clumsy of me. Are you all right, Mademoiselle Kregel?"

"Oh, I'm fine." She pointed to her bangs. "I'm quite hard-headed."

Blushing, he went on massaging his forehead; he could already feel it beginning to swell. He noticed how well dressed she was. The deep purple of her frock set off her coloring to advantage. "Please, please come in," he said. If she did not want to mention the meeting at the café, he would be guided by her discretion.

Julie Kregel took one step into the room and suddenly gave another little cry, slightly different from the last one, stifled by her hand.

He was alarmed. "But what is it?"

She nodded toward the wall. "That painting."

"Yes?"

"But . . . it's Max's!"

Decades later, sitting in the study of his house in Madison, Wisconsin, Professor Balassa wrote the following in a letter to a former student: "Perhaps you've noticed that life lived forward seems a matter of free choices—limited by necessity, to be sure, and seasoned with trivial coincidences, but free and under our personal supervision. Free will is a concept that depends on one's sense of a personal future. Retrospectively, however, these relations change; their proportions alter. The role of choice tends to shrink to that of a supernumerary—a waitress, a cab driver— whereas the parts played by accident, happenstance, and, above all, timing balloon into leading men and women. Who among us can claim to have chosen the most significant things about their lives: their work, whom they love, whether they marry, even where they live? I'm sorry. Such thoughts can only exasperate the young. This is old man's wisdom, knowledge that only further humbles the decrepit."

It is not unlikely that as he wrote this letter Balassa's mind had drifted back to that August morning forty years earlier when he had bumped heads with Julie Kregel at his door.

5.

"When we lived in Frankfurt my father kept a photograph of Michelangelo's *Moses* in his study; it was just a framed postal card. Max was eight when he drew that statue. It was a really exceptional likeness, but the thing that astonished us all was that he drew it from a different angle. You understand? He did it from the other side, the side not in the photograph."

"He was how old?"

"Eight . . ." She paused. "I was ten."

Balassa was gratified that she had contrived to interpolate something personal into the conversation. He was interested in her brother, yes, as she was concerned that he should be; but he was more interested in her and it pleased him that she should acknowledge it even indirectly.

"That is remarkable. So he became an art student. And that is how he came to paint my landscape, for a show at the school? And somehow it got into the hands of a job-lot dealer. But I wonder why he didn't sign it."

"Oh, that's not surprising. From the time we moved Max refused to sign any of his work."

"Why?"

She shrugged. "He called it egoistic, something that began in Renaissance. He used to talk about how admirable the medieval artists were for never putting their names to their work."

"Then it's a sort of religious scruple? For the greater glory of God?"

"Or misplaced modesty. I don't really know."

"When did he begin his formal studies?"

"That was after we moved. Back in Frankfurt he took private lessons. Mother insisted on it."

"Your father wasn't in favor of the idea?"

"Father made no objection, so far as I know. But he didn't exactly encourage Max either. I would say that he was indifferent to Max's work, though he had feeling for good art."

"Good art meaning the old masters?"

She smiled. "Father's tastes were formed in the last century."

Balassa looked her in the eyes and smiled back at her more frankly than an analyst should. An analyst, Rath had said, should wear what the Americans call a "poker face."

"And was he as indifferent to your accomplishments as your brother's?"

She threw up a hand and laughed. "What accomplishments? I only play the piano badly. Nothing to be proud of in the way I mangle poor Chopin."

Impetuously Balassa said, "I would enjoy hearing you mangle Chopin some time."

She looked over at her brother's picture and answered to the point but as if thinking of something else. "Perhaps you will."

Balassa pulled himself up straight in his chair and laid his forearms on the desk. Enough of this ridiculous flirting, he thought. "Mlle. Kregel, I would like to know more about your brother's early life, especially before you moved here. For example, did he seem to you a happy boy?"

"No. I think Max had a hard time of it at school. I know he would sometimes pretend to be ill so as not to have to go."

"The other boys?"

"Yes."

"Why?"

She looked at him with surprise. "Because we're Jewish, of course."

"Oh." Balassa thought. Ah, she is a Jewess. Yes, it's obvious now. He recalled a few incidents from his own school days, and he thought again of why he did not wish to return to Budapest.

"That's the reason we moved, though nobody said so."

"Had he any school friends?"

"Only one, a boy named Hermann Winckel. Max spent a lot of time with him. They played up in his room or in the backyard. Hermann was a sickly boy, pale with hair like straw. I suppose they formed an alliance, the two outcasts, the two weaklings. Then Hermann became really ill—I think it must have been tuberculosis. He was sent away and after that Max was on his own, except for us."

"I see. Any specific symptoms of being troubled? Bed-wetting for instance?"

She frowned. "Max was an odd little boy, I admit, but there was nothing of that sort."

Balassa made a note. "Would you describe your family as religious, observant?"

"Oh no. We only went to synagogue on high holy days and even that was just when we were little. I think Father looked down on those who took all that too seriously."

"All that?"

"Religion. Being Jewish."

"They are not the same, though?"

She looked down. "No, not the same."

"Hmm. Excuse me, but would you say Max was unhappy about about—being Jewish?"

101

Robert Wexelblatt

"Perhaps. It wouldn't be surprising, would it?"

"You said he's become—what? Interested in religion?"

"During the last year. I'm sure it has to do with what's wrong with him. I think it's a symptom," she said somewhat bitterly, "like bed-wetting."

Balassa made a note of that too. He was conscious of Julie watching his pen move across the page and so he wrote more slowly and deliberately than usual.

"How's that bump?" she asked suddenly, tilting her head to one side. "You really ought to have put some ice on it."

He rubbed his forehead. The swelling felt colossal. "It must look bad."

"Not so bad." She smiled again. He was becoming attached to that smile of hers. "A quail's egg, not a hen's."

"And you? No ill-effects whatsoever? Have I failed to make any impression on you at all?"

"I told you. My head's like iron."

Balassa ventured a guess. "Is that because you're the one who oversees the household, keeps things running, the hard-headed one on whom everybody depends?"

She raised her eyebrows and looked at him suspiciously.

"Well," he said, "artists are seldom practical and then you claim to mangle Chopin. Besides, you've taken it on yourself to try to help your brother."

"Well, it's true. I've got my father's head." She tapped her forehead. "*Ein Yiddischer Kopf.*"

Balassa made yet another note.

"What's that you're writing now? It makes me nervous."

"Just notes to help me, Mlle. Kregel. The more you can tell me about Max and about your family the better; anything could be a clue, a key. For example, was anything particular going on in Max's life when he began to behave in the way that's alarmed you? Was the change sudden?"

"No, I wouldn't say it was sudden, not exactly. Not overnight. He changed gradually, I suppose, and yet it didn't take long either. A matter of two or three weeks. He began to say these odd things."

"Such as?"

"Well, for example, one evening he insisted that he's older than me— even older than Mother."

"What?"

"Yes. At supper Mother happened to say that he was still her baby, something of that sort, and Max said that he was much older than the both us put together. Mother laughed and said he was being an absurd little boy. He just looked at her, the way one looks at a child who misunderstands things, with affection and pity. Later, when I asked him how old he thought he was, he put his hand on my shoulder gave a big sigh and said very quietly, almost under his breath, 'As old as Jewry.' I was stunned."

"That is significant. Can you recall anything else?"

"While he was able to work he told me that he could never again do a self-portrait. When I asked why, he said it was forbidden."

"Forbidden?"

"Of course I asked him for an explanation. Who has forbidden it, I asked him, but he wouldn't say another word on the subject. Soon after that he gave up painting and drawing altogether."

Balassa glanced at his notes. "Does he continue to read?"

"Oh, yes. He reads a great deal."

"Have you noticed any change in his reading habits?"

"Indeed I have. He used to keep up with the latest novels and art journals. He liked Michelet's history. But then he began to come home with musty old religious books—not just Jewish ones, but Christian and Indian too. Augustine. The Vedantas—and all in German, by the way."

Balassa nodded, as if this exactly confirmed his own suspicions. "I see, religion again. And the language of his childhood."

"And he began brushing his teeth six or seven times a day."

"I see." More notes. "Does he ever go out?"

"Yes, but very seldom. Only twice in the last week. Tuesday he went to the Luxembourg Gardens. I followed him. He sat on a bench like a pensioner. He really did look quite old sitting there among the prams and pigeons."

Balassa paused before asking his next question. "Girlfriends?"

"Pardon me?"

"Has your brother formed any attachments to women? Fellow students, perhaps?"

"Max is terribly shy. Even as a boy he would run to his room if any of my friends were visiting."

"So? No women friends at all?"

"Up till a year ago he would occasionally go out with friends. But there were no particular girlfriends I know of."

Balassa scribbled. "Do you believe, Mlle. Kregel, that your brother really thinks of himself as an old man, that he wasn't speaking just metaphorically?"

She considered the question.

He prompted her. "There was that remark to your mother, remember, and the way he looked to you in the Luxembourg Gardens—*like a pensioner*, you said. The prams and pigeons."

"Perhaps he really does believe he's old? Maybe even 'as old as Jewry,' whatever that means, but not simply an old *man*. No, it's something else and I can't understand it."

"Well," said Balassa, placing his hands on the edge of his desk and pushing back his chair like an accountant whose books have balanced. He turned to the picture on the wall, Max's landscape. "I like your brother's painting very much—and also, I confess, his sister."

Julie looked at him candidly, without blush, reproach, or surprise. He saw he had not told her anything she had not already guessed and wondered if they had been having two conversations all the morning long.

She tilted her head and narrowed her eyes. "You said you were also not French." It was the first allusion she had made to their encounter in the café.

"Hungarian by birth, stateless by inclination. And so here we are together, Mlle. Kregel, two strangers in the city with the finest food on earth. Might I persuade you to eat some of it with me? Dinner perhaps?"

She tapped her finger on her chin and knit her brows thoughtfully. "Yes. But not in a restaurant. I want you to come to our home. I've decided that's the way for you to meet Max. As I said, he would never come here."

It was an ambiguous invitation, but Balassa accepted at once.

6.

The air had grown less humid and Arno Balassa was in high spirits. Here he had a chance to become Julie Kregel's "beau" in a Paris cleared of both professional and amatory competitors; a challenging new case had been laid before him, one, it appeared, perfectly suited to his talents and interests. It would be grist to his mill; for the topic of the article with which he had been having such difficulty was religious delusion. He had already formulated a hypothesis about Max Kregel's state of mind, something to do with the father's death, the reversion to superstition, the missing girlfriends, the will to escape into the cocoon of a consoling Jewishness.

To Freud, religion is infantile. Its operation lies, he wrote contemptuously, "in depressing the value of life and distorting the picture of the real world in a delusional manner—which presupposes an intimidation of the intelligence." Balassa had the passage by heart. Religious feeling originates in the newborn's inability to distinguish between itself and its surroundings—thus the believer's feeling of oneness with the All—and is then reinforced by the child's need for refuge under the protective wing of a cosmic parent. The chief distinction between religious delusion and delusion in general is the former's near universality. "A special importance attaches to the case in which this attempt to procure a certainty of happiness and a protection against suffering through a delusional remolding of reality is made by a considerable number of people in common. The religions of mankind must be classed among the mass-delusions of this kind," the Master had written. In short, even a delusion accepted by all remains a delusion; a naked Emperor is still naked.

Balassa readily adopted this view. As a boy he had felt an antipathy toward religion; he detested his pious mother's enumeration of the eternal torments that awaited him should he neglect to clear his plate or tidy his room. Whenever he fell down she would be sure to say, "There, Arno! God punished you." It irked him to be dragged along to church where he had to attend to the pompous, bearded priests and breathe in cloying fumes. His was not the sort of intelligence to be easily intimidated. The love of science was his salvation; the will to demystify human behavior drew him to the study of medicine. Distaste for religion was one of the things that particularly attracted him to psychoanalysis. Religion he consigned to that eastern world he had been eager to abandon. It was, in large measure, because of the liberation psychoanalysis promised from all kinds of narrow-mindedness and provincialism, because of Freud's powerful alternative explanation of human existence, that he had made his way to Vienna as a secular pilgrim. To Balassa, religion was oriental and it was his intention to become a man of the world, which is to say a man of the West. Of all delusions, he believed religion the most pernicious precisely because so many people succumbed to it and had been doing so for millennia. Once asked the difference between a religion and a cult he had replied glibly, "About five hundred years, I should say." As the weightiest, most popular, and, so to speak, firmly rooted of falsehoods, the kind that is festooned with tradition, religious delusion was the most in need of being extirpated.

Balassa, like Freud, believed in a fixed reality which it is the purpose of the deluded to evade. This reality may be bleak but nobility lay in facing it. The tragic drama is true; the Gospels false. That reality might not be fixed at all simply did not occur to Balassa. He never thought that when he said an object was blue the person to whom he said it might see the object as blue-green. He now looked at Max's painting anew, seeing in it something repellent, not a delightful and sophisticated playing with images but mere derangement. There could be no shadowy middle ground for him between art and science, no place where art might extend reality without tainting its singularity. Perhaps, he mused, the father had been right to doubt his son's talent. Balassa liked modern art because he thought it truthful, not a matter of using the techniques of delusion to escape reality but the discovery of new means for penetrating the real, stripping it of mere contingencies, revealing its skeleton like an x-ray. Because he took it as axiomatic that delusion is a palliative and an evasion, he never thought that it could be horrifying. Because religion as a delusion was, by definition, a comforting illusion, it did not occur to him that one might be made less rather than more happy by faith. Nor did he suppose that the psychoanalyst also exercises a form of faith which is that if people would only submit to his version of the truth they would surely be set free to become happier with existence.

Meanwhile, Julie had invited him to dinner and he was happy.

"I will introduce you as my new friend," she said as she got up to leave, "and you can try to get Max to talk."

"And will your mother know the truth?" he had asked.

"But, Dr. Balassa, isn't that the truth?"

7.

He was let in by the maid, a stout, middle-aged woman who impertinently looked him up and down. He supposed that a dinner guest must be a rarity, though the house was large enough to hold scores of them. The place had a funereal opulence with its dark Biedermeier furniture, parquet floors, thick carpets and heavy drapes. But the foyer was cool, a welcome relief from the August sultriness.

This maid obviously considered herself a most important person, one who had the right to scrutinize all visitors to see if they could pass muster. "So you are Monsieur Barassa," she said, carelessly mispronouncing his surname. She was obviously in no hurry to let him pass; he began to anticipate an interrogation.

Julie appeared and asserted her authority by pointedly taking Balassa's arm. "Thank you, Marie," she said. Her scoop-necked maroon dress became her. Is that low bodice for me, Balassa wondered.

"Marie can be a brute," Julie whispered in his ear. "She's just being overly protective. We'd be lost without her; the pity is she knows it."

She conducted Balassa into a large drawing room where Madame Kregel was perched on the edge of a love-seat.

"Mother, this is my friend Monsieur Balassa, our dinner guest."

The woman held out a hand as white as her hair and breakable as Limoges. "A pleasure to make your acquaintance, Monsieur Balassa." Suddenly she looked at him with terror. "You won't take my Julie from me, will you?"

Balassa was uncertain that she was serious and, for lack of a better reply, offered a little laugh.

Julie saved the moment, making the joke after the chuckle. "But Maman, as you see I've brought Monsieur Balassa here, so obviously he cannot be taking me away."

Balassa took note that Mme. Kregel looked continuously to her daughter for clues as to how she ought to behave. All too clear a case, he thought ruefully. All the signs of impending dementia were evident: timidity, anxiety, absent-mindedness, that sudden, inappropriate remark. Later Julie told him that her mother had been the youngest of eight children and the only daughter. She had been raised "delicately," as Julie put it, educated well but not practically. From being spoiled by her father and older brothers she passed directly into the care of a wealthy husband who, if he did not love her as he might, certainly indulged her and propped her up. Not surprisingly, what he had supported crumbled at his death. "He gave in to her on everything. I used to think it was some sort of bargain between them." She shrugged. "Who ever knows the whole truth about one's parents?" "Few really want to," Balassa agreed with professional authority, "however curious they pretend to be."

No sooner were the introductions complete than Mme. Kregel excused herself.

"Pardon me. I must go and see Marie."

While her mother was in the kitchen Julie explained that Max was in his room and had been there all day. "He almost always comes down to dinner but it's hard to be sure. Mother's gone to tell Marie to fetch him. Max obeys Marie—out of habit, I think. He used to call her Sergeant Aubigné and make mock salutes behind her back."

"Does he know I've been invited to dinner?"

Julie made a face. "I'm hoping it will make a nice surprise for him."

"Then he knows nothing?"

"Well, I've told him I've met a nice man named Arno Balassa who is from Hungary. If he had asked about your profession I was prepared to make you a chiropodist. Fortunately, he didn't ask that. He asked if you were a Buddha or a Peste. Father encouraged Max's punning. *'Ein gut gezookt,'* he'd have said."

Buddha or Peste. Balassa raised his eyebrows. Nowhere in his experience or in his reading had he heard of delusional people making jokes. This was interesting. Also it struck him that yet another way of interpreting Max's landscape might be as a kind of visual punning.

"So, how did you answer him?" he said playfully. "Am I an Enlightened One or an epidemic?"

Julie, who had seated herself close beside Balassa on the couch, got up and took a few steps into the middle of the room. "Too soon to say." She raised her arm and pointed at him. "That's a very nice suit, incidentally."

Balassa instinctively looked down at his chest. "Thank you."

"Did you buy it here, in Paris?"

"Yes, but it's English."

"Ah. I thought so."

"And your dress is—"

She raised her hand teasingly. "It's far too late to compliment my dress, Doctor!"

Madame Kregel returned from the kitchen and immediately looked toward her daughter, who nodded at her, as if giving her permission to speak.

"Marie has gone to fetch Max. Then we can eat our supper."

"That's good, Maman. But perhaps Monsieur Balassa would like an aperitif?"

"Ah, excuse me. Of course. We have some excellent sherry. My husband was a connoisseur, you know, and he ordered cases of it."

"A sherry would be very nice. Thank you."

Julie went to a sideboard and removed a dark bottle, filled three little glasses, and set them on a silver tray. She then served them out, leaning low over Balassa.

"That is superb," he said after taking a sip.

"Of course," said the mother. "Yes, the very best amontillado. Didn't I tell you he was a connoisseur?"

There were heavy footsteps on the stairs and Max came down with Marie on his heels. He was dressed in black trousers and, despite the warmth of the evening, a loose sweater, also black. Balassa looked at him closely. He was tall, slightly built, dark-haired, and nearly as handsome as his sister. He did not appear nervous; Balassa could detect no tell-tale tics, only perhaps a kind of abstraction. He stared at Balassa but without evincing any surprise at his presence.

Julie, as if to reassure her brother, hastened to introduce the doctor. "Max, this is the Monsieur Balassa about whom I told you. I've asked him to supper. He's wearing a fine English suit, isn't he?"

Max refused to be teased about his clothes. His manner was not only equable but extraodinarily polite. He walked right over to Balassa.

"How good of you to come, Monsieur Balassa. Marie told me you were here and, as I said to her, the guest must be made welcome." Balassa thought he said all this suavely enough. The odd thing was that he extended his left hand to Balassa who then had to decide whether to take it with his right or his left. There was an awkward moment. Though he had to contort his wrist, Balassa gripped Max's left hand with his right. Mindful of what he had said to André Florel, he did not wish to begin by giving in to his new patient.

"How are you feeling, darling?" Madame Kregel asked. "You've been upstairs all day."

Her son glanced at her benevolently but did not bother to reply.

"Julie has not told me how you met," he said quietly to Balassa. "But then such things hardly matter."

"Perhaps not to others," Balassa replied, "but they matter a great deal to the people involved. I had the good fortune to meet your sister in a café by the Seine. She was eating an omelet and I was having a beer."

"Are you fond of beer, then."

Balassa smiled. "In so far it was the occasion of making your sister's acquaintance, yes."

Perhaps this riposte displeased Max because he turned on his heel and marched into the dining room.

Balassa had never experienced a more uncomfortable dinner, though the proximity of Julie mixed some pleasure with the awkwardness. Max ate silently and would take only the tiniest portions on his plate. Mme. Kregel fussed over him, encouraging him to eat more and complained to Balassa that her boy was too thin. "Just look at him!" she said tearfully. Julie tried mightily to begin a conversation between the two men. She ran through topic after topic. Art, music, politics, summer holidays in the old days, even the muggy weather. Balassa did his best to second her efforts. He made observations on the current government and what was new in the galleries, threw out leading questions, spoke of what the papers were saying about Germany. But nothing stirred Max until, spotting an old gilt menorah on a chest, the doctor took matters into his own hands.

"That menorah over there reminds me of the Jews in my homeland. They are a remarkable people, devout and learned," he said, "but, I'm sorry to say, terribly ill-treated. I think it's because they refuse to be like everyone else. In a sense, the Jews of Hungary insist on remaining exiles."

At that Max looked up at the chandelier and declared gravely, as if citing scripture, "The real exile of my people in Egypt was that they learned to endure it."

8.

Sex did not bring her closer to him. In fact, when Julie Kregel at last consented to let Balassa make love to her—it was in his bedroom and so the brother's dreamscape hung on the other side of the wall—he felt deserted, as if a climbing companion had wandered off just as they reached the summit. Where could she have gone behind those long, fluttering eyelids? Perhaps it was the airlessness of the room, he thought later, maybe she was simply overcome by lethargy or pleasure.

Does anyone pretend to comprehend the physiology, let alone to have mastered the psychology, of orgasm? Freud? Rath? Rank? Even they still show vestiges of bashfulness. What cold-blooded researcher has succeeded in unmasking Nature's boldest blandishment, written of it without recourse to metaphor, smirks, or sentiment? Yes, he had read of the fear of damaging the mother and the phallic triumph over the father, of little deaths and fears of being bitten by something so soft and melting, of everything as a symbol for coitus, the unacknowledged aim of architects, poets, plumbers. Now that he thought about it, Balassa was surprised how limited psychosexual theory was, how fanciful and how male.

He had been yearning for her for weeks, smelling her hair when he was able, touching her hand at every opportunity, parsing her smiles, pouts, the gestures of her body. It was like perpetually hearing the penultimate chord of a symphony. He began to believe this excruciating tension might never be resolved, that he had become lost among ambivalent provocations. This tension was more than sexual; it was ethical too. He was well aware of the risk the analyst runs from a patient's transference, had heard Freud himself thunder a categorical prohibition against any romantic attachment between doctor and patient. "Such a thing is ruinous, absolutely forbidden." But would it be wrong to sleep with a patient's sister, especially if the patient were unaware of being a patient? Was that also a transgression?

He thought about Julie's being a Jew. Did this make her still more desirable, exotic, risky? Well, they were all Jews; Freud himself was a Jew. The Kregels were so-called deracinated Jews, Western, completely modern. How could Jews join the avant-garde in the sciences, politics, the arts and at the same time persist in being the most backward people in Europe, a stiff-necked race who provoked hatred and believed themselves chosen above all others? "Dirty Jews" his mother used to hiss under her breath as they walked through the streets, yanking him away from a peddler as if fatal Hebrew germs might leap onto him, like fleas. Was there some atom of atavism in this recent preoccupation of Freud's with religion, some level below his obvious hostility? Was there some sort of radical reversion in what had happened to Max Kregel, some delusion about his ethnic identity?

As for Julie, she had given him an experience unlike any other. Making love to her was like arriving at the border of the Promised Land only to die alone, still in exile. Mangled Chopin.

As long as his orgasm lasted Balassa experienced a vivid waking dream. He found himself in an endless building of reddish stone. There were thousands of apartments, a maze with vast stone plazas, unexpected walls and pillars, posts and beams, low ceilings, no furniture, nothing alive. He seemed to be rushing through this abandoned edifice, accelerating with each ejaculation. He sped through what seemed like miles and miles of dressed stone. The palace was tremendous but also archaic, an infinite Babylon, a Persepolis without end.

There behind her closed eyelids could Julie also be rushing through this palace? Were they dashing toward one another through all these corridors? Or were they flying apart? He felt strongly that the distance between them gaped wide at the moment of release, that derangement of the senses. Was she awaiting him at the other end of a hallway or was she seeing chrysanthemums, candle sticks, soft rain falling on a garden? Were those tender ears listening to unmangled nocturnes?

Where had she gone then, and why did she allow him to make love to her at all? Would she do so if she didn't love him? We do not regret the things we cannot know, but those we might have. Even decades later he regretted that he never asked.

This perplexing affair ran concurrently with his efforts to pluck out the heart of Max's mystery, an undertaking no less puzzling. That Max was suffering from religious obsession, and almost certainly some form of delusion, Balassa did not doubt. However, its precise nature eluded him, nor did Julie have any suggestions. She would report to him about Max's diet, whether he was talking nonsense, mumbling to himself through dinner, or remaining silent. She wanted to begin paying him a regular fee and he had difficulty in persuading her that he could not accept payment.

"Is it because we sleep together?" she asked, hands behind her head.

"In part," he admitted. "But more because I haven't been able to accomplish anything."

"Well, if you do, you can expect a check. Tear it up if you like," she said with that smile of hers. Hard-headed.

Florel was right. To get anywhere he had to discover the individual nature of the delusion. He spent long afternoons in St.-Germaine, regarded by the mother with furtive anxiety and by Marie with open suspicion. Sometimes Max would not even come downstairs for supper, even if it meant disobeying a direct order from the formidable sergeant. When he did join them, he said little to Balassa whose efforts to draw him out were met either with snubs or gnomic replies. For example, when asked whether he ever felt the urge to paint, Max replied stiffly, "Painting is a vanity and, besides, one must be fully alive to move the brush properly."

Balassa persisted with his visits, increasingly troubled that he should appear under the pretext of being Julie's admirer when in fact he was her lover and Max's would-be psychoanalyst. He began to prepare himself, to study up. He asked Julie to discover some of the books her brother had taken to reading and searched out copies of his own. In one of them he discovered the sentence about the exile in Egypt. It turned out to be a remark attributed to Honokh of Alexandria, a zaddik from the East. He strove to win Max's confidence and came to identify his aim with being permitted to visit him in his room, his sanctum sanctorum. He began to picture Max's delusion as a thing, a looming object locked upstairs in that room. The images that infiltrated his dreams as the dust gathered on the chestnut trees and August drew near its close were not of Julie, but of keys and locks and bedrooms with black shapes in them.

9.

Balassa had already been out for his croissant and coffee. He had just gone into the bathroom when Julia phoned.

"I've been calling for nearly an hour." She sounded annoyed and a little alarmed but by no means hysterical.

"What is it?"

"Max has barricaded himself in his room. Mother's beside herself and Marie insists on calling the police. Can you come?"

"I'm leaving now."

He found a cab at the corner. In the ten minutes it took him to arrive at the Kregels' door he made up his mind how to proceed. He already saw himself bursting into Max's bedroom. Such an approach, of course, ran counter to his training but then nothing about this case could be called conventional. His patience was exhausted and his position unclear. He began to realize how much Max had infuriated him, how he would have liked to shake that slim frame, to squash that handsome face into reality.

Marie let him in and he strode right past her to the sitting room, calming down only when he saw Julie on the couch comforting her mother. The maid took up a position behind him with her arms crossed. Marie represented stupid violence. What was called for was intelligent force.

"Stay here," he ordered everyone and even Marie seemed to be cowed by his tone.

"The first door on the right," Julie called to him as he made for the stairway. "There's no lock. He's pushed something against the door."

Balassa marched up the stairs and knocked resolutely three times on the door.

Nothing.

Lowering his shoulder he began to push with all his might. Grunting and sweating he finally managed to shift the door a few inches. Then, setting his feet, he shoved more steadily from a lower angle. Now he could see the edge of a bureau. Had the stolid Marie been at his side it would have been an easy job. One more hernia-inducing effort and he had a gap just sufficient to slide through.

The room was hot and smelled terrible. Max was lying on the bed in his undershorts, staring straight ahead. He was unshaven and his eyes looked glassy. What Balassa felt was pity, and this surprised him. What had become of his anger?

He looked around the room. There were indeed a lot of books, most of them heaped up in one corner. He saw a folded easel, an armoire, a small writing desk, one armchair by the closed window. The foul smell was emanating from a porcelain chamber pot next to the bed.

"I'm truly sorry," Balassa said, only meaning to apologize for forcing his way in, but the sentiment somehow sounded more comprehensive, and softer.

Max turned his head and gave a little nod. Forgiveness? Indifference? Well, at least it was a response. There was hope in that. He had feared catatonia.

The doctor carefully closed the door and even moved the bureau partially back in place by way of reassurance. "Whew. There," he said. "Now we can talk." He seated himself in the armchair after first opening the window. "No women, Max. Just us."

Max turned his long body on the bed. He looked, Balassa judged, exhausted.

"Now, how old are you, Max?" He waited—five seconds, ten seconds, twenty. Would he get an answer?

At last, in a soft, hoarse voice, Max replied. "Older than everything."

Balassa, who had found it trying to wait Max out, was relieved to have gotten any sort of response, and this one was obviously significant.

It pointed to the delusion of agelessness, perhaps a morbid fear of death. He had prepared his gambit and it was time to use the story he had memorized.

"You know, Max, that I'm Hungarian. Well, in my country there were some famous rabbis in the last century, miracle rabbis, zaddiks, maggids. One of the most famous was Rabbi Yisakhar. Perhaps you've heard of him? Well, one night Rabbi Yisakhar was visited by a dead man, a member of his congregation. The fellow begged the rabbi's help. He said his wife had died and he needed money to arrange for a new wedding. This surprised Yisakhar who said, 'But don't you know that you are no longer among the living, that you are in the world of confusion?' The man refused to believe him until Yisakhar lifted his coat and showed him he was dressed in his shroud."

Balassa paused. Max gave no sign and so he went on, drawing the moral.

"The next day Rabbi Yisakhar told what had happened to his son. The boy was perplexed. 'Well, if that is so, Father, perhaps I too am in the world of confusion?' The Rabbi took his son; he embraced him and said, 'Once you know that there is such a thing as that world, you are not in it.'"

Max crossed his legs. "My sister says you are a chiropodist and a Gentile. So you are all about this world, feet firmly planted in a world of feet."

The doctor considered how he should reply. "It's true I'm a Gentile," he admitted.

Max continued in his soft, detached tone. Balassa had to lean forward to hear. "I will tell you a story too, an even shorter one. Once upon a time one of my favorite rabbis prayed this prayer: 'Lord of the world, I beg of you to redeem Israel. But if you don't want to do that, then redeem the Goyim.'"

Balassa considered. "I'm not a chiropodist," he said. "Nor am I a believer."

Max nodded. "Of course you aren't. So what's the game? Do you love my sister? Do you imagine you can make her happy?"

"I love Julie, yes, but who knows if I can make her happy? I do know that you aren't making her happy, or your poor mother either. So tell me, Max, why have you shut yourself off from the world? Why have you given up painting, suppressed your talent which, I must say, I admire? You huddle up here alone, heaping loneliness on your head like ashes. Can't you see that you are in the world of confusion?"

Max looked down at his bare feet. "This world is the world of confusion. Even a pseudo-chiropodist, a Gentile of extremities, must know that."

"Yet you are talking to me now."

"Because we are alone. Because you closed that door behind you. Now you are above the world."

Balassa began to feel as if he had already as good as attained his goal. His patient was actually conversing with him. The field was open at last. Yes, clearly the proper way to deal with Max was the frontal assault.

"Tell me about your father."

Max put his hands behind his head, a gesture which poignantly reminded Balassa of Julie reclining on his own bed.

"A man came to the rabbi of Kotzk complaining of his sons. 'They won't support me, though I'm old and weak and can no longer earn my living. I was always ready to do everything for them, but now they won't have anything to do with me.' The rabbi listened to this then raised his eyes to heaven. 'That's how it is,' he said. 'The father shares in the sorrows of his sons but the sons do not share in the sorrows of the father.'"

Are we to speak only in parables, wondered Balassa. "I don't understand you, Max. Do you feel guilty toward your father, perhaps?"

"I am my father's father."

"But how can that be?"

Max looked at the wall. "I am your father too. I am the father of the Jews and also of the Gentiles."

The monstrous idea came to Balassa all at once but he resisted the impulse to exclaim over it, to blurt it out; his professional scruples told him he must at all costs avoid showing surprise. One must enter into the delusion in order to defeat it. So, in a carefully measured tone, he posed a question.

"And what if you aren't God, Max? What if there is no God?"

"You're half right. After all, you say you're an atheist yourself. I agree there is no God. I am that God who no longer exists."

Balassa was stunned but knew he must somehow maintain his momentum and balance. "Excuse me, but if there is no God, which you grant, then you, who clearly do exist because you are lying on that bed, cannot be God. Surely you can see the logic of that, Max?"

"So it would appear. The world is stuffed with atheists, but they are of all kinds. One has to ask each of them which God it is that he doesn't believe in."

"But the world is full of believers, too—more believers than atheists."

"So what? The question is just as apt for them. Which God is it they believe in? Not me."

Balassa was confused but pressed on as best he could. "I take it you are a monotheist? The Lord is one?"

Max gave a wan smile. "I am what I am, which is the original mono-theist."

"Why should the one God reside in the Faubourg St.-Germaine?"

"Why not? You don't know where God lives?"

"Where is that, Max?"

"Wherever people let him in, of course. Should I move to your Hungary? Do you think they would let me in there?"

Balassa made to stand up. "You are ill," he declared with both anger and pity.

In response Max became passionate. "Much worse than ill! You ask if I'm a monotheist. Do you realize what montheism means? Can you grasp the unspeakable loneliness of God? No neighbors, no profession, no colleagues, no lovers, spouse, children, parents, cousins. People look right through me, are deaf to everything I say. Isn't that not existing? Isn't that the solitude of a forgotten God? The world doesn't want or need a God. This world prefers to rest in its confusion, its idolatry, in science and hatred. No, the sons never enter into the sorrows of the father!"

By the end of this speech Max Kregel was shouting loud enough to make the window rattle behind the doctor's ears.

10.

In September the sunburnt Parisians returned, including the oft-betrayed Mme. Desmoulins. On the afternoon of September tenth Julie met Balassa at the same café where he had first laid eyes on her, and explained that her brother refused ever to see him again. Also he had screamed at her, "Have nothing to do with that devil of a Hun. If you have to have a man then find some pious Jew, do it quickly, and have a hundred children. There's not much time." She had memorized his terrible words.

Balassa shook his head and laughed sadly.

"It's no laughing matter. I really won't be seeing you any more. I can't. There's no point now. I've arranged for Max to be sent to Doctor Florel's clinic at Rambouillet." She got to her feet and said adieu. Before departing Julie slipped an envelope on to the table. Balassa waited three days and then cashed the check.

Four months later Adolf Hitler was appointed Chancellor of Germany.

By January Balassa had attracted some new patients, two men with sexual difficulties, a neurotic friend of Mme. Desmoulins, even a poor lawyer convinced his daughters were plotting to kill him for his collection of African stamps. In February he finally completed his article on religious delusion. It begins this way:

Consider two states of affairs, A and B, where A is a healthy condition, B a delusional one. Normally one would say that when it becomes easy for a person to believe B and intolerable to believe A, and this temptation is accepted, he or she may be called delusional. Up till now it has been assumed that this "easy to believe" signifies such things as serving to glorify or spare the ego, palliative, consoling, reassuring, without pain. This is Freud's position and it must, of course, be given the greatest weight. This view of delusion depends on the fundamental analytic axiom of unconscious motivation. Thus Freud can say all religious believers express, and always have expressed, an unconscious wish for the protection of the father. The trouble is that unconscious motivation is like flypaper; it sticks to everything. In theory, the same view may be applied as readily to atheism as to faith. The atheist also chooses between an A and a B; we all do. Further, we have to admit the possibility that whether A or B is truly "healthy" may be a matter of convention rather than objective determination. The phrase "easy to believe" may not invariably mean that the belief is less painful for those who are deluded. On the contrary, a deluded person, greatly disturbed to be sure, may choose to believe the very notion that will cause him the most intense misery. . . .

Thanks to Janvier's recommendation, Balassa's forty-page article was published in a reputable journal. To its author's chagrin, however, it provoked no controversy. Florel sent him a congratulatory note, however, and the piece did furnish a useful line on his résumé. When he emigrated to the United States in 1937 the publication helped him secure an appointment to the faculty of the University of Wisconsin where he did little clinical work and led a lonely bachelor's life as the solitary Freudian in a department of hard-headed, unimaginative behaviorists. Two generations of students competed at mimicking his accent.

Through his correspondence with Janvier, Balassa kept tabs on the Kregels. From him he learned that Mme. Kregel succumbed to pneumonia in 1935, and that Julie married a businessman named Jules Goldfarb the following year. The couple was childless. As for Max, he was released from André Florel's clinic that same year. As far as Janvier knew, he did not resume painting but filled some minor position in Goldfarb's company. For several months he lived with his sister and brother-in-law but then moved to a small apartment close by the Goldfarb establishment.

This correspondence was interrupted by the war. After the liberation of Paris, Balassa mailed Janvier a huge package of warm clothing and good things to eat. In the accompanying letter he begged for any news of the Kregels. He had to wait two months for a reply. Janvier was grateful for the package and assured him that he and his family were all well. They had ridden out the two worst years with his wife's family in the south where conditions were a little easier. As for the Kregels, he had made inquiries about them. He quickly discovered that they were not in the city but he continued to ask around. By one of those unlikely coincidences with which Balassa must be familiar, it turned out that a family of his acquaintance happened to employ the Kregels' former maid as a laundress. Did he perhaps remember Marie? It was she who provided the regrettable news that he had to pass on to Balassa. In early 1942 Max, Julie, and her husband had all been rounded up and transported. All three had vanished into the East.

Blessant and The Dutchman

1.

I no longer see so well. I am losing the peripheries, and not merely of vision. In these last years I have endured ever more pinched circumstances. I have outlived my fortune if not my prudence. Even with my reduced expenses, cash often runs low by the end of the month; but beyond material constraints the scope of my attention too has been squeezed by penury and infirmity. I fear that my little flat, once my refuge, may become my cell. It fits me all too snugly, but as immovably as a gauntlet or a crypt.

It is customary for people entering on retirement to imagine they are taking leave of the world but, if they persist in existing too long, it is revealed that the world is leaving them. Then they turn sullen and querulous and become unbearable. To avert this fate I take my little walks to the nearby market and galleries, watch educational television programs, read two newspapers daily, dust off my sense of humor with Mme. Soulanger the concierge and the lively mongers at the market. I try not to dwell on my salad days. Nevertheless, something happened recently that has plunged me into a pool of sunken memories.

A few weeks ago I received a telephone call, quite an occasion in itself. I confess there is little utility in my keeping a telephone. Though it is really an extravagance, one easily convinces oneself the telephone is a safety measure. If one has to one can ring up the police, the fire company; if one chooses, one may even call the mayor, the Pope. But I seldom make a call and, unless an exchange is set up in Le Guet Cemetery, I am unlikely to receive many.

A young woman introduced herself. She said her name was Marie, same as mine. This Marie seemed peculiarly excited by my voice and begged to be permitted to see me; she wished, she said, to conduct an interview about my days as an artists' model. I could not help being intrigued, all the more so because Marie said she was American. It is my impression that it has been decades since liking Americans was chic. But despite what their profligacy has cost me, I have always liked Americans, or at least the idea of them. After all, an American is almost an idea, an idea that is always being formed.

As I was so well disposed by the young woman's manner, I suggested she pay me a visit the following afternoon at three. I prepared a little tea for us; I even bought a half-dozen petits-fours. Even before noon I had begun to remember things.

Marie turned out to be a post-adolescent with long, not excessively clean hair and rimless spectacles that were strangely becoming. Her demeanor was polite, frank, guileless, and her French nearly as good as mine. Apart from a pair of hideous work shoes, she was dressed like a prostitute—and not a very thriving one at that. I had to remind myself that, if only to make a space for their own prejudices, Americans began by freeing themselves from many of ours. Evidently, even the armoires of American girls are democratic. So what if she was badly dressed; this was certainly preferable to an attempt to deck herself out for me. Of course it is possible that a costume is precisely what she had put on, maybe even for my benefit. Her clothes made it easy to underestimate Marie and perhaps she was counting on this, calculating that I would speak the more freely to her. I confess that I could hardly take my eyes off the low-cut black frock and mesh stockings, the ridiculous plastic bangles and earrings in the shape of trout. Above all, I found myself fascinated by a small gold nose-ring she wore through her left nostril. I have noticed that recently young people, many of them college educated, have taken up this barbarous custom. Perhaps it is a revulsion with colonialism that makes the African practice so appealing to them, but in my opinion no longing for mutilation can bode well. I should have liked to discuss the point with her but, strange to say, I felt shy of doing so. It has been years since I conversed with anyone so young and I did not wish to appear even more of a relic in her eyes. Anyway, it was my role to enlighten her, not the reverse. Instead I asked for the story of how she had found me.

She was pleased by the question; her already luminous face brightened. "That was sheer luck, Madame Mercanton."

"Yours or mine, Marie?"

Marie blushed and stumbled through her explanation. "Well, you see, your name turned up in several of their letters. Of course I realized that lots of people would have seen them. I mean lots of scholars and researchers must already have pored over those letters, and it seemed to me that some of them would naturally have tried to track you down. I went to Professor Abrams—she's in charge of our Program—but Professor Abrams said she didn't know any articles that mentioned you, at least none in English, French, or German. She supposed you must be dead."

I smiled. "How morbid of the professor."

Marie giggled. "Well, it seemed likely enough. I mean those letters are over sixty years old and—"

"Please, my dear, no numbers," I said, then added, "I'll be eighty-three next month." From the look of her, she was astonished that the total of my years was not higher.

Once again I remarked the openness of her face. It was smooth as a polished apple, yet also like a wheat field which every zephyr causes to undulate. I liked this countenance of the prairies and felt sympathy for the ever-renewable resource of American innocence. Marie made me conscious less of my own age than that of my continent. I felt like the weathered public monument she took me for.

Her type I had seen before, on the streets, in the galleries. We get annual shipments of them, polite, wealthy, self-assured, carefully educated. She was wrong about the scholars seeking me out. No doubt, for the young women who come from America to study painters, Blessant and Steenkiste are as gloriously defunct as da Vinci and Titian. To judge by their casual appearance and deportment, their reverence is limited to Art History, a religion that makes few demands on their self-discipline. Marie was about the same age I was when I met Blessant and Steenkiste and I found her touching, quite unlike our European scholars who, in addition to being chiefly middle-aged males, study Art more or less as they might steel production. Her attention flattered me and, besides, she brought out something in me if not maternal then at least sisterly. Yes, it was not a little flattering to have a small portion of all that aesthetic veneration shed on me.

The child had compiled a whole roster of questions about Blessant and Steenkiste. Evidently she knew only vaguely of my connection with them, only that I had modeled for a time. She did not know that I had been their model for two years and that during this time I had lived with them as well.

2.

I was born into a respectable bourgeois family in Angoulême. My childhood was not oppressive, though I felt it to be. I had difficulties getting along with my mother who favored my elder brother Jules—Jules, my tormentor. Father, who was often away on business, inclined toward me. Once, having discovered my brother pulling my hair, he beat Jules in front of me. "Pull down your pants," Father commanded in a strangled voice. "You stay right there," he said to me. Then Father beat Jules's buttocks with his belt. I relished recalling this story for Marie without at all anticipating how she might interpret it.

It was chiefly to please my father that I did so well at school. To excel was easy, for I was good at my studies and had no trouble concealing my detestation of the nuns. My friends were of my own type, bourgeois, bright, restless. My particular talent was for mathematics, a discipline of which Father particularly approved and at which Jules was satisfyingly inept. I remember when I was about sixteen Father took me for a boat ride on the river and asked my plans and hopes. I told him that I would prefer being an actuary to a wife. He laughed at me but I could see that he was pleased. Two years later, when I had passed my bachot with honors and begged to go up to the university in Paris, there was a big row. "The University!" exclaimed Mother, "there was no offer of university to Jules." "Jules lacks aptitude," Father rejoined. By then my brother was working in Limoges at the furniture business he later owned and completely out of my life. The argument did not last long. I had Father on my side and Mother had to submit.

I adored Paris. If Angoulême dozed then the capital could not shut its eyes. At home people would gaze downwards, as if ashamed either to see or be seen, whereas in Paris everyone was always either examining their own reflections in the plate glass fronts of shops or looking each other up and down, devouring and judging. In those days shop girls and secretaries would buy one outfit a year, the most stylish they could afford, and wear it every day. You would be hard pressed to find badly dressed people in the city. Even at the Sorbonne the students made their cheap clothes look chic. How one dressed was meant to reflect one's tastes in art and politics. In those days Paris was the city not so much of light as of signs, where to live was to read. I learned to read with avidity.

In the spring of my second year I was attracted to a circle of bohemians whose disorderly lives thrilled me. I was careful to keep to the fringes however, being still too much the prudent provincial to tumble into trouble. My best friend at this time was Darcelle Desmolines, an art student. She wore her hair cropped short as a man's and, like my American namesake, blouses that showed off her bust. It was Darcelle who introduced me to Blessant and Steenkiste, the latter of whom she called simply the Dutchman. They were in their mid-twenties at the time, living in a loft sufficiently spacious and seedy as to be picturesque.

Apart from their talent, Blessant and Steenkiste fascinated the art students of Darcelle's circle because of the sheer improbability of their friendship. Indeed, it is still this relationship that beguiles the scholars so that one is never discussed without the other being mentioned. Blessant the flamboyant, intense surrealist, Steenkiste the reflective, analytic abstractionist—it was apparently a case of opposites attracting. Between them they divided up the world of the modern and made of their respective styles complements rather than enemies, a whole globe rather than two hemispheres. And yet when one looks at their work these so-called complements seem rather to exclude one another. I don't doubt that many of the students, dazzled by the proliferation of modernist styles, saw the personal harmony between Blessant and Steenkiste as a reassurance, perhaps a promise that integrity and wholeness had not been forever shattered by the Great War.

Blessant and the Dutchman had no money. Darcelle consented to pose for them in lieu of payment for lessons, though, as far as I could see, the lessons remained putative. I believe her interest was chiefly the Dutchman. Darcelle hated mathematics and yet, like many such people, stood in awe of those who had mastered its mysteries. She regarded me at once as a superior creature and one sadly lacking in human sympathies and deprived of worldly experience. One day she dragged me with her to the painters' studio, to "broaden my education" as she put it. She casually doffed her clothes as soon as we arrived.

When we got there at one in the afternoon Steenkiste was already drunk and he greeted us loudly. Darcelle he embraced perfunctorily. To me he bowed unsteadily then unsuccessfully offered to kiss my hand. The Dutchman continued drinking from a bottle of brandy for the next two hours of steady work. For his part, Blessant barely said hello to either of us and remained cold sober, painting with great concentration. At twenty-five he already had those two lines running up from the bridge of his narrow nose into his broad forehead. The comportment of the two painters surprised me after the fact, so to speak; for it was the quiet Blessant whose canvas seemed almost insanely manic while that of the extroverted Steenkiste took shape with Euclidean calm.

What did I do for those two hours? I observed; I took in the atmosphere which, while unfamiliar, conformed remarkably to the romantic images of nineteenth-century studios I had picked up from my reading. I also listened to Darcelle whose physical stillness on the divan did not prevent her from keeping up a constant flow of gossip and pretentious theorizing about art, Marxism, and cosmetics. Though neither man asked about me, Darcelle proceeded to tell them I was serious to a fault, had no boyfriend, and was a genius with numbers.

"That's good," asserted Steenkiste. "The whole of nature is numbers."

To this Blessant unexpectedly replied with the retort, "Pythagorean claptrap."

I thought Blessant good looking. I liked his seriousness, though I had difficulty squaring it with the picture he was producing in which Darcelle's body appeared molten, pulled apart, peppered with holes like a Swiss cheese. He had painted her flesh the color of a fresh wound; her short hair suggested a poilu's helmet.

With the Dutchman's picture, despite the fact that his inebriation repelled me, I could more readily sympathize. He had anatomized my friend's body into a set of forms and relations that would have seemed too strictly geometrical, except that the forms were not quite regular. Each rhomboid and triangle had a subtle curve as if to represent a vestigial humanity. Nevertheless, the attempt was clearly to abstract Darcelle into the most timeless structure. I fancied that through her he sought a desperate impossibility, nothing less than the Platonic idea of which the most beautiful of us is only a crude imitation.

At length Darcelle grew quiet and I grew bored. I found a copy of Gide's *Pastoral Symphony*, and began to read it.

3.

Marie consulted the next question in her notebook. "How did they treat you?"

"In what respect?"

She looked up. "Well, didn't you feel exploited?"

"Define exploitation."

She looked at me blankly, as people will when asked to give an account of the words they use a dozen times each day.

"Do you mean exploitation in the Marxist sense, my dear? Profiting from the surplus value of my labor? Or did you have something less commercial in mind, more emotional? Did they take advantage of me for their gratification, exploiting my youth and naiveté? I'm sure you don't want to know if one or the other slept with me but rather if they prevented me from going on with my studies, pursuing my own goals in life. Isn't that so, my dear?"

Quite naturally, the child was overwhelmed and I was sorry to have teased her.

"What about paternalism?" she asked, checking her notes. "Did you see them as alternative fathers, as substitutes for your own father's love?"

I smiled kindly and said, "Please forgive me, Marie. It is possible to extract so many theories from life but scarcely any life from theories. I loved my father and he loved me. It's perhaps true that in our relations with our fathers we women lay down certain patterns, certain expectations and also disappointments that do indeed color the whole of our subsequent experience. To be sure, the family is the first of our problems in life. And yet I cannot say I felt anything like a daughter to these men, or exploited by their production or submerged by their masculinity. I assure you that, even at your age, I did not lack weapons of my own. As I saw it, they were painters painting me, as I was a mathematics student being painted. Though his habits were anarchic, the Dutchman's pictures are themselves mathematical and, come to think of it, Blessant also yearned for harmony, insisted on it everywhere but in his work–his irritation with disorder was exceptional. So, he too had something of the serenely numerical about him. I felt a kinship, a sympathy. After all, haven't you noticed that we are all a little . . . divided?"

She put down her pen, baffled yet, I flatter myself, not unimpressed.

"Steenkiste abstracted you while Blessant distorted you; neither was able to see you as you are. Is this at least a fair statement?"

I shrugged. "Who ever sees us as we are, child? God?"

4.

About a week after that first visit to the studio Darcelle told me Blessant and the Dutchman had been asking after me.

"To tell you the truth, I think one of them is infatuated," she said slyly. I would not give her the satisfaction of asking which one. Frankly, I did not believe anyone had been asking about me, only that Darcelle wished to tease me. Provoked by a seriousness of purpose she envied and derided, it was my friend's pleasure to make up all sorts of disreputable adventures for me: larcenous sprees in Monte Carlo, spying for the highest bidder; she was always suggesting affairs with professors, saxophonists, taxi drivers. I often thought that I was the vessel for Darcelle's own wishes; for as I got to know her better I observed that her fantasy life was far stronger than anything she actually got up to.

In any case, I consented to go back to the studio with her. Why? Not entirely because I had been intrigued by Blessant's sobriety and Steenkiste's intoxication, or how their work inverted these personal qualities. My fondness for seeing the world clearly and, so to speak, without humidity made it natural that I should be attracted by the abstractionist's work, yet it was Blessant who drew me as a man. I liked the look of him. Though his pictures made no sense to me, his eyes did.

This time there was no work. "Keep your clothes on, Darcelle," said Steenkiste. "We all need a break." The Dutchman extracted two bottles of vin ordinaire from the cupboard and invited us to lunch with them on bread and sardines. As for Blessant, he said nothing and looked at me angrily. It was obvious that he was feeling as I was. The anger was because he resented feeling attracted to me and, worse yet, that I was aware of it. I had an urge to punish him for refusing to acknowledge his feelings though, paradoxically, it was this refusal that gave his feelings value for me. At that age, such matters are always games.

I lavished attention on Steenkiste. I begged him to take out all the pictures he had on hand. I made him unroll at least two dozen canvases and praised them in copious detail. Being untrained in art criticism, unlike little Marie, I had to make things up as I went along. "You must have calculated this angle very carefully to achieve such balance . . . . Yes, of course I can see how flatness is more honest than perspective would be, but the precision with which you suggest the decanter through the faceting is marvelous . . . . "

Meanwhile Darcelle, who was drinking a good deal of wine, began inveigling Blessant to dance with her. She hummed a provocative tango. At first he refused but then, looking at me with open hostility, he made a brave but ineffectual attempt. The poor fellow was as stiff as a dry stick.

The Dutchman asked me to explain Fermat's Last Theorem. "I have a particular reason for asking. Blessant over there is a descendent of Fermat."

Blessant blushed and retorted over Darcelle's shoulder, "Mathematics was merely a hobby of his. He was likewise a linguist and a lawyer. Three hundred years ago he was elected to the parliament of Toulouse where he is to this day famous for his integrity."

"And yet he worshipped Pythagoras," Steenkiste teased. I remembered the exchange they had had last time over Pythagoras. Pythagoras was evidently a private cause between them.

I proceeded with the requested explanation and continued until Steenkiste fell asleep on the divan. And then it happened while Darcelle was being sick out the window. Blessant asked me to return.

"I would be obliged if you would allow me to paint you, mademoiselle," he said as if he were making an appointment for a stabbing. "If you are agreeable you may pick any day you like."

"If I do come I won't take off my clothes."

He shrugged. "You may wear a hat or a burnoose, mademoiselle. To me it is a matter of indifference."

I liked him all the more because of the burnoose.

5.

"To pose for two painters," Marie said, "two highly talented painters —do you consider that it was a privilege or do you think that your autonomy was suppressed, your subjectivity pushed down as you had to keep still for them?"

"It's true that it's not easy to keep still but then neither insisted on immobility. After all, they weren't doing portraits for the National Gallery!"

"But you were a mannequin. What of your autonomy, your subjection to their will?"

"I did nothing except by my free will. It was canvases they painted, not me."

"It didn't trouble you to be looked at, scrutinized, to be the raw material for their fame? The whole history of Western Art is dominated by the male gaze which is invasive, which is penetrating. You have to admit that Blessant and Steenkiste were very masculine painters—that is to say, sadistic."

"If you go on like this you shall make me blush, child."

"The encapsulation of the female form, placed in a frame, torn to pieces by one, pulled this way and that by the other—"

"True, I suppose you could say that they were always trying to reconstruct me, but cannot reconstruction be a form of love?"

She perked up. "Ah, then you were more to them than a model?"

I asked her to go on but in another direction.

6.

Perhaps it really was a combination of love and hate, being watched and imaginatively maimed, pulled in and repulsed, perpetually captured yet forever running away. Who knows?

My passion for Blessant grew and still he would not respond openly. I began coming twice each week, each time hoping that Steenkiste would be out and that something would happen. But the Dutchman was always there, for he too wanted to paint me. You might think that they would compete for my approbation of their pictures but nothing of the sort happened. Roped together like mountain climbers, that is what Picasso said of his time working beside Georges Braque. However, while Picasso and Braque were painting in the same style, egging one another on rather than pulling in opposite directions, Blessant and Steenkiste always proceeded along parallel lines, the sort that we are assured will intersect at infinity.

I decided to make Blessant more jealous by responding to the Dutchman's habitual attempts at seduction. Between Blessant and me there was now an erotic power struggle. I could see to what fury my talking mathematics with Steenkiste drove him and whenever I permitted the Dutchman to touch me—under the guise of arranging my pose—Blessant's face darkened.

Then one Tuesday Steenkiste was not there. Blessant explained that his friend had been called home because his mother was ill. I was not sure that I believed him.

"How do you want me to pose today?" I asked pertly.

"Perhaps you could stand on your head."

"It's an idea," I replied coolly, "but, as you see, I am wearing a skirt."

"Maybe you would prefer to leave."

I went to his easel, picked up his largest brush, and broke it over my knee.

I moved in the next morning. When Steenkiste returned, he professed to be delighted. As for his mother, she had died.

Though in my inexperience I was unaware of it at first, Blessant was as poor a lover as he was a dancer. I could unlock nothing in him; only painting could do that. As for Steenkiste, he did not appear at all troubled by the noise of our lovemaking for the simple reason that he never went to bed sober or, on Thursdays and Saturdays, without a new partner from the streets.

Strange as it may seem, the irregular life I now led did not in the least disrupt my studies. On the contrary, the many hours I began to spend in the library made me rise yet further in my professors' estimation. In this respect, I was doing nothing to disappoint my father. Moreover, I was saving money on rent. In fact, I had begun to make money, for it was at that time that I undertook my first small speculations in foreign exchange.

In a few months Blessant's fumbling and constricted love paled on me, though I must say his painting became more flamboyant than ever. More sexual as well—and this was what vexed me most. I resolved to do some mischief and one morning, when he had tiptoed out for his customary coffee and brioche, I slipped into bed with the still unconscious Steenkiste. I had a malicious notion: Blessant would discover us and then I would see what happened next.

The Dutchman, however, was not really asleep. In fact, no sooner had I climbed in beside him than he erupted into movement, confessing his pent-up passion even as he acted upon it in the most convincing fashion. After all, how was he to have interpreted my action but as willingness? I soon found that where Blessant was cold on the surface and all heat underneath, a clumsy lover lacking in stamina and finesse, Steenkiste was a master of technique. To me, still so inexperienced (for it was to Blessant that I gave my virginity), Steenkiste was a revelation. Perhaps I did not act as I ought to have done but I confess that I was surprised, distrait, overcome, and before I knew it I eagerly responded.

7.

Whatever is written in those letters she found did not inform Marie of the extent of my relations with Blessant and the Dutchman. Though I was a little tempted to tell her, I thought better of it. The child was interested in Art History, not scandal. No matter how closely the two resemble each other it is best to keep them distinct. Perhaps, I mused, when she is safely back at Bryn Mawr she will ruminate on our interview and wonder. I like this image of little Marie at Bryn Mawr, which I imagine having picturesque Welsh stone walls covered by thick dark ivy, walls between which the golden daughters of the New World pursue the life of the mind untroubled by the reality of men, disturbed only by angry thoughts of men and their alluring repression, their penetrating gazes, their hostility to autonomy, their desires inscribed upon the female form. Brave but ambivalent thoughts in a female cloister.

"Nobody's in a better position than you, Madame Mercanton, to shed some light on the mystery of the friendship. What can you tell me?"

"Very little, actually."

But of course Marie already had her theory worked out. My task was only to confirm it.

"Wouldn't you say it was all about, well, completeness?" Here she looked down and consulted her notes. "I mean it looks as if neither man was able to reconcile art and life, to achieve wholeness, so that the incompatibility of their two styles became the origin of a mutual sufficiency."

"Mutual sufficiency?"

"A sufficiency that each constituted for the other. A sufficiency in no need of a supplement."

"What do you mean supplement?"

She smiled and shrugged rather condescendingly. "A woman, for example. A woman might have been disruptive to such a precarious balance."

"Yes," I said, revealing nothing.

"Or were they gay? You know, homosexual?"

I could not help laughing and yet, even as I laughed, I was wondering what my meaning was for them, what sort of "supplement" I had been.

"No, they were not homosexuals and yet they broke up as any couple would."

"Do you have any insight on the breakup?"

"Me? No, I can tell you nothing about that. Perhaps it was only the need to be on their own, or that what you call their incompatibility finally overcame that quality you call their sufficiency. Maybe they became exasperated by each other's habits."

"The breakup was a catastrophe," said Marie sadly, probingly.

"Was it?"

8.

The Dutchman had a manual. I found it one day in the bookcase, a much-thumbed, soft-bound pamphlet. At first I mistook it. I could not make out the Dutch and supposed the drawings to be erotic life studies of some sort. I even thought the book might belong to Blessant, so surreal did these images seem to me. And yet I soon realized that they were familiar, too familiar.

Steenkiste did everything mechanically, by the numbers. He drank by the liter and he made love by diagram.

Try to picture one of Plato's ideas. The best you can do is a number: 2, 4, 64. Numbers are immaterial, universal, invariable, perfect, bloodless. It's no use trying to smell or stroke them; you can't escape from them, only into them. Numbers are too indifferent to offer us softness, to give in to our curves or compromise with our imperfections. Taken one at a time nothing is simpler than a number—children count almost by instinct—yet their relations beget complexities beyond the grasp of even the greatest minds. We begin at one and wind up, baffled, at infinity. Steenkiste's paintings serenely if hopelessly aspired to be Platonic ideas, to escape the madness of curves and pliancy and decay. It would be wrong to say that he sought to turn me into such a dead perfection; I could more easily have forgiven him that.

The day after I discovered Steenkiste's sex manual I insisted on posing in the nude and that night I returned to Blessant's bed. I remember how he sighed while, only a few feet away, Steenkiste gargled brandy.

And so it went for two more years, back and forth, until I was ready to take my degree. During this time they began to quarrel with each other; they argued over everything except me. They didn't know what to do with me, though by then I had my own plans. All the scholars acknowledge that the greatest works of Blessant and the Dutchman date from those years.

I take some satisfaction in that, though not perhaps the sort little Marie would be prepared to appreciate.

I played with them. I drove them crazy, and the craziness reached its apogee on one particular night in early spring. I came in from a late class. They were waiting for me, each in his own chair, Blessant impassive, Steenkiste looking like a wounded animal.

He spoke first. "You have to choose. We've worked it out."

Then Blessant, "We're both proposing to you, Marie."

I could have laughed but I was gentle. I stood before them, feeling for the last time the familiar sensation of those four great eyes.

"Neither of you really wants me for a wife," I said quietly, "no more, in fact, than I desire either of you for a husband."

"Things can't go on as they are!" screamed Steenkiste.

"No," Blessant agreed.

"Very well," I said. "Then I'll leave."

Blessant was incredulous. "Leave?"

"I've accumulated quite a chunk of capital on the exchange, in a few weeks I shall have my degree, and you may as well know I intend to be married within a year."

9.

"Was your marriage a happy one?" Marie asked, having put down her notebook.

"Oh yes. Mercanton and I got on quite well. He was a colleague of my father's and he respected me."

She raised her eyebrows. I could tell what she was thinking. In this case, at least, she probably wasn't far from the mark.

"So your father chose your husband for you?"

"I suppose you could say my father offered him to me. Suggested him."

"And you had some money of your own? You were independent? You wanted a career?"

"I had been playing the currency exchange with fair success for two years. Mercanton was content to accept the condition that I be allowed a career. I worked at an investment firm for two decades."

"And children?"

"I regret to say there were none. I am alone in the world, my dear,"

I answered with forced cheerfulness.

Marie took up her notebook and pen. "Would you say that Mercanton displaced the two painters for whom you modeled?"

"In what sense displaced?"

She looked at me with a certain shrewdness, as if she might challenge my story. Once I was certain there was nothing in their letters to contradict me, I had admitted to nothing more than "a little modeling in my student days" for Blessant and Steenkiste. Nevertheless, Marie had her idée fixe; indeed, she had several.

"They were half-men and could never replace your father in your affections, not even taken together. So Mercanton was the perfect solution. Also, he took you as you were, his equal, even his economic superior. You insisted on power in your marriage."

I laughed dismissively. "You are pleased to be fanciful."

She pressed on. "Do you ever think of the cruel fates of Blessant and Steenkiste? Do you ever think of those fates as significant or symbolic?"

"What do you mean by fates?"

"I mean their losses, that Blessant should lose the use of one hand, that Steenkiste should lose the sight of one eye."

It was true that I had wondered about this when I found out. Blessant's hand had become paralyzed from years of gripping his brush too tightly. The Dutchman lost an eye in a bicycling accident. These disasters came within two years of my wedding, after the painters had parted ways; that is, at a time when their work had ceased to progress. "Self-parody" one scholar calls those senseless nightmares and abstractions empty of content that they produced after I left them.

10.

Marie has sent me a copy of her paper. I am discreetly referred to throughout as "Madame M." As was to be expected, it swarms with her pet theories, or those of Professor Abrams, theories in which a once-ferocious anger is already congealing into a kind of scholasticism. I will not say that I read it without learning a few things, though. At my age one can learn only from the young. But as I read what this armored young feminist said about me I wondered whether I had misled her, if I ought to have tried to set her straight on a few matters. Though I could have said more, would it have mattered? There was really little I could tell her that would have led her to a different understanding. She was determined to understand but only in certain ways. My objections to her paper, such as they are, may only be those of vanity as I see my particularity converted into something typical. But I would not presume to protest a single word. I wrote her a thank-you note. As I said earlier, I am fond of Americans. That sentimentality cost me a fortune in the inflation of the 70s when I ought to have dumped my dollars and bought yen.

In one section of her essay Marie develops a curious hypothesis about the masochism of artists' models. The theory is tautological in that she assumes masochism to be an indispensable prerequisite for being a model. After stating this theory she writes, "Madame M. vividly recalled for me an episode from her childhood when her father made her watch as he whipped her older brother on the buttocks for being cruel to her. Here we have a clear case of wish-fulfillment, of the daughter's projection of the forbidden desire to be beaten by the father while simultaneously being saved and protected by him. The pattern was established early. The longed-for duplicity of the father thus conceived was, for a time at least, satisfied by the two artists. In this respect it is noteworthy that Madame M. reports that she invariably posed for both at the same time."

Marie concludes her essay by referring to me as "the disruptive supplement" in the friendship of the two painters. She likes this odd word supplement. I am not certain what it signifies for Marie, but I am aware that if a supplement is not a Platonic idea and not a nightmare, neither is it quite a human person.

"As the disruptive supplement the model exists primarily as an object to be painted, to be inscribed; and yet as a female object Madame M. provided also the necessary subject for the best work of Blessant and Steenkiste, as she became the repository and vessel for all the meanings possible to distortion and abstraction."

In writing of me in this way has not my little namesake, though with the most sisterly of intentions, likewise abstracted and distorted me? Or can it be that forearmed innocence has seen more deeply than unprotected experience? Has this young American girl with a face as regular and naive as a field of corn looked into the encrusted equations of Europe, of love and punishment, and plucked out a solution that eluded me?

Arno Meer

A Short Preface

My two motives for embarking on this memoir are irritation and wonder. These are not casual grounds. Irritation and wonder are, in my opinion, the most vital of psychological states; that is, they constitute the essential sensations of living for those who are alive.

The capacity to be irritated is universal, though it differs in degree from species to species and individual to individual. What any given organism recognizes as an irritant also varies. For example, the anemone is constantly alert, relishing its ability to sense the slightest irritation through its polyps, ingesting the digestible irritants while endeavoring to hide from those that might digest it. The oyster fashions a pearl which is the embodiment of the myth of irritation itself, the sort of opaque beauty only protest can secrete. Conversely, a philosopher of the Cynic school prided himself on failing to notice that his foot was in flames. Irritation is moral as well as physical. Suppose you see a female separated from her offspring and identify equally with the frantic agitation of the mother and the sudden terror of the youngster. Should you be perturbed by this to the point of desiring that they be reunited, even that you yourself should perform the service of reuniting them, then you are proceeding from irritation. So, I am undertaking this memoir out of all kinds of irritation.

Wonder may take precedence even over irritation in the order of consciousness. No response to the condition of being alive is more rudimentary than wonder, which shoots through all your nerves at the speed of electricity and embraces not only the prodigiously varied external world but even your own stirrings, perceptions and thoughts, not excluding your wonder itself. Because my life has been full of wonders, then, I am undertaking this memoir.

Robert Wexelblatt

Why I Became an Artist

Well up on the list of irritants that have provoked me is the following sentence: "Suddenly cut off from his proper element and from the society of his own kind, we should not wonder that Arno Meer turned to art for solace."

The several presumptions in this cocky proposition, whose very grammar rasps against one's nerves, caused me pain when it was first read to me. I could think of nothing better than to dive to the very bottom of my pool and stay there so long that even Jane, unfailingly sympathetic and normally so equable, began to panic, striking the water with her palm and calling my name through the submarine sound system. We should not wonder that Arno Meer turned to art for solace.

I can claim some expertise on the condition of unintelligibility and so I say that not to be understood at all is tolerable. To be sure, for no one to understand you in any detail can be frustrating, particularly if one has the desire to communicate a detailed message; but at least when nobody understands you there are no false positions, none of those condescending grimaces or knowing nods. So long as one remains unintelligible the slate stands blank, its smooth emptiness inviting the possibility of perfect intelligibility.

It is important to understand, as I came to, that communion may come long before communication. In such a case, the condition of not being understood would not even be unendurably lonesome. What I am saying is that an understanding can exist with another being that may or may not be beyond words but which certainly comes before them. Precisely such a communion grew up between me and Jane months before the day of our celebrated breakthrough, so heralded in the media. To tell the truth, at the time this breakthrough left me worried, notwithstanding the many pains and reverses with which Jane and I had labored toward it and despite all it subsequently made possible. I feared that this new communication, disappointingly crude, might superimpose itself over the subtle depths which made it possible, that language might screen out what was in fact far dearer and better expressed without words. But I am getting ahead of myself. Let us return to the period of my isolation that allegedly made me take comfort in art.

Not to be understood at all is the real refuge, a gratification of one's vanity, a consolation for all that the world denies you (how it would rush

138

to heap up its gifts if only it understood!). Unintelligibility is a womb, an enclosure that recalls the prenatal lack of trouble with the universe. Not to be understood as completely as I was at first preserved me secure and distinct, out of any relationship complex enough to harm me deeply. My communion with Jane was purely positive, of course, aimed at only itself, without any of the deceitful or ulterior motives that language introduces. In other words, my condition as a subject remained discrete from my reality as an object. As an unintelligible object I was little more than a curiosity, free of the moral obligation to reveal myself as a subject. I was as self-sufficient and irresponsible as the dead air inside my beach ball.

Now, a pronunciamento such as the one cited above, an elucidation offered the public by a respected professional radiator of elucidation whose utterances take on the force of matters of fact, as if he casts a light as natural as that of the sun—this is irritating above all because it destroys one's solid unintelligibility in the worst way, putting a baggy and too hasty misunderstanding in its place. Not to be understood is tolerable, but to be misunderstood is not. This critic is evidently in love with the naive theory that all artists are estranged from their fellows and therefore serves me up to the public with an official stamp on my flank: Alienated.

I did not come to be an artist out of feelings of alienation. In fact, I did not become an artist in this critic's sense at all, for I hardly know what an artist is other than a being who makes artifacts. Among us, the emitting of interesting, threatening, comforting, pleasing, compelling, or occasionally lethal sounds is commonplace behavior. One can produce sounds for others, for oneself, or both at once. One can generate them in a playful spirit, to articulate desperate pleas, to exhibit joy, anxiety, affection, to manifest one's hunger, nobility, or wrath. Everyone has his or her own motives and style in the generation of sound. I will not deny that some are better at it than others, but to constitute any individual as an artist would simply not occur to us. The term presupposes a complex network of economic and social relationships, a vast and dynamic cultural history plus the variable connotations of a word which possesses an obscure magic and dubious glamour. If I am an artist, especially an alienated one, then it instantly becomes feasible to apply to me certain expectations, whether of admiration or scorn, to place me within a tradition or over against a tradition, to compare me with other artists, to slap prefabricated labels on my behavior, even to make allowances for my bohemian tendencies. The very idea gives me the sense of having swum inside a turgid lagoon where I am ensnared by mile-long tendrils of kelp.

Still, as I soon discovered, in one important sense it is true that I became an artist. Evidently, all that is necessary is for someone with the authority of this critic to declare me an artist and then I am one; although to my way of thinking this says more about the critic's alienation than mine. I believe it is only his own alienation from artists that makes him confident that he not only knows who they are, but is capable of thoroughly explaining them. Again I am digressing. The key question here is whether I turned to the making of music as a solace in my isolation, as the critic asserts. Of course I did, but that is by no means the only or even the chief reason.

One night I made a little rhapsody for my own diversion. It was nothing special. There was no one else to make it for and, frankly, I was exquisitely bored. Jane had gone away and nobody else was about. I was unaware at the time that my pool had been tapped. It was only later that I learned from Dr. Schultz that the tape of this little rhapsody had occasioned a scientific controversy. Like the critic, all the scientists had a pet hypothesis: it was a mating call, a sonar scan of my pool, a hopeless cry for assistance, an attack on the walls that imprisoned me, a complex mathematical formula, a way of clearing my sinus cavities, a philosophical monologue. Jane was the first to understand and I shall always cherish her words. "I told them I thought it was, well, beautiful."

As you might expect, once I made up my mind to begin serious composition there were enormous difficulties to overcome. For one, I had to limit myself to the comparatively narrow spectrum of sound accessible to my potential audience. This did not deter me for long. Everyone knows that limitations can be inspirational, a truth all the more true for me in whose existence enclosure had become the leading fact. Because I had beaten my head against its walls, my pool turned me from vain dreams of departure and aspirations of amplitude toward an appreciation of the possibilities of restriction.

Many have been surprised that I learned so much so quickly, but the reason is simple. To be sure, I had the capacity to learn quickly, but I had also only two alternatives to doing so: either to infantilize or to kill myself. Infantilization would have been easy and even Jane might have been satisfied had I done so, turning the succession of imbecile tricks that were proposed as my initial curriculum. Infantilization has its advantages: it keeps off despair. One can submerge oneself in the childlike joys of childish existence and even find in the thoughtless cycle of trick/reward/ trick/reward a kind of purpose, a way of pleasing others while gratifying oneself. Such a contemptible existence was no more appealing than suicide. Both were murders; both were final. Nor would it help simply to resist my environment, refusing to cooperate in the experiments of which I was the intended subject. So I sought for ways to make my intentions known.

One day Jane brought a radio and left it on beside my pool. She has always claimed that this was not a deliberate experiment, but I think this is only an example of her humility, for Jane is always eager to minimize her decisive role in my career. In any case, I made her see in the clearest way then available—double flips, ardent splashing, gentle nosing toward the radio—that this was what I wanted, that the one thing I yearned for was to listen. It was she who had the idea of reversing the wire-tap by installing three speakers through which music could be piped in to me.

I admit that at first I could not understand any of it. Everything seemed clumped into bales of barely differentiated noise. There was too much going on in too small a space; the sounds lacked scope to soar or dip or to strike attitudes. I could not make out what they meant to communicate. It all seemed to me dull and homogeneous, as if one should listen into a thousand telephone conversations at once. I smile to think of it now but it took me a long while to distinguish pianos from guitars, oboes from clarinets, cellos from violas, Brahms from Buxtehude. Orchestral music was a dense reef of sound with little extent but astonishing thickness. I fared better with chamber music, especially violin sonatas; yet my earliest preference was for choral music, the more ancient the better. The first time I really felt that I had grasped something was when a friend of Jane's gave her a recording of some recently discovered 11th century liturgical music. These strange monodies spoke to me in almost my own tongue.

Real comprehension of what was going on in all this music evolved only gradually and, oddly, for the most part along historical lines. I recall the satisfaction I felt when I was first able to differentiate between the keyboard works of Bach, which quickly became favorites, and the pieces of Chopin, which initially I found inscrutable. The *Preludes* gave me so much trouble that for a long while Jane was under the impression that I had become a fanatical Romantic because I asked to listen to them over and over. For a while I thought Mozart and Haydn must be the same

Robert Wexelblatt

appealingly lucid person. Beethoven, by contrast, leapt out of the speakers individualized and as it were fully-dressed. From Stravinsky, a much later revelation, I picked up a great deal. What a deep bag of tricks! Jane loved the Beatles yet it is not for her sake alone that I grew so fond of *Sergeant Pepper* and *Abbey Road*. But enough. The process is tedious to relate, though it was exciting to live through. World upon world opened before me and perhaps, in my mounting enthusiasm, I made too great a demand on myself to assimilate it all. I shall never be much of a musicologist.

Another technical problem that had to be overcome if I were to compose was to devise an efficient and comprehensible method of notation. I could never have done this on my own, but happily Dr. Schultz came to my assistance.

Dr. Schultz was paid to work with me. I was not paid to work with him, a fact which, when I teased him about it, he explained only with great earnestness. He told me he wrote a proposal and received a grant from a foundation. While I had no use for a grant, I would nevertheless have enjoyed getting one. As Dr. Schultz himself taught me, there is no validation to compare with money. Largesse, philanthropy, charity, patronage are all subtly gradated terms for the moving of money from one condition to another, from potentiality to actuality, from purposelessness to purpose, accumulation to disbursement, guilt to need, greed to glory. All these previously distinct forms of generosity or investment have, Dr. Schultz explained, now been homogenized, bureaucratized into the processes of grant writing, peer reviewing, the securing of recommendations, the organizing of documentation, and evaluation by committees. These proceedings are complicated and time consuming, and, once communication between us became more confidential, Dr. Schultz liked to complain about them to me. The subject obsessed him. His whole status and career, he would whine, were only as secure as the next grant or grant renewal; for grants once granted can be renewed or withdrawn depending on the grantor's satisfaction with the achievements of the grantee, the machinations of jealous competitors, or even on the appeal of other worthy supplicants. Dr. Schultz was thus a nervous man, entirely unlike Jane. I pitied him for being on such a treadmill, always scheming, perpetually writing new proposals or inflating his reports on the old ones, vying with others like himself in need of money to carry on work they believed vital. His life seemed to me dreadful, yet there is no doubt he had his uses. He taught me about anxiety, about how different a Schultz can be from a Jane. But above all he showed me how I could, with the aid of a cleverly programmed computer, record and even orchestrate my compositions.

And so it was a combination of my nature, my beliefs about the character of existence, and the growing enthusiasm I felt for the music played for me, plus Dr. Schultz and his grant, that led me to become the composer Arno Meer, to become what is called, with or without irony, an artist.

The Fascination of the Human

Human beings have long fascinated us, a fact which I have noticed they find flattering. The attentions of their domestic animals, dogs in particular, are unsatisfactory because of the suspicion that these are conditioned rather than freely given. By contrast, any sign of affinity for the human on our part is interpreted in our favor, yet in a typically duplicitous fashion, since it is really being counted in humanity's favor. That is, humans construe our fascination with them in their own way, not stopping to consider the nature of fascination, which is always a combination of attraction and repulsion. To be fascinated by something is to be drawn toward and at the same time disgusted by it. The reason why fascination is paralyzing is that it is the vector of two opposite and approximately equal forces. The completely alien is not fascinating, nor is the utterly common. From these we easily turn aside.

Fascination is like metaphor. Dr. Schultz introduced me to the concept of metaphor when he read me something he said he thought I might like. "To see a world in a grain of sand" it began. I did like it, very much in fact, but as I considered this statement I saw that its point was double. On the one hand, the world is round and stony at its core, not unlike a grain of sand; the world contains much but, comically considered, is only one grain among billions. On the other hand, there is no denying that the world is not a grain of sand. "A grain of sand is a grain of sand," I retorted to Dr. Schultz, who then exerted himself to explain metaphor to me. Without any embarrassment he told me that a metaphor is pleasing when it is an untruth that is also a truth. This striking notion was itself fascinating, a real glimpse into the human psyche: a soul that can be fascinated by repellent lies it sees as attractive truths.

I believe we have always sensed that human beings are descendants of those among our ancestors who chose to stay on land, though whether out of bravery or cowardice, out of love of the solid or distaste for the liquid, we cannot decide. Were they fearful of the deeps in which breathing is always problematic or curious to see what further developments the divorce between life and water might lead to? Some argue one way, others the opposite, but most hold neither opinion. Yet we all share this fascination with creatures who, to put it in human terms, are like far-fetched metaphors for ourselves.

Among the most repellent differences between us must be counted hair, hair growing out of skin; for it is hard to imagine a surer sign of imperfection. Even to humans, smooth and rounded contours are the marks of beauty and perfection. Nothing could be more repulsive or at the same time more pitiable than the sight of a human being trying to make his way through water, all kicking ungainliness and hairy limbs. What humans regard as swimming is to us as laughable and melancholy a spectacle as a dog trying to ride a bicycle. Even with tight rubber suits and fins fitted on their feet, humans, while apparently much improved, only the more surely betray their flaws. I do not mean their functional faults but their aesthetic ones. This covering up, this mimicry, only makes one the more aware of what lies beneath all the cosmetic prostheses.

Vanity is universal, but that of humans is particularly touching because of the human belief that only they are vain. Once a professor read me a speech from an old play about which he wanted my opinion. I was so diverted by the speech that I memorized it. "What a piece of work is a man, how noble in reason, how infinite in faculties, in form and moving how express and admirable, in action how like an angel, in apprehension how like a god, the beauty of the world, the paragon of animals!" It is beautifully said, I told the professor, and extremely funny. He was surprised that I found it amusing. I explained to him that all one needed was to substitute the name of any species one liked for the word "man" and this speech would seem as apt and splendid to them as it apparently does to humans. "What a piece of work is a tuna!" He seemed so taken aback that to cheer him up I added, "After all, which among us is not a quintessence of dust?"

About Jane

Let me begin with her body. For a long while it was the only interesting object in my pool. This body was less repellent than those I had encountered earlier. It was superior with respect to roundness and smoothness. I rejoiced that she did not go in for those rubber suits that conjure up what they hide. Jane covered herself only partially, with two brief garments, thereby showing, as it appeared to me, more candor and less shame. Still, I could not prevent myself from noticing that her smoothness was less than perfect. Only later did I discover that she actually shaved her body. Imagine how poignant this seemed to me, how flattering. As Jane was always quicker to understand me than anyone else, I assumed she underwent this perilous and painful daily scraping for my sake.

As I have already said, fascination has the two aspects of repulsion and attraction which may be understood as responses to that which one is not and that which one cannot be. Human hair fascinates us. The short hairs that grow close to the skin, either standing upright or mashed unpleasantly against the surface and marring its potential glossiness, are extremely objectionable; however, the longer hair that comes from the head is an entirely different matter, so different that it might as well be a distinct substance. By the strange mechanisms of fascination, as much as body hair seems to us ugly, this hair, head hair, draws us to it as to an aesthetic marvel, especially when it is very long and fine such as that growing from certain females, like Jane.

I have seen representations of those chimeras called mermaids, thought by sailors to be so voluptuous. All have precisely this long, fine, hair which flows about the head as if liquefied; indeed, as if it came to life only when submerged. It might surprise humans to know that such a creature is no less seductive to us than to a seaman; indeed, the figure of the mermaid might have been expressly devised as an imaginary being signifying a union between our two species, a reunion of what was separated so long ago. The first time I was shown such a picture I amused those around my pool by innocently identifying it as Jane, who confused me by blushing charmingly. It is not overstating things to say that my love for Jane began with the hair on her head, which underwater appears a dark reddish brown and moves with a more sinuous grace than the tentacles of octopi or the tendrils of the man-of-war.

Jane was assigned to be my trainer. At first, of course, I had no notion of the intended nature of our relationship. As far as I could see, she had been provided as a companion and playmate, less instructor than guide, less keeper than generous purveyor of endless quantities of fish. This last point should not go unemphasized. I was almost as dazzled by Jane's ability to produce fresh fish as by her tresses. Little wonder that I should grow attached to such a creature. I was willing to overlook her awkwardness in the water; indeed, before long I found it touching. All clumsiness in females is generally appealing to males, giving their hearts a pang, perhaps because it puts them in mind of the condition of pregnancy. Clumsiness combined with grace, however, is quite irresistible and in Jane the two were ideally juxtaposed.

We spent hundreds of hours together in my pool. I was not surprised when Jane displayed a keen interest in my skin. She seemed to love touching it, rubbing gently with her hand to appreciate its smoothness. This conveyed to me her natural admiration for a perfection she lacked, and out of common decency I examined her in return. Her skin, once I got over the preliminary repugnance of its roughness, was not displeasing to the touch; moreover, it had one quality I found attractive. It was covered by randomly distributed dots of pigment whose name I later learned was freckles. How delightful!

I should say that I realized at once that Jane was a female, a fact to which, in my distressed state, I responded with relief and gratitude. I have always been susceptible to femininity and Jane exuded it to a high degree, not only in the clumsiness mentioned above, but also through the quality of her voice, into all of whose nuances I was soon initiated. For us, sound has a singular intimacy, able to pass with little mediation from the core of one being to another. It is true that at first her words meant nothing to me, but her voice meant everything. Between us was a language beneath language, surer, calmer, an unshakable bridge—in short, music.

So Jane was my trainer and train me she faithfully did. However, in circumstances where the trainer cannot understand the trainee (dogs can be understood only too well), training must be a two-fold operation, full of subtle reciprocities. The illusion of training is that subject and object are irreversible, fixed by the verb: Jane trained Arno; whereas it is less obvious but nonetheless true that Arno trained Jane. Had this not been so then there would hardly have grown up between us that fundamental communion on which our later communication was constructed. The intelligible must always be built on the ineffable.

So Jane's training was a mutual enterprise. For example, if she required me to fetch a ball when she shouted the syllable "Ball!" I would, as she raised the ball to throw it into the pool, indicate to her where I would prefer her to throw it. If she wished to touch my skin, I would propel my head over the side of the pool to show her just where her touch would be most welcome. Needless to say, our water play was a great deal more complex than these trivial operations; for here I became aware of her fragility and trust, conscious of what a trifling affair it would be for me to break her bones or deny her air until she ceased to breathe. It was, in part at least, this sense of unused power that delighted me in our various water sports, during which I trained Jane to do such things as climb on my back or to be thrown—gently of course—into the air.

The need to love is powerful in us. This love naturally seeks for an object. So one loves first of all because loving is among one's capacities, and one can be fortunate or unfortunate in giving this love. But once the decision is taken, the process moves quickly, as love, though itself unreasonable, is adept at finding reasons for itself. As Jane's various fragrances became more familiar to me—her skin smelled lightly of sweat and soap, her hair of something indefinably glorious—each one became lovable. Her skin, her voice, her hair, her odors, in fact every occasion she gave for the use of my senses became alike delectable. To me she was nurture, beauty, amusement, stimulation, and sympathy, but the greatest of these was sympathy. I did not need to ask myself what I was to her.

Moralizing My Capture

I remember three explosions. The first was above me. It thudded on my back and forced me into the lightless depths on a swell of pain.

Now I had always prided myself on my diving. If someone called for a contest, I was eager to participate. I generally won too, able to hold out longer, bear more pressure, endure greater darkness and cold than my competitors. They bore me no ill will. They all appreciated the heroism of my abysmal dives. When I breached the surface they were waiting for me, glad to see I was all right, proud of my daring, quick to congratulate. Now I had been forced deeper than ever before. When the second explosion detonated even closer, I swam with it at my side, the pain feeling as if it had lodged in my right flank. I went fast, trying to outswim my anguish,

147

to escape the confusing bubbles and the frightful noise. What's happening, I wondered. Where is everybody? A gobbet shot by me trailing blood. Just the thing to draw sharks, I recall thinking before I realized with horror what it really was. I must have lost consciousness after the third explosion.

Humans in rubber suits and fins. Arms encircling, hands touching roughly, grabbing and turning me, fingers doing things. I was helpless either to resist or to help, nor did I know whether their purpose was harm or aid. I was swallowing quantities of water and breathing was nearly impossible. Then the sling was secured and I suddenly found myself rising clear of the water, groggy and aching. My fins flapped uselessly and I was unable to arch my back. My tail, normally so powerful and deft, hung down like something dead. I shivered. The air on my body chilled me through and through. I swung back and forth in the air then landed on something odiously slippery and solid.

Solid, liquid, gas: it is amazing that these three conditions should determine all the physics of our lives. Some believe that even in music there are the solid, liquid, and gaseous.

It was only an accident, they assured me much later and without so much as a display of embarrassment. You and your friends wandered into a testing area. Too bad, really. Nobody's fault. That's the way it goes.

There are many kinds of accidents, the worst being the coincidental; that is, when things that would be much better off not coming together do: a knife and your heart, a luxury liner and an iceberg, an asteroid and the earth—a depth charge and Arno Meer. The term *accident* is essentially a metaphysical alibi, short circuiting analysis by robbing an event of its ethical potentiality. Without the possibility of analysis the occurrence, no matter how decisive, becomes essentially uninteresting: it cannot be wrapped up in discourse; there are no borders to examine, no turning points between style and morality, no way to distinguish between intention and negligence. If I am to believe what they told me, then my capture (they favor the word rescue) was meaningless despite being the most consequential episode in my life.

There is something offensive in this incommensurability and yet I have to admit it has the starkness of truth. We were swimming, the depth charges were being tested. We were all intent on our own purposes while another purpose, belonging to no one, loomed up invisibly and overtook us all.

Well, I suppose life is like that. The decisions we make rough in the margins of our lives, but it is always the accidents that form its hard core. Meaning gathers around a kernel of meaninglessness. The pearl that we intend forms around the unintended, haphazard grain of sand in which we should indeed be able to see a world.

About My Home

Like the universe or a scallop shell, my pool is large enough for some purposes, too small for others. The pool proper is square with ample floor space on each side for my equipment, Jane, Dr. Schultz, and the others who come to see me. Overhead is a skylight that I am able to open and shut electronically. The sides and floor of the pool are painted to make the water appear a matchless turquoise. You might visualize the pool as the center of elaborate systems of drainage, grids for electrical wiring, ventilation conduits, several computers with their printers and modems, climate control devices, and my synthesizers. Dr. Schultz once referred to the complicated aggregate as a machine for living, a memorable phrase but one to which I objected. Not wishing to claim credit for the expression, he told me that machine for living was what a famous architect said a home ought to be. By then Dr. Schultz and I were capable of frank as well as urbane conversation. I told him I saw a disparity between a home conceived as an efficient mechanism for daily activities and one that amounts to more than a standing agglomeration of wood, wire, and concrete, one that can be drenched in the warm light of possession; that is, I told him that I thought a home should be a place that takes upon itself a weight of meaning exceeding its functions, a place about which one would, if ever one lost it, feel nostalgia. My understanding of old houses may be theoretical, but nostalgia I can appreciate in the most personal way.

This pool about which I can imagine myself feeling nostalgic, so tied up is it with music and Jane, with Dr. Schultz and our many break-throughs, both battleground and sanctuary, was not my first repository after the accident. That place was quite different, one to which I felt myself consigned owing to an unfortunate event, an event which made a hash out of any wish I might ever formulate.

This first pool was rectangular, a bit smaller than my present home, with rows of benches on two sides. It was not empty when I arrived. In it was Mugs. Mugs was a year or two younger than I, a bit smaller, and already thoroughly housebroken. How astonished I was to see him doing flips and fetching plastic toys whenever a human made some peremptory gesture and barked out his name. Poor Mugs didn't even do it just for the fish; he obeyed for the sake of obeying; it actually gave him pleasure to obey.

Mugs had been brought up in captivity; consequently, we had almost nothing in common. He judged me to be morose; I deemed him an imbecile. If the purpose of our cohabitation was for me to learn from Mugs it succeeded only in this: that I realized one of my alternatives was infant-ilization. Actually, Mugs was worse than a baby—he resembled the trained dog on a bicycle. Though I pitied him, I could not make myself care for him and repulsed all his childish efforts to win me over. I preserved my distance. After all, it was only too obvious what he wanted to win me over *to*.

I don't wish to exaggerate or seem ungrateful. At first it wasn't so bad being with Mugs. In fact, I was glad of the company, given how physically hurt I was, how helpless and disoriented. His constant nudging, though no doubt he meant it to be reassuring, irritated me and often hurt. I tried as best I could to answer his foolish questions and even made some efforts to educate him, but it was useless. Mugs did not believe what I told him and besides was simple minded. The longer I stayed with him the more his foolishness grated on and depressed me.

I had been there about two weeks when one morning a large number of small human children filed onto the benches on either side of the pool. A very hairy male human with a device for amplifying his voice talked to the children and shouted commands to Mugs. He also referred frequently to *Arno*, which was what somebody had decided I was to be called. Mugs really put himself out that day, flipping, twisting, fetching, splashing, diving, breaching, and clicking like mad. As for me, I was appalled by this shameless display of submissiveness, of undignified eagerness to please. I begged him to stop, but Mugs was proud of turning himself inside out for those squealing youngsters. He even tried to inveigle me to perform too, bumping against me by way of encouragement. Of course I did nothing of the sort. I merely basked, doing my utmost to show my contempt for the proceedings. That was the day my irritation with Mugs turned to disgust and I set myself to find some way to be rid of him.

My first thought sickened me almost as much as Mugs's per-formance. I actually considered killing him. I immediately pushed this thought away with compunction. However, it did seem to me that nothing short of violence was likely to free me from my circumstances. My second thought was therefore to kill myself but, as I've already mentioned, this alternative was less than appealing. Perhaps it would be enough just to rough Mugs up a bit, not so much as to harm him but enough to make it clear that we didn't belong together, that what I needed was to be released at once or at least given solitary confinement. I saw three drawbacks to this plan: a) that I would have to attack Mugs in cold blood, b) that given my impaired physical capacities the attack might not succeed, and c) I would have to rely on humans to understand what such an assault was meant to signify.

I was still puzzling over a course of action when the whole issue was resolved, and in a highly satisfactory way.

Mugs appeared to be in anguish as the winch's gears ground and they started hoisting me aloft (this time I was as cooperative as they could wish). I did not deceive myself that whatever he was feeling would last out the day. Even as I was being laid on my trolley I could see him giving in to the consoling caresses of his master. Mugs's feelings were like barracudas: narrow and capable of biting deeply, but not around for long. All the same, I gave him the most cheerful farewell I could manage. This took some self-mastery because, relieved as I was to be out of there, I was nonetheless filled with trepidation. Was I about to be released, moved into a worse situation, or what?

My apprehension increased in proportion to the dryness of my skin. The sensation of desiccation is more than just uncomfortable. It is akin to an anxiety attack. You feel yourself in danger of crumbling and blowing away, but at the same time you become so ponderous that your muscles can barely work. Everything slows down except your heart and lungs which accelerate the processing of oxygen, for there is now too much of it, air all around. Your whole being longs for the pliancy of the liquid world but feels only the nothingness of gases and then, still worse, the harsh and angular surfaces of solids.

Suddenly Jane was at my side. Her first act of kindness was to toss a bucket of water over my flanks. Her second was to lean close and croon "Golden Slumbers."

I know now that my pool was specially constructed, though not expressly for me. The designers were asked to conceive a laboratory for a

Robert Wexelblatt

wide range of experiments; the subject, to be chosen later, was in a sense the least important element of all that had to be disposed. Under one aspect, my pool continues to be this laboratory and nothing more; that is, the convergence of a number of "hard" and permanent systems with one "soft," replaceable center—namely me, Arno Meer. Considered in this way, it is absurd to call the pool *my home*. It could more aptly be called "my lab" by the scientists who use it as an instrument that properly belongs to them. As a sign, the pool would then signify something that excluded me. It would be static while I am dynamic, a transient feature, something moved in that could easily be moved out again. Jane could as well call the bus on which she rides here each day *her bus* as I could call the pool *my home*.

The difference between the pool as lab and the pool as home is that between something that contains me and something that is me, becoming the sign not for a set of experiments but of Arno Meer, much as his shell is the sign of the turtle. Conceived as a container (pen, corral, prison), the pool enforced on me the condition of passivity; it held a subject for experimentation aimed at increasing the knowledge of others. To envision it as my home I would need to make it a stage and myself the leading actor, protagonist of those little dramas called experiments.

The transformation of the pool from their laboratory to my home began even before I was aware of it. It started the moment I was lowered into its water, gleamingly turquoise and gloriously empty, like a miniature tropic sea the instant after its creation. I was simply overjoyed to plunge into the pool and I realize now it was this happiness that kicked off the metamorphosis. Joy is itself a species of possession: for the happy prisoner the penitentiary is hardly penitential. I swam around, I flipped, I splashed clumsily owing to my wounds, yet almost as gaily as Mugs with an audience. For me this was no performance but a way of declaring that the place was mine.

As I had foreseen, my subsequent persistence in making all experiments interactive, collaborative efforts revolutionized the politics of the pool. It was not built for me, but after a few weeks it might as well have been. I did not extrude it from myself, as the nautilus does its shell, but I did succeed in making it my refuge, my classroom and, in the fullness of time, my conservatory and studio.

Soirées Musicales

Composed, played, performed, listened to, appreciated, criticized, loved. These seven predicates can all be attached to music. Notice that with the first three verbs it is the active mood that predominates, in the last three the passive, while the fourth, the one in the middle, can be either. That is, listening to music is a greatly diluted form of composition and at the same time a feeble mode of criticism. Listening to music can be complex. At least it was for me.

It was from listening that I learned to compose, but it is no less true that it was from my attempts at composition that I mastered listening. For me, listening and composing flowed into one another. The more I did of one, the more I wanted to do of the other.

My muse is Jane, Dr. Schultz my mentor. All my work is tacitly dedicated to them. As for my masters, both wet and dry, they are beyond enumeration.

It was with an ironic smile that Dr. Schultz told me music has been called *the universal language.* "In so far as it is like mathematics or weeping," I replied wryly. Music that is universal is denatured music. It is music that is only a sign that blinks "music." When music becomes so characterless and abstracted as to be universal, then it strikes everyone the same way. Fifty violins raising the glucose level of a love scene, hokey arrangements of blues in elevators, easy listening piped into dentists' offices, Mozart in margarine advertisements—Jane has told me about them all, has played me tapes. My gorge rose. This was music that had ceased to be music in every sense *except* as a universal language. One does not listen to it; one does not even really notice it, unless one wishes to be nauseated.

No, I had no desire to create anything in a universal language. Understanding of any language is surely open to all, as my experience proves; however, there is no living universal language. What I sought in composing was not a way of communicating to everyone. Using sound to communicate is to music as grunting is to poetry.

The ideal relationship between a composer and a listener would be an understanding that precedes language, an intimacy that language can only disturb. Of course I am thinking of a specific embodiment of this ideal; it is the communion that existed between Jane and me prior to our famous breakthrough. There is in such a relationship ample room for ambiguity, richness, and empathy, but none for misunderstanding, duplicity, or sarcasm. In those early days especially Jane and I could be only ourselves because there was no language out of which to construct alternative selves, social masks or pretensions. Insincerity was impossible. We did not even have the means to live up to what we conceived to be the other's expectations.

False or uninspired music is always semantic, aimed at communicating, at making an impression. That is why it never sounds particularly good.

I scored my first composition for solo viola. It was a more formalized and disciplined version of my nocturnal rhapsody. From it I learned the perilously hard distinction between style and mannerism and something of the mathematics of form.

Next came a short piece for string quartet. From composing it I learned the nature of musical conversation and the difference between the half-measure of imitating the masters and the decisive one of robbing them.

My third piece was a piano sonata in three movements. From this piece I learned how to string musical ideas together like pearls on a necklace, like teeth in a jawbone. I also discovered what is possible for a performer, what is not, and the pointlessness of writing the latter.

My fourth piece was a suite for piano and clarinet. From this I learned methods for achieving balance and internal consistency in relation to the definitive musical qualities of repetition and variation (too much of either one and you no longer have music but either a dial tone or noise).

My fifth piece was a set of variations for solo piano. From it I learned nothing whatsoever because it was successful.

It is true that the *Concerto for Orchestra* is by far my "most ambitious effort to date," as the critics say, though without explaining the exact nature of this ambition. What was my ambition? To join the masters, of course. Anything else would not be an ambition.

An ingenious critic has given my work a kind of elemental interpretation. He begins by dividing up sounds into liquid and solid. Bowed strings, for example, are liquid, while percussion is solid. In piano pieces the right hand is liquid, the left solid; legato passages are watery, chords clod-like, and so forth. His next move is to essentialize the categories, as he puts it, which means to assign qualities or concepts to each type of sound. Thus the liquid represents such things as peace, unity with nature, the maternal, flux, playfulness, sexuality; while the solid stands for contention, aggression, struggle, confinement, rebellion, conviction, the simultaneous manipulation and resistance of materials, death.

In this way he attempts to read my music as dualistic, sometimes with forces balanced and reconciled, at others clashing or deadlocked. Something which ought to give even orthodox Manicheans pause is his eagerness to convert my compositions into narratives. Keys and motifs become characters, instruments events, development sections entire dramas. The sheer inventiveness of his article about the *Concerto for Orchestra* left me gasping for breath, as after too deep a dive. The review reads like the plot summary of a Russian novel. (Dr. Schultz chose two of Dostoyevsky's for me from the library's books-on-tape section.)

I could simply deny there is any truth to what this critic says, insist that my intentions were very far from programmatic, let alone novelistic. I might protest that I have never conceived of sounds as solids or liquids. But it would be useless. For this fellow I am a unique and entirely theoretical being and for a theoretical being nothing but a theory will do. Nor is there anything for him to learn from the horse's mouth, since he claims to base his interpretation on what I am not conscious of and this move is, of course, unanswerable.

What he is really doing is imposing the little he knows of my biography onto my music, a thing he feels well qualified to do, though he insists that I myself am unqualified to see any connection between my life and what I compose. What is essential to the critic is that I was rudely plucked from the watery world and set down in one he imagines to be solid (he knows nothing of my pool). He then presumes to find in these facts the root of the entire exfoliation of my music. Once he started down this garden path, there was no stopping him.

I cannot help feeling that this man longs to substitute his interpretation for my compositions so that what he has made will be more admired than what I have made. As for the latter, like most theorists he begins by setting aside the obvious, that what I have made is music, so eager is he to translate my musicality into the terms of a psychology he gaily believes to be unprecedented but at the same time quite simple.

I would enjoy meeting this very clever fellow, but I doubt he would embrace any opportunity to see me in the flesh.

The one unmentionable joy of composing is the power that one derives from being a composer. The notes, those who perform them, and even to some extent those who listen to them are all in my power, so long as I can keep it up.

Would I crave this power if my circumstances were not what they are? That is, to what degree is composition really compensation—not for social alienation, but for the absence of another sort of power or for being where such power is neither needed nor imaginable? Music is a way of relating to other beings, one that I can control and for which I even receive adulation. I ask myself, are these effects in danger of turning into motives?

In music I discover the world; in composing I discover myself. Sounds good, doesn't it?

As I swim slowly up and down my pool on a summer night with my skylight open to the moon, at ease with the loneliness I myself insisted on, far from others of my species with whom I recall taking such comforts as nature affords our kind, submerged in water though not the sea, subsisting on land but not solid ground, poised midway between buoyancy and gravity, having learned much and forgotten little, I conjure up sounds, harmonious and dissonant. I know my position and yet I am not discontent with its hopelessness.

Envoi

Why haven't I returned to the sea? I know I cannot complete this memoir without taking up the question.

I could blame my wounds, especially the deep gash on my right side that healed badly so that my flipper is permanently impaired. There are those who claim that this wound is actually the cause both of the break-through and of composing. It seems the alternative to alienation for those who need to see what I do as filling a lack is simply damage. No ability without debility—that appears to be their slogan.

Another theory: I have become humanized to such an extent that either I am no longer fitted for the unfettered life of the ocean or am fearful of spreading dangerous knowledge among my kind. This last point is still another instance of the inverted humility of humankind.

Yet another: I am following the imperative of my talent. I have a vocation. All artists love to do what they must, and in order to compose I have to stay put.

And one more: The scientists will never let me go because I have become, so to speak, an industry. I am their meal ticket—as they, of course, are mine.

I could add further to this proliferation of reasons (why overlook my deep attachment to Jane, for example?), and I would not trouble to dispute a single one of them.

Nor would I deny that the memory of leaping freely through the swells in the company of creatures whose perfection I had to lose to appreciate torments me with its sweetness. The camaraderie and exultation of our old diving contests, the charm of new pups, the deliciously tender flanks of their mothers, the salt taste of wild fish, the sumptuous marvels of submarine forests—all these and more I not only remember but strive to put into my music. But that is what I do. I no longer think of reclaiming them.

Can any of us deny that we are the equivalent of what we have become, that we are what life has done with us?

Arno Meer

Z

I've just been watching the fighting from the hotel roof. It's not exactly safe up there. Yesterday afternoon one of the second violins got half his head blown off. Wilhelm says the man's name was Heiser. I'll bet it was no stray round either. Some scared gunman who probably hadn't eaten for days or washed for weeks probably resented the idea of performing for such an insignificant audience, one bald-headed touring second violinist taking in the sights. When I went up I took Wilhelm's video camera and made sure that they got a good look at me pointing it. The guys with the assault rifles, the rocket-propelled grenades, those little portable mortars, and fifty-caliber jeeps like having their images recorded and, who knows, maybe flashed around the world. Celebrity is where you find it. Some even wave at me and strike Ramboesque poses. The "Hi, Mom" syndrome. If CNN turned a camera on me I could do it too.

"Hi, Mom. Here I am halfway around the world in the middle of some bloody revolution. Toodaloo virginity, by the way. The hotel's pretty nice, considering, but of course the concerts were canceled and we can't get out. I know. You're probably thinking I'm betraying all your hopes, throwing away chances, risking my life. But honestly, Mom, I'm only doing my best."

I'll turn nineteen next October 22. Three months ago, thanks to a four-year all-expenses-paid merit scholarship, I was starting the second semester of my freshman year at the University of Pennsylvania. Six schools offered me pretty much the same deal but Philly was closer to home than New Haven, Boston, Ann Arbor, or the Coast so I chose Penn. I was settling in nicely. I had a decent roommate and half-a-dozen friends. Academically, I was kicking ass and my playing was better than ever. I had hopes of being featured in the spring concert. Then, toward the end of January, I seduced the thirty-six-year-old conductor Wilhelm Kraus. His orchestra was on a tour. There were to be two performances at the Academy of Music, Friday night and Saturday. The eminent violin soloist

Robert Wexelblatt

who was supposed to play the Barber concerto with them came down with stomach flu at the last minute and all the other big shots they called were either booked already or also puking. So somebody desperate, the orchestra manager I guess, phoned the University and they sent me. As it happened, I'd been working on the Barber for the spring concert. That's just the way life is, the really *decisive* things anyway—luck and timing, sometimes good, sometimes bad.

Wilhelm was born in what used to be called The German People's Democratic Republic, East Germany, but now it's just the poor third of Germany. He makes jokes about the inept political indoctrination he endured in elementary school, but I can tell he kind of liked the idealism of a socialist society. Sometimes he's just disgusted by his own materialism. It's charming, actually.

The age difference doesn't bother me at all—in fact, I'm very fond of it, but it's on Wilhelm's mind. He's all the time reminding me how young thirty-six is for a conductor and in a way that suggests eighteen is ripe for a violinist.

"We conductors routinely live into our eighties, our nineties," he said to me yesterday, "and do you know why?"

"Four reasons," I say and tick them off on my fingers which he subsequently kissed. "All the aerobic exercise, frequent mnemonic work-outs, absolutely ceaseless public adulation, and plenty of power."

He nodded his head before smooching my fingers. Wilhelm has lots of good German conductor's hair and it flopped fetchingly over his forehead. He laughed a *gemütlich* laugh, the very model of a Teuton with both a sated libido and a gratified *Wille zur Macht*.

I had never seduced anybody before, let alone a celebrity. Frankly, I've always been suspicious of sex. I think the mistake most people make sexually is to confuse ends with means. A few years ago I realized that sex is a means contrived by nature to speed up evolution, a kind of technological breakthrough to replace slow and inefficient cell division. Nature contrived sex in such a cunning way that people think it's *their* end rather than *her* means. We want the cookie, but the cookie's just a trick—feel good, pay big or screw in haste, repent at leisure. I didn't intend to be tricked. As a precaution I went on the Pill before I left for Penn. That's our riposte to nature, our brainy counter-measure. Despite my looks it wasn't that hard to manage an intercourseless high school social life—guys are reluctant to hit on girls with grades as high as mine no matter what they look like—but I was worried about college, given all I'd heard and read. Still, I made it through the first semester with my maidenhead intact. I had my chances and enough beer to take one of them but nobody really tempted me. So maybe the seduction was just beginner's luck. Could be, but the fact is I've succeeded at everything I've ever really tried to do—so far at least. I suppose that sounds vain, but it isn't.

Ever notice the sort of things people like being praised for? For instance, my roommate Carla beams whenever someone says she's gorgeous. But I see Carla first thing in the morning. She didn't like it when I said she really knows how to dress and use make-up. My friend Kyle, he's a math major, just loves it when somebody says how *brilliant* he is. You should have seen the frown he laid on me when I told him how I admire all the effort he puts into studying. See my point? People prefer to be congratulated for things they aren't responsible for. They want to be told that nature lavished intelligence, beauty, and wit on them; they don't like hearing about perseverance, hard work, that they've done the most with what they've got. To me that's plain irrational. But then I'm a freak. I'm very rational. But I don't deserve any credit for that either. I know there's nothing praiseworthy about my being beautiful, level-headed, musically gifted, good in school, or even succeeding at seducing Wilhelm Kraus on the first go because I know exactly where all these things come from. I even know who was deprived of them for my sake.

WXYZ. That's what they called us—my parents and the newspapers. It was my dad's panicky little joke. You see, my mom wasn't getting pregnant. She'd had enough of means; she wanted the end. This was no problem for my father, who I think of as a means-for-ends kind of guy. In my opinion it wasn't necessarily that he didn't want kids; I think he probably didn't care one way or the other. As I see it, he was happy with the way things were but he didn't have the nerve to say so to Mom. Or maybe it was more than that, I mean that before *we* came along *he* got to be the child. Or maybe if there'd been just *one* of us he'd have stuck around. If I ever run into him, I'll have to remember to ask. Anyway, as I say, Mom did care. Big time. There she was—thirty-five, then thirty-eight. It ate at her. So she went to be tested and she made Dad get tested, too. This was nineteen years ago, remember; fertility therapy was still brandnew, semi-experimental. The doctors identified the trouble and told Mom there were things they could try. I can just see the way her ears must have pricked up. So, *without telling Dad*, she started taking this new drug.

And that's why she had four of us at once. Enough ends to swamp the means, you could say. She was forty-one at the time; Dad was forty-five. We came out one after the other, the two boys then my sister and finally me. Last but not least. WXYZ: Wystan first, Xavier second, Yvette third, and then yours truly, Zelda. It was Dad who called us WXYZ, like some easy listening station, his cute way of saying no more or rather too many.

So we spelled the end of the alphabet and, two years later, the end of my parents' marriage. Before I left for school Mom showed me Dad's note which she kept folded up in her satin jewelry box. I could have guessed. He had written one long self-reproach. This is the ploy of selfishness when it wants to be disarming and make a pre-emptive strike. The thing was typewritten which made you imagine the rough drafts. The way I see it, Dad must have figured he had about fifteen semi-good years left and being the father of the WXYZ quads wasn't even semi-good. So he took off to make the most of what he had left and Mom became poor, not that she'd ever been rich before. We moved in with our grandparents who did their best to take care of us but seemed simply overwhelmed. Both were dead in three years. We got to keep their house and the insurance money helped. Mom's job in the dress shop didn't pay nearly enough and she found another as an administrative assistant at a big paper company where she still works. The paper company paid better than the dress shop but, even cutting down expenses and having the house rent-free, we were still squeezed for money and space. To give him his due, for a few years Dad did send some cash but that dried up pretty quickly. No forwarding address. Maybe he seduced somebody too.

Does it go without saying that we all despised our names? No one more than me. I mean, really—Zelda? Wystan calls himself Buck because he says there aren't any English fruits named Buck. Xavier says he can live with Xav (Zave), but just barely. Yvette answers to Yvie (Evie) unless she's near the nadir of one of her mood-swings, in which case you have to call her Yelena Petrovna. This, I confess, was my doing. When we were about fourteen and I was devouring Russian novels Yvette's rapid-recycling manic-depression began to manifest itself. I figured such heroic, self-annihilating despondency demanded something Slavic. Dad's name is Peter. Or it was.

Yvette's manic-depression didn't show up until puberty hit, but Wystan's ADD was obvious a lot earlier, and Xavier's dyslexia. Both of them had asthma, allergies galore, were prone to ear infections, regularly got into trouble at school. From her first period Yvette's cramps were paralyzing (I had none). All three of my siblings got terrible grades, were badly coordinated, tended to be forgetful, clumsy. To be perfectly frank, they are not prepossessing specimens, not the sort anyone would find seductive. Wystan/Buck stopped growing at five foot four and weighs about a hundred and eighty pounds. He's got this flat, oily hair and the kind of complexion that goes with perpetually clogged pores. Xavier's height is normal but he throws fits (of rage? of spastic libidinousness?) and weighs just over a hundred pounds. Yvette is big, puffy, ankleless, and her hands shake because of all the medication she's on. So my siblings have no talents, no beauty, and nobody would call them bright. Don't get me wrong. They can be terrific, but I wouldn't say they're particularly sweet. I love them all. I think a lot about everything I owe them.

Sometimes I try to picture things back in the womb, especially on the day we were born, between four and four-nineteen p.m. I get this image of all the gifts of nature that should have been distributed equally among us somehow draining backwards, collecting in a little pool of residual amniotic fluid, and bathing me, the last, Zelda. I got all the good looks, the athleticism (I won three gymnastics tournaments before I developed these perfectly shaped breasts); I got the whopping I.Q., the winning smile (never a cavity while poor Yvette already has a bridge and both the boys need braces). I'm the one with the dry sense of humor and a musical talent that, if more equitably allocated, might have produced a creditable string quartet. While W, X, and Y can't even carry a tune I play the violin well enough to seduce Wilhelm Kraus, a guy who lives for music.

"It's just not fair," Yvette would moan sometimes, but she never got mad at me and, of course, I never argued the point with her. We were in total agreement. I had robbed them all but it wasn't my fault.

In tenth-grade Honors English I blew up when Mr. Villiers started in on how Oedipus, because of what he called his arrogance, his hubris, was guilty for marrying his mother and killing his father.

"Like hell!" I blurted out. Everybody turned toward me with big eyes. Even Mr. Villiers looked a little scared. I went on vehemently. "Isn't it obvious the whole thing's a set-up? I mean it all happened before he was even born." I had gotten a copy of *Oedipus at Colonus* out of the library; they never assign that one in high school. I opened it up and read Villiers the section where Oedipus says it wasn't his fault but the Fates'. "They knew; they, who devised this trap for me, they knew!" You see, he's

Robert Wexelblatt

whining but not unreasonably. Well, I had to see him as a victim, didn't I, and Antigone, Ismene, Eteocles, and Polyneices too. AIEP. As you can imagine, I have strong views on family curses.

Anybody can see at a glance why Pfrüde would never make it as a soloist. He looks too much like a sidekick. Pfrüde's an ideal concert-master, part virtuoso, part martinet, completely uncharismatic and eager to keep his snug berth for life. He works hard at concealing his resentment of me and I appreciate his efforts. Wilhelm treats him stiffly, though not without respect. Pfrüde prefers formality from both superiors and inferiors; he has a bureaucratic appreciation of stratification and decorum. I think it's fun to tease him.

"Herr Pfrüde," I said to him when he came to our table at lunch. He wanted to tell Wilhelm something but Wilhelm was talking to somebody else. "Do you know this one? What's the most important difference between a violin and a viola?"

As the Maestro wasn't looking he allowed himself to make a face at me, a sort of astonished/disgusted expression.

"The viola burns longer," I said. At that moment Wilhelm turned around and gave my arm a secret squeeze. Pfrüde noticed it, which pleased me all the more.

"Maestro," he said seriously, "I've been on the phone to the embassy again. They say they're still trying to arrange transport for us."

"That's good of them, but where to?"

"To the airport, of course."

"Isn't the airport one of the places they're killing each other over?"

Pfrüde looked ruefully down at my tuna salad. "It's possible a cease-fire can be worked out . . . a safe-conduct . . ."

All this to the pink-pink-pink of bullets striking walls, the not distant enough crump of explosions.

When Wilhelm announced that I would be joining the orchestra for the remainder of their tour Pfrüde was the first, as protocol required, to respond.

"And what of the young lady's studies at her university?"

Continentally condescending, that *her*. Wilhelm winced. Though hardly expressing a keen pleasure at having me around, Pfrüde was at least showing concern for my welfare. He made it sound like anxiety of the

164

avuncular sort.

I leapt into the breach. "I've taken a leave-of-absence." This was not actually true. I had played the Barber Friday night, spent Saturday afternoon with Wilhelm, played even better that night and had my wicked way with him well into Sunday (several times). This was only Monday morning and I hadn't even called Carla, let alone a dean. In fact, it hadn't occurred to me to take a leave, not even when Wilhelm proposed I join the tour; but now I considered it as good as approved, stamped, and explained to Mom. Under the circumstances how could the University turn me down? I'd be a nice bit of plumage in the music department's cap, wouldn't I? A real ornament of the institution when—if—I returned.

Perhaps you think calling what I did a *seduction* is too dramatic, too literary? You may suppose I'm an out-of-control brat who's read too much. No, I don't think so. How can a seduction be too literary when the only models you've got for how to go about it are books and movies? I mean, it's not the sort of skill you pick up at home, at least not from forty-five-year-old single mothers. Sexual attraction comes naturally, of course, but not the things people do about it. Anyway, for the record, here's how I remember it.

The phone call came around quarter to six when I might easily have been out. Another twenty minutes and I'd have been at dinner, which, incidentally, I never ate that night. It was hard to take in that Professor MacKenzie was telephoning me let alone what he was saying. At least he spoke slowly, clearly, precisely.

"Now, Zelda. They need of a soloist for the Barber tonight and again tomorrow evening. They'd prefer a local student, somebody young and promising. I told them that I have a very gifted pupil who by a happy chance has been working on the Barber. They were delighted and are willing to take a chance on you. As you can imagine, I have to phone them back right away and let them know if you're willing. What do you say? It's a colossal opportunity, Zelda. Feel up to it?"

I plumped down on my bed. MacKenzie, though encouraging, had never exactly drenched me with compliments. "'You think I'm very gifted?'"

He laughed. "I think you're up to it. Besides, if you agree I get two free tickets."

I had had crushes, of course, even in high school. In tenth grade a new boy transferred into our school. He was from Dayton, Ohio, which sounded to me like a clean, but marvelously romantic place. Dayton— sparkling city of dreams. He had dark hair and what used to be called an olive complexion. Because he was new I cast him as a brooding outsider and decided that he was glamorous in a sealed-off sort of way, the kind of bright young male I had found in many books, driven into himself to the point of concentrated, furious passion. The boy was placed into my honors English class and the first book Mrs. Roth assigned that January was *Wuthering Heights*. So what would you expect? Sexually, what I briefly felt for that Daytonian was purely mental; it only filtered down, so to speak. With Wilhelm it's the other way around. The mental part came last—it's still coming—but the sexual tug came at once, like a switched-on electro-magnet. When I saw him up there on that stage so close to me, lifting up my lyric passages with his strong arms, grinning at me during the finale like the god of music in a freshly pressed tuxedo, the music washing all over his sensitive European face . . . oh, my. Most musicians feel music physically, but you could see he felt every single note. His look of ecstasy during the first movement floored me. I wanted to see more of that; I wanted to be personally responsible for that ecstasy, not just through the medium of my fiddling.

I played the Barber as gut-sucking emotion; it was the first gambit of my seduction, though even I didn't yet guess what was afoot. That long opening melody, packed with nostalgia, became my siren's song, a soloist's striptease. The notes were secondary to the feeling; I felt I was playing essences. By the last movement I decided that Barber blessed our union.

Later on, at the reception, I could see it was going to be up to me sex-wise. Though he wasn't patronizing, Wilhelm "behaved like a perfect gentleman," a phrase women often use with disappointed irony. By then, of course, I was determined that he should be perfectly *im*perfect.

It wasn't easy but we were both under the spell of the music so that's what I used. I'm sure it must be an old story but the whole business was new to me and, so far as I could tell at the time, it was new to Wilhelm too. I know now he was married for a couple of years back in his twenties. The foolish woman made him choose between music and her. There had been women since then, naturally. I wouldn't have wanted him to be a novice. But with me, it would be different. "With you everything's different," he assured me that first night.

It was a night of nothing but firsts—my début. It was, for instance, that night I first caught on to the sexual character of my instrument. The violin's curved just like a woman (of the Mae West type), with apertures and guts that thrill. Rub them properly, lovingly, and you can hear the raptures of a soprano. The bow is just as obviously male: long and stiff, yet not unyielding, not without some tender give. If all goes well, if horsehair meets catgut with passionate sympathy, the male makes the female sing, as I indeed sang that night. I gave out with an involuntary trill that, I couldn't help noticing, had an encouraging effect on Herr Kraus. Thereafter, I believe he looked forward to this little operatic tribute; he was certainly willing to work for it. As for me, I won't say I discovered that my suspicions about sex were unfounded. No, what I did find out was the power of nature's means of getting us to make more of ourselves and why people want to make an end out of flesh, sheet, shudders. Willi was no more amazed at my voracity than I was myself. It was a honeymoon, that weekend, perhaps a honeymoon *avant le fait*. I discovered how to lose and find myself at the same time, a paradox I would have liked to think through. But thinking just wasn't feasible. No time for it. Or maybe I'm just too inexperienced to gain any distance, to push experience into abstraction. Anyway, my wishes weren't abstract; they were musical. What I craved was repetition and variation and that's what music essentially is, repetition and variation. Well, Wilhelm's a conductor with range. Beethoven, Rachmaninoff, Handel. He can make love *largo, allegro, maestoso—mai non troppo*.

We were lying in the big hotel bed on Sunday morning when I told Wilhelm about my being a quad. He didn't say a word. Instead he pulled down the sheet and began to examine me from head to toe like a dermatologist searching for tell-tale moles. I giggled as he ran his index finger all over my body and asked what he thought he was doing. "Shh," he said. Germans can shush very soothingly, incidentally. I calmed down, and he went on with his work. "No, it's impossible," he concluded, having worked his way all the way down. Holding my left foot tenderly between his conductor's palms he gave the arch a little kiss. "Such perfection can't be duplicated, certainly not quadruplicated. America is a country full of marvels but I refuse to believe it."

I laughed. "We're not identical. We're not a bit like each other, in fact. Four eggs, four sperm cells, forty-six chromosomes, a new throw of the dice every time."

He nuzzled my belly. "Tell me more," he commanded. The conductor wanted a cadenza, so I gave him one.

As I talked about W, X, and Y he lay my head on his chest and began to stroke my hair. I think he may even have shut his eyes the way I had seen him do while I was playing the Barber. Anyway, he listened the way musicians listen, every bit as attentive to over- and undertones as to melodies and harmonies.

Wilhelm quickly grasped what I suppose was the Big Undertone of my story.

"You think a gift confers responsibility and that every such gift must deprive somebody else. But you oughtn't to feel that way, Zelda. You didn't drive your father away; your siblings aren't troubled because of you, and that your mother had to struggle isn't your fault. You're completely innocent, Zelda. Just look at you!"

I knew I wasn't innocent at all, but I snuggled up against him. Who wouldn't?

"I hate my name," I said happily.

"Not me," he sighed.

W, X, and Y live at home with Mom. I'm sure it wouldn't occur to my brothers to do otherwise, even now that they're bringing in some cash. In September Wystan/Buck started a job in the mailroom at the paper company; Xavier bags at the supermarket. Yvette/Yelena alone yearns to go out into the world, but it's impossible. She's nowhere near well enough to hold down a job; it's only thanks to perpetual adjustments of her uppers and downers that she can function at all. Now that Mom got cable Yvette watches a lot of old movies. She talks to the cat, keeps the house spick and span, even does some cooking. I told all this to Wilhelm on the plane. He wanted to cheer me up and said that doubtless my sister's much less miserable than I imagine, that it would only be natural for me to project on to her how I might feel in such circumstances. I let him go on like this, let myself get angry, before, tight-lipped, I told him about Yvette's two suicide attempts. There we were at 30,000 feet, elbow to elbow, waves of sexual magnetism pulsing back and forth, and we couldn't even talk. I felt like crying but I never cry so instead I placed his hand on my thigh, and smiled as if I had forgotten all about poor Yelena Petrovna.

How can I put it? I feel connected to my siblings but at the same time disconnected too. The boys are easier for me to cope with; our relationship has clean outlines, like a comic strip. They worship me, are protective, proud of everything I do, how I look, speak, play. They carry around wallet-sized copies of my graduation picture. They both whooped and hugged me when I told them about the scholarship; they ran around the neighborhood showing the letter to everybody. For them it's as if I'm a different order of being. For them my good fortune is simply good, gratis, all light without shadows, a joyous thing that has nothing directly to do with them.

With Yvette everything's more complicated, shaded, maybe because we're both female, or because we were the last two out. I just don't know what to do for her. Her bouts of mania scare me. She talks to people who aren't there—Cary Grant, God, Dad, our dead grandparents, President Kennedy, Veronica Lake. Her depressions are terrible too, but in another way. She can hardly hold her head up and when she's awake she talks about breast cancer. "I don't know, Zel. I mean it's on TV all the time. *Every*body's got it, why not me? Or at least I could be *crippled*. Then people would be able to see what's wrong with me." The truth is I was dying to get away from Yvette. You can love somebody and not be able to stand being with them, right? Sometimes she looks at me in this funny way. I mean, it's spooky. It's as if she's always reminding me of something dreadful about myself. And, of course, that's exactly it.

Word is the hotel's going to run out of food soon. We still have water but the electricity's out. Just as well. It's too dangerous to turn the lights on anyway. One of the cellists got herself picked off by a sniper night before last. Another head shot. The phones aren't working either so there's nothing more from the embassy. Pfrüde's turned despondent and careless. According to Willi he got drunk last night and confessed to Ursula, one of the first violins, that he's almost sure he's a homosexual but has never done anything about it. He's been moping around all day and didn't even show up at lunch.

Things begin to crumble, morale to crack.

There's a baby grand down in the lounge. Wilhelm makes me practice for an hour every afternoon, but I don't know enough music by heart and all the scores we have are orchestral. I'd love to play sonatas with him. Yesterday he played Bach and Schumann for me, but I was more impressed by the way he does Debussy and Ravel. For a German he's amazing with the French repertoire. He has such a light touch, and not only on the old eighty-eight either.

169

Robert Wexelblatt

How did I ever manage it?

There was a reception at the orchestra's hotel after the Friday night concert, lots of local big shots, gallons of white wine. I pretended I'd had too much to drink. I told Wilhelm, who stayed gallantly—paternally—by my side all evening, that I couldn't go back to my dormitory until I felt better. I asked if I could rest and suggested his room. He looked at me quizzically. He knew (and knew that I knew he knew) that I had drunk hardly anything at all. Did I feel then how lonely he was, just him, divorced, with all that music and adulation? Barber and white wine may have gotten to him too, of course.

I was cautious, not that I knew how to be anything else. I took my time, brushed against him, spoke hardly at all, let him get accustomed to the idea, let the outrageousness seep out of it, kept myself a mystery. I waited for his scruples to resolve, or dissolve. Around midnight I went to the bathroom and, on a sort of calculated impulse, took off my clothes and put on the bathrobe I found hanging there, one of those luxurious white terry cloth jobs. I kept telling myself I was making a good career move. I wanted to assure myself of an ulterior motive so that later on I would be able to feel guilty about what I was doing, if I needed to.

Yvette says mania, when you feel enough exultation to lift an apartment house, is far worse than depression. Could she have meant that my mania is her depression, that her bouts of suicidal melancholy are easier for her to endure than my prospects of happiness? I'm not sure how much I want to be happy, or how much happiness is what I really want. But that night I for sure wanted the Maestro.

Wilhelm tried to explain to me why they're killing each other out there. He said it's hard for me to understand but easy for him, a German. I asked why. "My country has always churned out good music and bad politics." He sounded proud of it.

According to the Maestro, "No matter what they say it's all about power."

"Politics and music *both*?" I asked pointedly.

He looked momentarily baffled. It had obviously never occurred to him that the music he loved and the politics he loathed could have any-thing in common, or that his love of conducting might have its source in his getting to order four score people to hold a crescendo.

Beauty is power, intelligence is power, power is power. Music,

170

politics, human relations—are they all just about power? W, X, and Y are powerless. Mom had no power to make Dad stick around, no power to make him pay. I'm powerful because they aren't.

Willi is becoming anxious about the fighting. He says he's worried he's put my life in peril. I told him that we're in love and so we're already in danger.

"Do you think someday you will forget me?" he asks.

I arch an eyebrow. "Will you become one of those aging conductors who collect young soloists and give them all fur coats afterwards?"

"What an awkward conversation!" he exclaims impatiently. "Let me make love to you."

I wonder, is love power or is it the renunciation of power? Can it be both?

We've been stuck here a week now and the musicians are starting to stare at me. I can see the resentment in their eyes, especially the women's. They all look brittle from the strain, but it's unfair for them to put their fear into an envelope addressed to me. Is it my fault if a whole nation wants to revert to the state of nature?

Sheets, clothes, towels all need changing. The hotel smells sour, smells of unwashed people, cabbage, dust. They're rationing food now. A few stray shells have hit the building and, though the damage is light, violent death loiters in the corridors. Everything looks grey and vulnerable. I think I see why they resent me. I've taken their Maestro from them, made him happy and therefore oblivious to their terror. He should be leading them through this nightmare just as he would a frightful Mahler scherzo, but instead he's always with me. Two new lovers: we're the only beautiful, vital things around here.

Willi really is beautiful. He tells me sad lovely stories of his old conservatory, funny ones about the secret police. Today I asked about his parents and he took a deep breath. "They lived through all the bad years. My mother just became more and more meek but my father grew cynical about everything except music," he said. Music was the ground on which my idealistic young Willi uneasily met his dad. "Father thought music had nothing to do with anything human, as though it were a big white angel that sits up in heaven and looks down on us with pity. Father loved music because he was a misanthrope. I'm not like that. I see music as the essence of humanity raised to perfection—not looking down but up!"

I'm not sure I would like Wilhelm to love me the way he does music, to see me as the imperfectly human raised to a Platonic idea, all the sex notwithstanding. It makes me jumpy to think this might be exactly how he *does* see me.

Can seduction end in anything but disillusionment?

There are rumors of intervention—the UN, US, NATO, the Pope. We have no radio or TV, only these rumors.

Today Pfrüder, evidently restored to his former dignity, came to our room at the head of a delegation. He looked at me with open scorn. Pfrüde too has a will to power, of course, only it's twisted and not at all like Willi's, which is healthy, straight from the shoulder. He said they needed to speak to the Maestro alone. Needed, wanted, insisted on. I left without a word and was a little disappointed Willi let me.

Most of the hotel staff have left, but those without families have been staying on because it's safer. I went down to the lounge where I found the assistant manager, a man of thirty with a face like an envious undertaker's wearing a black suit about two sizes too large for his slat-like frame.

I asked him what the fighting was about.

The question seemed to annoy him. "The civil war has many causes, mademoiselle." He made an impatient gesture with one long arm.

"Really? Isn't it fundamentally about power?"

Annoyance and impatience merged into contempt. I was so naive and his people were so complex; all Americans are infants. "Of course it is about power; that is self-evident."

"Oh?"

"Power is merely the leaf, mademoiselle, the roots go far deeper. How could you understand? People do not always love one another; they also hate each other, sometimes for centuries. Yes, of course all wars are about power, all wars are about economics, but also all wars are religious wars and therefore about hatred."

"I see you're a philosopher," I said to make light of his bombast.

He shrugged, got up, then turned on me, spit out a parting shot. "You Americans and your endless pursuit of happiness! You always get the best of everything, don't you?" Then he marched off in the direction of the kitchen.

It was a pointless, nasty exchange and yet it really was philosophical. I would have liked to call him back and tell him about W, X, and Y who, despite being American citizens, do not pursue happiness, who do not see it as their birthright. But also I was reminded of one of those early Greek philosophers the professor in my Humanities class, eager to get to Socrates, had ticked off in his introductory lecture. This was one of those archaic philosophers whose speculations about the cosmos the lecturer made seem silly: the world is made of fire, water, air, green cheese. But, as I recollected it, this fellow said there were two principles that governed everything, one that pulls things together—a centripetal force I remember he called Love—and another that tears everything apart. I forget what he called that one. Anyway, this idea doesn't seem so silly to me now. Apart, together, apart, together. It explains a lot.

W - Z, Wilhelm - Zelda. No X or Y between us, those protean algebraic ciphers, unless X and Y are the two armies, the conductor and his orchestra. W and Z are pulled together; X and Y yanked apart. It doesn't make a balance, only a tension.

It's clear Pfrüde and his delegation have spoken pretty bluntly to Wilhelm. He was pale afterwards, and, worse yet, evasive. The little he did say made it easy to guess the rest. It's to be me or them. This is an orchestra that *elects* its conductor. I'm up against the damned German People's Democratic Republic.

Are they unnerved, jealous, feeling puritanical? Willi won't tell me what they had to say about me, how I must look to them—like an opportunist, a spoiled brat of an American, an insatiable nymphet. Am I in a war of love or hate? Having everything means others have nothing. Do W, X, and Y love me and do I love them? Does loving do anybody any actual good, or is it just better than hating, better than nothing?

I'm beginning to think that sex can't hold even two people together. It may be necessary but it's not sufficient, and what's not sufficient eventually isn't even necessary. Too bad.

Even a concerto is a kind of contest, a war, a negotiation. The harmonies are not more frequent than the antiphonies. The one and the many. Together, apart.

Last night the firing was sporadic, light arms only. Willi and I didn't talk much; we didn't even try to make love. At dawn the city was silent, as if after a massacre of love.

Robert Wexelblatt

An hour ago a man from the embassy came to tell us that there's to be a negotiated settlement, that we will be able to fly out this afternoon.

I can't help it. I'm longing to see W, X, and Y.

Steppe Story

I took my time over breakfast, lounging at a small white table on the roof of my hotel. From this perch I could look straight down on the broad boulevard. The asphalt ended at the steps of the Town Hall, an odd building, dignified but so squat it resembled a bank gently squashed by a passing giant. The waiter who refilled my coffee cup smiled with anticipation, for I had been tipping lavishly, a sound policy in unfamiliar locales. Rather to my surprise, this trip was proving pleasant as well as profitable. I already had one signed contract and my new customer had treated me to a decent dinner the night before. Arslan Erkut was an eager booster, facile talker, conceited about his business acumen. He struck me as excessively proud of his Italian suit, prosperous paunch, even his receding hairline. Erkut was unctuous and studiously Western. He made me reflect that if appearances are deceiving it is because people take care that they should be. I had several questions about the suddenly booming city which he dodged. He deprecated the past as he excused himself to answer his cell phone. Erkut was anxious I should esteem him as he did himself, as a man of the future.

Wearing a long apron, the proprietor of a café pulled back his shutters, took a seat at one of his own tables, leaned forward, opened his newspaper. Two pensioners with walking sticks settled on a bench near the Town Hall and began to argue contentedly as they watched the morning progress. The first cement truck of the day growled its way like a noisy beetle on to the boulevard. Cranes bristled into the cloudless sky, tracing a ghostly skyline. Trucks pulled on to work sites. Workers in yellow hard hats unloaded them, examined yesterday's footings, scaled scaffolds, made ready their tools, while others stood around waiting for orders from the foreign foremen. Three boys desultorily kicked a ball against an unfinished wall. No women were to be seen on the streets, no girls. A few of the most elderly, shrouded like black friars, would emerge later when the donkey carts arrived at the open market loaded with vegetables, fruit, and fresh meat.

Robert Wexelblatt

It was in August that the director called me to his office. The firm had chosen to send me to this place at the edge of the steppe "just to gain a foothold," as he blithely put it, handing over a copy of a sanguine report on the region's prospects. That afternoon, following a little research of my own, I begged that the trip be postponed a few weeks. I had been right. The blistering heat and notorious wind of the summer, said to drive people like me mad, had dissipated. Since my arrival the weather had been temperate, the few brisk gusts off the grasslands refreshing. It was harvest time. Erkut was condescending toward the bulk of his compatriots. "I fear our new skyscrapers are going to be filled up by peasants in neckties for a few years. I say so not because I am myself a peasant—as you can see, I am anything but a peasant. My own people have always been merchants." On the subject of his family's line of work he was expansive. "Trade was the glory of our past and it is now the hope of our future. Trade is universally held to be the path to peace, to prosperity, the model of human relations and the highest calling of men. Wouldn't you agree?" He rubbed his chubby hands together and grinned at his own perspicacity. "It is wisdom to build on the desire for profit as it is justice to give alms; but for the alms one first requires the profit. Wouldn't you agree that it is mad to try to arrange things the other way around?"

All concrete and glass, these new buildings were without ornament and ugly, like so many toasters with windows. People had been living here for a millennium yet it looked as though somebody had taken it into his head to throw the place up the week before. Yet when I turned my gaze away from the boulevard and the two blocks on either side of it, there were crooked lanes, shanties with red geraniums in window boxes, gates of peeling planks, open cooking fires and closed courtyards. The immense sky pressed on the flat land. It was almost a relief to see so much activity despite the disappointing results. A few hectares of tomorrow, acres of yesterday; the affluence here was sudden and uncertain. The positively globalized Erkut was an exception, of course. The locals looked perplexed as plate glass, advertisements, and street lights mushroomed; they made me think of old folks bewildered by the antics of their grandchildren, yet impressed.

"You are leaving tomorrow?" Erkut inquired.
I told him my intention was to stay one more day, that I had an

appointment the following afternoon.

He hesitated. At first, I thought it was so that I would tell him with whom I'd be meeting, then I realized that he would surely know with whom. "Very well, then. I will wish you a bon voyage. May I trust you will give us a good report?"

I assured him I would. His anxiety was genuine. He seemed to regard me as an emissary from the paradisal world of commerce.

"Tomorrow—"

"Yes?"

"I was just thinking. Tomorrow you may perhaps see something, something that may puzzle you."

"What do you mean?"

"It's nothing."

"Nothing? And at what time will nothing take place?"

Erkut did not like being teased. He made a dismissive noise. "A local tradition of no interest, thoroughly ridiculous in fact. You will certainly have better things to do. You will have your appointment to prepare for."

"When did you say?"

"Around noon," Erkut grumbled and began to explain his plans for a petrochemical plant.

Four men without yellow hats wrangled ladders from street lamp to street lamp, rather carelessly draping each with a faded strip of blue bunting. At the top of the steps leading to the Town Hall three policemen knocked together a small wooden platform. The air grew sultry. From the plane trees spared by the builders broad leaves hung like satiated leeches. Then, without warning, the wind blew in from the steppe. Leaves were torn from the trees and the table next to mine, which had an umbrella stuck through it, toppled over. Down among the unpaved lanes washing blew from the lines. Even the cranes trembled perilously.

I had slept late. When I went down to the lobby to look for a newspaper I was greeted fulsomely by the hotel manager. He offered me a day-old London tabloid and an even older *Herald Tribune*. I asked about what was to occur around noon and where. He was no more eager than Erkut to talk about the matter but said it would be at the Town Hall. I supposed it must be a harvest festival of some sort. These businessmen and hotel managers took themselves to be superior, scorning anything

it might be a religious rite which it would be unseemly to discuss with an
infidel, even one who leaves gigantic tips.

I took the tabloid, checked my watch, and asked if I might have
breakfast served on the roof in half an hour.

A police car pulled up in the center of the boulevard, lights revolving
and siren sounding, but only briefly. The workers abandoned their jobs
and what traffic there was pulled off the road.

From all over people began to pour on to the boulevard. Slowly, like
spilled molasses, the crowd spread itself out on either side of the avenue,
men and boys at the front, women and girls behind as if from a unanimous
shyness. In a travelogue I had read a quotation from a Frenchman who
claimed that, underneath these robes and behind their courtyard walls, the
women dressed as they pleased and exercised absolute power over their
men. I thought this a vulgar and unoriginal fantasy on the traveler's part.
Though I had no idea what went on behind courtyard walls, it was plain
that these women exercised no authority at all, except perhaps the power
to make their men perpetually apprehensive for their honor.

I could hear nothing. Either the people whispered or were silent.
Maybe it is a state funeral, I speculated, or the commemoration of a hero's
death. Erkut, no doubt, would be in his office, chattering on his cell phone,
checking his e-mail, or calculating prospective assets. He was not the man
to care for dead heroes.

No one looked toward the Town Hall or the platform. Everyone was
craning their necks, staring down the boulevard and past my hotel. I
looked around for the waiter, but he was gone. I got up and went to the
edge of the roof, steadying myself against the simoom.

Again the police car sounded its siren and, at this signal, a peculiar
thing happened. The men stepped back and the women came to the fore.

Then, just below me, a man with a shaved head made his way up the
middle of the street. He was dressed in soft boots, a leather vest and wide
trousers which ruffled in the wind. His clothes were in tatters but the man
was very erect. He marched past the police car, taking no notice of it.

A man I took to be the mayor emerged from the Town Hall and
climbed the three steps to the platform. He was holding a basket with a
long strap and something on a chain, perhaps a medal.

The stranger now glanced quickly to the left and right, not at the

178

people but at the new buildings and the cranes. When he turned to look back at the hotel I saw that he had fantastic mustaches. His narrow eyes struck me as unimpressed, even disdainful.

He stepped on to the small dais and confronted the mayor who bowed slightly, as if it pained him to do so. The mayor said a few words which I was too far off to hear. The strange man stood beside him, arms magisterially folded. The mayor concluded his remarks, handed over the basket, then quickly placed the chain around the man's neck. Next he pointed to the women and girls, who lowered their eyes. The mustachioed man gave a curt shout, loud enough for even me to hear, and spit at the mayor's feet. Looping the basket's strap over his neck, he climbed down from the platform and walked at a measured pace back the way he'd come, this time not deigning to look right or left. As he passed, the women stepped behind their men. Soon he was out of sight.

The police car's siren rang out one last time as it pulled away and the crowd scattered, citizens to their narrow lanes, workmen to their jobs, the mayor inside the Town Hall.

The whole business was over in ten minutes.

Jedvet Envil was a short, slight man with an intelligent face, the small lines around his eyes making them shine the brighter. He wore a crocheted skull cap, almost the same white as his hair, an embroidered vest over a dazzlingly white, collarless shirt, and well pressed gray slacks. I arrived five minutes early for our appointment, and the young male secretary rather officiously asked me to wait. But Envil would not hear of it. His door was open and he sharply told his secretary to send me in directly. He rose to greet me, politely offering both coffee and sweet tea which I declined.

Envil's appearance and manner could hardly have been more different from Erkut's. He was certainly at least as clever but his shrewdness was of a quieter, more assured sort, his temperament more equable, his manners old-fashioned. I had been eager to meet him when I learned that he was the wealthiest man in these parts as well as the prime mover behind the new policy of pursuing foreign investment. He didn't look the part of a tycoon. Erkut tried hard to do so, was flamboyant, in a hurry, delighted to dismiss the past and grab at the future with both hands. Envil's manner was not at all rushed. He had repose, as though assured that the future was bound to show up, like me, at his doorstep. His office

179

also could not have been more different from Erkut's overly-lit premises in one of the new towers. He did business above a large wooden warehouse in a neighborhood of small factories blocks away from the bustle of the boulevard. Where Erkut surrounded himself with new, sharp-edged furniture and hung abstract paintings on his white walls, Envil's office was more like a scholar's study. It was dimly lit and beautifully decorated with carved furniture of dark wood, silk pillows, and fine carpets. Two high bookcases dominated the room and the pictureless walls were painted a muted rose.

He asked if I were enjoying my stay and my opinion of the new hotel. I knew he owned it and was able to compliment my accommodations sincerely. Envil spoke little about the future and more guardedly than Erkut had. He had a surprising amount of information about my company at his fingertips. In short, we were both well prepared and soon set about our negotiations. I laid my proposals before him and, while he said he found them enticing and might have a few propositions of his own to our mutual advantage, he was not yet prepared to commit himself. For this he apologized courteously though not profusely, promising a definite reply would be sent to my firm within one or, at the most, two weeks.

As he seemed in no hurry to dismiss me I brought up the subject of the ritual I had witnessed that morning. Not wishing to offend him by showing too much curiosity, I came at it indirectly.

"I had a pleasant morning. I took a late breakfast on the hotel roof."

"Unfortunately, even what we believe is past does not always like to let go. I fear the wind will have disturbed you."

"Not at all," I assured him. "However, I was puzzled by the ceremony at the Town Hall. Were you there by any chance?"

"It is an annual event."

"It seemed rather solemn."

"Yes," he allowed, "solemn. A solemn remembrance."

I tried to draw him out. "Who was that outlandish fellow with the mustaches?"

Envil gave a little shrug, picked up a black Pelikan fountain pen and began toying with it, as though he would have preferred not to discuss the matter but was obliged by courtesy to answer. "That man may be the last of his race. It is not improbable."

"What, if I can trouble you further, was being commemorated?"

Envil paused then looked at me with a smile both pained and ironic. "Our salvation," he said. "Our humiliation."

In airplanes you are nowhere, only between; but what you are between is airports and these are so identical that the sensation of placelessness begins before liftoff and persists after landing. You only arrive when the doors to the parking lot slide open and the raw air hits. How could the city's new terminal help but be just like those the world over? The heat and the wind vanished as I entered into this denatured, intermediate realm. The clothing was international, the seats and lighting and air-conditioning; only the faces proclaimed a history.

Envil had reluctantly given me the facts, all the while playing with that pen of his and scarcely looking at me. I can't deny that he had arranged these facts into a story or even that he had stated its moral before he began telling it. All the same, the facts needed to be thought about because morals aren't quite meanings; words like salvation and humiliation are too abstract.

As everybody knows, centuries ago all the cities of the steppe, the great and the mean, were overrun by ferocious nomadic tribes from the east. They were plundered, razed, their populations raped, enslaved, and slaughtered. These tribes conceived and gave birth in the saddle; both the men and the women drank horses' blood and could hit a mark with their arrows at fifty yards. They were merciless creatures who swept like the wind across the treeless steppes. What had become of them? They settled down, of course—what else could they do?—and for a generation or two became overlords. But it didn't take long for them to succumb to their conquests, mingle with merchants and farmers, marry the daughters of craftsmen and camel-drivers, to give up their recurved bows and their centaur-life.

According to Envil, his city alone had been spared.

"We were the last to be attacked," he explained. "The men were terrified by the news of what had happened elsewhere. Since to resist was to provoke annihilation they chose submission."

As the wind battered leaves against the window, I waited for him to go on.

"The barbarians bore down on us at just this season of year, with the last of the hot winds. The men hid a little food but most of it they heaped up before the gates. Then the women and girls were driven outside the walls and lined up beside the harvest. The men barred the gates and cowered inside the walls. The wind carried the stench of the barbarians before them. The clouds of dust they raised could be seen for hours before they arrived."

Envil now spoke as if he were there and looked as though he could still see that terrible cloud of dust.

"The barbarians reined in their horses. At first they were stupefied by what they saw, then they turned indignant. Instead of assaulting our walls, they pissed on them, shouting insults and laughing."

"They carried off the women?"

Envil looked at the window. "No. The food they took—in fact, they returned every year to take our food but—the females they would not touch." He spoke abjectly, as if the past were more real to him that the cranes and the glassy tower blocks a quarter of a mile away, as though he himself had cringed behind the old walls. "They would have nothing to do with women who bred such cowards."

So the nomads had never stormed the city. They continued living on the steppe nearby, kept up their skills for a time, gradually turning war into games, tended their livestock and went on demanding their annual tribute even as their power faded and their numbers dwindled. In shame and gratitude the city maintained the ceremony until the food and the gold became mere tokens. The women are still ritually offered. Who knows what revenge they take on their men in private or even whether they know revenge is due them. And what of that dignified beggar in the wide trousers and soft boots? Perhaps he lived alone with his flock of filthy goats, but he had been reared in a tent made of hides, taught to demand his yearly basket of groceries and brass medal and to show contempt for the city-dwellers, though perhaps even he could no longer say why.

On the Boughs Our Bodies Shall Be Strung

I was sure I'd come too late.

Even from the outside the house—half-timbered, gabled, its once-white stucco turned to gray—appeared to be in mourning. In spite of the sultry air, the curtains were drawn; the grass was growing wild. A light rain fell from heavy clouds so low they looked like boulders about to crush the horizon.

A woman I took to be the professor's daughter answered my knock at once and seemed to recognize me. "Please," she said solemnly, ushering me through the foyer and into the living room where a hospital bed had been set up for the old man.

I had not seen many corpses but I was in no doubt that I was looking at one. The professor lay flat on the bed, his eyes closed, his skin the same pewter color as the stucco and the clouds. My immediate thought was for the daughter. Her father must have passed away in the few moments it took her to answer my knock. What a shock for her, I thought, and was almost glad I was there to support her, but at the same time I regretted coming at all. I glanced behind me; she must not yet have seen. The old man's chest was still and his big hands lay splayed on the blanket like rakes. What most drew my attention, though, was his nose. It was sticking upward as if it were an independent being, glad to be liberated from the defunct, dissatisfied face. Its armature of cartilage was clearly visible. The old man seemed to have collapsed into himself, but that nose—how it fascinated me—looked positively alive, thrusting up as though it wished to take a stroll around the room.

I had received a letter from the daughter three days earlier. Though imposingly formal in tone, it was likewise a plea from the heart. I was informed that her father was near his end, that I had always been one of his favorite students, and that it would be an act of charity for which she would be eternally grateful if I could arrange to pay him a final visit. But I would have to hurry. The doctors said his time was short. So, not without difficulty, I rearranged my schedule and came.

Standing there before the dead man I was uncertain what to do and hesitated at the foot of the bed, bracing myself for the daughter's wail of grief. But she came up and stood silently beside me so that we resembled two parents looking down on a newborn's crib. Her profile was unreadable —serene or indifferent, I couldn't tell. Dressed in a long black skirt and a white blouse, her hair pulled carelessly up on her head and held there with a tortoise-shell comb, she had the air of an intelligent spinster, a school-teacher from early in the last century.

"I think . . . I'm afraid . . ." I stammered, but she put a steadying hand on my forearm and directed me toward the chair set next to the bed. As she did so she leaned her face close to mine—there was a faint odor of lilies-of-the valley—and whispered in my ear.

"Shh. Just sit down and talk to him. Tell him something. Anything."

"What? But can't you see he's—"

"Something you remember from his lectures would do, or even one of those nicknames you students gave him."

"But can't you see?"

"Shh," she whispered again and pushed me firmly down into the chair. "Go ahead," she insisted. "Please."

I couldn't bring myself to address the corpse and turned my face toward her. "I'm sorry. His nickname among us was The Stork—well, *Der Storch*, actually."

At that the old man coughed three times and rotated his head. His face, in which the lines were deeply set and that had looked as immovable as jade, broke into an unsettling grin. "So, you've come at last," he croaked as if he really were a stork. I remembered that disapproving irony from my student days. "No," he went on, "no, it's very kind of you. You can't imagine what it means to see my old pupils. You're all grown up and now it's you who run the world. How can you find the time for a superannuated relic like me? And yet you keep coming. It's so gratifying. Just yesterday it was Pfeiffer. You know, he's chief engineer of the waterworks now, and the day before that . . ." he trailed off and, with round-eyed desperation, looked over my shoulder. I had nearly forgotten the daughter but she was seated in a high-backed chair by the door, knitting.

"The day before yesterday it was the Bishop, Father. Remember? He told that old joke of yours about the jackal and the goat."

"Ah, how could I forget?" The professor chuckled. "The jackal certainly got the better of that goat, didn't he?"

184

The daughter shook her head at me, rolled her eyes, crossed her needles, and slowly mouthed: "*Other way around.*"

"Well, and now you've come to see me."

"Yes. It's good to see you, Professor."

"Tell me, how are things with you? Have you settled down? You have a nice plump wife, do you?"

"No, Professor. I'm not married."

He wagged one long finger at me. "You devil," he said. "So, tell *Der Alte Storch* what you remember from the old days."

The old man's challenge made me feel as if I were back in his class; my mind went blank for an instant then battened on something ridiculously trivial.

"I often think of the day you explained the difference between placing an adverb before or after a verb. We were all lost until you gave that clever example."

"Hee, hee. I remember how you all laughed—because the example was improper." He attempted, without much success, to raise his voice. "You hear that, my dear? Improper."

"Yes, Father, I heard. What was the improper example?"

The old man smiled encouragingly at me and nodded, certain that I could remember the example, granting permission for me to speak improperly in front of his daughter.

"You explained the distinction by contrasting two sentences: *The young man accidentally brushed against the young lady's shoulder* and *The young man brushed accidentally against the young lady's shoulder.*"

"Full marks." The old man was delighted. He cleared his throat—a terrible sound—and proceeded to speak exactly as he had in class so many years before. "In the first sentence, the young man is innocent; it's merely an accident that he brushes the young lady's shoulder. But, in the second sentence, there is a hint of another possibility; namely that he was aiming at something other than her shoulder and only accidentally brushed it on his way elsewhere, so to speak. Now that's appreciating the subtleties of style."

The daughter clicked her tongue out of irritation or disgust. If he heard, the old man chose to ignore it.

At this moment there was a knocking on the door—no, a real pounding. The daughter leapt to her feet and ran from the room.

The old man lay back down, breathing shallowly, and gave me a wink. "That will be the Bishop," he hissed hoarsely.

And in fact I caught a glimpse of a tall man in the foyer wearing a clerical collar. His arm was around the daughter's waist. I heard them going up the stairs.

The old man managed to raise a forefinger. "Tomorrow it will be your turn," he said then fell back against the pillows and closed his eyes. He lay still for so long that I carefully put two fingers on his wrist. I felt a faint fluttering like that of a tiny, trapped moth.

I made to get up but the old man, his eyes still shut tight, said, "No, don't go yet. Tell me, can you remember in which circle of Hell Dante puts the suicides?" It was no different in class; he was always tossing out unexpected questions. His curriculum had no boundaries.

"I'm afraid I can't remember, Professor. Was it the sixth?"

"Not bad. It's the seventh, quite far down. He tosses them in with the blasphemers and the perverts—above all, with the murderers. Does that seem unjust? Well, consider that part of what makes us modern— which is to say, faithless—is that we distinguish between violence against others and ourselves. Dante made no such distinction, all life being the property of God."

"Professor," I said nervously, "perhaps we could talk about something else?"

"Such as your wife?"

"I told you I'm not married."

"So you did. No wife, no children. You know, it was hard to keep my hands off them."

"Pardon me?"

"The young women, of course. There were times I could scarcely hold my hands in check. You can't imagine how I sometimes yearned to kiss their necks."

I was shocked. "And did you brush against their shoulders? Accidentally?" I asked, not disguising my bitter disillusionment.

The sly look on his face was disgusting. "Once in a while. Quite accidentally, as you say."

"Oh, naturally."

"You're quick to give your grades, aren't you? You're certain that teachers should be sexless and that suicide's no sin."

"Suicide . . . suicide's the end of a tragedy," I said pompously.

The old man turned away from me. "Speaking trees," he said in a strangled voice. "It's horrible. What if I should convince my daughter to let me die? Wouldn't that be a sin?"

"Not a sin, but it would still be wrong. Plato and Aristotle were no Christians but you yourself taught us they both considered suicide cowardly."

"You amaze me. What a splendid student you were! *We ought not to quit our post without permission of Him who commands us; the post of man is life.* Fine words, yes; and yet Socrates, the patron saint of old professors, was himself a sort of judicial suicide. He'd resolved that he was a dead man before his trial began. How else could he have been so marvelous, so provoking to the Assembly? 'Death,' he said, 'is the only subject,'" but a cough interrupted this incipient lecture.

When he was silent I told him what I thought. "I agree with the fellow who said all healthy men have thoughts of suicide."

Taking a breath he drew his hand slowly across his mouth and his eyes swam up at me as if he were drowning. "That's because you are not only modern but still young. Modernity wears off in time, just like youth."

"Professor, I don't understand you."

"Because you don't wish to. The same act is not one thing—can be love or lust, bravery or cowardice."

"There was an English actor who killed himself out of boredom. That was selfish and despicable."

"Yes, yes. I know the case. But unlike you, he was married several times, and to spectacular women," the old man chided. Then his tone changed again and he looked frightened. "It's hard to stay alive. It's terribly hard to keep me alive; and yet you can see for yourself what my daughter gets out of it, what she's turned into."

"What do you mean?"

He shook his head petulantly. "Ach," he said, "what am I saying? She's a wonderful child and completely devoted to me."

"Yes?"

"You know," he said querulously, "I never wanted to retire. They forced me out. I waited for the president's office to be stormed by hundreds of alumni, for his desk to be buried under a mountain of indignant letters from my former students, from people like you . . ." He looked hurt. "Now, when it's too late, when I'm as good as dead, you all come to assuage your guilt and seek absolution from the victim who was once your benefactor. You make up to my daughter—I'm not blind—

because you think this is a way to get at me, to propitiate, to please me. But I can tell you it won't work." His eyes opened wide and he tried to raise himself on his sticks of arms, the pajama top falling away from his thin chest. I could see he was worked up and meant to shout at me.

Just then I heard steps descending the stairs, the front door open and shut, and the daughter hurried in, adjusting her skirt. When she saw the old man's contorted face, red with anger, she rushed to his side and put her hand on his forehead. "Father, you must calm yourself," she murmured soothingly; but the old man's eyes were already glazing over and, instead of the denunciation he had no doubt intended to hurl in my face, a rattle came from his throat. I jumped to my feet but the daughter, with her eyes still fixed on her dying father, seized my hand and raised it to her mouth; then, with a terrible tenderness, she bit into it.

Elected Silence

1.

Between June 17 and July 20 of my fifteenth year I didn't say a word.

My month of silence began when my older sister Leda unjustly accused me of lifting a charm bracelet from her jewelry box, the most off-limits item in the house.

At about two in the afternoon of the day after school ended, I was out in the yard, reclining in the hammock and paging through a copy of *Seventeen* when Leda banged out of the screen door, arms menacingly crossed, and advanced on the hammock. The indignation shimmering off her would have done Émile Zola proud.

"All right. Give it back. I mean right now."

I put down the magazine and replied mildly. "Give what back?"

"You know damn well what."

"No, I don't."

"My charm bracelet, moron."

"I didn't take your charm bracelet," I observed reasonably.

Leda took a step closer, too close, brushing the hammock with her hip, making it swing a little.

"You're lying! I *know* you took it. Give it back. Now!"

Leda had received said charm bracelet for her last birthday. It was from Joe Wessenhal. Joe was a big good-looking senior with a lot of straight black hair and fair prospects of a basketball scholarship. In romantic matters I had the cynicism of the innocent. In my opinion, Joe's estimation of Leda was ludicrously inflated, and her opinion of him was correspondingly fatuous. The bracelet was an emblem of their adolescent misapprehensions. Each dangling charm held a particular, private significance. I had been let in on some of this because Leda craved someone to confide in and brag to. For example, the silver piglet was a token of something that happened on their first date, the tiny ballet shoes commemorated a dance they'd attended, and the little orange basketball was self-explanatory. My personal favorite was a heart from which the red enamel was flaking away. I took the flaking as a portent.

Leda stood trembling with hostility and grief beside both me and herself. That she had been careless with this crypto-engagement ring was inadmissible; consequently, Leda was convinced that her jealous little sister must have boosted it. For twenty hours this crime constituted the center of her world-view.

But I hadn't taken the bracelet and the next day she found it in her sock drawer. She was also wrong about my being jealous of her. My mind, such as it was in those days, wasn't focused on Leda's love life but on my own immediate future. I wasn't sure what to do with the two months of summer vacation, apart from the threatened family trip up to some woody house on some northern lake.

Leda hollered at me a little more and concluded lamely and meanly with a grand declaration. "Of all the things that are bad in this world, having a nasty little sister like you has got to take the cake."

To Leda I beat plague and genocide. Up till then I hadn't been fully aware of how much she detested me. It was a revelation. I had no reply. I didn't even bother reiterating my innocence.

My sister stalked off toward the house, putting as much hatred as a popular high-school girl can—and this is considerable—into each step, every twitch of her shoulder. Normally, Leda tended to slump but I remember how that day her spine formed a perfectly plumb exclamation point.

When my mother, all too quick to believe her first-born, came out to say much the same sort of thing to me, accusing me with no more evidence than Leda's whining, I said nothing at all. My silence began as petulance, I suppose, a childish protest against injustice and frame-ups. I've never been able to watch movies in which people are falsely accused of crimes. A world like that was simply unacceptable to me. I wanted to go on being a healthy animal. I suppose I sensed a threat to my condition if the moral order could be so casually cracked. To such a world I had nothing to say.

2.

"You're not going to talk, not to *any*body? You're just going to sulk— is *that* it? Personally, I think it's overreacting, but if that's what you want."

I sat on my bed, attending not so much to my mother's words as to the little shifts underneath them, the cajolery, mockery, and sarcasm. But I said nothing.

"Are you going to write us notes from now on? Is *that* it? Notes? And what are you going to do about your friends? Are you going to talk to them but not your family? Are you planning to keep your mouth shut all summer? Is it because you *hate* us? Is that it?"

If you don't answer, all questions become rhetorical. Mother's questions piled up like bricks, a tottering stack that was meant to fall over and flatten me. I had to agree with her in part. It had only been one day and already I felt I had pushed things way too far, that I was being not only willful but foolish. Still, there was a thrill in knowing that I had unbalanced the household.

She got up from the bed, which rose like a wave, and stood in front of me almost as an enemy. "Look, Leda *found* the bracelet!"

The night before, Father, informed of my misbehavior as soon as he arrived home—not about the lost bracelet but my provoking silence—had come to reason with me. It was a pleasure to listen to him, really; the even flow of his logic was like that of mechanical time itself, regular and smooth.

"Now, Ellie, this is just childish. What's more, it's not right. If you won't communicate with us, won't let us in on what's up with you, you'll begin to feel more and more cut off. So will we. Look, it's like the telephone. When it rings we *have* to pick it up, don't we? It's our duty. We're not meant to stay locked up in ourselves. Sure, we all have times when nothing seems better than just that, to crawl into our skin as if it were a sleeping bag and zip it up. Everybody feels that way sometimes. It can even be good for a while, pulling in, clearing our minds. You go into yourself and find things, straighten yourself out. You dig things up. But then you have to share them. You have to reassure us, Ellie. We love you. We need to know you're all right. If you don't talk to us then we'll start imagining things, none of them good, either. Silence is supposed to be golden, I know, but gold's malleable. You can make any shape with it. What's up with Ellie? Is she going to dye her hair blue and stop eating roast beef? Is she planning to run away with Mr. Barnum and Mr. Bailey? Is she having cramps? Has she converted to Islam or Buddhism? See what I mean?"

Mother's questions were intended to overwhelm me; Father's were meant to make me laugh. If I laughed then I would surely talk. He was right about that. One chuckle and my little game would be over. I sensed that there are no comic possibilities in silence itself, only in silent movies where the fullness of speech is turned into feverishly broad gestures, physical screams, corporeal escapes, preposterous passions. Silence that sits still, as I sat on my bed, just isn't funny.

I put my hand over my father's and smiled at him. I was grateful that he had not yet reached the stage of anger, though if I persisted I suspected that eventually he would.

Of course they made Leda come and apologize to me. I didn't care about Leda's contrition and this surprised me because for years my sister's moods had been the weather fronts of my life. So, I discovered that my silence was no longer aimed at Leda, not even at cosmic injustice. If I had gone mute as a protest then I could no longer say what my target was. I couldn't say anything. All I knew was that the longer I went without speaking the more the going on became an end rather than a means.

I was in my room before dinner, reading a book by Mary Renault, when Leda interrupted me in a way that proved in advance that whatever came next would not be sincere. This was okay by me. I've never rated sincerity all that highly. I prefer integrity. Leda, unfortunately, had little of either.

"All right," she said ungraciously. "I'm sorry. Okay? Got it? I was wrong. Mea maxima culpa. The bracelet must have fallen in the drawer. I was upset. You can understand that, can't you? And now Mom's going on about how this is all my fault and you're so supersensitive and all and I have to fix it. I'm fixing it. So you can start talking again. Okay?"

I wasn't and I didn't.

Leda looked at me in a new way, as if for the first time I had her full attention. "You're getting scary, Ellie."

Scary? This was intriguing, my first intimation of the power to be gained by simply shutting up. It could frighten people, your sister anyway. But why? Because if talking reassures, as Father said, then not talking does the opposite. If I did as they wanted, if I spoke, this power would instantly vanish. Not only that, but I would surrender something else I couldn't even name to myself because what it amounted to was, in a sense, acquiring a self.

Leda threw up her arms. "Go on then. Be a freak. I don't care."

But anyone could see that she did.

3.

I ate what was put in front of me.

"Do you want more applesauce?" Mother asked, but I was not to be so easily tricked.

"God," she whispered.

"Are you going to see Maureen or Jackie?" Father asked.

I didn't reply. In fact, I had been wondering why I hadn't heard from my two best friends since the day school let out. Three days was an unprecedented hiatus for our triad. Would I have talked to them? I hadn't yet decided.

The dinner conversation was a play, an astonishing one. My parents were more desperate than I thought.

Mother delivered her line breezily. "Oh, didn't I mention it? I ran into both of them at the market yesterday but I told them she'd given up talking to people."

I took note how my presence had been sucked out of this sentence, how my silence gave permission to pretend I was somewhere else, locked up, dead.

"Were they relieved?" Leda asked with an unpleasant grimace in my direction, a look that said "moron," but which at least brought me back to life.

They expected me to respond; they reckoned that whatever sacrifice I was making couldn't withstand the loss of Maureen and Jackie, my dearest intimates, the ones I giggled with and told everything. Were they right? My silence was ridiculous and exasperating but, they must have thought, it was only a family matter, a sibling snit, a tussle between me and Leda.

I remembered how once, when we were playing Monopoly, an argument started between Maureen and Jackie. Maureen said Jackie had counted the spaces wrong on purpose and had really landed on Park Place where she had a hotel. Their voices had risen up the scale pretty quickly. They both appealed to me. I turned the board over.

What would they have thought when my mother told them I'd gone mute? Would they worry about me? Would they take it personally, thinking I didn't want to talk to them? Already I realized that's how people took silence. Silence is the greatest occasion for interpretation and so for misinterpretation. Father was right. If you don't pick up the phone people think you're blowing them off. So, what about my best friends? Would I talk to them? I wouldn't have to use the phone. I had only to walk over to Maureen's house, to Jackie's. I turned the question over. Did I have one duty here or two? The duty to talk everyone understands; but if there is a duty to be silent, then no one understands it.

I got up and began clearing the table. I took my plate and glass into the kitchen and looked out the window over the sink, feeling perverse and cut off, but also stubborn. Whatever it is I was buying I felt willing to pay the price. I wanted to go to my room and read, back to Mary Renault, to an ancient world with dangerous gods in it. I wanted to escape into words that were printed, silent words. I wanted the world to fall away from me.

As I passed by the table my mother growled, "You're grounded, young lady." Father looked away, embarrassed. Leda stared at her dessert plate, looking neither triumphant nor in the wrong. I sensed their helplessness and bafflement but without sympathy.

4.

My father, a thoughtful and clever man, wrote me a letter. Fourteen-year-olds who do not go away to boarding school or summer camp, whose parents aren't yet divorced, seldom receive letters from their fathers.

Leda handed me the envelope. She had picked up the mail on her way to the yard for a little tanning. "Here," she said. I'm not sure she noticed the return address.

I was bowled over. I liked that he didn't slip it under my bedroom door or press the letter into my hand when he got home from the office. Why? for the same reason you don't slip Christmas cards into the neighbors' mailboxes.

The letter came toward the end of that first week, when Father was still being light-hearted, still believed in the reversibility of what is so malleable, when my silence had not yet turned into the stone guest at the banquet. His impregnable good humor helped me bear up. Just because you're pushing against something doesn't mean you want it to be overturned.

I had seldom seen my father's handwriting. It was regular though by no means easy to read. Even on his business stationery the blue words looked intimate. I found the physicality of his writing touching. It was as if by moving away he wanted to draw closer. Though he was not sitting on my bed he was addressing me more confidentially and with respect, in a way no one else could see or hear. It was the letter of a loving father and a man of affairs. I pictured him in his law office on the fifth floor of the Filbert Building, efficient little Mrs. Ardekian in the outer office behind her big IBM Selectric and the telephone console. "Hold all my calls," I imagined him shouting from the doorway as he shut himself inside to write to his beloved, obstreperous Ellie, the apple of his eye.

"Dear Ellie," he began. I might have preferred "Dearest," but Leda was entitled to half his love; in fact, being the first-born and not incomprehensibly mute, perhaps she was owed more than half.

"I need hardly tell you your mother and I have been very worried about you."

The movement of this first pawn did not delight me. This sentence struck me as stiff; worse yet, it asserted a united front, as if whatever followed should be taken as coming from Mother too and would lack any individuality, which, I thought, is the only thing that makes a letter worth reading or writing. The "I need hardly tell you" was particularly unpromising. It wasn't a real phrase but a piece of soiled merchandise about a century out of date. I had a vision of the two of them late at night, sharing their worries about me between the sheets. They weren't just worried either; they were "very worried." I've never found the word "very" of any use and I mistrusted it even then, a nervous couple of syllables that add nothing.

"Your mother is afraid that there is something the matter with you, that you have become abnormal. I am writing to you because I want to communicate and am hoping that this letter will get your attention."

He neglected to say whether he shared my mother's fear of "abnormality," which I took to be a euphemism for wacko. But that he ascribed the suspicion only to Mother at least opened a slit between them, so it made up a bit for the first sentence.

I took the letter out into the yard. It was three pages long and I wanted to read it in the open air, undisturbed. Leda, in her turquoise bikini, lay on a beach towel near the hammock and so I plumped down on the back steps. If she wanted to she could watch me read it.

"You are at a difficult age, an age when there are big changes to deal with. I know this. I am aware that teenagers often slam their doors, claim to be misunderstood, can't understand themselves, bury themselves in books, get into scrapes or worse, push boundaries."

One personal anecdote, one recollection of his own puberty, would have done the job better. Show, don't tell, I thought.

"But this silence of yours is something else, Ellie. You refuse to talk to us, or even to your friends, and soon we will no longer talk to you. You will become a kind of ghost. It's dangerous."

He went on about this peril for most of a page. In the end, what he wrote had an act-or-you'll-be-acted-upon tone to it. He wasn't threatening me exactly. It wasn't control he was after—that was more in my mother's line—but a kind of growing terror he wanted removed. I could sympathize with him because I respected his motives and relied on his love but at the same time I relished the hazardousness of what I was doing. It was certainly no worse than hopping on the back of some greaseball's Harley or sampling cocaine.

Coming to the end of his letter, which even he must have felt to be a Hardingesque plea for normalcy, my father must have paused. Perhaps he took down a Bartlett's from among his law books because suddenly he was quoting Plutarch at me: "In silence there's a worth than brings no risk." This was a new tack, belittling the big thing that had taken over his little girl's life, shaming her. But Plutarch so obviously didn't apply; my silence wasn't that of some Porcius Pusillanimous cringing in the back row of the Senate. It was right up front; I was risking my family and friends— even *he* said I was in danger of turning into a ghost, which is a being without any vital connection to where she is, who can neither touch nor be touched. No, he knew silence wasn't riskless even if he wasn't certain what or who was at risk.

"So please, Ellie," the letter wound up, "please stop giving us all the silent treatment before it goes too far. Your always loving father . . ."

I looked across the yard at Leda, supine on her bright beach towel, and saw what a good figure she had. I was, comparatively speaking, a stick. You only had to look at her to see that hers was the outer world, a world of boys and noise, dates and mates. Was my world that of silence, an inner world?

5.

People accept routine and so anything that becomes routine will sooner or later be accepted. Having proved the ineffectuality of joking, pleading, tickling, disapproving, warning, even sympathizing, my family behaved as if they no longer expected me to speak. I was tolerated when it was necessary, ignored when it wasn't. In a matter of days I had indeed become a sort of ghost hovering around the house.

Maureen stopped by and, when I wouldn't say anything to her, went off in a huff. Jackie, quickly informed by Maureen that I had gone all weird, didn't even bother to visit. I didn't mind being written off but I was shocked by the speed with which it happened.

When my parents invited the Langebornes over for a July 4 barbecue Mother ordered me to stay in my room. "I'll tell them you're ill," she said. It was a sad-sounding reproof, and her face suggested that she wasn't sure if she would be fibbing. I had to remind myself that my silence had made me an object of some fear, as unreadable as a drunk in a subway car. Then she added something. Without hope she said, "Unless you promise to behave normally." I was glad she hadn't given up on me entirely and smiled but stayed up in my room all the same.

Leda did give up on me. Nearly from the moment I had failed to respond to her apology she had adopted a policy of ignoring me. I could see that her silence with me was supposed to be a mocking mirror of my own, as when children repeat each other's words; but her silence was all too intelligible. Mine, on the other hand, was not, even to myself. But I persisted; I went on as if I were on a journey with a destination, as if this were all about something. In the meantime I read like a fiend.

The week before we left for the lake I began to read poems. I was looking through some of my father's old college books and found a paperback copy of *Immortal Poems of the English Language*, edited by Oscar Williams, first published in 1952, the one with all the pictures of the poets in little ovals on the flyleaves. There was the intelligent John Donne and gorgeous Gene Derwood, red-lipped Elinor Wylie and soulful Dante Gabriel Rosetti, bird-like Shelley and glamorous Byron. Some looked like flappers, others like businessmen or pirates. I could see nothing outward that they had in common and yet all were poets, all six hundred years of them. I commenced to read the book straight through, from Chaucer to Dylan Thomas. The experience was nothing like the tedious hours we had spent in school over "O Captain! My Captain!" or "Stopping By Woods on a Snowy Evening." I still have the book, crumbling and yellow and completely unglued.

Some of the poems I found appealing from the first; quite a few baffled or bored me but, out of my silence, I learned to read them, to be quiet with them, even to let them read me. Silence had made me sharper about language. I learned to see through words but also to weigh them as a jeweler does diamonds. I saw for the first time that a poem is a series of choices; in other words, I began to think like a poet myself, from the other side of the text, so to speak. Up till then, I realized, words had been opaque, setting up a screen between me and the actuality of things. For example, if somebody said I had on a "nice dress," the dress, with all its stitching, all its embellishments, became a blur under the dirty lens of "nice." Even worse was my own prattling, all the thoughtless, unchosen words I had spoken that had no mass or meaning: "You're crazy, Jackie" or "The capital of Guatemala is Guatemala City."

The power of real speech depends on that of non-speech; that is, words have to grow out of silence the way music does. How quiet is the meadow before Gray says, "The curfew tolls the knell of parting day"? How empty was the night before Vaughan rose up on tip-toe to confess, "I saw Eternity the other night"?

It was in Williams' splendid little vade mecum that I began to suspect where silence was taking me, what it is for.

6.

My father came home from work early one hot Friday afternoon and we packed up the car and drove to the northern lake. I listened to them in the car, heard them straining to keep the words coming. Father was buoyant, full of boyish but forced anticipation. There would be fishing and water skiing, hiking and, if we wanted, there were supposed to be stables nearby, he promised. Rainy days? Like all the best summer rentals, the place would be overflowing with books and board games. Since the lake was ringed by summer houses there were bound to be other young people around. We would make new friends. A bedroom for each of us girls, even a hot tub, according to the rental agent. "The family that's braised together stays together," he quipped and looked over his shoulder at me.

Leda hadn't wanted to come at all. She would have preferred to be near Joe Wessenhal but Joe had betrayed her by taking a job as a camp counselor. So her feelings were mixed: she didn't want to spend two weeks in the boonies with the three of us, but she didn't want to work either. She spoke mostly about what she was going to do when the two weeks were over, sounding determined to make the worst of things. My father had a fine time cheering her up. "Maybe you'll find a guy even bigger and prettier than Joe," he teased and Mother threw an elbow into him. She coped by devoting herself to organizing the packing and provisioning and preparing for a thorough sanitizing of everything. The lake was what my father wanted, not her. She couldn't say so but neither could she help making it clear, if he wanted to see it. Nobody ever said exactly what they meant. In fact, I'd come to understand that few conversations are really aimed at what my father called communicating. They are rather a sort of simulation of it, meant to provide the kind of reassurance insects get from touching antennae. Most talk is simply a way of not being alone. In my opinion, really to talk to somebody ought to demand at least as much discipline as not talking at all.

The house was spacious, low slung, and made of dark timbers smelling vaguely of creosote. It was overhung by huge pine trees. Brown needles lay all over the roof, making it look thatched, and on the ground. The darkness of the wood, the shade of the pines, cooled the July air. Here, I thought, was a silence grander than my own, less deliberate, without any taint of will or anguish. There was a big stone fireplace and five bookcases, mostly filled with paperback murder mysteries and thrillers. We arrived at dusk. Mother headed straight for the kitchen and my father went to check out the hot tub, which had rusted out, then made for the dock and the motorboat. Leda slumped off into the larger of the two non-master bedrooms then quickly vanished into the bathroom we would share. I went down to the lake, sat on the bit of pebbly beach and watched my father mess around happily with the boat and his fishing gear.

"Ellie, come over here," he called.

I walked out on the dock.

He kept fooling with the outboard, not looking at me.

"Are you very unhappy?"

I shook my head.

"What?"

I went back to the house and helped Mother put things away. She didn't say anything much beyond, "Here, put this there."

My bedroom had a terrible reading lamp beside the bed. It was too small and not bright enough so that you had to scrunch over in the bed and even then it was hard to see a whole page. In the night I stole into the living room and exchanged it for one of the bigger lamps.

199

7.

That my father preferred me to my sister was as certain as that I preferred him to my mother. I had known this since I was quite little, from the age when such knowledge first becomes decisive. Consequently, I knew that it was my father who suffered the most from my silence but also that he was the one most compelled to pick at and interpret it. Silence is like a difficult poem that dares you to interpret it. My mother, sister, and friends were careless readers, but not Father. To him my shutting up must have appeared not merely a dereliction of normal social and familial obligations, but a pushing away of his love, an intimate turning of the back, a betrayal. After all, weren't we allies in the family wars? I had deserted him and chosen an inaccessibility which looked like neutrality, indifference. He had gone so far as to write to me, to joke with me, to let me have my way, and I didn't respond to any of it.

That silent month fell between two of my periods. Without the smokescreen of my own whining and babbling, during this time I became more observant but I had also grown even more self-centered than my sister. Leda was only a conventionally selfish late adolescent female who is good-looking and popular, with normal complaints and aspirations; whereas to me the term "self-centered" applied with every ounce of its weight. Who is not the center of the universe? Certainly not spirited fourteen-year-olds and surely none of the 150 poets who had composed the 447 immortal poems in Williams' anthology. My reading insisted that the only way out of self-centeredness is love, but I wasn't so sure about this, not if love was what bound Leda to Joe or my father to my mother. I was young enough to think that I could hold back indefinitely and so keep myself intact.

Love is both a noun and a verb, a being and a doing. Where my father was concerned that month, I turned the verb into a noun. I suppose most of my confidence came from his paternal love which is a sort of trust. I kept myself well wrapped up in this trust and took it for granted. After all, the dreamer doesn't dream about the blanket that keeps her warm. Besides, it didn't seem to me that loving my father required that I speak to him. Poets knew how to speak about love; in fact they said it all a bit too well. But what enthralled me was their words, not their loving.

Silence gave me waking dreams; that is, I was more conscious than I had ever been and yearned for more of it, but this sudden lucidity was, just like that of a dream, detached from the world. The connection between what went on in my swarming mind and the busy world could only be language. So silence led me to words, to the stentorian compilations of Whitman, the luscious voracity of Keats, the dexterous duplicity Frost. I had gone south only to find myself called to the north. What else is a writer but a beguiled reader with the nerve to emulate?

As I read through Williams' book I formed a resolution. If I could somehow find such words of my own then I would speak because there would simply be nothing else to do. Silence and I would release our strangle-holds on one another. But the silence would always remain nearby, ever accessible, a place I could visit, like a dark house by a northern lake.

8.

I did everything in silence. I got up on water skis, I swam, I hiked up a mountain. Leda and I even spent an afternoon riding horses, walking them through woods and cantering across fields. We all went into town one night to eat and watch a movie. But I was restless, waiting, and so was my father. I overheard a conversation between him and Mother.

"I think we should take her to see somebody. I really do."

"Be a little more patient," he replied forlornly.

One morning he took me out fishing early, just the two of us. That Leda and Mother were still sleeping made me feel virtuous and hardy. We motored out into the middle of the lake; he baited the hooks, and we sat quietly for half an hour.

"You've made me think, Ellie," he said finally, "I mean think about silence. I've decided there are three kinds. There's the silence that's just being absent. Some day you'll go off to college and then I won't be able to talk to you unless you pick up the phone or answer my letters." He laughed but I thought guiltily of the letter I had already failed to answer. "You know, when I was in college I had this friend who burst into my dorm room one night and announced that he'd just figured out he was God. I asked him how he made that out. 'Well,' he said, 'whenever I pray I always end up talking to myself.'" He glanced at me to see if I was repressing a laugh. "Okay. That's number one. Then there's number two. This is being silent not because you're absent but because you're present—you know, like when Leda's got a hair across her saddle or Mom's put out with one of us. The cold shoulder, sending us all to Coventry. These days they call it passive aggression, and that's what I thought you were up to at first. But it's gone on too long, Ellie. Too long." He began to fool with his tackle box, still not wanting to look at me, abashed by his own seriousness, I guess. "So now I think there's maybe a third kind, which is a choice, a sort of social suicide. I don't understand it, though . . . . Are you *ever* going to come out of this?"

I fixed a smile on my face and waited for him to look at it. I nodded once. It meant, "Sure, Dad, just not yet."

Later, before we headed back in, he surprised me by pulling a piece of paper out of his jacket pocket. It was folded in a small square. He opened it carefully, glanced at it, refolded it, and tossed it to me. He had written down a quotation from somebody named John Tyndall. Much later I looked Tyndall up in the library and was surprised to discover he was a Victorian popularizer of science, though evidently a pretty humble one. "The mind may be compared to a musical instrument with a certain range of notes, beyond which in both directions we have an infinitude of silence."

In jumping up to kiss my father I almost overturned the boat. He laughed but I wasn't yet fifteen, wouldn't allow myself to be mocked, and had all I could do to keep from crying.

That night my parents were invited to dinner by a couple of pluto-crats who owned a huge white house across the lake. Perhaps they wanted to lord it over their neighbors who merely rented or maybe they were just sociable. Leda and I, well provided with food, various commandments of the Thou-Shalt-Not variety, and a phone number, were to be on our own until around 11 p.m. Shortly after our parents left, dressed up in uncon-vincing summer colors, Leda got on the phone and pretty much stayed there. Leda on the phone does not afford edifying or musical listening. Even through a closed bedroom door I could hear the diphthongs and conspiratorial laughter of the sought-after girl. What she really craved was Joe but she had to make do with talking to her friends long-distance about Joe and complaining about "this hell-hole" and "the mute moron," a phrase she enunciated with particular emphasis. Alliteration, I had discovered, provides fairly cheap effects.

I had to get out of the house. I took down the lantern that hung by the back door, got a book of matches from a kitchen drawer, gathered up my Williams—the less my family talked to me the more the poets did—and also a bottle of something from the highest cupboard. With the lantern in one hand, the bottle in the other, and Williams under one arm, I headed for the dock. I felt like drinking and reading and generally howling at the new moon, whose monthly renewal, whose period, was supposed to be a cosmic simile, an echo of my own.

The pines rose black against the clear sky, mobbed with stars I could never have seen at home. The silent night was like my own silence, disclosing much and nothing at the same time. The lights of the houses across the lake danced across the water and made me think of the agile, well-dressed couples, dancers in old movies, of my own promised adulthood, still so far off. I arranged the lamp and, to the sound of little whomps as the boat rose and fell, settled down to read.

I was well advanced in the book, deep into the nineteenth century. I read a couple of poems by Thomas Hardy and liked them the first time through, feeling I had understood both tolerably well. The next was a long poem by Sidney Lanier, "The Marshes of Glynn." This I didn't care for at all; in fact, it was the first for which I hadn't wanted to thank Mr. Oscar Williams. Lanier's verses were cluttered with every one of the devices we'd be tested on in English class, assonance, alliteration, onomatopoeia; there were irritating archaisms, relentless rhythms, ponderous rhymes. Lanier, it seemed to me, did badly what Poe had done better. On top of this, it has to be the soggiest poem ever written. I got as far as the rising of the moon on page 457:

And the marsh is meshed with a million veins,
That like as with rosy and silvery essences flow
    In the rose-and-silver evening glow.
    Farewell, my lord Sun!

I lay the book down by the lantern, opened the bottle of whatever it was, and took a big swig, as if it had been Pepsi-Cola. I had never tasted hard liquor before and it was awful, burning and sour. I dutifully took another hit anyway. I drank because I thought I ought to, because my life seemed to be running down some inward drain, because weeks of silence had furnished me with some of the prerequisites of the solitary drunk as well as the poet. That is, I was beginning to have a self but also to want to forget it.

9.

I woke up late and more than a little woozy, but also exuberant, the way you do when suddenly recalling some unprecedented midnight achievement, an orgy or giving birth. As I reached down to the floor beside the bed, I could hear them all at breakfast and felt a million miles away, as if I had absconded years before and become only the kind of memory that no one bothers mentioning, not because it's too painful but too faded.

I had slipped back in and hidden from Leda. If she had smelled the alcohol on me she would have told. Had I remembered to put the bottle back? I hadn't drunk all that much really, just enough.

It had been marvelous, opening like a lily, turning inside out. I lay still and recalled the dream-like scribbling, the swift second thoughts and rearrangements. How long had it all lasted? The stars, the words? Ever since, writing has always seemed to me to take place outside of ordinary time, and this is one of the reasons getting started is so difficult; for how can the timeless kick in at 2:45 on a Saturday afternoon?

What language can do, I suppose that had been my theme, or correcting language so that it should do it, finding how to speak as a way of pounding through and not just up against all the walls in the world. Loosened by booze and, in a negative sense, inspired by Sidney Lanier, I had pushed away turbid music and strained metaphors but at the same time sensed that some kind of music is compulsory and metaphor inescapable, because language, at least once you renounce its abuse and visit it in books of poetry, shows itself to be a tissue of metaphors, filaments bound to the world of dirt and doorknobs. Even the most abstract nouns—administration, education, bureaucracy—barely hide a tactile thingness. You see a girl serving up food and medicine, a man with a stick goading cattle into their runs; you can picture the despondent supplicants lined up outside the office, the overheated air, the aroma of inkwells and rubber stamps. Not to evade all this is good, and not to let others do it, either.

I lay for a few more minutes listening to the clink of knives against plates, thump of mugs on wood, the peevish just-awake voice of Leda, my mother's replies, cut sharp as finger sandwiches, Father's soft baritone, teasing them both. From this string quartet I had made myself a truant. Now that my silence was going to end I already missed it a little. Still, it thrilled me to know my absence was about to be over, and why.

I read through the last draft, could think of nothing to change, and got up to brush my teeth. For such an occasion one's mouth should be as clean as possible. Also, one ought to be properly dressed. I chose a pair of chinos and a cotton pullover one size too large.

They all saw that I was holding a piece of paper, holding it up in front of me like a chorister. Leda looked away, Mother frowned, Father appeared both glad and anxious. But the really enchanting thing was that all of them were silent.

I took one more step forward and read aloud my first poem:

I could tell you what the night was like,
the moon a lemon rind, a sour
tequila sky nauseated with stars;
but that is not my style.

I go in for plain speaking. So:
it was merely dark; I was simply drunk;
the moon was a lot newer than my style
but far older than your metaphors.

10.

Four years and two months later, when I was at last off at college, I sat in my small dormitory room and wrote a letter to my father. The next morning I mailed it to his office, where Mrs. Ardekian would put it aside as not pertaining to business. I asked if he remembered the first letter he had ever sent me and said I was sorry for taking so long to answer it. What followed was chiefly a mixture of apologies and thanks, a kind of critical review of my adolescence; in other words, just the kind of soup a dutiful daughter might eventually serve up to a much loved, much missed father.

There was a great deal for which to be grateful, I said, and plenty of which to be ashamed. Of that month he found so terrible and baffling, and to which he brilliantly never alluded, I said that perhaps it merited both gratitude and shame. I had since learned the difference between the silence that is chosen and the wordless loneliness that is not and added that I was in for more of the latter. But while I was sorry for causing him anxiety back then and for cutting even for four weeks the skein of words that tied us together, a string that had begun with my first stuttered da-da,

I could not be whole-heartedly contrite for what I had done. I had gained too much by it and it was hard to muster up remorse for what made me grateful, what had given me to myself. Could he understand that, thinking of an arduous future full of carefully chosen words, but when I would never be so intact, so sealed-off and safe, I felt some affection for that old shame?

I wound up this way: "Maybe you'll remember that, in that sweet and desperate letter of yours, you quoted Plutarch at me. Well, I want to reply even to that and so here's an even more obscure Roman saying: 'I have often regretted my speech, my silence, never.'"

Leuterre

I.

The mayor was more than satisfied by how the day had gone and enjoyed telling his wife all about it over their aperitifs. The evening before, she had the pleasure of pointing out that hospital administrators, even those with ambitious and charismatic husbands, do not take mornings off for photo opportunities with visiting dignitaries. The mayor was not a calculating man yet he was a man who calculated. Well, he had thought with a mental shrug, such a wife, politically astute within her feminist limits, was an asset, particularly to a conservative male who delighted in shooting small game.

Things really had come off well at the train station, considering the steady rain. June's weather can be so changeable. A crowd of perhaps two thousand showed up. Being in the main literary enthusiasts and university types, they were not exactly raucous, but they did cheer when he presented the framed certificate and the oversized, gold-plated key. Especially gratifying was the presence of so much media, with their cameras and lights; there had even been a helicopter. Krantz's doing probably. The coverage stamped the event as of national—even international—significance. It was just the sort of off-beat story that could be used to close a newscast on a pleasantly insignificant note anywhere on the planet.

The great novelist had declined to speak at length but he was gracious in accepting his honorary citizenship and the key and at least produced an audible thank-you. Leuterre could be proud; it *was* proud. His city looked good; *he* looked good. Krantz had been right to advise him to seize the opportunity, peculiar though the whole business undoubtedly was.

Krantz had come to his office in a state of exhilaration just the week before, clasping two of the national dailies to his narrow chest. "Yesterday three members of the National Academy of Arts and Letters proposed Richard Kord for election," he declared.

"So what?" said the Mayor, who had never known what to make of Kord's work and its queer relation to his city, though he had been apprised of Kord's contributions to tourism.

Krantz remained standing as he explained the matter in his annoyingly clever and condescending manner. A good thing he lacked even a drop of the Mayor's charisma; he'd make a formidable rival.

"There's a provision in the by-laws of the Academy excluding non-citizens."

"Quite proper. And so what?"

Krantz broke into a grin and held out one palm like a smug teacher of geometry. "And so we make him a citizen. We get the Council to offer Kord honorary citizenship in Leuterre."

"Would the Academy buy that?"

"Who cares? It's good for us."

The Mayor considered. "And what if Kord declines our offer? We'd look pretty foolish, wouldn't we? And don't forget that a lot of voters aren't exactly big fans of Mr. Kord."

"First, there's no need to make the offer public unless he accepts. Second, I think he will accept."

"He's been invited to visit before, hasn't he?"

"Oh, plenty of times. But only by literary organizations and booksellers. Not by us. I really think he'll come."

"How about the University? Haven't they been after him for years?"

"I'm not saying it's guaranteed, just that you should trust me on this. It's his chance to get into the Academy, to be the first foreigner to do so. It raises his profile and his publishers will love it. Besides, we do owe him a lot. If he didn't exactly put us on the map, at least he's responsible for a lot of people coming here. Your constituents do a tidy business in literary tours. The connection's been a clear benefit. This is a win-win, as they say over there."

"Not everybody's going to think so. Not everyone thinks we owe Kord anything. In fact, some think just the contrary. And a lot of them are my supporters."

"Philistines," Krantz snapped dismissively.

II.

When she was sixteen Leda Lirette read her first book by Richard Kord and decided that she would someday write a doctoral dissertation about him. Given her nature, talents, and the fact that she lived in Leuterre, it was not remarkable that, even at such an early age, she should be absorbed by Kord's books or that, her good looks notwithstanding, she considered herself fated to become an academic. What was surprising was what she wanted to write about.

At twenty-three Leda knew what all the critics had said of Kord's work. There was praise for the human scope of the novels, the range of characters, the inventiveness of his plots, the breadth of his historical imagination; for Kord had a firm grasp on Leuterre's long history from its origin as a Roman garrison to its present post-industrial sprawl. She had read theoretical critiques of the experiments with narrative method in his short stories and novellas, elucidations of the symbolism that made his work transcend the local, whole monographs on the dead authors who had allegedly influenced him, his use of liturgical structures, speculations on his religious and political views, articles purporting to explicate the deeper meanings of this or that passage in his work. Leda was as impressed by all this as anybody else, as, for instance, her thesis advisor, Professor Van Orden. Professor Van Orden, however, was dubious about Leda's proposed line of research and pressed on her the need for "a practical focus" and the obligation to make an "original contribution to scholarship, no matter how modest"—in other words, she wanted Leda to aim low. She suggested Kord's use of the first-person plural and how it connected him to various nineteenth-century writers or perhaps the influence of Herman Melville, a subject which, in her view, had hardly been exhausted. But what Leda craved was to pluck out the heart of what was most mysterious about Kord's work, its *how*—how did he know so much about the city —and, still more, its *why*—why did he write about Leuterre at all, Leuterre and nowhere else.

Kord's latest book, *Leuterre by Night*, was a collection of intricately related stories, each set between dusk and dawn in one of the city's neighborhoods. The characters were of every age and social class, from a toddler to a senile widow, from a homeless immigrant to a corrupt bank official. There was violence and love, sacrifice and loneliness. Not all the neighborhoods were familiar to Leda, but the ones she did know were described, as always, with correct street names, recognizable landmarks and, above all, those little details that thrilled the locals, such as the small butcher shop that sold a particular kind of liver sausage or the rules of a complicated game involving two tennis balls and a garage door only played by children in a four-block section of the Rheinach. Kord was precise about school uniforms and restaurant menus, the shape of church steeples, forgotten local saints whose feast days were kept by a handful of old women. Into one story he even worked a little stand of beech trees frequented by boys and girls who knew there are no better trees for climbing than beeches. Leda had played there herself. Everything was correct, as if Kord had been writing in plein air, so to speak, as if he'd devoted his life to soaking up the local color and the life of a medium-sized city which never seemed to Leda as rich as it did in Kord's books. Leda had devoured the stories in a single sitting.

Leda Lirette had been one of those precocious children with whom the public schools find it difficult to cope, except that her brilliance was not in mathematics, chess, or music—those lofty athletics of pure reason in which success requires a miraculous sort of brain and no experience of the world. Leda did rather poorly in math, in fact, but she was a brilliant reader, extracting so much meaning from what she was assigned in school that each new teacher, grading the girl's first essay of the term, accused her of plagiarism. As a result, Leda developed a horror of injustice in general and false accusations in particular. She was physically incapable of sitting through a frame-up movie.

By fifteen she had taken her education into her own hands, working her way through all the classics neglected by the official curriculum, to the puzzlement and sometimes the consternation of her parents, who would wonder why her bath lasted an hour, only to find the girl, neck-deep in tepid water, lost in Thucydides or Goethe. It was for her sixteenth birthday that an aunt gave her Kord's *The Urban World* and she was hooked. Up till then there had been for her a sharp and even reassuring separation between literature and actuality, what she read and where she lived. Reading Kord, she was astounded by the disregarded world around her and enthralled by its transformation into words. It was as though Richard Kord had thrown magic dust over Leuterre, metamorphosing the banal and ordinary city into a place as profound and full of wonder as St. Petersburg or Mississippi. For Leda, reading Kord's work was delightfully dissonant because it mixed the commonplace with the exotic and infused the everyday with the mythic.

Now he was here. He would be giving a public reading and she was determined to meet him. Professor Van Orden might not be interested in her ambition, might scoff at the idea of a mere child solving the well-guarded mystery, but Leda had a hypothesis.

III.

The Mayor was still in a good humor. Settled in his easy chair he considered his guests and thought about the symmetry of the two couples, a brace of congruencies all dressed up. The University Rector and his wife had been his guests for dinner and he would be theirs at the University. The Rector's wife was a distinguished professor, his ran a hospital—four accomplished people who were no threat to one another. His wife looked quite feminine tonight; he was happy she had chosen to wear the pearls his mother had given her. Professor Van Orden and her husband the Rector looked reassuringly just like what they were. He checked his watch.

"It's very good of you to come," the Rector was saying. "We seldom get to see you at university events."

"Thanks for that 'get to,' Rector. But really this is a civic event. After all, Kord's our city's unofficial laureate. May I get you another sherry?"

The Mayor's wife stood up and scowled a little. "That's exactly what's wrong," she complained. "Kord is our laureate and nobody has any idea why. Besides, he's not exactly flattering about us, is he?"

Professor Van Orden, who did not use her husband's name and was keen that everybody know she had been a professor before she married, spoke as she might at a seminar.

"Quite true, Madam Mayor. Kord has singled us out and, given his talent, it's an honor. To be sure, it's an unasked-for one but did Paris ask for Hugo or Prague for Kafka? I'd say he's given us our due. No more and no less."

"Excuse me, it just makes no sense and I don't care for mystification. What does he say when people ask him about it? They must ask him all the time."

"Ask him what?" said the Mayor, turning his head from one woman to the other.

"Why he writes exclusively and incessantly about Leuterre when he doesn't even live in this country, let alone this city."

"Oh," said Professor Van Orden, "on that point he's said a variety of things."

The Rector laughed. "Kord once said, 'It's a wonderful town.' Thought I might use that tonight."

"So it is," the Mayor chimed in congenially. "Wonderful."

"He's said other things too," added Professor Van Orden. "I've read all the published interviews. He said 'Why not?' He said, 'Leuterre is reality.' He said, 'I prefer not to say.'"

"Prefer not to say?"

"Yes. And he told one interviewer, 'Leuterre's a vast subject. I haven't come near exhausting it yet.'"

"Some joke," said the Mayor's wife.

"My favorite answer is the simplest."

"Which was?"

"'Leuterre is what I write.'" The professor raised a finger. "Notice, he doesn't say it's what I write about."

"As if he made us," said the Rector, amused.

"Well, he certainly doesn't flatter us."

"No, my dear. We're supposed to flatter him."

"Precisely. What for? It's like having to thank a stranger for sending you a present that's too big, too ugly, and too confusing."

"Complex," corrected the professor softly.

"And why's he here now?"

"You know why, my dear."

"Just to get into the Academy? I don't believe it. Kord's world-famous while our Academy's an antique, a club for sycophants and back-stabbers. Why it's just a relic of cultural nationalism as dated as—as celluloid collars."

"Or telegrams," added the Rector helpfully.

"My wife's not a fan of Kord," explained the Mayor superfluously. "She thinks he's some sort of voyeur. Apparently he wasn't very kind about her hospital in one of his novels."

"*Intensive Care*," said Professor Van Orden, who answered questions even if nobody asked them.

"Didn't read it myself," said the Mayor complacently.

"It's actually very moving," said the Rector, who had liked the book; moreover, he had the feeling that he hadn't been holding up his end of the conversation.

The Mayor checked his watch again. "We really ought to be on our way. So, Rector, how do we do it? What's the drill?"

"I thought you might want to make a few opening remarks. As you say, it is a civic event. Then I introduce Lucille and she introduces Kord. He reads, takes a few questions."

"Unless he prefers not to," scoffed the Mayor's wife.

"Yes, if he chooses, he takes questions. And then there's the reception. We're using Stiegler Ballroom. Light refreshments. Pleasant chatter. Then we all go home."

The Mayor's wife was determined not to let go of her displeasure. "You don't think that's a little excessive, a bit, well, heraldic? He introduces you, you introduce your wife, she introduces Kord?"

"Well," mumbled the embarrassed Rector.

"She's got a point," the Mayor chimed in. He had, out of prudence, been looking for a chance to agree with his wife about something or other. "Just keep it short, Rector, and I'll do likewise." He turned to Professor Van Orden. "Not you, Madam. Of course. You're our Kord expert, after all. We'll all be listening closely to you. Maybe taking notes."

IV.

The reading was open to everyone at the University, but Leda begged Professor Van Orden to arrange for her to get into the reception.

"You're quite the little terrier, Leda. Well, it is an opportunity not to be missed, I agree."

"Yes, Professor. Most definitely not to be missed."

"I'll see about it. After all, if you're going to make him your special subject you've a better right to be there than, say, Rhadamanthus."

They giggled like a pair of adolescents. Rhadamanthus was Professor Hadiquet, an unpopular medievalist who, even if he was not the misogynist he was rumored to be, always wore bow ties. Except to his face, nobody used his real name.

Leda arrived at the auditorium early. She wanted to claim a seat in the fourth row, close enough to the stage but not so near as to have to crane her neck. Her copy of *Leuterre by Night* was in her large handbag along with a legal pad, three ballpoints, and a note in an unsealed envelope. Professor Van Orden had called to tell her that not only could Leda attend the reception but that she would personally accompany her to the ballroom and introduce her to Richard Kord. She was amused by

Leda's childish squeal of delight. "In my day it was John Lennon and Mick Jagger who made us wet our pants; not Böll or even Yevtushenko," she mused nostalgically but said nothing to embarrass either Leda or herself.

Leda had a long wait in the fourth row. The hall eventually filled to the rafters and not only with university people. At last the principals took the stage, marching out, she thought, not unlike a firing squad escorting a condemned prisoner. She was surprised that Kord was dressed so informally, in a sport jacket, black jeans, an open-necked shirt. He looked younger than fifty-seven, younger even than he did in the grainy photograph on the dust jackets of his last three books. This depicted him in a loose greatcoat seated on a park bench staring at the ground like a defeated infantryman. There were blurs in the background of two pedestrians and three cars. It was a poignant image, in Leda's opinion, suggesting individuality to the point of isolation. She examined him as he took his seat. Kord was lean and tan, the way some Americans were. With a thrill of interest and disgust she wondered if he could be one of those foreign authors who made it a point to seduce young women wherever they went.

The Mayor spoke pompously but briefly, saying absolutely nothing but in just the right key. The Rector was hieratic, as if announcing the Nobel prize or the death of a monarch, but he too kept it brisk. Professor Van Orden, however, approached the podium with a sheaf of papers, laid them on the lectern, and took out her reading glasses before pausing to look over the crowd. It was exactly what she did in class.

"Your Honor, Rector, ladies and gentlemen . . . I was about to refer to Richard Kord in the usual fashion as our honored guest but it seems to me a question whether he is *our* guest or we are *his*."

It was a promising opening, Leda thought, but unfortunately the professor then turned to her notes and the next sentence—a real python even by Van Orden standards—lost the crowd irretrievably.

"The modern novel and the modern city have always been closely conjoined, mingled even in the social and economic substructure that brought both into being, but never as intimately as Leuterre and the works of Richard Kord, so much so that he has made us see in how many respects a novel is a city; that is, a concatenation of the accidental and the deliberate, of chance and consequence, clusters of human beings, high and low, in an incoherence made intelligible and orderly by plots, by the choice of hero or heroine, the very choice all of us make when we open our eyes each morning."

The professor persisted in this vein, making an analogy between traffic patterns, street grids, and narrative structure, dropping big names like Balzac and Dickens, Dostoyevsky and Proust, and generally wearing her learning as heavily as possible. Kord, she went so far as to say, had done for their Leuterre what Homer had for Ilium—or Dante for Hades. Through it all Leda kept her gaze fixed on the author himself. He sat very still, looking not only as if all this had nothing to do with him but as if he'd gone stone deaf. The speech contrived to be fulsome and technical without really coming to any point. At length it petered out and the professor called on Kord to read a story from his latest book, which he dutifully stood up and did. He read well enough but without any effort to dramatize, to draw his listeners in. The audience listened, if not reverentially, at least politely. Leda had been curious about which story he would select. He chose the one about the unemployed man who, just to get a little warmth, wanders into a university lecture on a February morning and ends up making a stunning speech about economics. The story was set in the very auditorium in which it was now being read. At first Leda thought this was just a bit of cleverness but then she saw a deeper significance in it; for Leda Lirette never failed to get the literary point of anything. It came to her in the form of a simple sentence of just four words: There are two auditoriums.

Professor Van Orden would have done better to have stopped after that first sentence of hers.

Stiegler Ballroom was a linoleum-floored cavern that, so far as Leda knew, had never witnessed anything as festive as a ball. It was now divided by red curtains in order to create a more intimate space; that is, one that would be crowded. Serving tables had been set up and covered with starched white linen cloths. Students in short jackets and black trousers stood at attention behind them as if guarding Buckingham Palace and not stuffed mushrooms, mini-sausages, tea, coffee, and the second-rate wines favored by university caterers. As receptions are planned to last for only an hour or so there were no chairs for sitting and chatting. The affair was the usual see-and-be-seen, look-over-your-interlocutor's-shoulder, balance-the-food-and-drink sort of thing. Like ants around dropped candy, people clustered about the most important personages, the Mayor, the Rector—above all, Richard Kord.

Robert Wexelblatt

Professor Van Orden, true to her promise, had taken Leda in tow and made straight for the novelist; but, in their passage across the ballroom, she was accosted three times by colleagues who wanted either to praise or take her to task for her remarks. The annoyingly insistent Professor Moreau, who apparently wanted to give a lecture of his own, would not let her go. "An actual city, of course, is not a novel," he said. "You know this perfectly well. Naturally. Still, when sitting down to read— or, I venture to say, to *write*—one can't foresee all the contingencies to come, the accidents which must nevertheless not appear to be accidents . . ."

Leda stood impatiently at her professor's side, glaring at Moreau who wouldn't stop: "Perhaps, as you imply, the god of the city is indeed a novelist, but, if so, he's a god who can only play at pre-destination and you know—would be perfectly lost without the collaboration of his characters who . . ."

Leda opened her bag and took out the envelope. She felt as she did when, as a child, she was first taken to see Santa Claus, cajoled into sitting on an alien lap to disclose her heart's desire. Her hands were damp.

Finally Professor Van Orden cut Moreau off. "Maybe a city's just a novel without a plot. Please excuse me, but I've promised Ms. Lirette . . ."

Richard Kord graciously thanked Professor Van Orden for her introduction, flattered her by alluding to one of her publications, then fell silent, looking curiously at Leda, who blushed.

"This is my most brilliant student, Leda Lirette, and she intends to write her doctoral thesis on you, Mr. Kord."

Kord's eyebrows went up and he gave a goofy little laugh, as if the notion of a doctoral dissertation devoted to him was, of all conceivable notions, the most absurd.

Leda had never met a famous author before, especially not one she had been reading most of her conscious life. To her, Kord's work meant so much and it partook so much of the eternal that it was impossible to imagine it being composed by this particular body sitting down in some physical place on a day that had an actual date. Up close Kord's face looked nice, thoughtful, less open or blank than those of younger Americans she'd met. She mumbled a few words and pressed her envelope into his extended hand.

Kord opened the envelope at once and read her note. Leda took one of the ballpoints from her bag and handed it to Kord. He gave another little laugh, more embarrassed than amused. He took the pen, raised his knee, rested her note on it, and scrawled something.

"What's this?" said Professor Van Orden jovially. "An autograph or an assignation?"

Leda, having succeeded so far, was emboldened to say, "I haven't had my autograph yet. If you would, Mr. Kord?" And she reached again into her bag, pulling out her copy of *Leuterre by Night*. Kord took it and wrote a dedication on the flyleaf, then, with a mock click of his heels, bowed and returned first the pen, then the book, and finally her note.

Leda placed all three smartly in her bag and said, "Your most devoted reader in all Leuterre." Then the audience was over. Now she couldn't wait to get away from the professor who was bound to ask questions. It was the Mayor's wife who came unexpectedly to her rescue.

"Splendid job, Professor," she said, wine in hand, and, manifestly, some quantity inside, "not that I had any idea what you were talking about."

Leda excused herself hurriedly and headed for the least lit corner of the hall. She opened the book first.

To Leda from an Ugly Duckling, Richard Kord.

That, she thought, was clever of him, to be suggestive and not at the same time.

Then she opened her note. Kord had scribbled: *Ten tomorrow morning? Lobby of Hotel Kristall*. Above it she had written: *This isn't your first visit to Leuterre. Will you meet me tomorrow?*

V.

The rain that had let up overnight returned in the morning but Leda's spirits were anything but sodden. She awoke feeling like a gambler who had played a successful long-shot. And, the payoff was yet to come.

Her seventeenth-century seminar met at ten-thirty. One of her most earnest classmates was to deliver a paper on the disputes between John Donne and Robert Bellarmine and Leda had no hesitation in cutting it to go to the Hotel Kristall.

She dressed with care, tempted by but rejecting a green sundress in favor of her best jeans, a cream silk turtleneck, low-heeled boots, and her new jacket. It was a student's outfit but stylish and not cheap.

By eight o'clock both her parents had departed for work which left her plenty of time to collect her thoughts and get to the hotel. Then the doubts began. Why had he agreed to the meeting so readily? Did he have designs on her after all and was that why he had chosen his hotel? With shame she recalled Professor Van Orden's tasteless disjunction—"autograph or assignation?" And why, even if she was right, would Kord, who had for decades evaded the very questions she meant to answer, tell a green grad student the truth? *Why Leuterre*, she would have to ask. What was to prevent him dismissing her with . . . *Why not*? or *Because*? After the reading he had declined to take questions, pleading tiredness. He made a joke of it: "I hope you will excuse me. Anyway, my experience is that the natural scientists are right. All questions have answers, but most of the answers are wrong." But then she reflected that, for all Kord knew, she had actual information, not just an inspired guess. She had countered mystification with mystery and the gambit had worked. It would be tricky to let him persist in this delusion but not impossible, and she could avoid lying outright. She had to say as little as possible and let him do all the talking. Maybe it was just to tell her—to tell somebody—that he had come to Leuterre. It wasn't entirely improbable. She didn't believe he'd come because he yearned to be elected to the stuffy Academy. It was like Einstein applying to the plumbers union.

On the tram, watching Leuterre unroll through the droplet-covered window, it was natural to think of how Kord had written of this boulevard, of Frunzi Square, how he had depicted a crowd and the weekday traffic near the lycée, told the history of the cathedral and the scandal behind the monument to Count de Vide. One day in class Professor Moreau, indignant that they knew nothing of the Dreyfus Affair, indicted her generation. He said that to them "nothing's real until it's on television." It was meant mockingly and yet there was a truth in it he didn't intend, that nothing is fully real until it is imagined because perception is an aggressively creative act. One need not do the imagining oneself but somebody must. That was what Kord had done for her. Before reading him she had felt she lived nowhere. This was the real source of her great, simple idea. No one could have so much feeling for a place without having been there. But the emotional power of a place is owing to what has occurred there, especially what has happened to us in it. Therefore she deduced not only that Kord must have been in Leuterre before but that something indelible had befallen him. It was simple logic.

The Hotel Kristall is a baroque pile situated on prime real estate. It sits on the Inner Ring, across from both the Opera House and the Rosenheim Gardens. As she walked up the broad pavement to its golden doors Leda's mind was in high gear. Not too many years before a young woman dressed as she was would probably not have been admitted to the lobby of the Hotel Kristall; at the least she would have been sneered at and frowned upon. Now she simply waited for the doorman to do his job. It fortified her confidence to have this huge specimen dressed like a field marshal hold the door for her and touch his cap. Then she remembered this was exactly what Hannah Adler had thought when entering the Kristall to commit her first adultery in *Neither Father Nor Lover*. How many scenes had Kord set in the hotel? Always he associated it with sexual entanglement, the decadence of the privileged, the pretensions of parvenus. In his books nothing really good ever happened in this hotel. Why had he chosen to stay there? Of course, she realized, Kord didn't choose. He was the guest of Leuterre, after all, and could hardly have been offered anything inferior to a suite at the Kristall.

Inside, Leda found herself in another world, one shut off from the noise and glare of workaday Leuterre. The lobby was a marvel of soft shade, soft air, soft sounds, soft furniture and carpets. Even the carved wood of the reception desk and the display case of antique crystal appeared to be melting. She scanned the place, looking for Kord. She checked her watch and cursed herself for being five minutes early. Impatience might take her down a peg in Kord's estimation—if, indeed, there was an estimate to be diminished. What should she do if he actually made a pass? It would be awful and yet here she was. She ought to have prepared something graceful to say, something clever, humane, sharp and gentle all at once.

She was staring at the sleekly groomed desk clerks when she felt a touch on her shoulder, tentative and light.

"Good morning," Kord said sheepishly, ducking his head. "Hope I didn't startle you."

He was dressed in blue jeans and a tweed sport jacket and looked even more informal than he had the night before.

"Not at all. No. Good morning."

Kord seemed ill at ease and struck her as more curious than anxious. He didn't leer at all; in fact, he seemed almost boyishly shy. What now?

"Have you had any breakfast?"

A splendid question. Leda felt relief, even gratitude.

"The coffee here, like everything else, is the absolute superlative, the very best."

They went into the café which was almost empty. Kord directed her to a booth at the rear. It was next to a window that looked across the boulevard to the very Rosenheim Gardens where Hubert Beifeld had murdered André Fassenet in *The Big Deal*.

When they were settled Leda said, "Thank you for seeing me, Mr. Kord. It's a privilege."

"Is it? Well, it's quite a privilege for me to be the subject of a doctoral dissertation. Also to meet such a dogged researcher, Mademoiselle. So, you found the police record?"

This jolted Leda. Best to smile and say nothing, she thought, and treat the question as rhetorical. She smiled at Kord slyly, like a journalist guarding a source.

A waiter came and they ordered coffee. Kord asked for a plate of brioche and croissants. Leda was relieved not to get the fish-eye from the waiter. The cliché, *old enough to be your father*, zipped through the nebula of thoughts in her busy head. All the sources said that Kord had never married, that he now lived somewhere in New England, and alone. Yet he wrote brilliantly about women. What did the man do about sex? In his books it wasn't joyous, at least not for long; it almost seemed to her that he punished self-surrender and openness.

She still hadn't lied to him. "Why don't you fill in the blanks for me?" she asked invitingly. It was worth a try.

"I suppose I should be surprised nobody found out before. Frankly, it's a relief. I grew sick of the mysteriousness long ago but it seemed best just to let it ride. Besides, it's not easy to explain, me and Leuterre."

"What's the idiom? I'm all ears?"

"How about your dissertation? If I fill in all the blanks you'll have to change subjects."

She smiled and, true to her method, stifled a reply. If the man had brought himself to the point of making a confession, he was more apt to deliver it to someone who isn't talking herself. She was determined to do her utmost to be a vacuum in order that he should fill it.

"All writers are guilty but life," he said, leaning his head back against the seat, "isn't like those detective novels where the guilty have a single premeditated motive. The very first story I wrote, unpublished, was about Leuterre. *Before the Night Train* I called it and it was terrible. I tried to figure out why. There were plenty of reasons; there always are. Most of all I made the rookie error of confusing what happened with what's true. I'd tried to reproduce a memory rather than to imagine an action. A memory's like a finished object, a doorknob or a baseball—easy enough to put your hand around the outside of it."

Leda was bewildered and said so. She held up her bag. "May I take notes?"

Kord shook his head. "I'd prefer you didn't. Not that I want more secrets. If I wanted secrets we wouldn't be here. It's just that taking notes is what interviewers and college students always do and then I can't just talk to them; I begin to arrange things for their notebooks."

"All right," she said quickly. "Tell me whatever you want, in any order you like."

"And you'll just listen? Good. I once read about this old Jewish man. He'd made it to the States after the war and started a business. The business took off and he made a fortune. He married and had kids and then grandkids. He bought a big estate on Long Island and traveled everywhere first class. The thing was he always kept this little suitcase under his bed. Understand? When I was young I was always looking to escape, not because I was insecure but because I didn't feel I belonged where I was. I was supposed to be somewhere else. Maybe it wasn't belonging where I was that turned me into a writer. At least it made me a conscious being. My family moved from the city to the suburbs when I was twelve. Up till then I'd been a healthy animal—all playgrounds and the guys and pop music. But then I became unhappy, a new experience for me, and I didn't understand it except that I knew it was important and that I wasn't really eager for it to end. Reading was like that for me in those days too—I mean, I didn't understand what I read yet I could tell if it was good. Dostoyevsky was good. Flaubert was good. Kleist was good. I wanted to work my way right through the classics section of the library but the truth is I read all those masterpieces the way lonesome people wolf down science fiction and historical romances. It's quite possible to read good books in a terrible way. Pure escapism. The books made me yearn for a richer life, deeper depths and higher highs. Anything but the bland boredom of my suburban adolescence. I felt like I was holding my breath, a caterpillar doing time, hoping to turn into something that could fly."

"How did you get to Leuterre?"

"So, the order does matter, eh? Linear narrative? Okay. By the summer between my sophomore and junior years in college I'd saved up enough to bum around Europe and by then my parents weren't exactly inclined to dissuade me. Found a cheap charter that left the day after my last examination. Got the wash-and-wear shirts, the backpack, the blue blazer and this book by a guy named Frommer, *Europe on $5 A Day*. The Bible of its time and place. Every American under thirty had a copy of Frommer so we all ran into each other everywhere we ate or slept or gawked. At five bucks a day I calculated I could manage ten weeks. I've hardly gone anywhere since, I mean just to travel. I suppose I used up all my wanderlust that summer when I became a ghost. All right. Now, Leuterre. It was just a layover on the way to somewhere else, of course, somewhere prettier, more famous. Even Frommer didn't have anything to say about Leuterre. I arrived in the morning and was going to take the night train out. So I walked around. I marched down that boulevard out there, strolled through those gardens over there."

"Forty years and nothing's changed on the Inner Ring?"

"A hundred and thirty-five years, actually."

Nothing is more tedious to the young than their elders' nostalgia. Leda was uninterested in Kord's adolescent peregrinations; she wanted to hear about that police report she was supposed to have found.

"So that's when it happened? When you were here in the Inner Ring?" Still no lies.

"No. I went further out looking for cheap eats, all the way into the Rheinach. I was checking out a greasy spoon when this girl in a miniskirt came up to me. She was pretty and I knew absolutely nothing. She took my hand, mentioned a price, and I went with her. I was lonely. People looked through me. Becoming a little more invisible every day for two weeks had turned me into a ghost—and what seemed worse, a virginal one. The hotel she took me to wasn't much like this palace and the transaction didn't take long. I'd just gone back out in the street when, stunned rather than gratified, this hysterical man with a policeman in tow dashed right up to me, pointed in my face and began shouting. So far as I could make out I'd punched his wife and robbed his jewelry store."

"Didn't they search you?"

"Sure. On the spot. Didn't seem to matter. You see, I had on a blazer and it was blue. That seemed to be the chief point."

"Did they beat you up, the police?"

"No, but they scared me. Took my passport and my belt and locked me in a cell about the size of, and with much the same smell as, a beer keg. That's how I described it in that first story. Fancy sentence structure and all. Three hours later a woman came into the station. They told me about it later. Said that she hollered that her daughter's no-good boyfriend was a thief and she had proof. She produced the engagement ring he'd swiped. She even had his blazer, blue like mine, but with pockets crammed with bracelets, necklaces, and brooches. The police fetched the jeweler to identify the loot then they turned me loose. They were kind enough to tell me what had happened but not so gracious as to apologize. They handed over my passport and belt. I figured they'd throw the arrest forms away."

"You left the next morning, then?" Leda said quickly, telling herself there was no such thing as a lie of omission.

"Bye-bye, Leuterre. Good riddance, I thought. And yet, Mademoiselle, I've never really been released. As you know."

Leda finished off the last of her coffee and bit into a croissant. It was ineffably light and buttery, a croissant from the other side of the moon.

"So because of that afternoon no—because *of a half-hour forty years ago* when you lost your virginity and got arrested—you've stayed in Leuterre? Mentally, I mean. Emotionally."

Kord spoke seriously. "Not *this* Leuterre. *My* Leuterre."

"I don't quite—"

"Oh, it looks just the same. I've gone to a lot of trouble to make it so. Research. It's all scaffolding, though, to be torn down as soon as the building's up. I've got maps, photo albums, telephone directories, annual reports from the electric and water companies, from any number of companies. I have census figures and subscribe to all the newspapers and half a dozen magazines, including your University's literary journal which, I regret to say, publishes a phenomenal quantity of execrable poetry. I've read all the chief histories and own all the museum catalogues. Then there's the omniscient Internet, our vast collective memory. Amazing what you can find there. Soon nobody'll have to remember anything."

Leda nodded encouragingly.

He pointed at his head. "My Leuterre is a place I made for myself, one where I can imagine I belong. That it's not the purest act of imagination, I admit; but it's still sympathy plus invention, still seeing what isn't visible. It's something, an occasion, a motive. I can say both 'Leuterre, c'est moi' but also 'Kord, il n'est pas Leuterre.'"

Was he honest? "Is Richard Kord your real name?"

Kord looked taken aback by the question then laughed. "Sorry. I got carried away. I'm not used to speaking so freely and it's a little intoxicating. Of course Kord's my real name. Wasn't it on the report you found? It was my grandfather who followed the American custom of changing names. Americans don't just re-invent themselves but also their posterity."

As you have ours, she thought. "He didn't by any chance come from Leuterre, that grandfather of yours?"

"Not even close. He came from Russia. A fine place to leave, a country with absolutely no talent for happiness. But what novels!"

"And you live all alone?"

"What a question. Don't we all? Well, I do now, anyway. Or you could say I live in Leuterre, at least when I'm not here."

"Here, there?"

Kord made a wry face. "Mademoiselle, the only way I ever found to tell the truth is by lying. And I've tried to tell as much of it as I could."

Shocked by a sudden surmise, Leda sat up straight. "And has all this been a lie? Another Leuterre story?"

Kord picked up a brioche, took a bite, chewed it, swallowed, all the while looking her in the eyes, the way liars don't. "Is my work a failure of the imagination or a success? Have I invented Leuterre or has this city dreamed me up? Do I belong to it? Am I its newest citizen only because I'm so alienated? Am I still missing that night train?" He leaned back. "Well, Mademoiselle Leda Lirette, why don't you tell me?"

Salisbury

The unanticipated death of Josh Martin owing to the equally unexpected collision of his twin-engine Cessna with an upstate power pylon set all the talent-mongers in commotion, not excluding Jay Horrocks.

"Get your butt over to that studio," he cried in his Hitler-on-the-phone voice. "Believe me, kid, you're perfect. Perfect. So just don't screw up and you're in, working for life."

"For life?" I queried politely.

"Well, next best thing. Hell, it's Josh Martin. Look, the call's for two so, damnit, get going and let me know after. Got it? You write that address down?"

There was a sign in the lobby: Josh Martin Audition - Fifth Floor - Studio 19. Nineteen is my lucky number. I would bounce the ball nineteen times before every foul shot and eventually the guys got sick of fouling me.

Vivaldi was playing on the elevator, a concerto for two oboes and orchestra that was unfamiliar to me. I rode up and down until it was over. I watched half a dozen would-be Josh Martins get out on the fifth floor before joining them. Vivaldi's my favorite composer, my favorite Italian one anyhow. The auspices were almost too favorable. Imagine, my lucky number and Vivaldi on an elevator.

Going up and down like that I picked up some interesting sociology. For example, I discovered that network people are either young and manic or old and manic. The old ones are more manic mostly because they are trying to conceal their oldness and some are pretty successful at it. In what is oxymoronically called the Entertainment Industry people get demoted as they age. Experience is incompetence. The elevator starts at the top; it ought to be called the demoter. Programming chiefs are usually about twenty-three; they work their way down as they lose touch with the pubescent audience and burn out. With writers it's a little different. As I discovered later, they tend to be older men, cantankerous eccentrics. Some of them don't even bother with hair-weaves or those faded stretch blue jeans. They are comparatively independent spirits with a keen sense of being exploited no matter how much they make. Their superiority and cynicism can be bracing and breathtaking.

I could see right off that the audition was going to be unconventional. True, I had never before auditioned for a soap opera—or "daytime drama," which is the preferred euphemism for the product—but still, one doesn't expect a grand jury. I supposed the entire cast must be there. Unlike Jay Horrocks, who has undiscriminating viewing habits, I had never actually seen *Salisbury*, but it looked like a big gang to me. Save for the very young director in cowboy boots and pony tail, the three rumpled writers, and the Olympian, heavily assisted producer, the rest of the gang looked sure enough like actors and actresses, or, more precisely, like the sort of people who populate soap operas. Very pretty, fantastically coifed, impeccably clad. The young men were absurdly handsome, the older ones trim and prosperous-looking, the young women big-haired, ferociously feline, and roughly evenly matched, the older women either soft as the beds in the better Paris hotels or hard as false teeth.

This crowd all sat more or less together while our bunch of about two dozen unemployed males was directed up to a raised stage and into a suitable number of stackable chairs arranged as if for a school assembly. So, in effect, we were two audiences on two stages; it struck me as odd, metaphysically speaking as well as physically.

The director stood between the two groups and talked to us a little evasively. He began plainly enough.

"Now everybody here loathes auditions, I'm sure," he said ingratiatingly. "That you guys hate them goes without saying, but we don't like 'em either. It's a hell of a lot easier to fire people than to hire them," he added in a take-it-from-me tone. "Now, some of you may know our show and some of you may not. I wouldn't say we're one big happy family, of course"—here there were chuckles from the regulars—"but we do have to live with each other and that's why the whole cast has shown up this morning. Josh Martin wasn't just anybody. Josh wasn't just Audrey's husband, Daphne's lover, Keith's uncle, Letty and Horace's eldest son, Chief of Thoracic Surgery at Salisbury General, the suspected murderer of Sylvester Sloane, or the rest of all that stuff. Josh was—or is—one of us, as I said, and we all miss him . . . and not just from the show either. And we're going to go on missing him until he comes back to us, maybe through one of you. Josh Martin can't be written out of *Salisbury* and so, for all intents, purposes, and ratings, Josh Martin's immortal. The plane crash was a real accident. Not in the script . . . ."

"What's this jerk talking about?" whispered the guy to my left. I took it as a rhetorical question. The fellow to my right was actually taking notes on a little spiral pad, the kind the eager kids used to write their assignments in.

"Now, what we want you to do is simple enough. No reading of lines, no playing of old scenes. We just want you to socialize with us, get to know us, live with us for a day, that's all."

At this point there was a rumble from our side, while the other half of the arena remained impassive. The director hastened to explain as best he could.

"Look, it's simple. For the time being you're all Josh Martin. Now Sam here's one of our writers and he's prepared a little bio of Josh for you to glance over. Sam?"

One of the disheveled writers crossed over to our side and silently handed around photocopied bundles headed *You Are Josh Martin*. This done, he turned away from us with the disdain of the white for the blue collar.

"Now," barked the director, who seemed fond of this transitional, attention-focusing word, "now, you've got ten minutes to read that over and then we'll get started."

Salisbury, as quite a lot of people know, is the longest running soap of all time. Beginning back in the pre-Cambrian epoch, it flourished among the dullish blue-green algae, miraculously survived the great extinction, worked its way deep into pre-history; during the Cretaceous, Triassic, and Jurassic periods it was popular with the gigantic reptiles but even more with the little mammals; narrative complications multiplied as brains swelled and choice displaced tropism. By and by, *Salisbury* plied its course through the tedious afternoons of the troglodytes, figured in Second Maccabees and certain pages of Suetonius, put in hard hours beside the Venerable Bede, and so even to this present day. From epics stamped out around campfires to rude plays, from broadside ballads to the racier ladies' magazines, from the radio at last to network television where *Salisbury* has finally found its promised land which lies just on the other side of the electronic keyhole.

And always at the center, at the still point in the middle of the vortex, was Josh Martin.

Now I was Josh Martin.

Josh Martin's biography is not much like mine. For one thing, his childhood was scarcely more than a pleasant rumor, his adolescence merely something Letty or Horace might allude to in an organ-drenched moment of nostalgia. The truth is that Josh, like Athena, had sprung to life full-grown from the network's mammoth brow, a kind of standard-issue white American professional haute-mesomorph, malleable as silence and every bit as golden, with a whole passel of past but absolutely no moral development to hinder the commercial exigencies of his unpredictable entelechy. Bluntly put, life passed through Josh as cheap goulash does through an imprudent tourist. To be sure, Josh Martin is a character and not a person. And yet nobody, not even the hard-headed Jay Horrocks, spoke of him that way. Hamlet you play; Josh you evidently become.

I myself was born in the customary fashion, between feces and the other thing, a few years after John Kennedy was shot dead. My father adored Kennedy, and being a good Catholic Democrat kept a framed picture of the fallen President above the little desk in the basement where, in his declining years, he did the daily crossword puzzle. The portrait hung next to the BVM Herself. To me they looked like an ideal couple, and why not? Kennedy was a lot like Josh Martin. That is to say, historical legends are more like characters than people. Like characters you pretty much have to take them on faith; to have a good time you've got to suspend your disbelief. Faith breeds immortality, after all. As I see it, for both Josh and JFK myth trumps fact.

I was sent to a parochial school named Holy Cross where the nuns were either tough, senile, or both. In my day most of them were still reeling from Vatican II. With catechism and apologetics, confession and holy days of obligation, Lent and Advent, I drank in the rich stew of an Irish Catholic boyhood and emerged an atheist haunted by all the usual ghosts and odors: sickening incense against the dusty smell of plush pews, boiled corned beef mingled with attar of cooked cabbage, cheap perfume wafting around white Easter bonnets, the must of decaying missals, the alcoholic laughter and alarming keening of wakes, an ingrained weakness for knee socks, the unbeatable sensuality of Bishop Butler's *Lives of the Saints*. In time I became a wise-ass and fell in love with the stage in tenth grade when I landed the part of Floristan Dunphy in *The Bleeding Heart*. I began to use my head. In a couple of years my intellectual rebellion won me a scholarship to Northwestern's Drama department. Even before graduation I had a couple of commercials on my résumé: Long John Silver's seafood and something called Gauntlet after-shave—"throw it down tonight." Then, having attained a bachelor's degree and lost various virginities, I made a bee-line for the Big Apple.

Josh Martin grew up, or at least has always existed, in Salisbury, scion of an old-money family that had resided there since the afore-mentioned pre-Cambrian era. Salisbury is in no particular state of the Union; indeed, no other geographical locations are ever mentioned in Salisbury, not even the United States of America itself, God bless it. Salisbury endures in a sort of ever-changing eternity. Clothes, slang, musical tastes, diets, furniture fads, epithets, and sexual mores are invariably up-to-the-minute, and yet Salisbury is simultaneously exempt from history, a sort of with-it bourgeois paradise. Unacquainted with poverty, Josh passed all his medical exams without studying for them. With me it was different.

My first year in New York I lived on peanut butter, coffee, and Lucky Strikes. I occupied a squalid room a half a step lower than the slightly less sordid studio apartment I later moved into most unhappily with Belinda Wilderstein. That's where I was living when Josh Martin ran into his upstate pylon.

I was dividing my time between waiting tables at a dive called La Nouvelle Heloise and absorbing rejection at auditions more conventional than *Salisbury's*. New York had reached the end of a slushy, slate-cold January. I was sleeping in my overcoat and had no money to support even trivial vices, but I was still so young and Irish that misery only made me romantic, failure sentimental, hunger witty. How was I to grasp what lent Josh Martin his inexhaustible and peculiarly Anglo-Saxon charm?

One night I found under the slops a staggeringly generous tip from a herd of conventioneers I had served with facetious gusto (waiting at La Nouvelle Heloise taught me the resentment of a peasant but was good for my acting). Feeling flush, on the way home I decided on the luxury of a beer and went into an upwardly-mobile bar on West 87th Street. The place was more crowded than I expected at that hour; I had anticipated that the would-be polo players, corporate rock climbers, and ladies with shoulders like fullbacks would be sleeping the sleep of the well vested. It was impossible to say if people were alone or together. I noticed Belinda nearly at once—self-contained, appropriately raven-haired, shapely and so short she had put her bum on her rolled trench coat to reach the bar. The stool next to her was free and I had an impulse almost worthy of Josh himself, whose kind of place it was anyway.

I sidled up, splurged on a Bass, and asked Belinda if she could name the seven dwarfs.

She turned toward, or perhaps on, me. "That a crack about my height?" she said with savage and wholly disproportionate defensiveness, a reaction of which I ought to have taken closer notice. Her hand went reflexively for the trench coat.

"Huh? Oh," I chuckled, "no. No, I was just trying to remember them all—you know, Doc and Grumpy and Sneezy . . . ?"

A stupid line, you'll say, but Belinda had been a compulsive student and could not resist giving any answer she knew.

"You probably forgot Bashful," she said, heedless of the romantic overtones, establishing a bond, breaking the ice and grinning at me—exactly as if she were quite sane.

In only a week I was living with her, enthralled at first by what I later learned to call her mood swings. Like Cleopatra and Mary, Mary, Belinda was quite contrary. She was also from Philadelphia and was starving for some as yet unnamed art. She didn't have a job, and she didn't write or paint or sculpt. Belinda examined things. She did this with the eye of an artist, her scrutinies being stored away to use later in the grand multi-media agglomerations she would stay up designing on deluxe water-color-ist's paper. She examined, to pick just one example, bricks.

Belinda started in on me one ordinarily crazy night as I was trying to sleep after a heavy bout with Heloise. "Well, what do you actually know about them?" It was always worse when she began with a question, for this meant that she had part of her meandering mind fixed on me. "If I were a brick, would you lay me more often? After all, Irishmen are all bricklayers at heart, aren't they? In Philadelphia It's Kelly for Brickwork. Ever hear that one? Kelly's daughter Grace laid actors and princes; her daddy laid bricks all over the goddamn city. Bricks are cool, full of earth karma. You bake them like cakes but they're rough, like dead fish. Stand a little distance away and a brick wall looks like Jehovah's order itself, but if you get up real close the thing's sloppy as hell. Bricks are inhuman, but what's more human? They're man-made, like you infrequently make me.

Bricks're like a child's blocks. They're like an army, all uniform but all individual, a bunch of potential casualties for the wrecking ball. Bricks never touch each other. Brick sounds a lot like prick . . ."

Belinda got a check every month from Philly. She took a lot of pills. Belinda was mad and getting madder. But I had nowhere to go and, to tell the truth, the woman frightened me. I was scared to move out, scared she'd track me down. She grew daily less predictable, spoke more strangely, spent more of her allowance on pot.

In Salisbury the women are all a little like Belinda, at least in their capacity for obsession and hostility and jealousy, albeit they are decidedly saner. Illnesses in Salisbury are comparatively straightforward, not just physical but becoming. Only minor, transient characters take drugs. Nobody smokes anything anymore. Nothing harder than white wine gets drunk. Needless to say, vice flourishes all the same.

At the expiration of the ten minutes allotted for absorbing the hopelessly complicated life-story of Josh Martin, the director motioned us through a large metal door into another studio. Here he ticked us off in groups of six as if for a Czarist firing squad and sent each platoon, by turns, to stand before a bank of stage lights. While this line-up was in progress the cast of *Salisbury* made its way in behind us and milled about sociably, like people in those paintings of big eighteenth-century parties or slave auctions. *Salisbury's* cast was much too large to fit on the little screen all at once. In Salisbury, parties are kept intimate, except for weddings and funerals, which can occur in segments.

The producer and his train of assistants, the director, and those sardonic, sallow, and silent writers scrutinized each crew of Joshes as Belinda herself might have, then consulted like judges at a beauty pageant. After that the director personally informed about a quarter of my compeers that they were, not to put too fine a point on it, no longer Josh Martin. The physical requirements of the job were pretty strict.

After the first cut, the rest of us were released, sent off to party. Salisbury opened wide its collective arms and took us to its collaborative bosom. The socializing centered around a folding picnic table with an exiguous supply of crackers, cheddar, and flat soft drinks in plastic champagne glasses.

I was heading for the food when a man about ten years my senior, with straight blond hair and a tip-top physique, came up to me with arm

Robert Wexelblatt

outstretched and an army-buddy grin. "Well, how the hell've you been, Josh?"

I was startled, of course. "Uh—fine," I managed and shook his hand.

"Haven't seen you up at the Club in weeks. So what's doin'?" Here the man leaned close and leered expectantly. I was fascinated by the unnatural waves in his hair. "Cecilia tells me something rather exciting might be going on with Audrey." I tried hard to recollect the last paragraph of Josh's Byzantine bio.

"Oh, you mean that story about Audrey's being pregnant?"

His eyes brightened theatrically. "Then she *is*?"

I took a stab. "Hey, even *that* wouldn't keep me off the first tee, Waldo."

Fortunately, it *was* Waldo, Waldo Emerson the golf pro at Salisbury Country Club and a minor romantic complication. Lucky for me he laughed.

One of the writers emerged from behind Waldo's wide pro's shoulders. He was making a note. I flattered myself that he looked impressed with my reply. I supposed it was not lost on him that I had cleverly ducked the pregnancy issue, kept the rumors alive, upped the suspense. Surely there were weeks of episodes left to be milked from a dubious pregnancy, not to mention resolving the question of paternity.

My second encounter was more challenging. A stylish woman in her mid-twenties with lethal green eyes, auburn hair done up like a rococo cornice, and a face that would intimidate Redford approached with a phony smile and whispered through her resplendent teeth, "I can't wait any longer, Josh. I've got to see you tonight or it's all over. You understand?"

This was clearly an emergency and, almost as clearly, this had to be Daphne, the low-born, scheming, but undeniably delectable mistress who coveted Josh's name, trust fund, and Porsche.

"Look, Daphne," I whispered back, all the while keeping a grim smile on my face, "don't threaten me. It won't work and I won't stand for it. All right, if I can get away, I'll see you at your place tonight, but no promises. Got it, sweetheart?"

Daphne appeared taken aback by Josh's assertiveness. Well, after all, I figured a guy with Josh Martin's advantages, one accustomed to slicing into people's thoraxes, a man who piloted his own twin-engine Cessna, no matter how incompetently low, ought to behave with a degree of self-assurance.

Thus did I dispose of Daphne, who flew off to torture the fellow with the spiral notebook, leaving me a few moments to myself. Chewing a cube of cheddar I observed the director who was having a hell of a good time sending yet another Josh into outer darkness. For the first time, I allowed myself to think Horrocks might be right. Maybe I was right for this part. But what would it signify to win this ludicrous game, to be on, or in, *Salisbury*? "You Are Josh Martin." The portentously existential, Stanislavskian insistence of this proposition resonated for me with Horrocks' queer remark about "working for life." To my agent it must mean ten percent of a hefty and steady thing, but to me it sounded a bit like one of Sister Rose Emelda's curses, though with Sr. R. E. it was generally a matter of an eternity of molten sulfur.

Rose Emelda was one of the senile nuns, or so we nine-year-olds instinctively concluded. Her specialty was visions. She had two or three of them on a middling day. These revelations were always associated with water. According to Rose Emelda, the Virgin Mary spent most afternoons hanging out by the third-floor water fountain in order to inform her of our countless sins and also how much we would have to pay, sometimes down to the penny. The Intercessor as snitch.

"Tommy McCracken!" she would bawl after a pause for refreshment. "The Blessed Virgin appeared to me just now and told me all about the mortal sin you committed with last month's *Playboy* magazine. That's going to cost you seven hundred big ones, you filthy little pig, unless you come up with another dollar for the Pagan Babies. And as for you, Georgie Farrell! I know all about the horrible thing you tried to do last Friday night with one of the girls from St. Agatha Merici's . . ."

Our putative sins being invariably sexual, were, for the most part, incomprehensible to us. In later years, I speculated on how the world must have been for Rose Emelda, little more than a cheap envelope which opened up to reveal lurid, perfumed messages written in peacock-blue ink. And so it is in my field too: the world always loves imagination more than imagination cares for the world. To Sr. R. E., her pupils were really no more than optical illusions, a kaleidoscope that changed every year, illusory subjects next to the reality of her Lady, the actualization of lust, and the finality of deserved damnation. Hell was far more real than Holy Cross Elementary School, Paradise closer than the Boys' Room at the end of the corridor.

Robert Wexelblatt

Under slightly different circumstances—a less devout mother, a more forthcoming prom night—Sister Rose Emelda might well have become one of the pious fans of *Salisbury*.

"This is right weird," said the pretty fellow on my right. "*Weird*. Anybody mind if I don't smoke?"

In the seat behind us the discussion had turned dietary and evangelical.

". . . Tofu and leafy vegetables, and of course *lots* of oat bran, which is the real secret. You hear about the Iceland study?"

"*I* mind," piped up the driver, who was slow for a guy with such a good job, such a heavy foot.

In his sky-blue brand-new network-leased six-cylinder Dodge Caravan he sped us and his cigar deep through the gathering rush hour, drove through the ditch of the Cross Bronx abattoir with savaged Plymouths and Toyotas rusting under the high forsaken bridges. I looked out on the sepia tenements just beyond the walls fouled with graffiti, and those terrifying tenements seemed not to belong to our time, but embodiments of either the city's immigrant past or its post-nuclear future. In our van we had the velocity of survivors, climbing fast towards the suburbs, outrunning the shock wave.

We four remaining Josh Martins were all on our way to someplace called Salisbury.

"It's not so well known that *Salisbury's* now being taped completely on location," the director had explained in the entre-nous whisper of a CIA spy master. "Now, what we've decided is that we're going to take you four finalists there, probably just for tonight. I assume you can all go?"

He waited. Nobody said a word. I groaned a little; inwardly I groaned.

Belinda, on a hair-trigger at the best of times, would be frantic, electrostatically charged. I could imagine her howling down the stairwell like a bereft mama coyote. I saw her burning my clothes, ripping up my borrowed *New Yorker*. I smelled her overdosing on nutmeg and Valium, puking, calling the cops, blaming me. "If you go I'll kill myself." The oldest threat, full of lascivious spite. She played this trump card at least once a day.

"I need to make a phone call," I said.

234

"Okay, Josh," replied the director. "Come with me." He was very polite but as I followed him his back looked annoyed.

He took me out into the corridor, into a private office, and ordered me to make it snappy. "We're leaving in five minutes, with or without you."

At first I thought Belinda had barely listened or, better yet, didn't care. "Okay," she said breezily, "so then if you don't get back tonight I'll see you tomorrow." I thought I was off the hook and started to put the receiver gratefully down. But I was too slow. "Didn't you notice I've got a cold? Can't you hear it in my voice? My head's all mucussy, totally stoppered. It's because I was standing outside this church all afternoon talking to this priest, Father F . . . ." It sounded like his name might have been Florsheim. "He told me about your whole set-up, about the Sodality and about canonization. He told me about the little Rose of Lima." It was here that Belinda's voice began to rise like a banshee's. "You must remember her? Rosie. Little Isabel-Rosa? Remember? She was afraid of the sin of vanity because Rosie was sore afflicted with beauty. She was in love with suffering and Jesus. So little Rosa cut off all her hair, blistered her pretty little face with chili peppers, rolled her perfect little hands in quick lime, slept on broken roof tiles, wore a hair shirt with iron nails all over it and a crown that had exactly ninety points facing inward. Dead at thirty-one. First saint in the New World. My kinda gal that Rosie was. Belinda's patron saint. Imagine a line of Rose of Lima cosmetics for the masochistic maiden . . ."

I pardoned myself and hung up before Belinda could start threatening to douse her perfect tiny face with hot chili.

Salisbury (Salisbury?) lies somewhere in southern Connecticut. Like the police cars on the turnpike, like Mozart's grave, it's unmarked. Perhaps it wouldn't matter if it were, since Salisbury looks pretty much like the rest of southern Connecticut. It looks affluent and hyphenated: tree-lined, richly-lawned, security-systemed, air-conditioned, two-car garaged, double-glazed, sky-lighted, rear-patioed, pseudo-Tutored, apple-cheeked, rock-gardened. Salisbury looks exactly like, well like *Salisbury*.

We pulled up at dinner time. The four of us had been discussing dinner on and off for about twenty miles, the carnivores along with the herbivores. Not even unemployed actors can subsist on a bit of cheese and a few crackers. So we talked about food, what the network would lay on for us; besides, professional etiquette demanded that we steer clear of discussing the job.

The director and the rest of the gang had beaten us in their sports cars and touring sedans, though not by much. We could see various vehicles making their way into driveways, garage doors flying up all by themselves. I pictured the cast of *Salisbury* masquerading as a cortège up Route 95, all in a row, headlights on. Josh Martin's funeral procession. Josh is dead; long live Josh.

Our van turned off a macadamed lane and crunched onto the circular drive of a dark, half-timbered mansion. Blue-black spruces loomed like caryatids on either side of a brown portico. Creamy orange light of the sort one sees in pumpkins shone through leaded windows behind the heavy landscaping. We Martins stepped out onto the fine gravel of Salisbury, actors in an acting land, just as dusk was giving way to night. The Caravan peeled out and the front door of the house opened to reveal the director, his slim frame immensely amplified by a long fur coat of the sort found in Jack London stories. He greeted us seigneurially. I saw two writers in loose sweaters and wry faces hanging just behind him.

"In here," invited the director, jerking his thumb like a boss of longshoremen. I noted the increase in his authority which came with the change of venue. So we went into Dracula's Castle, which was dark all the way up to its slate roof.

The foyer had real marble tiles and an old chandelier. A good Hudson River School picture hung over a small French table. The walls were painted a tasteful light grey. We were directed into a no less elegant and clichéd den off the entryway—large Tabriz rug, two maroon leather club chairs and matching tufted couch, home entertainment unit, brass lamps, even a pipe rack. We all plumped down without being asked.

The director frowned, then nodded to the one of the writers who was not lighting a cigar to distribute a sheaf of stapled papers. This fellow had the look of a dissipated frog—bald, superior, full of flies.

"Okay," said the writer in a voice redolent of Jersey, "I'm giving you guys this to look over. It's all part of the test, but life's a bit of a test, innit? You learn this stuff and then we send you off to eat. That's a test too, so easy on the cheap Chablis." He turned toward the vegetarians on the couch. "I've only got three of these, so you two'll have to share. Sorry. We didn't expect so much talent." This crack caused his colleague the cigar smoker to guffaw and cough.

What Josh Martin Knows read the new handout and a random chunk of it went more or less like this:

Audrey's little sister Dahlia is thinking of posing for pornographic photographs in order to assert herself against her mother and older sister; the photographer may be Josh's old enemy, Gregory Lacombe, the very same Gregory Lacombe who, six years ago, ruined things between Josh and the beauty queen, Dallas Denton. According to a confidence from Dr. Lance Kilton, who has befriended Dahlia, a little plot-tangent named Tiffany Weathers stands in need of an abortion, and Josh suspects the shadowy Lacombe is behind her predicament. Horace Martin's business empire is teetering on the edge of collapse after the big Brazilian co-production deal fell through owing to the machinations of Lambert Wilson, Daphne's half-brother and quondam fiancé of Annabelle Pearson. Normandie Kilton, the long suffering cousin of Lance, has contracted AIDS from the accident victim she tried to save the night of the Albemarles' wedding rehearsal. . .

And so on and on through eight single-spaced pages.

My head swam from both hunger and detail until the shining moment when the secret of *Salisbury*'s deep structure finally revealed itself to me. The thing was fractal. The endless proliferation of plot-devices, jealousies, affairs, resentments, diseases, intrigues, lust, and greed seen close up was intentionally bewildering in order to give the appearance of freshness and invention. What next, one wondered. But, from the proper distance, every swatch of *Salisbury*-time actually resembled every other swatch. Each moment in *Salisbury* resembled every other moment. The incessant story was finite though the finite episodes were endless.

The lively realm of drama, as I had learned in school, has lots of provinces with sharp borders. Tragedies, comedies, cop shows, basketball games, infections, and law suits all derive structure from their ordained catastrophes, meaning from their dénouements. Without an ending there is no drama, only home movies. Follow Oedipus to the bathroom after he rips out his eyes and the tragic effect is sorely diminished. The dialectic of drama must complete itself theologically, legally, medically, even sexually. The roller coaster rises to its ineluctable climax then hurtles down to the end of the line, all energies coming to rest. Not so with *Salisbury*. *Salisbury* has no end. So, while drama is an abstraction from life,

Robert Wexelblatt

Salisbury, as all its fans know, is a substitute for life. It is life heightened but not exalted, impeccably dressed but neither purified nor cleansed. *Salisbury* is not a because, it's an instead.

I studied the complicated contents of Josh Martin's mind—not, after all, so different from what clogged my own. Gradually, I began to comprehend that Salisbury was courtship without consummation, experience without wisdom, motion without progress, existence without death. World without end. Amen.

The others were sent elsewhere but, for me, dinner was to be had at the Ferrers', a couple recently wed after Arthur had foiled the attempted abduction of Cecilia by agents of her ex-fiancé Bruno Scintillo, now safely incarcerated for an indefinite number of episodes. The Ferrers were due for a stretch of happily-ever-after and, to share their bliss, had invited Father Conwell, who had married them, Seth and Dora Thomas—Dora being Cecilia's step-sister and matron-of-honor—along with their old friends, the leaders of the Salisbury young married set, Audrey and Josh Martin.

"But where's Audrey?" Cecilia wanted to know right at the door.

"Aud sends her regrets," I answered, fussing with my coat, stalling. "She was really looking forward to this all week, but you know how Audrey is."

Both Cecilia and Arthur looked at me, united in puzzlement.

Somebody called in from the living room. "There's nothing *wrong* between you two, is there?" I presumed this must be Dora with her notoriously big ears and love of gossip.

"Of course not, Dora," I said with ironic indignation, as if she had made a joke in poor taste. Flailing a little, I added that Audrey couldn't make it because she was over at her parents' taking care of her little sister, the crypto-pornographic Dahlia, for whom I invented nothing worse than a dose of stomach flu.

"Hey, there's a lot of that going around," offered Seth helpfully and with a smile I found particularly winning. "Come on, Art, get Josh here a drink."

Cecilia took my coat.

At this moment Father Conwell came in, complete with black gabardine coat, grey muffler, dog collar, and red nose.

"Well, Josh," he said with exactly the sort of reproachful enthusiasm

238

I remembered from the ecclesiastical figures of my youth, "it's good to see you. How long has it been since—?"

"Too long, Father, too long." I did my utmost to appear ashamed. Despite their insatiable worldliness, the Martins are supposed to be devout at heart, sympathetic goodies. One or another of them had even been known to pray at the ends of particularly distressing episodes.

The priest, supplied at once with a drink, approached closer, getting into a single frame as it were. "A little bird tells me that Audrey might be with child, Josh—but where *is* your charming wife anyway?" He looked around as if she might be hiding from him.

I side-stepped the annoying pregnancy issue again. "Oh, Audrey had to stay with Dahlia tonight. Dahlia's come down with some awful stomach flu—you know, the one that's going around."

Arthur brought me a drink; Dora hung at his side like a microphone. "Say, how's *Audrey's* stomach been, Josh?" asked Arthur crudely, but—to my amazement and relief—Dora told him not to pry.

Nevertheless, prying was the main purpose of the dinner party, Josh Martin's being the tight lid in question. They were all pretty good at it, too. They kept me on my toes.

For example, over the fruit cup Cecilia contrived to mention Daphne in a pointed fashion. Daphne, it turned out, lived only two doors down.

"I was taking a letter to Lahoma down to the mail box this morning and I ran right into Daphne. We had coffee. Now, she didn't exactly say so, but she sort of intimated that she might have some really big news soon. Frankly, she seemed bursting with it, but you know Daphne—she's so sly. I couldn't get another word out of her."

Everybody looked at me. I coolly gulped a segment of grapefruit and stared right back at them, as one might just before, say, a commercial. After a pause during which nobody said "Cut!" I asked Cecilia how much better marriage to Arthur was than engagement to Bruno.

Father Conwell dropped his spoon and Dora choked a little, enough so that Seth had to strike her sharply on the back. "Cut," I whispered to myself.

Supper proceeded along these lines with hints about Horace Martin's business reverses, the Albemarles' separation, rumors about the return from up north of the redoubtable Dallas Denton. "I'll bet you remember *her*, Josh!" I parried, I blocked, I played dumb; I was on the defensive all through the soup and roast chicken. However, over dessert, hunger appeased and patience eroded to a mere patina, I went over to the attack after ostentatiously polishing off the Chablis, which wasn't all that bad.

"Father Conwell," I began rather loudly, "Cecilia here tells me that the Higgins boy—you know, Brian, the red-headed one?—that Brian Higgins says you assaulted him after Mass last Sunday. Anything to it?"

Before I got an answer from the confounded priest, I swiveled toward Dora.

"Dora, there's a good deal of cash missing from Amanda's dress shop. Now Amanda told Audrey that she noticed it missing just after you left on Thursday. Coincidence?"

"Josh!" cried Seth, rising slightly in his seat.

"Oh Seth, give me a break. You must know your bride's a klepto, don't you? She's been pinching things since she was no higher than this table. Besides, you're lucky the Williams girl who used to babysit for you decided not to press charges."

I was getting into it. Improv class was always my favorite. It was time to go and I wanted to make a grand exit. If I remembered correctly, I had a late date two doors down. For my parting shot—and I hoped the writers were tuned in—I rose, made for my coat, and turned on my flabbergasted host and hostess.

"And by the way, Cecilia, maybe you should know that it wasn't Bruno who hired those thugs. It was. . . ."

"My God! Who?" demanded Dora, who was quickly back in her character of Queen Gossip.

"Why don't you ask Arthur," I said, heading a little unsteadily for the foyer.

I retrieved my coat smartly from the closet and, as I closed the door behind me, I heard a faint "Bravo." I think it was a blessing straight from Father Conwell. From his lips to God's ear, as Belinda used to say when imitating her Granny Wilderstein.

It was plenty cold out, but a nicer cold than in the city, softer, healthier, the sort of frigidity enjoyed by the affluent at their ski resorts. I filled my lungs with bracing Salisbury air, stepped onto the gravel and wondered idly if, after my *coup de théâtre*, I were still Josh Martin or not. Then I spotted the Porsche parked at the end of the circular drive. I knew it was red but it looked plum-colored in the light from the street lamp. The license plate read JOSHM and the door was unlocked. After briefly looking this way and that, I climbed inside and let myself slide onto the soft Bavarian leather. I had never been in such a car. That the keys were in the ignition only confirmed my intuition that I was still in the running. I was a finalist—maybe even *the* finalist.

I started the engine and raced it a little. I confess that the sports car thrilled and frightened me, not unlike the prospect of becoming Josh Martin. I decided on a test drive, let out the brake and, more gingerly, the clutch.

I headed slowly down the empty street, picking out Daphne's house, the spoil of a dirty divorce dating from the High Renaissance. The house was well lit; there were even little lamps set next to the flagstone path leading to the front door as if it were a landing strip. Josh's landing strip. I shifted into second gear and nosed around the corner with the mail box for letters to Lahoma.

This was the first time I had been alone all day and, sitting there in Josh's Porsche, I meditated; I allowed my mind to race as I had the powerful motor. I began by recollecting an image.

Lamont Johnson had been one of my pals at Northwestern. He was the best improviser I'd ever seen. When we were flush we would go into Chicago together to take in a show or grab a good meal. Late one chilly afternoon as we were slogging down Goethe Avenue in a gathering snowstorm Lamont broke into song and dance. First it was Ray Bolger's "Once in Love with Amy," then, as the snow piled up beyond soft-shoe depth, the whole of Gene Kelly's "Singin' in the Rain." Suddenly he switched to Iago doing the handkerchief scene (I was Othello) and then he wound up improvising a terrifying dialogue at a crowded bus stop. He was the black rapist-murderer-heroin addict jiving me, his white parole officer. Lamont loved this sort of thing; he simply adored the intensity of being on and he was on most of the time. "Life," he once told me when we were drinking, "life's a musical comedy."

The connection between this memory and my present situation was obvious enough. *Salisbury* wasn't merely shot on location; Salisbury *was* a location. The cast lived in it and, like Lamont, they too were on all the time. They weren't characters searching for an author to lend their disorderly lives form and significance; they were characters for whom the authors searched, whom the authors—old, as they might be—were too young to have created and so they led the authors by the nose. I began to see how it might happen, how years on *Salisbury* could become one's life, how everything that was *not* Salisbury could grow pale and vapid. The possibility of joining the cast struck me in a new light—theologically, so to speak. What these people wanted wasn't an actor, but a soul. Now an actor's soul isn't worth all that much under ordinary circumstances; he's accustomed to losing it provisionally, to surrendering it a bit at a time. But this was something different, something with an odor of finality. To be Josh Martin required not rehearsal but renunciation.

I thought of Belinda; that is, of getting away from her. Why did I want to be rid of her? Because Belinda was mad. But what was her madness? Wasn't it the inability to *act*, to set any distance between herself and herself? No one is ever as earnest as an insane person. Salisbury, I thought, is merely the reverse of Belinda Wilderstein; Salisbury is the inability *not* to act. This was the principle behind all that had happened during the audition, and I was now astonished by how thoroughly I had given myself to the game. I was a pig in shit. Of the two fates, I clearly preferred this one, preferred being perpetually on, preferred televised immortality, being born again, newly baptized. I preferred to infuse Josh Martin with what soul I had. Besides, I loved his car.

Believe it or not I also thought of Shakespeare. I had always considered the secret of his genius to be that he was an actor. It was obvious to me that he adored writing plays as only an actor could. Negative capability and all that. Not the absence of a soul, but the ability to invest it in a wildly diversified portfolio. As soon as Will stopped acting he ceased writing too. Hell, either he stopped acting or he went on doing it for a dozen years in some place called "Stratford."

As I pulled up in front of Daphne's I wondered whether Audrey really were pregnant with Josh Martin's child. I mean really and truly.

Daphne opened the door wide for me. "Well, it's about time, lover." Her tone, like her motives, was mixed. At once indignant and melting, she wore a short white terry cloth robe, all too loosely belted and, so far as I could see, nothing else but a pair of furry slippers. More TV clichés, I reminded myself, but all the same I needed steadying. Hackneyed imagery or not, here was no Wilderstein. If Belinda was a battered Civic, Daphne was Josh Martin's Porsche. She didn't look quite mortal standing in the doorway's golden light; she looked air-brushed. We went in. A fire burned picturesquely in the white brick fireplace. A single lamp shone on the first click of a three-way bulb. Bill Evans wafted from the hi-fi.

"What took you so long?"

Now what would Josh Martin do, I found myself wondering for the first time that day. This was a nearly fatal error.

"Damnit, Daphne," I announced stiffly, throwing one arm up to indicate exasperation. "I got here as soon as I could. Did you expect me just to blow off the Ferrers or what? As it was, I walked out early."

My voice was inappropriately loud and Daphne winced at it. "Don't overdo, sweetie," she whispered into my ear. She was right, of course; I was overacting. With a little thrill, I realized that she must be on my side.

Daphne stepped back as a vixen might from an awkward rabbit. "Come on," she said, "let's take that big coat off. It's nice and warm in here, isn't it? Isn't it nice, Josh? Just you and me. For a change let's not fight about anything."

I allowed her to remove my coat and even to begin toying with the buttons on my shirt. I stood as still as Saint Sebastian.

"It's silly but I was really afraid you wouldn't come," she cooed in the brown sugar voice of the Other Woman. She pouted. "You were such a beast this afternoon, you know. Really Josh, you're a big big bad bad bear."

What the hell, I thought as Daphne pressed up against me and looked up through her preternaturally green contact lenses.

"Only a teddy bear," I said cooperatively and pulled her the tiny bit closer that was possible.

Daphne's bedroom was heavily draped and surprisingly well lit. It reminded me of those chaste sex scenes on TV which the engineers contrive to light up in blue, making the viewer imagine it's pitch black. Daphne's enormous bed was big enough to spend a weekend in. And it was soft and cool and subtly perfumed, just like Daphne herself, who quickly slithered between the rose-colored satin sheets with her robe only fractionally covering up her magnificent torso. Despite all this, she was talking about the plight of my father's business empire.

"We've got plans," I sighed and rolled onto the bed beside her. "Something to do with the South Koreans," I added with real effort, then surrendered myself to gravity and other forces of nature as Daphne lay back, smoothed her telegenic hair over the high pillow, and rotated toward me the whole of her luscious bitch-goddess form.

The doorbell gonged three shattering times.

Before I could come up with anything more inventive than "Damn!" Daphne was vertical, pulling her robe around her. "Sh, sh. You stay here, honey, and keep completely quiet. It must be Salvatore. I have to see him. He said he might be over tonight."

"Salvatore?"

"My new lawyer, sweetie. Only a minute. I promise I'll be right back."

Then she was out of the room, shutting the door behind her, dashing down the stairs.

I lay in the middle of the land of counterpane and soon heard loud but unintelligible voices from downstairs. Both voices were female. *I understand the fury in your words, but not the words.* Shakespeare again. It was doubtful there could be a female lawyer named Salvatore, especially in Salisbury.

"...of my way! I *know* he's here. His car's right out front," insisted the higher and more hysterical of the two voices and this was followed at once by a confused clattering on the stairs. I braced myself and thought fast, but of nothing.

The bedroom door was flung open as only bedroom doors can be and a blonde woman in a trench coat—a faint recollection of Belinda Wilderstein's—stood backlit on the threshold.

Audrey.

"Oh Josh!" she cried, staggering.

Fortunately, I still had my trousers on and I leapt up to catch the woman, my wife, before she collapsed. This act was virtually instinctive as was, I suppose, the shock wave of genuine guilt I felt.

Audrey was shorter than Daphne, taller than Belinda. She looked like Grace Kelly in her prime. As I deposited her in a chair I could hear Daphne on the stairs, marching up remorselessly.

Audrey was in full tears, big ones on both cheeks. "I wasn't with Dahlia," she sobbed. "Bill called me with the results of the test." She looked up at me, pausing just long enough for Daphne to reach the doorway. "Oh Josh, I *am* pregnant!"

I froze.

Daphne took one giant step into her bedroom. "What a coincidence," she said with magisterial nonchalance. "So am *I*."

Then everything stopped—time, language, the wave-like photons of diffused blue bedroom light. It wasn't a commercial break; it was more like Friday afternoon. There wasn't time for any number of questions: who was Salvatore really? can you name all the seven dwarfs? is Audrey better looking than Daphne or just more virtuous? did Arthur actually set Bruno up? exactly how far is Salisbury from Stratford?

"I've got it!" I shouted, breaking the spell like Prince Charming.

Both women looked at me with hard expectation. Behind me the heavy drapes faintly stirred as from a freshening breeze.

"I've got it," I repeated, directing my words to all four walls, all four corners of Salisbury. "I was in a plane crash. My twin-engine Cessna collided with a power pylon. I survived the crash but I've got amnesia! I can't remember anything. I don't know Audrey, let alone Daphne. Hell, I wouldn't even know I'm Josh Martin if somebody didn't tell me."

The director was the first out from behind the drapes. "You're Josh Martin all right," he announced. Then the two writers emerged, bent over, a couple of dwarfish, smirking evangelists, taking careful notes.

The Artist Wears Rough Clothing and
Carries Jade Inside

1.

The slant of light beaming through the bay window into the living room proved it was two o'clock on a Sunday afternoon. I went closer to the window. My all-American dream house was situated at the top of two broad terraces. The lawn was thick and I could make out a huge viburnum, colorful spirea, dark rhododendrons, darker yews, a variety of hosta, well mulched beds of roses, hollyhocks, hibiscus. The ample living room was furnished very much to my taste. On top of a taupe carpet sat two café-au-lait leather wing chairs and a matching couch as long as a basketball player, tables of good polished wood. An old Chinese landscape painting hung over the couch. In the distance three tiny sages make their way up a mountain, there's a village in the middle, and a bamboo forest in the foreground.

A car pulled up in front of the house. Two women and a man climbed out. Like my dream house, they too were American. The middle-aged woman was a real-estate agent, the couple potential buyers. I noticed the sale sign by the bluestone stairs. But this is *my* dream house, I thought greedily.

Would they have rung the bell or simply used a key if I hadn't hurried to let them in? "Oh, hello," said the realtor. She didn't appear at all surprised to see me. I was now in some perplexity. Was I selling this house? Should I show these people around, withdraw discreetly to a bedroom? But what I wanted to do was drive them off. I was certain the house was mine; it felt familiar despite the fact that I'd never seen it before, like a new edition of somewhere I had lived. That is, the house was at once new and old, mine and not mine. I had the sense of recovering from amnesia, recognition suddenly filling what had been vacancy just a moment before.

They came in all smiles and moved about quickly, eager to see everything, chatting.

Robert Wexelblatt

"Hello—"
"So nice—"
"Yes, beautiful—"
"Lovely carpet—"
"May I take—"
"Oh, yes, look—"
"The view, exposure—"

We bustled in an awkward cluster in the direction of the kitchen. In the hall there was a closet. The closet door swung open and out stepped my father. For a moment, everything froze as in the children's game of statues.

My father was wearing proper Western clothes; in fact, they looked just like David's clothes. The gray tweed jacket fit him perfectly, the mole-skin trousers well pressed, the brown loafers shiny. He wore a blue broad-cloth shirt and a striped tie. Father looked as neat as a pin from the head down; however, his long hair sprang wildly away from his head on the left while on the right it was matted as if with mud, nor was he clean shaven.

"Mai-Ling," he said in a low voice, looking delighted. He was remarkably chatty. "Yes, my dear, it's me all right. I've been waiting for you in that closet. I suppose it's childish, but I wanted to surprise you. That closet's actually larger than the attic where I painted the pictures for *A Daughter Is A Chrysanthemum*. You never saw them, but your mother did. I returned to watch her find them where I'd hidden them. She cried. Well, what can you expect? Tears weren't the effect I'd aimed at, though. Rather the contrary. Your mother was like Cleopatra in Shakespeare's play. She'd figure out my mood then adopt the opposite. If I were grumpy, she'd be cheerful. If I were cheerful, then she'd be morose. So, when she looked at those light-hearted pictures of a girl and her father, she cried. You might think it was because she wasn't in the pictures. Her absence was meant to be a presence, but this may have been too subtle for her. When I was refined, she'd be obvious. When I was crude she'd be delicate. You get the idea. And so it went, our marriage."

I was an inch taller than my father but still I lay my head between his cheek and shoulder. I felt I was crying though in fact I was dry-eyed. If I was weeping it was happening somewhere deep inside, somewhere one does not ordinarily cry. I felt the warmth of his hand on my back.

We had forgotten all about the three people standing so near us. However, the real-estate lady, a woman of tact, touched the arms of the

248

man and woman and, with a tender smile directed at me and my father, whispered, "Come. They'll want to be alone." And then they were gone.

Father said, "Was I too rude? Well, maybe, but the point had to be made. I can hardly wait to show you the kitchen, my garden, and just wait till you see the home-entertainment room."

My dream house was taken.

2.

My American name is Vivian Chu Lin. I am married to David Lin, a geneticist who studies yeast. We have two sons, Kevin and Brian. Kevin is a gifted pianist, not quite a prodigy but almost. Brian loves playing soccer and baseball; he is rather good at math. Neither boy has much time for painting and still less for poetry. They live in three worlds at once: the family, school, and their own brother-world from which everyone else is excluded. I have a job at the same university where David has his laboratory. I advise graduate students. I enjoy my work but understand it has its limits. That is, I am there to serve the ambitions of others or to counsel and console those whose ambitions exceed their capacities.

I have a nice ordinary life, helping the students, driving my sons to practice, games, concerts, keeping house, listening to my husband anguish about his grants. I have my worries too, but I'm careful not to ask too much of David in this respect. I don't complain because I dislike taking up too much room. I could never drive an SUV, for example.

I came to the United States in the early 80s to study social psychology. David and I were introduced by a non-Chinese couple. I respected his seriousness of purpose; he talked earnestly about how microbiology was going to improve the world. Yet David could also be funny. He made faces and told jokes, like my father. He was particularly amusing about having parents who pushed him to Americanize yet not to speak English at home, who drove him relentlessly to succeed yet forbade him to socialize with young people born outside of Little Shanghai. David is irreverent but also discreet, a winning combination. He knows what matters and what doesn't.

I was born in the Big Shanghai. The city has always been the most cosmopolitan in China. I would never call myself sophisticated even now, but I was far less so when I arrived and just able to hold my own at the university. I knew I was on my own and that I must meet people. When my mother said goodbye to me, she made it clear she didn't expect to see me again and she was right. With David I felt so comfortable that I even ventured a few jokes of my own. I steered clear of politics. I set out to please David's parents and knew just how to do it. They found me submissive and modest. David thought me exotic. This is what he said the first time he kissed me, exotic. To me, David was purely American—open, optimistic, generous, big, innocent. Because they relegate history to their theme parks and bearded professors, Americans lose their innocence over and over. It always seems to grow back.

Professor Wendy Marquis was raised on an Iowa farm. She told me that when she was eight years old she was taken to visit an aunt in Chicago. The aunt took her to a museum which had a collection of Chinese furniture, pottery, and painting. "I was hooked," she said with a giggle. She is now a professor of modern Chinese history. She sought me out, knowing only that I was from China. She likes to practice her Cantonese with me. Whenever she asks about my childhood and teenage years I am polite but evasive. She goes on asking anyway. This too seems to me an American trait, this persistent curiosity.

Wendy Marquis fancies that she is herself a little Chinese, that she was born in the wrong place or lived an earlier existence in China. In fact, she is far more like David than like me. I sometimes wish I could be more like her, could treat the past as a finished object, like one of those vases she collects.

There are tasks to which we are deeply averse but which we know we can't escape. When Professor Marquis asked me to deliver a lecture to her class about growing up in the PRC during the Cultural Revolution, my hands began to shake and then my insides quivered as well. I saw myself on a dais, childish faces fastened on me. Perhaps my trembling was invisible; in any case, Professor Marquis took no notice. As I found it impossible to refuse her outright I said I would think about it but in such a way that she would understand I was only being courteous. Nevertheless, the task had fallen on me and I believed that, no matter how I struggled or how much the prospect terrified me, I was already bound to it. Like a criminal who's been cornered, I looked for a way out.

3.

This one was an animated film.

"Notice the calligraphy," whispered Father as the title, *Emperor*, filled the screen. "Don't you find it dignified? Nothing trendy or new-fangled. And pay attention to how well everything is drawn. Every line in this film is made to count."

We sat on two recliners, our legs before us, each with a bowl of microwave popcorn and a Coca-Cola. My father liked things just so. And he was right about the lines. Everything was exquisitely drawn. The motion of the film was unusual. It moved across the screen like a wind or waves of convection.

The emperor was being carried out of the Forbidden City. His litter was surrounded by fierce guards, all heavily armed.

"It's the Emperor Shun Yang-sun," Father explained. "You may not know of him. His reign was brief and ill-starred. He's fleeing not only invaders from the north but a couple of pretenders as well, one from the south and one from the west. His plan is to gather his forces in the provinces."

On screen, the imperial procession is making its way through the countryside. Everywhere peasants bow so low as the Emperor passes that they see only the legs of the cavalry's horses. There is the sound of horses, the murmurs of the people, the grunts of the soldiers.

Two of the guards have caught a spy, or someone accused of spying. He is dragged before the captain of the guard who orders him beheaded on the spot. The man is a barefoot peasant who screams and screams. Then, even as the man's mouth opens wide, everything falls silent. We see the man's open mouth; we see his head pushed brutally down; we see the axe slowly move from right to left. This motion of the axe is elegant, at once light and heavy. A gong sounds which makes you think of the bursting of blood. Then there is the sound of steady rain and, indeed, from right to left rain gradually fills the screen.

The litter-bearers are struggling in the mud. They cannot go forward and the litter is set carefully on the ground. The guards set up camp, beginning with the imperial pavilion. A shrunken old woman picks her way through the sodden guards as they work. She looks as determined as a badger. Whenever one of the guards is about to spot her, she ducks behind another. In the teeming rain she makes her way right up to the

Emperor, who is still sitting in his litter, contemplating his plight.

I feel anxious for the old woman, worried that she will be discovered and instantly beheaded. The guards are in a foul mood. The Emperor still sits in his litter, but now dusk has fallen and a lantern shines behind him. His silhouette is cleverly drawn so as to convey both preoccupation and fear.

The old woman worms her way so close to the Emperor that she is able to tug at his silk robe. The Emperor cries out and the woman is instantly seized. The captain has already raised his sword when she cries, "Stop!"

Taken by surprise, the man hesitates and the Emperor slowly turns. He looks at the old woman. We can see his face is full of disdain. Still, he orders the captain to stand aside.

The Emperor's voice is deep and cruel. "What is it you want, Granny?"

The old woman contemplates the Emperor's face, which we cannot see, which, for us, is still in shadow, a blank.

The captain yells at her. "Hurry up! The Emperor is waiting, you broken old wok!"

The old woman ignores him. She speaks directly to the Son of Heaven. "My grandson is dead. My son is dead. My husband is dead. In the wrong order. And all thanks to your wars."

"The Emperor has no time for this," snaps the captain.

The old woman turns on him. "If he's got no time to listen to a suffering old woman, then how can he be emperor?"

Again the gong sounds. Again the archaic, courtly calligraphy fills the screen. The End.

"Quite a fine thing," observed my father with an appreciative nod, "the drawing in particular. Still, it's rather abrupt and some comic relief wouldn't have hurt."

"It's almost . . ." I hesitated to make a judgment.

"Yes?"

"Well, it reminded me of something. That's all."

My father tossed some popcorn into his mouth and munched. "Me too. It has the brevity of a parable, which is what it aspires to be."

My father and I often watched films together in the dream house.

The first one he showed me had also concerned an emperor. Deep within the Forbidden City he is told of a peasant who lives far away on the frontier. This peasant, who has only a few square yards of land to till, had refused to bow down when the emperor's glorious name was mentioned. The peasant dared to shrug. The emperor sends out a thousand armed men to chastise the peasant. "No offense is trivial," he says sternly. It takes the men a long month to get to the peasant's hut. They haul the man out, beat him, yell at him, and cut off his head. As it rolls on the ground, the head declares that the emperor is an impostor. "The true emperor," says the head, "is among you." The men stuff the head into a wooden box and set off on their return. On the way each is suspicious of the other; each wonders if it is he who is the true emperor. Why not? It doesn't take long before they begin to fight. They kill each other until only one is left, an officer. He returns alone with the head to the Forbidden City. He is shown into the emperor's presence. Before the astonished guards can stop him, he draws his sword and stabs the emperor in the heart. As the guards close in the foolish officer tears open the box and holds up the head. "Tell them!" But these are his last words.

"That," said my father, "is what I call a revenge tragedy."

My favorite is about a rich merchant, his wife, and two concubines. The man is distinguished and handsome, the ladies all beauties of different ages. At the beginning of the film the women find all sorts of petty ways to make each other unhappy. They are always competing, and so the merchant too is unhappy, his house so unbalanced that he can take pleasure with none of them. Then there is a turning-point, a sadness out of which happiness grows. The younger of the concubines becomes pregnant but while the merchant is away in the province of Shun she loses the baby. The two other women help her, console her. After this the wife makes a speech. "From now on," she declares, "I intend to do everything I can to make you two happy. I hope that you will do the same." Each tries to find out the others' dearest wish and fulfill it. The younger concubine craves apricots out of season; the other desires a blue dress; the wife longs for a rare variety of rose bush. As for the merchant, he longs for a son. One by one, all their wishes are fulfilled. It is never clear who gives birth to the boy. He calls all the women "Mama."

When not watching films, Father and I spent time together walking in the garden. We would cook elaborate dinners in the kitchen. Only once did he permit me to peer into his studio at the top of the house. The light up there blinded me. It was all windows and skylights. The ceiling was so high it was easy to imagine oneself in the sky. I saw an enormous canvas turned to the wall. He quickly shut the door. "Time for a movie," he said. Most of all Father liked to watch films with me.

"These are heavenly films," he explained after the conclusion of *Emperor*, "never released on earth."

After *Emperor* faded out I expected to do the same myself, as was the custom at the end of one of these celestial films; however, this time my father took my hand, as if to hold me back.

"I know all about the invitation," he said. "The one from the woman professor."

"You do?"

"Naturally. I know what I know but also what you know."

"That's an unsettling thought."

"Indeed, it is. It rather embarrasses me to know so much, as if I were a successful interrogator."

"Well, what do you think?"

"It's you who are reluctant, not me. You're afraid. But remember, I won't be there. I'll be here in this house."

"But those people can't possibly understand."

"Excuse me, cara Fiorella, but isn't that why you've been asked to speak? So that they *will* understand?" He stroked my arm for a bit then deftly changed the subject. "You know why you've been visiting me?"

"I've given it a lot of thought."

"Yet you've neglected to discuss it with your husband, right? Well, what? Do you think it's because the professor asked you to give a lecture? After all, your first visit was that very night, wasn't it?"

"That's what I thought at first. But no. I think it's because we're now the same age."

He broke into a happy grin. Over the years, despite everything that happened, I always remembered him grinning, smiling, laughing. "My bright little chrysanthemum's done it again. Do you wonder I always wanted to show you off? *Apple of my eye* is a lovely expression, though not Chinese."

I took the occasion to ask about something that had been troubling me. "What about your grandsons? Are they apples too?"

"Those two I love on principle."

"That sounds rather abstract."

"That's so," he admitted. "It can never be the same as with you, of course. Now, what about this lecture? You could do as superficial a job as the professor asked. What did she say? A few details, take a few questions?"

"Her low expectations make me feel ashamed."

"You're remembering what I told you all those years ago when you were twelve, aren't you?"

"I did my best to dismiss what you said. But when Professor Marquis asked me to speak, those words of yours came back. I admit it. Even worse was remembering the way you looked at me on that frightful day. Your sweetness has proved more durable than my perverted virtue; your forgiveness is more implacable than my childish certainty."

"If you were in China you'd feel shame but here in America it's guilt you feel. The one looks around, the other inside. It was easy for me to forgive you."

"I don't have the right to forgive myself," I wanted to say. But I had already begun to fade.

4.

I did tell David about Professor Marquis' request but I didn't wish to tell him about my father and the dream house. I found keeping a secret from him difficult, as it would be if I had a tumor or an affair. Perhaps I underestimated David but I doubt he would understand my being a living spirit who travels each night to my dream house at the top of two terraces, a top-dollar mansion with a perfect garden, a huge flat-screen high-definition TV, and an artist's attic studio with an apparently unlimited ceiling. What if I told him my father was residing there, that it was located in what could only in the crudest terms be called the after-life? How would he have responded? He would be like Sigmund Freud, another scientist who likewise began with big hopes about making the world happier. David knows little about my father but he is content with that little. He has constructed a narrative about me and my life in which he occupies the role of sane hero. In his view, the China in which I was born was plainly mad. This diagnosis is far too simple, of course; but, as David once said at a dinner party, it covers the facts. He believes the country is now coming to its senses, *li* by *li*, so to speak, and this pleases him. Again like Freud, like all scientists, his hypotheses are precious to him and he relishes having them confirmed.

"It's just that you're so shy, Viv. Why not give a little lecture for

Marquis, take a few questions, get it over with? It's not such a big deal, is it?"

For me, the deal is colossal; for me, the deal has no horizon.

My mother gave me some of my father's papers when I left China. I keep them in a fireproof box such as is used for deeds, wills, and birth certificates. One of the most touching items is this poem written in pencil in minuscule characters on the back of a railway ticket to Wuhan.

> On the most terrible day of my life
> the clouds were kind enough to divide the
> sky for me and even the sun, less indifferent
> than usual, deigned to smile. As for the
> mountains, they almost begged to be climbed.
> Children called to come play with them in the cellars.
> In short, the world's kindness could still be discerned,
> like written-over verses; but before
> even one game could be started, the first
> foothill scaled, I was put on this train.
> So it's not so bad, not so bad. On the
> train I found this pencil stub, this crumpled
> ticket, this poem. The poem
> has made a sensible suggestion.
> Escape, it says, and we'll roam the countryside.

Chu Hsi-Wei, my father, actually did escape from that train; he did indeed "roam the countryside," as the poem romantically suggested, for nearly two months before he was caught. The people who arrested him were like David, people of science who simplified matters by calling him mad. Or perhaps they were good people looking for a way to spare him further pain. Maybe they were art lovers who admired the work of the notorious black artist Chu Hsi-Wei. Anyway, he was put into an asylum. For good behavior he was sometimes allowed to draw. My mother was permitted two visits. During the first Father told her what had happened to him and slipped her some of his work, including the ticket to Wuhan. By the time of the second visit he was dying.

5.

Down the hall came the electronic noises, the *cools* and *oohs* and *ughs* of the boys at their video game. David, in the sweatshirt and jeans he put on the moment he got home, sat at the table watching me empty the dishwasher. His gaze made me nervous; before I'd been to the dream house I would have felt something different being studied like that. To break the silence I asked how his two new post-docs were working out.

"Fine," he said flatly. "How are things with you, Viv?"

"Oh, I'm fine too." Even to myself this sounded too cheerful. Just like a post-doc.

"Really? So you're not planning on telling me, then?"

I turned with a handful of forks. "Tell you what?"

David laughed in an unhappy way. The merchant, his wife, and the two concubines had laughed the same way in the first half of the heavenly movie. It wasn't a bitter laugh, not aggressive or dismissive, though it had in it something of all three. There are no words to describe such a laugh but there's no mistaking it, and David's version made me want to cry. There's an old saying: secret shared, a bond, withheld, a wall.

Now my voice sounded tiny. "All right. Once the boys are in bed."

We sat in the living room. David patted the couch but I took a chair across from him. He would try to comfort me and I did not want it. I didn't tell everything. But of what I did tell the part to which my bright husband attended most closely was the terrible thing that had happened in January, during my twelfth year, that of my first period.

"You have to understand how un-Chinese a father he was. I mean that he spent lots of time with me, bathed me, took me with him, fed me. He drew me all the time and made up stories just for me. My father adored me and he had the knack of looking at the world through a child's eyes. He was so much fun even when he wasn't being funny. You think it was just a mad time in a crazy place. But my father believed in the Revolution and had helped to advance it with his work. He thought it was going to make everyone happier, even the bad people, as he once told me. When things first became difficult he said to my mother, 'Big storms throw off little storms. In the same way, within every big correct revolution there are bound to be little, incorrect ones. Best to take as little notice as possible. Such things pass quickly. It's the big storm that matters.'"

"Sort of a violent metaphor," said David, raising both arms over his head and stretching his back the way he does. It was true. My father understood that the Revolution was a tempest that would destroy as well as create. What he wanted was to mitigate the destruction, especially of the art-forms he admired and carried on in his own style. He wasn't against the necessary demolition, but he wanted to salvage these archaic things from the wreckage on which the splendid building would be erected. He felt the same way about the unnecessary proscription of Western art, which he also could turn to his own purposes. The most famous example was the picture of Mao which hung for a time in the Art Institute. It was patterned after Caspar David Friedrich's *The Wanderer above the Mists*, yet it also suggested traditional Chinese landscapes with its mountains and fog, pictures like the one of the three ascending sages that hung over the couch in my dream house. But my father's picture was problematic. It wasn't just that the picture resembled a celebrated Western painting but that it depicted Mao alone, the Red Army, represented by a few reverent officers and men standing behind him on safer, less sublime terrain. Read politically or malevolently, this iconography was ambiguous and when the time came was used against him.

As conditions worsened, my father did his best to toe the line either out of conviction or expediency, which are not always easily distinguished. Late at night he and my mother would have long talks about what that line was. In those days it wasn't easy to say. He would show her the cartoons he was considering having published. All of them made her afraid. In earlier years it was his cartoons that made him famous, though soon they were to be used against him. Now only the crudest political images were welcomed—the coarser and stupider the better—and the sort of elegant work my father did was denounced as formalist, elitist, and, worst of all, Japanese, deriving from the *manga* tradition of the hated invaders. But it was impossible for my father to draw inelegantly. It went against the grain.

His poems had to be just as carefully vetted. It was typical of him to chose a lowly subject to make a lofty point. One I remember was about an iron lock on a warehouse gate. The poem expressed indignation about this lock:

> One cunning piece of metal belies
> All the goodness of the wallflowers.

The people are the wallflowers—humble, numerous, innocent, flowering—while the lock denotes the evils of private property and the insidious suspicion of comrades.

My father struggled to keep his head above the rising water, so to speak, to swim the perilous Yangtse even as his colleagues began to go under. But all the care he took to censor his own work was secondary. There were two things that made his survival possible. The first was the protection of a high official named Kung; the other was the love of his students. And so, when the world turned upside down, when the foolish lorded it over the wise, the young instructed the old, and denunciation became the order of every day, the first blows fell on others but not Father.

The effect of being spared told on him. He wore a look of perpetual anxiety and increasing self-disgust. It was hard, this waiting for the "little storm" to blow over. During these months he once again drew one of those tiny pictures he liked to make just for me when I was little. I now understand that these pictures were escapes into delight and freedom, works in which he could indulge his various styles while depicting the commonplaces of our home and neighborhood. But this picture, the last, was entirely different. It showed the usual father and daughter pair but this time they were not in our Shanghai neighborhood, not even in a city. Hand in hand, they picked their way across a half-ruined footbridge as the sides of the impossibly steep gorge loomed like fists above them. *And so they continue on their way* was written at the bottom in his admirable calligraphy. I no longer have the picture. It wasn't lost. I myself tore it up.

The first attack on my father came in a leading newspaper article. Why? The high official had withdrawn his support, which had become a danger to himself. That same day my father's favorite pupil, already a Red Guard big-shot, made a speech against him at the Institute. Well, after that the floodgates opened. It was arranged that the next day he would be physically hauled out of the Institute, paraded around town, and criticized. Detachments of Red Guards were detailed for this work, including the one from my school.

David is a perceptive man and knows me better than I thought.

"You denounced him, didn't you?" His eyes grew bigger. "You were one of those little Red Guards with their little red books?"

I bowed my head. I hadn't even had to tell him.

The last time I was with my father was on that icy afternoon at the Institute, just before he vanished on the train. He had already been beaten and paraded and was now in the ox-pen. In the short interval between the ritual chanting and his being taken away to the train station, we had a few moments together in the courtyard. I stood with my classmates, yelling with the rest. I wanted the others to hear me call him a reactionary, a counter-revolutionary Confucian, and what-not. I did my best not to look at him. But my father never took his eyes off me and the moment I looked back he motioned me to come to him. Of course this was the last thing I wanted; I wanted to stay with my classmates. But squatting down in the pen, bleeding and bruised, he still managed to look me in the eyes, as if nothing else existed but the father and his little daughter who is a chrysanthemum. I can't possibly express the kindness of that look. It drew me to him. "Listen to me," he said in a whisper that was somehow louder than the screeching mob. "You've done a terrible thing. If you'd done it out of maliciousness I could correct you. But you're convinced you've acted virtuously. So it's the best in you that's performed the worst. This nobody else can correct. So you will, some day, have to correct yourself."

6.

It is ten in the morning. My father is not in the house. I search every room. I rush up the stairs calling out to him. The door to the attic studio is locked. I had never seen a lock in the house before. It reminds me of the lock on the warehouse gate. In a panic, I pound on the door, but there is no reply.

I rush back down the stairs and out into the garden and there I find him down on his knees, pulling weeds. He has an old straw hat on his head. He doesn't stand up.

"I couldn't find you," I complain, discharging some of my desperation.

"Even here there are living things that have to be removed. That's the harsh discipline of beauty, my dear," he says then pulls a comical face to show me that he was only pretending to be pompous.

I offer to make us some tea.

"Yes, that would be nice," he says, digging up a dandelion.

As I turn, I hear the sound of a tennis ball being struck. It's coming from the other side of the privet hedge.

"There's a tennis court?"

"That will be your mother playing with Mr. Cheung."

"What?"

"You never wondered why she wasn't here?"

"You mean you've . . . separated? That can happen here?"

"Mr. Cheung is a very nice man, not so demanding. He was a shirt-maker in Hong Kong and counted among his customers no less a personage than David Niven. Once, he had an order for six shirts from Bob Hope." My father made a droll face.

"Shouldn't I go and see her?" I asked uncertainly.

"You could, certainly. But there's not much point. Not just yet. You see, she lives in a different house. With Mr. Cheung. Your mother and Mr. Cheung are devoted to their morning tennis. I don't think they would like to be interrupted."

I accept this, though I can't say why; even my parents' separation seems entirely natural. Perhaps I would visit my mother later.

"I'll just get the tea, then?"

"Yes. That's good."

I bring a tray out to the patio and we sit together under the blue umbrella with our cups of green tea. My father smacks his lips and says the tea is good and then, perhaps reminded by the tea, he says he would like to recite a poem, a special one which was written long ago by his namesake. "This poem means a great deal to me. You might say it changed my life. It's a poem about what it meant to this other Hsi-Wei to be an artist. The verses are honest and modest. A parade of pictures, actually. Cartoons. Listen closely."

> Tendrils thin as new snakes
> undulate upon the inlaid table.
> No desire for sudden noise
> disturbs the Lord Shi-Yueh
> taking green tea with his friend.
>
> In the scarlet bedchamber
> a man turns to his wife
> and speaks of some incident
> long past. Her gentle nodding
> is like sunlight on gold roofs.

The family sits in the garden.
From the railing of the foot-bridge
the littlest child pushes pebbles
into the shallow running brook
while two ducks stop to watch.

In his study underneath the
dumpling shop of Mrs. Shang-Kiu,
Hsi-Wei the calligrapher
paints these images in his
bumbling bird's-foot characters.

"How do you like this poem, my dear?"

"Very much," I said. "It does make me think of those cartoons you used to make, the little ones. You're like that other Hsi-Wei, aren't you? You both make pictures and poems. You too wanted to live underneath a dumpling shop, didn't you?"

My father nodded to show he appreciated my insight. "You see, this poem is a letter. At least that's what I thought when I first read it as a boy. It's funny to think of it now, but back then I believed the letter was meant for me, simply because this bumbling calligrapher and I shared the same name." He laughed. "His subjects are homely. The sublime is never political. Anyway, writing of this sort is what your David might call—what's the word?—*non-biodegradable*. Yes?"

"I suppose David might like it," I said defensively. I wasn't sure whether my father approved of my husband. Perhaps a wife can never be certain about this and, while it makes her anxious, there is also something not displeasing in it, as if the love the two men feel for her will be more secure if they don't love each other too much.

My father asked if I had looked for him in his studio.

"Yes, of course. When I didn't see you—"

"I supposed so. I'm sorry I locked the door. It's only because I didn't want you to see the painting before it was finished."

"What painting?"

"I call it the January painting. It's just a picture of my home town in winter. Would you like to see it, or would you prefer a movie? I've got a new one, just in. It's about a courier who carries a message from the Emperor to the southern army. The message is inscribed on his scalp."

"No, Father, no couriers and no movies. I would much rather see your painting."

7.

The students appeared anything but bored, though by now I took hardly any notice of them. Professor Wendy Marquis sat at the rear, her back straight, her manner rapt. I was approaching the climax of my lecture which had turned into something else, something that could have a climax.

Events moved quickly during that time, I said. It was intense which means that more important events occurred in a shorter time. Some of what happened to my father I discovered only much later, some my mother disclosed before I left to come here. A certain high official named Kung, once my father's admirer and protector, met with a delegation of Red Guards and formally withdrew his support, explaining it away as a tactic he had used to draw out my father's reactionary tendencies. He proclaimed the struggle against wrong-thinking reactionary elements in the arts must be pressed. My father was the chief target but by no means the only one. Virtually the whole of the Art Institute's remaining faculty came in for a pasting. These were all artists of great spirit who even under the worst conditions found ways to continue working. The painter Xi Pang-Kai, during his banishment to the countryside, drew on cigarette papers. Upon his release from forced labor Hueh Kai-Fung claimed to have painted no less than two score canvases in his head, which he then set about executing. The imprisoned sculptor Pu Shi-Yeh, denied any materials on which to work, used a discarded child's scissors to carve splinters of wood pried from the walls of his cell.

The so-called struggle-sessions went on everywhere in those days. We young people were in an unimaginable state of euphoria. The certainty of misguided idealism is a powerful drug. Each competed to be more terrible than his or her comrades, to show herself the more ardent revolutionary. In fact, it was risky to be anything less than fervent. Even children were quick to accuse and so settle private scores. Reactionaries, spies, and wrong-thinkers could be anywhere and under particular suspicion were the families of those condemned.

As I talked, I experienced again that poisoned air of universal suspicion. That epoch of zeal and betrayal marked the real triumph of my father's lock on the warehouse door.

The day he was seized was January 21, a frigid day. Everything had obviously been worked out in advance. He was taken straight from his classroom and marched into the crowded courtyard. What a blow it must have been for him that the Red Guards should be led by his favorite student, a stuck-up seventeen-year-old named Jiang. This young man barked the customary formula at my father: "Prepare to receive criticism from the revolutionary people!" A placard was hung around my father's neck. "I am a Western agent," it read. After the ritual denunciations he was thrown in the back of an open truck and driven around the city. The whole time people—especially the young—screamed at him, threw stones and vegetables; they leapt up and down with enthusiastic hatred. From time to time the Guards in the truck beat him to please the crowd. Finally they drove him back to the Institute and shoved him in an ox-pen. Here Jiang announced that there was to be a traveling struggle-session. For this purpose my father would be transported to his home town, where the first of these sessions was to take place on the grounds of his former elementary school. Then a remarkable thing happened. My father's former favorite recited from—of all things—the *Tao Te Ching*. He was, after all, well educated and no doubt carried away by the day's activities wished to show off for the crowd. He recited at the top of his lungs:

> Banish learning, discard knowledge:
> People will gain a hundredfold.
>
> Banish benevolence, discard righteousness:
> People will return to duty and compassion.
>
> Banish skill, discard profit:
> There will be no more thieves.

Jiang meant to give Lao-Tze's words the worst meaning, to twist the Tao to his revolutionary ends, appropriating the sage as Mao's precursor. My father, crouching in his pen, calmly raised his hand and called out. "Chi-Hung, why don't you finish the passage? Can you have forgotten the rest?"

Jiang was nonplused. Perhaps he had already begun to realize that he had made a serious error. My father completed the quotation for him:

These three statements are not enough.
One more step is necessary:

Look at plain silk; hold uncarved wood.
The self dwindles; desires fade.

The enraged and frightened Jiang instantly ordered my father dragged from the pen and beaten yet again. I was there. I saw and heard. Snow began to fall. It was after that last beating, after he'd been put back in the pen, that my father spoke to me for the last time. The last time I saw him he was being hauled off to the train station.

He arrived at his home town early the following morning. The distance from the station to his old elementary school was ten *li*, a long way, especially in the cold wind, over the snow and mud for which he was not properly dressed. The whole way was lined by screaming peasants, townspeople, and joyous children out for a holiday, imitating the grown-ups. What might have been a sentimental journey, a famous son's nostalgic and triumphant homecoming, was turned instead into a gauntlet of shame.

On the school grounds he was yet again denounced at length. His sins against the people were all spelled out. Then his head was shaved and a kind of paper dunce cap put on it. He was given a pail of water and an old broom made of twigs and ordered to clean the floors of the classrooms. Honest work they called it. My father, I'm told, comported himself throughout with dignity. What's more, he did a thorough job on the floors.

Fame was my father's undoing. He didn't seek it but it found him out. It must have been as he washed the classroom floors that he composed this poem. He wrote it down later and gave it to my mother when she visited him.

I went to the slide projector. My father's calligraphy on the pulpy creased paper appeared. I translated:

A broom is my brush today.
My once-proud calligraphy evaporates
On the schoolroom cement.
Sketched in crude strokes
Evergreens at dusk, birds on bamboo.
My name too is written in water.

> The hare hides from the high hawks.
> Why didn't I do the same?

At the end of the day he was put back on the train for the return to Shanghai. Somehow he managed to escape from the train. He ran off and for a time roamed the countryside like a holy fool, dirty and with wild hair, drawing charcoal portraits of peasants for rice. When he was captured, he was officially declared to be mad and placed in an asylum. It was there he made this cartoon, perhaps his final work, my father's last word.

Again I went to the projector. The slide showed my father's world-turned-upside-down cartoon. He had drawn himself with his feet on the ground, his head bowed in apparent submission. Hanging above him is a mob of children with open mouths, arms raised in anger.

I then reversed the slide. Now it was the crazed children who appeared to be stuck in the frozen mud while my father hovered above them, looking down compassionately from the heavens. Their arms were raised to him in what now seemed like longing, their mouths open in supplication.

But, I was thinking, this wasn't his last work, not his last word. That was the big painting at the top of my dream house. The canvas was as long as a railway car. In fond detail it portrayed the entire topography of his native region, its mountains and paddies, rocks and streams, everything made pure by freshly fallen snow. You had to look hard to make out the squat elementary school in one corner, harder still to see the little figure surrounded by tiny children.